The Beast Insid
The Second Boo

An Urban Fantasy Novel by David Horrocks

The Beast Inside Series:
The Beast Inside
The Beast Inside: Blood of the Forsaken
The Beast Inside: Blood Queen

Cover Art and Design by:
Kristyn McQuiggan of Drop Dead Designs

Edited by: Judie Horrocks, Bob Horrocks and Jonny Horrocks
Special Thanks to: Kate, Nils and Conor

About the Author

A British born author living in the United States, David Horrocks has a passion for writing, wanting nothing more than to share his ideas and stories with the world. The first novel he published was 'The Beast Inside', which he has expanded on further with other novels and short stories. The art of writing is an outlet in which he pours his heart and soul, hoping to bring the enjoyment of reading to everyone who picks up his books.

Copyright © 2018 by David Horrocks

All rights reserved. Except as permitted under the U.S. Copyright Act of 1976, no part of this publication may be reproduced, distributed or transmitted in any form or by any means, or stored in a database or retrieval system, without the prior permission of the author.

This book is licensed for your personal enjoyment only. This book may not be re-sold or given away to other people. If you would like to share this book with another person, please purchase an additional copy for each recipient. If you're reading this book and did not purchase it, or it was not purchased for your use only, then please return it and purchase your own copy. Thank you for respecting the hard work of this author.

This is a work of fiction. Names, characters, businesses, organisations, places, events and incidents either are the product of the author's imagination or are used fictionally. Any resemblance to actual persons, living or dead, is entirely coincidental.

TABLE OF CONTENTS

Prologue: Somewhere beneath the surface. *4*
Chapter One: To dream of drowning. *13*
Chapter Two: The empty grave. *23*
Chapter Three: The hunter or the hunted. *43*
Chapter Four: A little southern hospitality. *57*
Chapter Five: Skeletons in the closet. *71*
Chapter Six: The learning curve. *84*
Chapter Seven: A home within the chaos. *99*
Chapter Eight: The forsaken one. *113*
Chapter Nine: That sinking feeling. *129*
Chapter Ten: The hand that feeds. *142*
Chapter Eleven: Out of the woods. *161*
Chapter Twelve: The performance of a lifetime. *177*
Chapter Thirteen: A sudden reversal of fate. *192*
Chapter Fourteen: The show must go on. *209*
Chapter Fifteen: A pain long past. *222*
Chapter Sixteen: The hunt goes on. *234*
Chapter Seventeen: A most secret meeting. *250*
Chapter Eighteen: Nowhere to run. *267*
Chapter Nineteen: Judge, jury and executioner. *281*
Chapter Twenty: Waiting for the dawn. *292*
Chapter Twenty One: An army of me. *306*
Chapter Twenty Two: The lair of the dead. *318*
Chapter Twenty Three: A friend in need. *335*
Chapter Twenty Four: A meeting of minds. *352*
Chapter Twenty Five: The calm before the storm. *370*
Chapter Twenty Six: A flaw in the plan. *384*
Chapter Twenty Seven: It all came crashing down. *399*
Chapter Twenty Eight: Life after the fall. *413*
Epilogue: The queen of her castle. *432*

PROLOGUE: SOMEWHERE BENEATH THE SURFACE.

"I can show you all the wonders of the world." Sam didn't recognise the woman's voice, but her words were sweet like honey. Trying his best to respond, he found that his voice wavered and his words failed him. Caught in the moment, he was completely enthralled by his companion. A warmth rushed through his veins, soothing him faster than any drug. He knew that he was dying, but it didn't matter as he had wanted to die anyway. It was his final wish. He was tired of living his life so full of regret. Weary of the world, and sick of feeling sorry for himself.

The warmth was soon replaced with the chill of the grave as it spread out through his body. Death was something that Sam had once believed would feel a little more permanent, but the nameless woman had promised him so much more. "This isn't the end. It's the beginning of something much greater." For some reason Sam believed everything the woman said, confident that her words weren't just full of empty promises.

As the last of his life ebbed from his open wound, Sam no longer felt regret. Everything was sure to be better now, as he was going to have a clean slate and past mistakes were no longer of consequence. He was strangely content and free of worry. Death was a truly liberating experience. Memories were fading, making it difficult for him to remember how he got to this point. He barely even remembered the dangerous mix of pain meds and alcohol that he had consumed not all that long ago. Had the unusual woman rescued him from that, or was she there as a reaper to claim his soul as he transcended into a new plane of existence? Maybe he was just high and was hallucinating all of it, but this felt all too real.

There was nothing now but the blackness of the void as Sam's organs ceased to function and his spirit began to float out into the ether. He had expected pain, but other than the initial shock, he felt nothing of the sort. It was a strangely peaceful experience that felt like it was meant to be, as if he was always meant to die. A second voice unexpectedly pierced through the veil of darkness that obscured his senses. It belonged to a girl that he recognised instantly. The girl who had at one time been his closest friend before he screwed everything up. Alice Delaney, the broken girl who he had once loved, but who was unable to love him in return. "Wake up, Sam! You're not dead, you're just sleeping!"

Sam awoke with a start, gasping as he took a deep and unnatural-feeling breath of stale air. He couldn't see anything at all, causing a sense of unease to take over. His mind was clouded with confusion, making it difficult for him to focus on anything in the darkness. Either his eyes were failing him, or he was stuck somewhere without any source of light. Feeling groggy and weak, his body resisted any attempts to move. It left him with a dreadful feeling of helplessness and he hated it. He had always hated feeling vulnerable.

Trying to remember how he got there, Sam did his best to recall his last few memories of that night. Yes, he had been mixing alcohol with stolen medication, and had passed out on the sidewalk. He knew that he had wanted to die, but had felt regret when his life began to fade until something else happened. His heartbeat had slowed and he convinced himself that it was the end. He remembered hearing footsteps, a woman's voice, and then nothing. Had she taken him somewhere afterwards? There wasn't much else in his memory after that, so he couldn't be sure. At least there was nothing else of importance that he could remember. Just falling unconscious, his mysterious companion, her promises and then waking up here, wherever here was.

Summoning all his strength, Sam tried to push himself up into a sitting position, but his head met with a hard and impassable surface, causing him to slump backwards. He struggled to reach out to the sides with his arms, and they too hit something. They were thinly padded walls of some sort, with the same above him too. He was surrounded on all sides by the same soft material covering what sounded like wooden walls beyond. The situation seemed more than a little odd.

Gathering his thoughts Sam tried to work out what was going on. And then it struck him. He was lying in a coffin, likely deep underground. Panic set in. If he was in a coffin, then he was surely dead. But if he was dead, how was he even able to think about being dead? Sam realised that despite the stress that he felt, his pulse wasn't elevated. In fact, he had no heartbeat at all.

That confirmed it. He had died and this was either hell or some sort of purgatory. Sam discovered that he didn't appear to be breathing either. Yes, he had taken a breath before, but it hadn't felt natural to him. It had felt strained, like he had forced his lungs to take action out of habit instead of out of necessity. So he wouldn't be running out of air any time soon, but he was still trapped six feet underground in a rectangular box, with no hope of anyone coming to his rescue.

Sam was worried that he was doomed to rot away in his wooden prison. He was almost tempted to resign himself to that fate, as he believed that he deserved it, but a voice in the back of his mind screamed for him to escape. He was hungry, so painfully hungry and he needed sustenance. The hunger was a dull ache that started in his stomach, spreading out through every inch of his body until he could think of nothing else. He may not have needed to breath any more and his heart may have been nothing more than a shrivelled, useless organ, but Sam apparently still had to eat. The intensity of his hunger gradually built up inside of him and took over his mind like a beast breaking out of its cage. He needed to feed, and he needed to do it soon.

A burst of energy came out of nowhere, fueled by a desperation that caused Sam to claw at the lid of his coffin. He tore at the cloth, ripping it to shreds as he continued to scratch at the varnished wood beyond. It was slow going, but the voice in his head refused to let him quit, and so he scratched until the surface began to splinter. He didn't stop for a second, even when his nails began to break and his fingers bled.

Something about the box reminded Sam of a recurring nightmare that had started at an early age and had carried on into his adulthood. Every night he had been imprisoned in a featureless wooden room and nothing he did could set him free. In the morning he would often wake up feeling more exhausted than he had been before he went to bed. It was as if the room had been real and he had never actually slept. The image of the empty room had haunted him throughout the day and tortured his very existence. As if that wasn't bad enough, Sam now found himself within an even smaller box and this time it definitely wasn't a dream.

It took every ounce of strength that Sam had, but he managed to crack the wood. It would take some time, but he was beginning to believe that there was a real possibility of surviving the ordeal. A handful of dirt fell through the fracture in the coffin lid, and before he could react the crack began to widen, opening inwards as soil began to pour through at an exponential rate. In his desperation, Sam hadn't thought that far ahead and now was unsure whether or not he had the energy reserves to continue the dig upwards, but that didn't mean that he wouldn't give it his all. The soil was heavier than he had anticipated as it began to cover his entire body from head to toe with its crushing weight.

It wasn't long before the lid had given way completely, collapsing in on its occupant. Sam scrambled into action, reaching upwards and doing everything he could to pull himself up through the layers of earth. Once he could no longer feel the wood of the coffin, he quickly realised that he had become disorientated and didn't know which direction to tunnel in order to reach the light of day. Clumps of dirt and stone were in his eyes, up his nostrils, and pushing in through his mouth. It was everywhere and he found that his clothes were weighed down by the soil that permeated them, tearing them at the seams as he kept on clawing through the ground in the hope that he was heading the right way.

Sam managed to keep himself going. Not just because of the hunger that he felt now, but because his own survival instincts were kicking in. 'Just keep digging, Sam.' He would have told himself out loud, but he didn't want to have his mouth completely full of soil. 'Dig. You can do it. Just dig.' And that's what he did. It felt like he was going upwards, but he had been turned around and there was no way of being sure. 'Don't think about it. Just keep going.'

As there was no place for the dirt to go, Sam couldn't pull it past him. He had to push upwards, using his arms to pull himself through. It might not have been tunneling in the traditional sense but it seemed to be working. He had to be running on pure adrenaline by now, if dead people still had adrenaline. Wherever his extra energy was coming from, he sure did appreciate the boost.

Time had lost all meaning within the confines of the earth. Minutes could have been hours for all that mattered. Sam had no concept of such things as he struggled on through the never ending wall of dirt. It had to be further than six feet to the surface, or maybe he was digging horizontally. Every time he tried to stop and find his bearings, the soil around him seemed to tighten its grip, and so he couldn't take a break or rest even for a second. He had to keep going. He had to keep on pushing through.

Sam's arms hurt and his legs threatened to expire, but he wouldn't let them. He would only give them a break when he could see the sky with his own dirt clogged eyes. For a moment he wondered if he was in a marked grave and whether or not it said the words 'rest in peace' upon the epitaph. If it did, this was certainly not what they had in mind. He wasn't resting and he felt anything but peaceful. Instead it felt the planet itself was trying to keep him down there. It was Sam versus the world, and he was going to fight tooth and nail until the very end. There was no giving up, not now. Not ever.

There was no telling how long it had taken him. No knowing how long he had been within the earth's grasp. It could have been a lifetime for all Sam knew, but just when things seemed like they couldn't be more dire, his fingers breached the surface. He could feel the cool air brushing his fingertips as they protruded out through what must have been the grass beyond. He was close to obtaining the freedom that he had fought so hard for that he could almost taste it. Just a little bit more work and he would be free of his own grave.

Sam placed his hands on the flat ground above him before

pulling up with all that was left of his might. Weary arms were closely followed by his head, eyes opening slowly as he could finally smell something other than the soil in his nostrils. It took a second for his vision to clear, but all he saw around him was yet more darkness. Sam wasn't greeted by daylight, rather the stars of the night sky. As he suspected, he was buried in a graveyard and it was one that he recognised too. He wasn't in Seattle anymore, the city in which he had given up all hope. Instead he now found himself in his hometown of Birchfield, Kansas. A place more familiar to him than any other.

Sam clambered up through the grass, grabbing at its blades in an attempt to drag the rest of his body into the open. It was a struggle to pull his legs up, but after one last ditch effort he was finally free of his prison. His body had never been so beaten up or exhausted, and he couldn't tell if he was bleeding or if he was just damp from water in the soil, but he didn't care. Freedom tasted so sweet.

Somehow managing to roll on to his back, Sam peered up at the moon, its crescent shape relaxing him in his moment of triumph. Tilting his head backwards, he could see that he had dug his way straight up as he was lying by a large and relatively new gravestone that bore his name. There were dead flowers decorating the floor in its immediate vicinity, having likely dried up some time ago. The engraving on the stone was upside down from his perspective, but Sam still managed to read it out loud, his voice sounding tired and gravelly. "Here lies Samuel Isaac Mitchell. Our beloved son, missed dearly. Life is not forever, love is." It was an odd feeling, reading his own epitaph, and one that he would likely never forget.

Sam wondered where to go from there, but decided that he was in no rush to do anything else. His stomach grumbled in protest, sending shooting pains through his already sore limbs. He was still starving and would have to deal with his hunger soon, but before that he wanted to see his parents. He wanted to let them know that they hadn't lost him and that he was okay. Well, he might be dead, but at least he wasn't completely gone. Sam was sure that he wasn't a ghost as he had a corporeal form, but if he wasn't a spirit, what was he? Something told him that he would have plenty of time to find out. Perhaps his mom and dad would have some answers. With that thought in his mind, he clambered to his feet and made a vague attempt at dusting himself down, although his effort was in vain as the dirt clung to his clothing and refused to be dislodged.

Sighing loudly, Sam shakily made his way out of the cemetery with weary legs, past rows of crumbling, unkempt gravestones and between the creaking old trees that bordered the unnervingly open area. He squeezed between the rusted railings that led towards an old short cut that he remembered from his childhood and made his way down the familiar streets in search of home. Sam hoped that his parents would be happy to see him and felt nervous at the thought of seeing them again. He had a nagging feeling that it had been quite some time since they had last laid their eyes upon him. Unfortunately for him, it had been much longer than he could have ever guessed.

CHAPTER ONE: TO DREAM OF DROWNING.

Aaron knew this place. It had haunted him for longer than he could remember, as if nothing had existed before it. It was a place that had changed him and there was never a chance of going back to being the kid that he was before it all happened. Twenty years had gone by and yet he could never shake the feeling of fear that had overwhelmed him in that little suburban house, nestled between the trees of Edison Heights, New Hampshire.

Barely turning nine years old when it began, Aaron had hated living in that house ever since the day his family had moved into town. It never felt like home to him, and he sorely missed his friends back in Michigan, but his parents had to go where the work was, something that was difficult for him to understand at the time.

The house had been built in the sixties and still had the old, tobacco smoke stained wallpaper that his mom plastered over with new coats of paint. However, no matter how much she tried to modernise the decor, it still somehow managed to smell damp and musty. It didn't help that the scented candles and air freshener that Aaron's mom used did a far better job at making him feel sick than actually masking the dank odour.

There was something distinctly off about the building, but neither Aaron's mom nor his dad could sense it like he could. There were noises at night as he huddled under the relative safety of the covers of his bed, hiding from anything that might come for him. Running water could be heard where there was none and a constant tapping or maybe even a dripping sound that his parents seemed oblivious to. They just said that it was an older residence with its quirks and that he would settle in soon. The trouble is, he didn't. He never adjusted. Aaron knew that he wasn't the problem though, it was the house, or rather something within it. The old house never welcomed him and it certainly never became his home.

Trapped within the freshly painted halls of the old house that twisted impossibly and glowed with an unnaturally greenish hue, Aaron knew that he was in the nightmares that infested his mind on a nightly basis, yet he still felt fear. It may have just been a distant memory, but it still felt real. He thought that it would have faded through the years, but the vivid images set before him had only intensified, becoming corrupted over time with new, more bizarre experiences.

Aaron had no control over his surroundings and was doomed to relive the horrors of his past encounters with the supernatural. Once again, he found himself as he once was, nine years old and all alone, wandering through the mists of unfading memories, wearing pyjamas that he hadn't seen in years. Aaron had witnessed so many terrifying things throughout his life, but nothing quite so overwhelming as this. His first encounter with the paranormal. The close encounter that changed everything.

Wet footprints led along the crooked floorboards, reaching out into the darkness of the hallway that stretched far into the unknown. Aaron felt a call, starting as a whisper that urged him to step forwards, his own bare feet treading in each puddle as if he were retracing his own steps. He was unable to resist, knowing full well that he had walked that path before and that he was doomed to walk it again. The water between his toes felt cold to the touch and chilled his skin like ice, sending a shiver through his body. He tried his best to ignore the sensation, keeping his attention focused on where the footsteps were leading him.

In the distance, Aaron could make out the shape of a familiar doorway. It seemed normal enough, with the pale white of its painted surface seemingly untainted by the swampy, green air of the hall. The polished brass of the handle almost sparkled in the failing light, inviting him to turn it to enter into the room beyond. As he approached, the hallway around him faded from view until there was nothing else but him, the door and an ever expanding puddle of water that was protruding outwards from beneath the doorway itself. The sound of a running faucet could be heard clearly now, with its source originating from somewhere on the other side.

Pausing for just a moment, Aaron could feel his heart trying to break free of his chest, his lungs inhaling and exhaling with force. He felt weak and clammy, and his legs wanted to give out underneath him, but still his hand reached for the door. His arm outstretched, Aaron could feel himself shaking as he began to turn the handle. He took one last giant breath before pulling the door open, a flickering light escaping from the room beyond.

Before Aaron could react, a torrent of water burst through the doorway, knocking him off his feet as it swept him back down the hall from where he came. It engulfed him completely, dragging him back into the murky green and causing him to lose sight of the door. A raging river filled the corridor, leaving him dazed with no sense of direction and no source of air. The hallway soon disappeared from view again as walls were stripped away and he found himself surrounded by nothing but water, his immediate area illuminated by a dull green light.

Aaron couldn't breathe. He desperately needed to, but it was impossible. There was nothing for his lungs to take in other than the icy cold water that numbed his body. He tried to swim but something stopped him. It was holding him there and refused to let him move. All he could do was thrash his arms and legs, but it didn't help. There was no surface or pockets of air. He tried to think, but his mind was racing a mile a minute, making rational thought impossible. Closing his eyes, Aaron attempted to calm himself, but it was no use. He was in a panic and the only way to stop it was to escape, but he knew that there was no hope of that. After all, he had gone through this nightmare a million times before and knew exactly what was coming next.

Resigning to his fate, Aaron opened his eyes again and came face to face with a girl, approximately nine years old. Her brown eyes were wide, pupils dilated, as she stared directly into his. She silently screamed out for help, her wild, dark hair floating around her as she struggled in a similar manner to Aaron just a few moments before. He knew the girl, as he had seen her many times before. He knew how her story ended and it sickened him every single time.

Aaron couldn't help the little girl, even though he wanted to. It was far too late for that. It had always been too late, which is why this was the worst of his nightmares. He was always the witness and never the saviour that he wanted to be more than anything. He watched as she gasped for breaths of air that would never come and as her body began to convulse. All he could do was watch as the life faded from her, as he was powerless to do anything else. All he could do was watch her die. In this particular tale Aaron was unable to play the part of the hero and he hated it. It had been his first true lesson in life. Not everyone could be saved.

****

"I'm sorry!" Aaron yelled at the top of his voice, unaware of where he was.

"What the fuck, man!" Came the surprised response as the truck swerved on the road for a split second before quickly recovering.

Opening his eyes, Aaron could see the annoyed expression of his foul mouthed friend who he had startled with the sudden outburst. "Oh... Sorry, Tommy. I must have been dreaming..." Aaron said apologetically as he sat up straight in his chair, adjusting his seat belt with one hand and rubbing his neck with the other. He knew that he had been sleeping awkwardly as he felt sore all over and had been sweating profusely. The fabric of his t-shirt had been drenched and was stuck to his skin. The ache of his jaw signified that he had been grinding his teeth again and they really didn't have the funds right now for an emergency trip to the dentist.

"Dude, you look terrible. Like you've seen a ghost or somethin'." Tommy looked worried, but true to himself he soon swapped his look of worry for his usual goofy looking grin. "Then again, you always look crappy. That's why people say I'm the good lookin' one."

Although he was still feeling somewhat disturbed by his dream, Aaron managed to flash a smile in return. "Whatever, Tommy. You're full of it." With a loud sigh, he stretched his legs as much as possible. They had been on the road for hours and even the spacious interior of their pick-up truck felt cramped after a while. They had only stopped for gas, the occasional bathroom break and to change drivers despite Tommy's protests, never spending enough time out of the truck to fully recover from the drive.

Taking a moment to check out the scenery as it passed them by, Aaron saw that the open fields of Kansas had given way to rolling hills and woodlands. The truck rumbled along a paved, single lane road, passing a sign that signalled that they were nearing their destination. Birchfield, Kansas.

Tommy used his left hand to roll up the sleeves of his red and black plaid shirt, keeping his other hand on the wheel to steer. "I don't think I'll ever get used to this freakin' heat. Promise me we can go somewhere colder after this..."

Tommy wasn't wrong. The nightmare wasn't the only reason that Aaron found himself sticking to the beaten, tan leather of his seat. The dashboard display showed that the temperature was in the high eighties and the humidity was nearly unbearable. The air conditioning in their old pickup truck hadn't worked in years, so they had cracked the windows open to compensate. However, the sticky, humid air wasn't helping to cool either of them down very much.

Aaron shifted in his seat, sitting himself up straight and groaning a little from the aches and pains brought on from his nap. He took a moment to stretch his arms out in front of him before leaning over to reach under his seat for his old, grey laptop which he pulled out with some care. Placing it on his lap, he flipped open the screen and turned it on. A beep sounded as the computer whirred to life.

Tommy glanced over at the laptop, seemingly interested in what his friend was up to. "So you finally gonna tell me about the case?"

Aaron gave a quick nod. "Sure, just a sec. It's booting up." A minute later and he was entering his password on the login screen, unlocking access. He proceeded to open a number of different documents and his web browser, complete with multiple tabs that he had previously bookmarked. Local news reports, addresses and all sorts of compiled data that had taken a while to collect. He took a moment to organise the windows on the screen in order to make them all visible at once. "Right, what do you want to know?"

Tommy almost groaned in response. "What do you think? Gimme the goddamn details!"

Reading through the information, Aaron began to spout out anything that he found relevant. "Let's see... Birchfield. Small town in Kansas. Young adult, one Samuel Mitchell, breaks in to his old family home and assaults the new occupants. He then escapes the scene and flees town after a violent confrontation with the local police."

Tommy raised a hand from the wheel and held it out towards his friend in exasperation. "Please tell me you didn't make me drive all this fucking way for some petty crime!"

Aaron stayed focused on the laptop monitor. "Come on, give me some credit... We're not here to waste our time playing cops."

Tommy grunted. "Okay, so spill!"

"It'd be faster without interruptions." Aaron sighed in response.

In complete silence, Tommy replied by pretending to zip his lips together, quickly followed by a thumbs up.

"Right." Aaron clicked on the browser, separating two tabs for an obituary and a news report before expanding them both to take up the majority of the screen. "Here we go... Samuel Mitchell was identified by an officer on the scene who was close friends with the family. He claims that 'the boy barely recognised him'. The interesting part is that Samuel has been dead for over a year."

Tommy chimed in. "Bloodsucker?"

Aaron quickly shot down that theory. "No. Over a year and the grave had only been disturbed the same night. Open casket funeral during the day, so it couldn't have been a vampire. He was in the ground for far too long."

Tommy's eyebrows raised questioningly. "Corpser?"

Aaron examined the news article some more. "Nope... Zombies are brainless killing machines, not much for conversation. It seems that Mr Mitchell was talking up a storm. He may have been confused, but he was still somewhat coherent."

Tommy slammed both his hands down on top of the steering wheel, catching Aaron by surprise. "Shit, I don't know then!"

Aaron rolled his eyes. "Relax. That's why we're here. We'll find out what we're dealing with and then... deal with it. Maybe it's a changeling or maybe even something new... Or maybe the guy was just a doppelganger."

"Right! Crazy ass lookalikes!" Tommy exclaimed, stepping on the gas and causing the truck to roar forwards at an accelerated rate. "The sooner we get there, the sooner we can get to the fun part!"

Aaron didn't have time to respond and knew exactly what was coming next, as his friend turned on the stereo, twisted the volume control and started blasting out one of his favourite metalcore tracks. As if that wasn't enough, he wound down the windows further, stuck his head outside and yelled his usual obscenities as he jammed his foot down on the gas pedal. "Fuck you, monsters! Your balls are mine!"

Powerless to stop his crazy companion, Aaron closed his laptop and slumped back in to the damp, sweaty leather of his seat as Tommy began singing along to his obnoxiously loud music, while simultaneously drumming on the wheel. With their luck, the cops would pull them over and take them in for questioning before they even had the chance to look around town. After all, why would a couple of guys from New Hampshire be out in the middle of nowhere? And why was there a crate of guns, knives and all manner of pointy objects locked away in their truck bed? The police would never understand or believe the real reason behind it. No-one would. It was just another typical day in the life of a hunter.

CHAPTER TWO: THE EMPTY GRAVE.

Walking shoulder to shoulder with Tommy, Aaron could see the yellow police tape that cordoned off the grave site as they meandered between the weathered stones of the graveyard. It was early evening, and the intense heat was finally starting to let up as the sun hid itself behind some thick cloud cover. The pair had stopped and booked a room at a motel in town, taking the time to shower and change out of their sweaty, travel clothes. A fresh t-shirt and clean pair of jeans later, and they were ready to get to work.

As they got closer to the site, Aaron could see that some police officers were still nearby, but they seemed to be wrapping up for the day as they carried shovels and other such equipment back to their vehicles. A small excavator sat next to a pile of dirt, just on the other side of a large hole in the ground that must have previously been the grave of the supposed late Samuel Mitchell.

Without a second thought, the pair of them ducked under the tape to peer over the edge of the hole in the open ground. Sure enough, an unearthed wooden coffin lay at its base, partially obstructed from view by a few handfuls of soil. The most unusual thing about the coffin was that the lid had somehow splintered outwards, as if someone or something had broken out from inside. The interior seemed to be full of soil as well, as it had likely filled the void left by Samuel Mitchell's missing body.

Aaron turned to read the gravestone, confirming to himself that they were in the right location. "Samuel Isaac Mitchell. We found it."

"No shit..." Replied Tommy in his usual snarky tone.

Aaron crouched down to take a closer look at the hole and sighed. "I wish we got here before they destroyed the place."

His friend moved next to him, leaning over his shoulder to peer inside too. "Yeah, man. I hate when th..."

Tommy was cut short by a booming voice that spoke with harsh authority, causing them both to freeze on the spot. "What in God's green earth are you boys doing here? This is an active crime scene! I should have you both placed under arrest!"

Tommy raised his hands slowly as if it was a robbery. He had been in jail on more than one occasion and always tensed up when dealing with law enforcement, quickly turning into a mute. It was for the best after all, as he had a habit of talking himself into trouble, not out of it.

It was Aaron who was first to break the through the silence. "We're sorry, officer. We didn't mean any harm."

The gruff, Southern accent of the policeman replied a little softer than before. "You boys aren't from around here. What brings you to town? Other than trespassing and interfering with official police business."

Aaron had to think fast. He hadn't prepared an excuse, so it was handy that he was a quick thinker. "We're Sam's cousins... His mom was worried?" He didn't mean to make the last part sound like a question, but he had panicked. Fortunately for him, the cops in Birchfield were used to folks being honest. It was a little different from the law enforcement back home.

"Oh, well why didn't you say that before? You boys should have introduced yourselves from the get go. How're Simon and Olivia coping with the news?" The man sounded genuinely concerned.

Aaron relaxed, slowly turning towards the cop while presenting his friendliest smile, whereas Tommy didn't move, his muscles still tense as if he had been turned to stone. It took a quick nudge from Aaron to snap him out of it, causing him to spin around to face the officer with a grimace plastered across his face. It was doubtful that he would add much to the conversation. At times like this, Tommy was completely useless.

Aaron cleared his throat. "Fine! Well... as much as can be expected. They were talking about maybe coming back to town." He was going off what little information he had available. The Mitchell's had changed their address to some place in Florida and now had a baby girl too. "But the new baby makes things difficult for them."

The officer examined the pair, checking them out over the top of the rims of his aviator sunglasses. He ran a finger along his moustache before smiling warmly. "I heard they had a little one. I couldn't be happier for them." He took a big step forward, shaking each of their hands in turn with a firm grip and rough, calloused palms. Tommy's handshake looked as uncomfortable and awkward as his stance. "Sergeant Bob Ellis. I'm in charge of the case."

"Aaron Mitchell." Aaron gestured to his companion. "And this is Tommy."

There wasn't a single word, nor sound from the statuesque Tommy.

"Not much of a talker, is he?" The Sergeant chuckled, eyeing Tommy up once more.

"No, sir..." Tommy finally interjected, albeit with a weak and shaky voice. He couldn't even manage a fake smile and just looked out of place.

Aaron came to his rescue. "This whole thing hit him hard. He's had trouble processing it all."

Sergeant Ellis nodded his acceptance, placing his hands on his hips. "Well gosh darn it... I understand. You boys in town for long?"

Aaron nodded. "Just until we find out what happened with Sam."

The officer tipped his hat back, scratching his temple. "Might be waiting a little while. The investigation could take some time... It's a little on the unusual side."

Aaron decided to take a chance, using the cops pleasant demeanor as an opening. "Can we please meet the victims? We want to apologise for our cousins behaviour."

He tried to sound sincere, but could tell by the change in

expression on Sergeant Ellis' face that he had overstepped his bounds and caused instant suspicion. "I can't have you disturbing those nice folks any more than they already have been. There's already been too much of a ruckus about the whole thing, small town and all."

Aaron did his best to recover the conversation, but found himself quickly stumbling. "We'd be quick. It's really important for us to make sure that they're alright and we've got a few questions about Sam."

Ellis frowned. "Those folks have enough to worry about without being questioned by strangers, however pure your intentions."

His answer peaked Aaron's curiosity. "What did Sam do to them?"

"You're out of line, son!" The Sergeant barked his displeasure.

Aaron kept the questions coming, trying to catch the officer off guard. "Did he bite them?"

His tactic seemed to work, if just a little. "Now how would you know about something like that?"

Tommy mumbled something unintelligible, pointing towards the officers arm and catching Aaron's attention. "What's up, Tommy?"

He spoke a little louder and clearer this time, still pointing down at the cops arm. "Did... did he bite you too?"

Aaron looked exactly where his friend was pointing, and sure

27

enough the police officer's sleeves were rolled up, displaying a bandaged forearm that he hadn't noticed until it had been pointed out to him.

Sergeant Ellis didn't appreciate being the center of attention and snapped at them. "What of it?"

Aaron tried to examine the wound from a distance. "Is it a puncture wounds or a regular bite mark? Does it itch?"

The officer looked puzzled. "What kind of stupid question is that? Of course it's a 'regular bite mark'. He's a human being, not some sort of rabid animal." He seemed to study Aaron's face for a moment. "You two seem to know more about this than you're letting on."

Ellis looked back and forth between the pair of them. "You're not his cousins, are you... Maybe I should take you down to the station for questioning."

Aaron raised his hands defensively, trying to diffuse the situation. "That's not necessary, Sergeant. We're just... We have an internet blog about weird goings on and... were just curious."

Sergeant Ellis huffed, crossing his arms in front of his chest in annoyance. "I should have known... Nothing but troublemakers and thrill seekers. Get out of here and stop wasting my time before I arrest you both!"

Tommy was ready to move and turned to walk back towards the truck. Aaron on the other hand stood his ground. "So there's nothing unusual about the bite at all?"

There was obvious frustration on the Sergeants face now as

28

it turned beet red. "No. As I said, it's a 'normal' bite, if you can call a man biting another man 'normal'." He raised an arm and angrily gestured towards Tommy, his other hand resting on his gun. "Now get the hell out of here and stop wasting my time. Don't make me tell you again, boy!"

Feeling a little stubborn, Aaron followed through with one final question. "Do you know where Sam went?"

The officer was almost spitting now as his voice raised in to a yell. His movements were increasingly animated as he waved his arms around wildly. "He skipped town! Like you boys will if you know what's good for you! This is a small town with friendly and trusting folk. We don't need your kind here causing trouble! If I hear you've been disturbing the peace, I'll put you both in a jail cell and throw away the key!"

Finally taking the extremely unsubtle hint, Aaron turned and hurried to catch up with his friend who was still walking away through the graveyard. Even though he was in a rush, it didn't stop him from getting some final words in as he called back to Sergeant Ellis. "Thank you for your time, Sergeant! Enjoy the rest of your day!"

Sergeant Bob Ellis declined to answer, merely grunting instead. He stood there sternly and stared at the two of them as they wandered back to their waiting vehicle.

Tommy elbowed Aaron in the ribs with some force, not hard enough to wind him, but just enough to cause him to stagger. "Dude, you almost got us in serious trouble. You're a dick." He spoke quietly enough to make sure that only his friend could hear his words.

Aaron grinned widely, mimicking Tommy's infamously wicked smile. "Oh, I know. I learned it all from you."

They both stifled a laugh, trying to look serious as they knew that they were still being watched.

"Hungry?" Aaron asked, opening the passenger door of the truck.

Tommy nodded. "Always! You know me."

"Unfortunately..." Aaron's witty reply came much quicker than either of them anticipated.

As Tommy got in the driver's seat, he stopped for a moment and stared at his friend in mock anger. A second later and they broke down into a fit of hysterics.

Taking a few deep breaths to recover, Aaron brought up the area map on his phone. "Come on, there's a diner down the street with decent reviews."

Tommy simply nodded. He turned the key in the ignition and began to drive down the gravel path towards the exit. As Aaron looked back, he could still see Sergeant Ellis glaring at them as he cradled his wounded arm. From the way he was acting, it definitely didn't seem like a normal bite at all.

****

Whatever happened to them, no matter what each day held,

Aaron could count on his best friend for one thing. Tommy Hughes knew how to stuff his face. No-one else could see things that would turn most people insane and still be able to fill their stomach to bursting with a full stack of pancakes. It had luckily been a quiet day for them so far, which meant that Aaron was able to keep his food down too.

Aaron sat quietly, sipping his coffee as his best friend jammed fork fulls of food in to his face without chewing much in between mouthfuls. Tommy was working on a massive plate of food across the booth in the retro styled, fifties diner they had found, that had clearly seen better days. The decor left a lot to be desired and the fluorescent lighting was far too bright. Despite the state it was in, the restaurant seemed to be popular with the locals and was pulling in a decent sized crowd.

"Did you see the size of the bug that hit the windshield? It was as big as my fist!" Tommy was in his element and didn't even stop for a sip of his soda to wash his food down. He loved to eat, which was hard for some to believe as his fast metabolism left him slim and athletic in build. Some people had all the luck. Aaron actually had to work out to stay thin and didn't eat anywhere near as much as his friend.

"Remember Bradley Wells?" Tommy's thought came out of nowhere, with his mouth still stuffed to almost bursting.

Aaron queried his friend's question with a raise of his eyebrows. "Sure, but why bring that up now? It's ancient history."

Finishing his mouthful, Tommy considered taking another

bite but thought better of it and decided to play with his food instead. "Well... he had that invisible thing that followed him around, watching out for him."

Aaron remembered it like it was yesterday, when in reality it had happened over fifteen years ago. "His 'guardian angel' or however he put it, yes. That's the first time you started to actually believe me about supernatural stuff."

Tommy loaded up his fork and prepared himself for another huge bite. "You mean I thought you were a fuckin' lunatic and needed help. But yeah, we never worked out what the hell it was... You think we'll have the same shit luck this time? I've no idea what's with this Mitchell kid."

Smiling thoughtfully at his friend as he stuffed his face once more, Aaron laughed. "We've come a long way since then, Tommy. The Shadow House, the Gulag, Tsang and his creepshow motel, that vampire nest in the foothills... even the farmhouse."

Tommy's face quickly changed from a look of wonder and amusement to an uncomfortably somber expression. "Christie..."

A feeling of guilt washed over Aaron as he realised that mentioning the farmhouse wasn't the brightest idea. "Sorry..." He paused for a moment, sipping his coffee. "My point is, we've been through all that and more. We've learned a great deal and have grown from our experiences. If we encountered Bradley now, I'm sure we could solve the mystery before his dad pulled him out of school."

Tommy put his fork down on his empty plate, having finally

polished off the last of his food. "So you think we'll find out what the hell kinda monster this guy is and track him down?"

Aaron nodded. "Exactly. It'll be a cakewalk."

Leaning back, Tommy dabbed the edges of his mouth with his napkin before taking a long and noisy sip of soda through his straw. "If it's so easy, genius, what do we do next?"

There wasn't time for Aaron to answer before they were drowned out by the loud conversation of some gossiping locals just one table over. "Ah heard it was the ghost of the Mitchell kid, coming back from the dead to kill his folks, but they weren't there no more." The statement came from a particularly loud and arrogant man, dressed in denim overalls.

His skinny friend didn't take long to voice his own noisy opinion, tweaking the peak of his old baseball hat. "Nah. Ah heard he was dug up by some drifter and they're goin' 'round wearin' his face." Aaron and Tommy stayed silent, listening for any possible truths in the hearsay, but not taking much stock in the rumour mongering of suspicious townies.

A well dressed woman, who was sat at a seperate table with her husband and two boys, decided to turn her head and join in. She addressed the others with a clear feeling of superiority. "Actually, I overheard that the Mitchell's boy was brought back by demon worshippers and that he acted under their evil influence." She seemed more than pleased when all other conversations ceased and all the attention fell on her. It was if she had waited her whole life for that moment and that she didn't waste a second.

The woman stood up from the table, leaving her husband slack jawed with embarrassment as she adjusted the bun of her hair and proceeded to preach as though she was all high and mighty. She seemed to revel in the moment and was quick to come up with new ideas. "It's obvious that the police are hiding the truth from us! The evil girl has come back to town and has brought her witch cult with her!"

Someone called out from the other side of the diner. "The Delaney's girl?"

The woman nodded enthusiastically, gesturing in the direction that the voice had originated from. "The one and the same!"

A wave of whispers passed around the room as everyone seemed to suddenly agree with her, with no actual evidence to back up her words. Aaron and Tommy exchanged a nervous glance, realising that they were out of their depth. They knew that they didn't belong there and hoped that no-one would notice them tucked away in the corner.

The woman continued her rant, wagging her finger as she spoke. "She's come back to corrupt our children and kill everyone else. She'll harm us just like she did the Mayor's boy! The devil girl is back!" It sounded as though she was trying to incite a riot or invoke mob justice, even though there was no obvious target within sight.

Everyone within earshot began to gossip between themselves, their murmurs increasing in volume as new theories were tossed around. It was then that the woman realised there were strangers in their midst and she turned everyone's attention towards

34

the unprepared Tommy and Aaron who had been keeping a relatively low profile up until that point.

"And what do we have here?" The woman strolled over with the confidence of a tyrant as the talking in the room died out around her once more. She stopped just shy of the edge of their booth and looked at the pair with accusing eyes. "You're both new in town... It's interesting that you both turn up when trouble starts. I suspect that you're in league with the Delaney girl, aren't you? What do you have to say for yourselves?!?"

Aaron didn't have an answer as he knew that she wouldn't believe anything that he had to say.

Tommy didn't even look up at the woman as he took a sip of his drink, placed it down on the table and spoke clearly and calmly. "Listen, lady... We just got here today. We haven't done a thing, so why don't you walk back to your table, sit the fuck down and spend some quality time with the beady eyed swamplings you call a family."

The woman's jaw dropped as she was left feeling flabbergasted, but she still somehow managed to come back with a retort. "I should have expected such blatant rudeness from out of towners... but this proves it! You're in league with the cult, I know it!"

Tommy didn't like being accused of something that he didn't do, yet he still refused to even acknowledge the woman by looking at her as he spoke. "You still here? I guess it's true what they say about people from the south... Slow in the fuckin' head."

Aaron almost facepalmed. "Tommy, don't..."

It was too late. He knew that Tommy didn't mean what he said, as they had made plenty of friends on their travels in the Southern States, but his friend knew how to push people's buttons. The guy was a well practiced jerk, but he also had a certain talent for angering crowds of people.

The woman was clearly mortified by Tommy's words, but her husband wasn't the one to come to her defence. "That's no way to speak to a lady!" The bellowing voice came from an overweight man in a tank top, sat at the counter near the kitchen with his back to the room. Behind him, the waitress and cook had ceased all activity to watch the events unfold. He pushed himself up from his stool and turned to face the strangers from New Hampshire, using the thick hair of his forearm to wipe his mouth clean. "You take that back and then get outta here before we throw you out!"

Aaron gulped. The man towered over everyone else in the room, but his sheer size didn't phase Tommy one bit. He just tensed his fists, ready for a brawl as he looked over with an unsettling glint in his eye. "Sit the fuck down, Hightower! Just finish eating your greens like mama told you, so you can grow big and strong like a real boy!"

The giant of a man shook with rage and Aaron was pretty sure that he was close to charging at them. However, today was their lucky day, as the door to the diner swung open and Sergeant Bob Ellis walked in on the proceedings. "What in the God's name is going on here?" The Sergeant didn't look pleased, but his powerful presence seemed to instantly pacify the townsfolk and caused Tommy to freeze up, finally shutting his big mouth.

The large man sat himself back down without a word and even the loud mouthed woman made her way back to sit with her family who looked as though they wanted to pretend that nothing happened. They all appeared to have a great deal of respect for the authority of their local police force, despite any complaints.

Aaron cringed, looking back at the Sergeant who was making a beeline for them, while Tommy stared back down at the table, trying to ignore the fact that they were mere moments away from being carted off to the police station.

"I had a feeling you two couldn't stay out of trouble." Sergeant Ellis' shadow loomed over them as he stopped at the edge of the table where the woman had been not long before. Aaron could feel the eyes of everyone in the establishment staring at them, their untrusting gaze boring holes in to the side of his skull. "Stand up and leave without another word." The Sergeant was clear, concise and straight to the point. "You two are coming with me!"

****

"I want you boys to promise me one thing." Sergeant Ellis wasn't happy, but for some reason he wasn't dragging them to jail and that was good enough for Aaron. He had escorted them out of the diner and into the parking lot where he stood them both next to his car, away from prying eyes.

Aaron answered quickly. "Yes, sir. We promise."

He nudged Tommy who blurted out his own response. "Promise. Yessir."

The officer stared both of them down, neither wanting to make eye contact and attempting to avoid it at all costs. "If I tell you what you want to know, you need to leave town and don't come back. The people here are God fearing Christians and they don't like strangers much. It's for your own protection as much as theirs."

Aaron wasn't so sure of himself anymore, but he still had a desire to know more. "We'll leave, sir. But if I may ask, what happened here? They mentioned a girl?"

Ellis sighed loudly, removing his hat to allow himself to scratch the top of his head. It was dark outside now, so his aviators were now tucked away in his shirt pocket. "Alice Delaney... Quiet girl and Sam Mitchell's only friend. They were thick as thieves as children, but then her parents were killed by a drunk driver and she moved in with the Mitchell family. Not sure what happened after that. They grew up, graduated and Sam ended up leaving town, but she stayed behind. Got a job at this very diner."

Tommy and Aaron looked at each other and then back to the Sergeant with renewed interest. They waited patiently for him to continue. "Well then news reached town that Sam died. Drug overdose or some such. It was a crying shame... His folks were heartbroken and left for family in Florida."

Aaron knew this part of the story, but found himself increasingly curious about the girl in the story. "And what happened to Alice?"

The Sergeant put his hat back on, shaking his head slowly. "With Sam dead and the Mitchells gone, the poor girl had no-one. No idea why she didn't just go with them, but I kinda wish she had. She was quiet and kept to herself. Kind of an outsider in town, you see. People knew her, but she was still a stranger. She was just odd."

Sergeant Ellis began to pace a little while they stayed still watching him intently as they listened with open minds. "We got called to the diner as there was some incident between Alice and the Mayor's son, Drew. She claimed he'd assaulted her, but she wasn't the one beaten half to death in the bathroom. There were no witnesses, but she was distressed and I was inclined to believe her. The Mayor didn't take kindly to the whole situation and turned the whole town against her, using his own influence to demonise the girl in their eyes."

Aaron found that he was beginning to understand, but felt disturbed by the fact that the people could be easily swayed to open hatred. "The Mayor has that much power over them?"

The Sergeant nodded. "He's well liked. There's a reason he's been Mayor for so long."

Aaron felt sorry for the girl. "So Alice became an outcast?"

Ellis shook his head slowly. "Always was one. She never did fit in here. They chased her out of town soon after and she never came back."

It took a moment for Aaron to ponder on the subject, but something about what the clientele of the diner said came to mind. "Some of the people inside seem to think that Sam Mitchell came back from the dead to kill his parents and that Alice Delaney's controlling him. Do you think any of that is true?"

Sergeant Ellis almost laughed, but quickly stopped himself as he thought about it further. "Little Alice? Heck no. The girl loved Simon and Olivia. She was harmless enough, just misunderstood." A look of dread crossed the man's face as he thought about it more. "I did see Sam the other night though. I'm certain it was him. He spoke to me, but he was all confused. Kept hollering about how hungry he was and then there was the biting..." It was easy to see how disturbed the officer was by what he had seen as he absently scratched at the bandage on his arm.

Aaron gently eased his next question in to the conversation. "We want to help him, but we really need to know where he went. I promise he won't come to any harm." Tommy looked a little confused, but let Aaron continue regardless. "We want to find Sam as much as you do."

Sergeant Ellis looked at them both again, examining their faces as if he was trying to commit them to memory. "As I said before, he loved his folks. My guess is he's heading down to see them. I may have let it slip to him that they moved..."

With a thankful smile, Aaron spoke softly. "Thank you, Sergeant Ellis. You've saved lives today."

Sergeant Bob Ellis didn't seem convinced, but he did appear

to be somewhat relieved. "There were sightings of him near the rail line. I'm guessing he stowed away and is long gone. It runs from coast to coast, so it's a straight shot from here to Florida. The trains are slow, so if you're quick you might be able catch him along the way."

The rail line meant that Sam was travelling down a set path and should be easy for them to track down, but he had a head start. Despite his advantage, it looked like their luck was finally picking up. Aaron felt truly thankful for the Sergeants help. "We really appreciate it. And I promise we won't trouble you or anyone else here anymore. We'll leave first thing in the morning. Right, Tommy?"

His companion didn't manage much more than a stutter. "R... right, yeah."

The Sergeant nodded his satisfaction, stroking his moustache with his thumb and forefinger. "Don't go venturing out tonight. I can't keep my eye on everyone in town." It was sound advice. Tommy had angered the locals and there was no telling what they would do without the presence of the local police. It was best not to tempt fate and avoid as many people as possible.

Aaron thanked the Sergeant once more and hopped back into the truck with Tommy hot on his trail. "Let's head straight to the motel. I don't want to run into the wrong people... We should leave before sunrise too."

Tommy nodded, not having fully relaxed from their last encounter with Sergeant Ellis. He would need time and Aaron understood that. Tommy had seen the darker side of law enforcement growing up and had the scars to prove it, both mental and physical. There were some things he would likely never get over or recover from.

On the bright side, they now had a target and destination, with a new case to give them purpose. In the morning they would head east, following the rail line with the hope of catching Samuel Mitchell before he made it to his parents home in Florida, or failing that, be able to track him down in the Sunshine State itself. The hunt was on.

CHAPTER THREE: THE HUNTER OR THE HUNTED.

The last few days had been a little rough, but Sam had finally made it to his destination of Fort Lauderdale, down on the southeast coast of Florida. It had been a long journey of self discovery, and he had learned a great deal about this new existence already. However none of it could prepare him for the trials that were yet to come.

The train that Sam had jumped aboard near Birchfield had only taken him so far, as a fallen tree on the line resulted in unbearably long delays. Adapting to the situation, he abandoned his original plan and hid himself within the trailer of a semi truck. He had overheard the driver talking on the phone at a gas station and had discovered that he was scheduled to transport grain to a depot close to the town where his parents lived.

Sam was convinced that it was going to be an easy ride across the country after that, however things hadn't gone so smoothly since then either. Newly emerging weaknesses threw a wrench into his plans, as they brought with them a need to adapt quickly to difficult situations as they arose. It had been an exhausting few days since his departure from Birchfield, but he had eventually emerged from his trials in triumph.

A great deal of the problems that Sam encountered along the way had stemmed from an emerging allergy that appeared to come out of nowhere. When exposed to direct sunlight, he would break out in a rash that covered any parts of his skin that the sun's rays had touched. It wasn't all that painful at first, offering nothing but a mild discomfort and he wasn't too bothered by the itching that it caused, that was until open sores began to develop due to extended exposure. After that, the 'pox' as Sam called it, became so unpleasant at times that he learned to avoid daylight whenever possible. The symptoms took their toll and resulted in him only wanting to move around at night, operating under the light of the moon and stars instead. Although it was during the daylight hours that the second part of his affliction would also come into play.

In the dark, Sam felt alert and ready for anything, as if he had the strength to take on the world. However, during the waking hours of the day he felt weak and apathetic. It was a draining sort of sickness that sapped his energy and made him want to hide away. The way it made his body feel was nothing short of strange, but he managed to push through the exhaustion, as tough as that could be at times. It was the kind of tiredness that couldn't be overcome through the usual rest and relaxation. He no longer needed to sleep in the traditional sense, instead feeling strong and alert again as soon as the sun had set.

As if Sam's vulnerability to natural light wasn't bad enough, there was one thing that controlled him more than the rising and setting of the sun. An intense hunger grew inside of him, boiling up from somewhere deep down. This ravenous appetite had become so insatiable that it left him powerless to resist. He had been hungry before, but the hunger that humans experienced didn't come anywhere close to this. Sam used to be able to keep his wits about him, but now he struggled to think of anything other than feeding. Finding the source of his next meal was something that motivated his actions first and foremost, and those gluttonous thoughts couldn't simply be ignored.

It didn't take Sam long to discover that it was no longer food that he required. He didn't eat like a human anymore, which made him realise that he wasn't one any longer. He could consume food if he wished, but it left him bloated and didn't satisfy the hunger. Not only that, but he would have to expel whatever he had ingested within a few hours, through any means possible, or face some extremely unpredictable and unfortunately unpleasant consequences.

No, Sam's body craved a different form of sustenance. Not meat, nor vegetable, but the life force of all living beings. Blood. The lust for blood had become his true master and he was its unwilling puppet. He could obey its will and thrive, or ignore its call and suffer an excruciating pain that would only intensify over time. If left unchecked, he was sure that it would eventually cripple his body, fast becoming a fate worse than death. Nothing could be worse than being imprisoned in a decaying corpse in excruciating agony as he denied himself his only salvation.

It wasn't all bad however. Sam was physically stronger than before and much faster than he had ever been in life, even at his peak. His hand eye coordination was fine tuned to a level that he had previously believed impossible and his senses had reached another state entirely. It would have been a truly liberating experience had he not been left feeling imprisoned by the new limitations that had been imposed upon his body.

Ingesting blood wasn't so terrible either. The taste of it was a revelation and nothing else in the world could compare. Drinking vitae straight from the source felt unbelievable in more ways than one. It was remarkably delicious, and the way that it made Sam feel was intoxicating. It left him with a feeling of euphoria that he hadn't felt since... Well, he hadn't felt it since the day he died, and apparently that was quite some time ago. The blood wet his tongue and trickled down his throat, causing him to lose himself in the moment. It was as if nothing else mattered to him. He didn't care about anything else in the world, until it was all over and he came to his senses once more.

However much Sam enjoyed the experience itself, the thought of sinking his teeth into human flesh still made him feel a little queasy. He had to convince himself that the whole process was just a means to an end, but that didn't help him forget the atrocities that he had committed to survive. He had only managed to feed a couple of times so far, but the act had been somewhat problematic. It was as if his mouth wasn't quite designed for the task, and the mess it made was horrific.

Sam was certain that there was still a great deal more to learn about his recent changes, and he had an inkling that the knowledge would come to him in time. It was exciting to know that there was still so much left to discover and that every night could bring fresh understanding. The upcoming weeks and months were likely going to be a long and gruelling transition period with a steep learning curve. Unfortunately, Sam still didn't have a notion of what he had become. He wondered if anyone out there knew what he was, or if there was anyone else like him. If not, was he doomed to wander alone? The uncertainty of it was terrifying.

Sam was sure that he would never be able to forget those that he had harmed, no matter how much he wanted to. He could still remember the look on the woman's face as he bit down on her neck, and the deafening screams that followed. The cries had penetrated his soul and had left a permanent scar. He didn't like hurting people, but it seemed to be integral to his survival now. Sam genuinely felt remorseful, but he wasn't ready to give up on himself yet. Not again.

The struggle wasn't all that Sam remembered from the night of his rebirth. The woman's husband had been there too. He had pulled a gun and soon after he too found himself at the mercy of Sam's vicious bite. He couldn't recall how he had managed to overpower someone so much larger than himself, only that he had. There had been a child present too, but they were small and far too weak to be worth the trouble. However, that child had called for the police and soon after Sam had found himself at the mercy of Sergeant

Bob Ellis.

Sam had demanded to know the truth. Why were those people in his house? Where were his mom and dad? He had been yelling for answers, but none had come. He just wanted to let his parents know that he was okay, but no-one had been willing to help him. And where was Alice? Was she okay? He desperately wanted to talk to his best friend. No, he needed to talk to her! He needed her to tell him that everything was going to be alright! Sam felt awful for cutting her out of his life and he wanted to make amends, but no-one was willing to help him! He just needed some help!

The woman had cried out, the man had threatened him and the little girl had burst into tears, but in his confusion Sam just couldn't understand why they wouldn't help him. He couldn't comprehend it. At least Bob seemed to offer some support and guidance. At least that's what Sam thought he was trying to do. It's not as if the events were clear in his mind.

Sam remembered Bob. He knew him as one of his father's oldest friends and the Sergeant had been part of their lives for as long as he could remember. The look of surprise and disgust on the man's face was sobering and helped him regain at least some of his composure. However, his brain was still clouded from the voracious hunger and he had struggled to hold a conversation. Bob had tried his best to calm him, as another cop left to call for an ambulance and most likely some backup.

Sam couldn't recall if the Sergeant had let him go, or if he had somehow escaped, but he did remember that someone had mentioned his family moving to Florida. They must have moved there to be near Auntie Jane and so he knew that it wouldn't be hard for him to find them. Auntie Jane was extremely active on social media and shared pretty much anything about her life, much to the annoyance of others.

After that, it had been just a matter of fleeing town and hopping in to an open shipping container aboard an eastbound train. Sam wasn't sure if he was being followed or not, but he didn't want to take the risk. He was hopeful that the police would treat the case as a local matter and they wouldn't involve the State Troopers or even the Feds. Bob Ellis wouldn't turn him over, would he? He wouldn't put others on to his scent. Despite what had happened and how he had acted, he had to believe that a family friend wouldn't betray him.

****

Nothing seemed more strange to Sam than creeping through the bushes in the middle of the day to spy on his own family. Hopefully the neighbours wouldn't call the police to report the strange man lurking on the property. He wasn't ready to knock on the door outright, announcing that he had mysteriously returned from the grave and that all their grieving was for naught.

Sam felt like a creep, but he didn't know how else to see his mom and dad before they could lay eyes upon him and jump to conclusions. Then again, what conclusion could they possibly come to? That he faked his own death? That he was some sort tormented spirit coming back to haunt them? Or maybe they would think that it was some sort of government cover-up and that he had been in hiding all this time. The truth of the situation wasn't exactly easy to comprehend or even accept. He had come back to life, for whatever reason, and he had to make the most of it.

  The sun was high in the sky, causing another rash to break out across Sam's body, and his only defense against it was the dirty shirt and tattered suit that he had been buried in. His surprise visit could have waited until after nightfall, but he desperately wanted to see his parents and wasn't willing to hold out for even a few more minutes, never mind several hours.

  To help remedy the situation, Sam had managed to salvage an old hooded sweatshirt by digging through a nearby dumpster, using it to replace the plastic tarp that he had been sheltering under up until that point. The hoody smelled like rotting trash and offended Sam's overly sensitive nostrils, but the extra layer offered the protection that he sorely needed. He knew that he looked like a hobo, but it was just a temporary measure that would have to work until he located a fresh set of clothing.

  It was supposed to be unbearably hot in Florida, but for some reason Sam didn't really feel the heat. His limbs were weary from moving about during the day, but he didn't seem to perspire at all and he felt as comfortable there as he did anywhere else. He had become accustomed to humidity growing up, although he would still sweat on exceptionally hot days, but it didn't seem to phase him at all now. Sam could sense the extreme temperature, and yet he didn't suffer from it. There was something about the lack of moisture on his body that was strangely unsettling, but he chalked it up to the changes that he had been going through. Perhaps it was just a phase, or maybe it was a permanent part of his transformation and he would be immune to any changes in climate in the future. There was no way to be sure.

The house itself was very different from the one Sam had known growing up. It was definitely smaller, with three bedrooms instead of four, and a single bathroom instead of two, but the size wasn't the main difference that he had noticed. The shape of the building was off, as it was only a one story building, with no basement to speak of. To his knowledge, houses in Florida tended not to have them due to the swampy nature of the landscape. The yellow painted walls of the house definitely screamed 'Sunshine State', and were a far cry from the plain white siding of their old home in Kansas. There wasn't much of a yard either, with a few withered shrubs, some overgrown bushes and a chain link fence separating them from the street by only a couple of feet.

Sam imagined that the new living conditions took a while for his parents to get used to. He was sure that they must have felt a little cramped and closed in for the first few months at least, but he knew that his mom would have done her best to decorate and make the place feel like home. What was it that she used to say? "Home is where your family is." Yes, that was it. How could he forget?

Scrambling on all fours, Sam squeezed in between the leaves of a particularly thick bush outside what he believed to be the living room window, and that's when he saw them, surrounded by familiar looking furniture in a familiar setting. He resisted pressing his nose up to the window to get a better look, deciding to peek through the bottom pane while trying to remain as inconspicuous as possible.

Sam could see them clearly through the dirt stained glass. His mom, his dad and to his surprise a baby dressed in pink. A little girl. A sister. His first thought was that his parents had decided to replace him, but that idea quickly passed and he soon realised that they had taken what chance they could to live a happy life following his unfortunate death. It must have been difficult for them to cope and he wished that he could take their pain away, but that just wasn't possible. He couldn't change the past, but perhaps he could ease their sorrows by revealing himself to them. However, he would have to time his appearance perfectly to avoid any further upset.

As Sam pondered the situation, he realised that his parents weren't alone with their daughter, and that they had visitors who he didn't recognise. They were two young men by the look of it, both in their late twenties at least, but it was hard to tell as they had their backs to him. Both of them were sitting on the old, leather couch that his dad used to take naps on, right across the wooden coffee table from his parents and within arms reach of them. Sam didn't know who they were, but he was instantly filled with feelings of distrust. His instincts flared up as a warning that these people meant to cause him harm. They must have known that he was alive and were there to take him in, but who did they work for and what were their intentions? They sure didn't look like cops or the FBI.

Observing in silence as the scene unfolded before him, Sam bided his time and tried to gather as much information he could. He was still attempting to work out what was going on and tried to listen in, but it was impossible to filter out the sounds of the local wildlife, passing cars and someone's dog barking in the distance. He was left feeling frustrated as he found himself unable to hear anything from inside other than muffled voices as they were drowned out by a cacophony of unfiltered noise. All he could do was quietly observe as he tried to hypothesise what was actually being discussed.

Sam's parents were sat close to each other as his mother held her baby girl against her chest, her other hand brushing hair from her face. They seemed to be fully engaged in the conversation with the two men, but they weren't acting distressed or upset in any way. Sam took a moment to just take in the sight of his family. His father had more grey hair than he remembered, but other than that he hadn't changed one bit. He was squinting through his glasses as he nodded in response to something that was said, adjusting the collar of his beige polo neck shirt. As for his mother, she didn't look all that different, although she did seem tired. Her smile was what he remembered the most and it hadn't changed one bit. She was still the same woman that he knew and adored, and it was wonderful to see them both, even at a distance.

Sam felt a little guilty when he looked at his sister as he didn't feel any attachment to her at all. After all he didn't even know that he had a sibling until just a few moments ago. He had grown up as an only child and recalled asking for a brother or sister on more than one occasion, but he had let go of those feelings a long time ago. He didn't know the girl, but he wanted that to change and hoped that he would soon have the chance to introduce himself to her. She would have the opportunity to grow up knowing that she still had a big brother instead of just being told about him. It was a dream that could become a distinct possibility if he played his cards right.

Getting lost somewhere in his mind, Sam almost forgot about the strangers that were visiting his parents as his thoughts dwelt on a future with his family. It was then that he came to realise that Alice wasn't with them and that she was still nowhere to be seen. She had become part of their family after her own parents had died, and yet she wasn't present in the room. As shy as she was, she wasn't the sort of person to hide away while there were visitors as she considered it to be rude.

Maybe Alice had gone out somewhere, but where could she be? Knowing her, she could have been off exploring, but the city didn't offer the same solitude that she used to enjoy out in the country. Maybe she had a new job and was at work, or perhaps she had enrolled in college and was finally getting the education that she had always desired. Sam vowed that he would wait all day if he had to, just to get a glimpse of the friend who he missed with all his heart.

Sudden movement inside the house caught Sam's attention, causing him to focus on the outside world once more instead of the maelstrom of thoughts that were swirling chaotically in his head. The conversation between his parents and the mysterious men had ended as they all stood up from their respective chairs. Hopefully this meant that the strangers would be leaving and that he could relax a little as he formulated a plan.

Now that everyone was moving around, Sam was able to see the men who his mom and dad had been conversing with. The tallest of the pair was slim and athletic, with his dark hair smothered with gel to keep it locked in place. He was what most people would consider to be good looking, with a boyish smile that Sam presumed would make women swoon. However, his casual sense of dress and general demeanor made him seem rough around the edges, as if he was trying too hard to be a bad boy. A plaid shirt, jeans and work boots were simple, yet impractical for local temperatures, implying that he wasn't all that smart.

The slightly shorter of the two was also relatively slim, with longer hair that stopped a few inches above his shoulders. He was better prepared for the hot climate, with a red t-shirt that was adorned with a simple white design on the front, plain cargo shorts and matching red sneakers. The odd, yet inquisitive looking individual didn't share the same swagger as his friend, instead seeming a little more uptight. He had a distant look in his eye that gave the impression that he had seen some things in his life that had changed him irreversibly. Sam knew that look, as he seen it in the mirror on more than one occasion.

Taking the time to observe both men as they shook his father's hand and said goodbye to his mother, Sam still couldn't identify either of them and had no recollection of ever meeting them before. He found it troubling that he still had no clue as to who these people were, why they were there or even where they had come from. Unfortunately, he didn't have a chance to find out more as the taller man caught sight of him in the corner of his eye, drawing the attention of his companion as he waved his arms dramatically. Sam could hear the yell from where he rested, his face almost pressed against the glass of the window. "Aaron, it's him! He's fuckin' here!"

Sam knew that he had messed up. He had gotten too close to the window and had been spotted there. The problem had arisen as he had been far too curious and hadn't waited patiently as he originally planned. There was a split second decision to be made of fight or flight and he went for the one with better odds of survival for both him and his family. It was time to run away from there as fast as he could. It was time to run for his life.

CHAPTER FOUR: A LITTLE SOUTHERN HOSPITALITY.

"Are you boys sure you don't want something to drink?" Mrs Mitchell definitely had the warm and welcoming attitude of someone from the south. She was always so pleasant and it didn't seem to be forced at all.

"No thank you, Mrs Mitchell." Aaron said, with a level of politeness to match.

"Please, call me Olivia." She smiled warmly, patting her baby's back as she held it gently in her arms.

Tommy was a little less refined in his response. "Nah, I'm good." He was trying, but polite conversation had never been his forte.

Mr Mitchell was the friendly sort too, but was a little less open with it than his wife. "So how did you know our son?"

Aaron looked over at Tommy who was slouching on the sofa right next to him. They made eye contact for a second before Tommy nodded his head in the direction of the Mitchell's, as if he was trying to tell Aaron to answer the question.

Clearing his throat, Aaron did his best to answer, formulating lies as he went. "We met Sam in Seattle and took him under our wing. We tried our best to help him but... Well, we're sorry for your loss." He felt terrible for lying to the Mitchell's faces, but they had to get a foot in the door so that they could get their hands on the information they needed. As bad as it made him feel, lying was unfortunately part of the job.

Tommy wasn't a great actor, but this time he somehow managed to pull through. He genuinely seemed sorry for Sam's death as he spoke. "His passin' sorta hit us both hard."

Olivia's sadness was written on her face, but she was grateful for their kind words. "Oh... Well I'm sure you did everything you could. Thank you kindly."

Mr Mitchell placed his hand on Olivia's back to reassure her before looking over to Aaron through his circular framed glasses. "So what brings you to our neck of the woods?"

Thankfully, Aaron had ready planned his next response. "We couldn't make it to Sam's funeral, but he meant so much to us. To be perfectly honest, we were in town on vacation and wanted to come and pay our respects."

Olivia smiled warmly at the pair of them. For some reason, Aaron couldn't help but admire her fading beauty. She was of Italian descent, with tanned skin and deep, brown eyes that he could get lost in for days. Twenty years ago, he imagined that she would have been quite pretty and the sort of woman that he would have dated, but the years had given way to wrinkles, the odd grey hair and dark circles under her eyes that made her look weary. Aaron had to stop himself from looking at Mrs Mitchell for too long, averting his eyes every time he caught himself staring. Life on the road meant that he had no time for relationships and that he was often left feeling lonely.

Mr Mitchell was oblivious to Aaron's wandering eyes as he replied. "Well we appreciate the thought. Are you in town for long?"

Tommy was a little less tactful this time, shaking his head as he spoke. "Not if we can help it."

The Mitchells both looked a little taken back, glancing at each other in confusion before peering over again.

"What Tommy means is… We don't want to miss our flight." Aaron tried to focus on Mr Mitchell as he spoke, not wanting to get caught looking at Olivia with dreamy eyes. Her flowing dress was distracting and that inviting smile was almost too much to bear. It seemed that he was developing a taste for older women.

Mr Mitchell was a little older than his wife, but not by much. He looked like the kind of guy who had a great deal of responsibilities as he worked hard to support his family. He dressed smartly to keep up appearances, was clean shaven and was definitely a bit of neat freak. His Southern drawl was much more apparent than Olivia's, but he tried his best to enunciate as he spoke. "That's alright. We know he didn't mean any harm by it. He's just a straight shooter, right fellas?"

Aaron nodded, smiling widely. "That's one way of putting it."

Olivia arched an eyebrow with curiosity. "Is there anything we can help you boys with while you're in town?"

Aaron tried to keep his thoughts clean, reminding himself that they were there to do a job and that these kind people had lost their son not all that long ago. He instantly felt guilt for his attraction to Mrs Mitchell as she was a grieving mother who was just trying to get on with her life. No-one expects to lose their child, and eighteen was an awfully young age to die. Aaron and Tommy had come to the house expecting to find Sam there, or maybe even his parents covering for him, but these people weren't capable of deceiving anyone.

"We just wanted to warn you about some vicious rumours we heard while passing through Kansas on the way here. It was all over the news out there." Aaron had changed from a possibility of an interrogation to full on damage control. He didn't want to hurt these innocent people.

"We already know…" Came Mr Mitchell's speedy reply. "My friend Bob called us himself. He's a Sergeant in Birchfield's Police Department." He sounded annoyed, but his feelings weren't directed towards them and so Aaron let him continue. "He claimed our son was alive and that he'd dug his way out of his own grave. I knew the man liked to drink, but really… It's terrible to even think such things, never mind calling us in the middle of the night." Furrowing his brow, his mouth became a stern line. "I told him that he needed to get some serious help and lay off the moonshine."

Mr Mitchell wrapped his arms around his wife and child protectively. Olivia reciprocated by resting her head against his, causing Aaron to feel even more awkward about his previous thoughts. He could tell that Tommy was swallowing back his words, stopping himself from saying anything about the undead or anything else along those lines. Sighing loudly as he let his wife go, Mr Mitchell looked at his guests apologetically. "I'm sorry, you really don't need to know about our troubles. I imagine you have enough on your own plates without us adding to it."

Aaron was actually relieved that they hadn't believed Sergeant Ellis. Their lack of belief meant that the job would be less destructive, or so he hoped. "That's okay, Mr Mitchell. We understand that you've gone through a great deal over the past year. Sam was a great guy…"

Tommy coughed, covering his mouth and playing it off as if he did so unintentionally. Aaron wished that he could kick his friend for his reaction, but thought better of it as he didn't want to arouse any suspicions.

Olivia gently patted her baby on the back, rocking her back and forth as she rested the little girl against her chest. The baby placed her head against her mother's neck, cooing a little as she relaxed in her arms. The woman seemed to enjoy listening to the sounds that her child made, a smile returning to her face. "I'm sure that Sam would have been happy to know that you cared enough to visit. I wish we'd met under better circumstances."

Aaron gave a polite nod. "I'm just glad that we got to know him while we could."

Tommy nodded his own head in agreement, mimicking his friend. "Yeah, it's a damn shame. Maybe we can exchange stories or someth..."

Cutting his friend's sentence short, Aaron decided that they weren't gaining anything by staying there and slowly stood up to leave. He wanted to leave the Mitchell's in peace and get on with the hunt without disrupting their lives any further. "Thank you so much for taking the time to talk to us. We should really get back to our vacation and let you go about your day."

Tommy stood up next to him, stretching his arms as he suppressed a yawn. The Mitchell's rose in unison, with Mr Mitchell extending his hand to Aaron across the coffee table. "Thanks for stopping by. It's been a pleasure meeting you boys."

Aaron shook his hand and bowed his head respectfully as Mr Mitchell turned to shake Tommy's hand as well.

Olivia held her baby with one arm, quickly waving to the pair with her free hand. "Feel free to stop by anytime. Our door is always open to friends of Sam." It was obvious from her tone that she meant her words. Anyone or anything that reminded them of their boy would be welcome and have a place within their house.

Only one person in the room had noticed the face staring at them all through the window as he turned to leave. Before Aaron could say his goodbye, Tommy had started waving his arms around as he yelled in surprise. "Aaron, it's him! He's fuckin' here!"

The Mitchell's were completely stunned, but Tommy's shouts had already awoken the baby. As the little girl began to cry, Aaron found himself turning to look out towards the window. True enough, a face looked back at him in terror, barely visible for a second before it vanished from sight. If it was Sam, he was on the run now and they had to think fast.

Aaron felt terrible. He didn't know what state they would be leaving Mr and Mrs Mitchell in as they made their exit. His words failed him as he looked back at their shocked faces and completely blanked on what to say to excuse themselves. It wasn't exactly the polite farewell that he had in mind, but there really wasn't time for that now.

Tommy was already powering his way out of the front door and into the street before Aaron could even react. The door handle slammed against the wall, the surfaces crashing with a horrendous bang that only served to make the baby wail even louder. As he sped through the entryway of the air conditioned house and into the blistering heat of the outdoors, Aaron found that he had been left in Tommy's dust. His friend was already half way down the road and making his way towards a nearby alley.

Mr Mitchell called from the living room, but Aaron couldn't make out what he was saying. Whatever had been said, he was sure that their welcome had been rescinded, as even good country folk had their limits and this sort of anti-social behaviour was usually frowned upon. Aaron prayed that his and Tommy's actions wouldn't cause any trouble for the family and that they wouldn't have second thoughts about their doubts towards Sergeant Ellis' story. It was better that they remained clueless about Sam's current existence and that they believed that he was still six feet under.

Tommy disappeared behind a wooden fence and down the

alleyway that he had been running towards. He was hot on the trail of Sam Mitchell and nothing could stop him now. It was times like this that Aaron was glad how fast his best friend was. Tommy would either catch up to their target or corner him somewhere down the road, allowing them both the opportunity to confront their quarry and find out exactly what they were dealing with.

****

"Man, that son of a bitch is fast..." Tommy had doubled over, resting his hands upon his knees as he wheezed loudly. They had been running for miles under the midday sun and were both out of breath. Aaron had only just caught up, having lagged behind for most of the chase. Tommy had always been faster ever since they were kids. There was no shame in it, he was just a natural athlete.

"You... aren't... kidding..." Aaron could barely speak, only managing single words in between breaths. He felt faint and could see stars as they had exerted themselves a little too much in the heat. Neither of them were used to the humidity and they were drenched from head to toe in sweat. It would have been disgusting if they weren't so distracted by the disappointment of their quarry getting away.

"...Where the fuck did he go?" Managing to force himself back in to a fully upright position, Tommy had started the hunt again. He was peering over bushes and looking behind trash cans, searching for anywhere that Sam Mitchell could have been hiding. When it came to physical activities, he often had the edge and would always be the first to recover. It was especially true now that he had given up smoking. If he only gave up his drinking habit too, then he would be almost unstoppable.

"Well... we can definitely rule out him being a vampire..." Aaron had almost caught his breath now too, but exhaustion was setting in. The high temperatures were really taking a toll on their bodies.

Stopping his search, Tommy turned to his friend with interest. It hadn't dawned on him why they couldn't be hunting a 'bloodsucker' as he called them. "Why's that?"

Aaron took another big gasp of air and pointed towards the sky. "It's just after noon... and he didn't burst into flames."

It took as long for Tommy's brain to catch up as it did for Aaron to catch him while running. "Oh shit, you're right! Then what the hell is he?!?"

Aaron shrugged. "I have no idea..."

It was obvious that Tommy was mad about Sam getting away as he started pacing back and forth across the alley. "How the fuck does someone just vanish like that?"

Tommy was extremely dedicated. Aaron had never met anyone else with the same level of determination as his friend. They had survived against impossible odds together and both of them had become stronger because of it. Each of them had their quirks and differences, often getting into fights, but they knew that they would be friends right up until the end. Nothing was more important to them than their loyalty to each other. Aaron understood the motivation that pushed Tommy forwards, but he also knew that he had to be the voice of reason. It was his job to protect his friend from himself, making sure that he took time to rest and recuperate. Without him, Tommy would likely forget to sleep and would push himself to the point of collapse.

"That's what we're here to find out..." Aaron tried to soothe his friend by thinking logically. "Let's regroup and come up with a new plan of action. A little more research could help too." His tactic seemed to be working as Tommy began to slow down a little.

Tommy had been a happy go lucky guy once upon a time, with no responsibilities and not a care in the world. That was until the day that he met Christie Reece. They had a special connection that Aaron was admittedly envious of. Everything that she went through in life, Tommy went through it with her. Both of them had suffered through her ordeal at the farmhouse and he had been the one to help her get through the aftermath.

Tommy's on and off relationship with Christie through the years hadn't been the easiest thing for him to deal with either. It was a raging river of heated emotion that was impossible to control until the day that Christie died and Tommy lost almost everything. Suspicious circumstances, they said. Being accused of murder had almost broken the poor man, and the way the cops had treated him in jail... Aaron was sure that he wouldn't have made it through the ordeal if the same thing had happened to him. Tommy was definitely the strongest of them, but he still needed friendship and support.

Something small bit Aaron's neck, causing him to slap at it absentmindedly. He pulled his hand away and looked down at his palm. Squashed flat against his skin, a mosquito twitched as it hemorrhaged blood. That was the last straw, he wanted to go back to the motel and plan their next move. Aaron had had enough of Florida for one day. "Come on, let's go."

"No way, dude. We almost fuckin' had him!" Tommy scowled. He was never happy giving up on the hunt when they were so close.

Aaron looked his friend directly in the eyes and spoke with tired frustration. "It's hot, I'm tired and the insects are having a feast!"

It was clear from his increasingly relaxed posture that Tommy wasn't going to argue about it this time. He must have realised that he felt the exact same way now his rush of adrenaline was wearing off. "Fine... but you're buying the first round."

****

It was dark when Sam finally decided to emerge from his hiding place beneath the pavement, having wedged himself into a storm drain under the main street. He didn't want to risk being spotted again by whoever the men were that had chased him from his parent's home. They clearly knew more about him than he knew about them, but that didn't matter as long as he could stay one step ahead of them.

Sam didn't know where he was walking to at first, hobbling down the dark streets of the neighbourhood. He was on autopilot as the hunger began to rise inside of him once more. He hadn't fed since arriving in town, in fact he hadn't eaten since that night in Birchfield and he seemed to be paying for it now. His stomach hurt and his head was getting cloudy. He needed sustenance soon or he would lose control to the voice that lurked in the back of his mind.

It wasn't until he had arrived that Sam realised where his hunger had taken him, his face and hands pressed up against the cooling glass of the window as the heat dissipated in the night. He could see his parents in the living room, cuddled up together on the couch. It looked as though the baby had been put to bed as they sat there enjoying each other's company. They seemed to be having a serious conversation, most likely about what had occurred in that very place just a few hours prior.

At first it wasn't clear to Sam why his legs had taken him there until a stabbing pain reminded him of his need to feed. He had been drawn there like a moth to the flame, staring into a house that felt familiar to him, yet strange at the same time. He knew that it was stupid to return to the scene, but he couldn't resist. All he had to do was open the door and walk inside where he would be greeted with open arms. His parents had always loved him and he had loved them too, but now they were just food. From where Sam stood, all he could see was easy prey. He knew that his mom and dad would be happy to see him and they wouldn't realise what was going on until it was too late. He could bite down upon their flesh and drain them dry without much of a struggle.

The anticipation was difficult to ignore. Sam couldn't wait for the coppery taste of blood to trickle down his throat and fill him with a burst of power that currently seemed to be waning. He wanted to feel that renewed vigor flowing through his veins, his whole body screamed out for it. He desired that sweet liquid more than anything he could remember, and something about that fierce craving suddenly scared him.

"No! Wait!" Sam wasn't sure if it had been a voice inside his head, or if he had spoken the words out loud, but it quickly brought him back to his senses.

How could he think about his parents that way? Sam felt a sense of self loathing and disgust at even considering his parents as nothing more than a quick and easy meal. In that moment he knew that he couldn't have a normal life with them as they would always be at risk. What if he couldn't stop himself? He would lose two of the people who meant more to him than his own life, and he would leave his sister without parents. Or worse, she would grow up and he would kill her too. Sam knew that he was a monster to even have looked at them that way. It seemed that his humanity was getting dangerously close to being snuffed out.

Stepping away from the window, Sam fought back the hunger, trying his best to keep it at bay. He had to get as far away from there as he could, and so he decided to run away. With no destination in mind and knowing nothing of the local area, he just picked a direction and ran. He would keep going until either his body gave up or until the morning sun burned him so badly that it wasn't possible for him to keep going. Sam swore in that moment that he would never put a member of his family in harm's way again. It was better that they believed he was still dead and that they never saw him again. Samuel Mitchell, for all intents and purposes, no longer existed. It was better for everyone that way.

CHAPTER FIVE: SKELETONS IN THE CLOSET.

It was the same dream that haunted Aaron night after night. That same childhood memory where he stood, a little boy once more within the darkness of the bathroom. It was the place where the wet footprints ended, the same place that they always led him and where they always would. It was in that very room where such a terrible act had once been carried out with such malice that it ripped a hole in the world. It left a tear in the very fabric of the veil that separated the living from the dead. There had been consequences to those actions, and a secret that was left to be uncovered. It was a somber tale lost in the sands of time, and yet the story hadn't ended there. It had only just begun.

The only source of light within that pitch black room was a faint, green glow that barely shone through a narrow gap beneath the door. However, Aaron's attention wasn't focused towards the light, but to what hid beyond the shadows. He found himself being drawn away from the doorway and up to where the the light was reflected back. The object that beckoned to him was a mirror set in the wall above the ceramic sink. The mirror's glass was clouded with condensation, the centre of which had been marked with a small handprint, the shape pressed upon its smooth surface.

Stepping up onto a wooden stool to gaze into the reflection, Aaron could see that the image was all wrong. Although he could still see himself within it, the room on the other side was strangely different. The wallpaper wasn't quite right, with an old flowery pattern that had begun to peel instead of the plain painted walls that his parents had chosen. A single light bulb hung from the center of the ceiling, filling the mirrored world with a flickering light that gave birth to a feeling of unease.

Quivering with fear, Aaron reached over the sink to lightly touch the mirror, placing his own hand on the cold glass. As his palm rested against the surface, the room around him seemed to shift. It felt as though he was being drawn into the reflection and through to the other side. He soon found himself in the mirror world, the same peeling wallpaper and erratic bulb swaying from the ceiling as its power fluctuated at irregular intervals.

As he turned to face the room behind him, Aaron could see that the empty space had been filled with a large, antique bathtub. It was full to the brim with murky waters that began to overflow and spill onto the stained tiles of the bathroom floor. Unable to resist his own curiosity, he overcame his fears and stepped down from the relative safety of the stool where his bare feet met icy cold water. The chill moved up from his feet and spread throughout his body, sending shivers up his spine. As unsettling as it was, he continued to walk through the expanding pool of water towards the bathtub beyond, its faucet still running as it continued to top itself up with a seemingly endless supply.

As he made his approach, Aaron found that the water in the bathtub was so thick with scum that he was unable to see much at all beneath the surface. It wasn't until he reached the side of of the tub that he could see the shape of something lurking below. Skimming the surface with his hand, he cleared off a layer of unidentifiable slime that had made it impossible to see any deeper. It clung to his fingers, refusing to give as he made a vague attempt to shake it off.

The opening Aaron had made allowed him to see clearly what had previously been obscured from view. Somewhere deep beneath the ripples in the water was the face of the same girl that he had seen night after night for years. She lay motionless at the bottom, her long hair spread out around her with arms outstretched as she called for help from beyond the grave. Aaron couldn't hear her cries, as they were drowned out by the decades that separated them, and yet he still felt compelled to come to her aid.

Trying his best to reach down into the frigid depths, Aaron quickly found that his arms were too short to reach the girl who stared at him, eyes wide and full of despair. He was so close to her, yet too far to take her hand. The tips of their fingers brushed, but he couldn't stretch far enough to take hold. Refusing to give in, he leaned over the edge and plunged his head underneath the water, his shoulders following close behind. It was then that he felt the push of someone much bigger and stronger than him, forcing him downwards. Into the bath he fell, sinking fast as he was pushed deeper and deeper.

Fighting to break free, Aaron found that he had lost sight of the girl. He looked around frantically, but she was nowhere to be seen. It seemed that he had taken her place and now found himself submerged within the bathtub instead. He kicked and screamed in a panic, but his actions only served to replace the air in his lungs with a liquid that would soon steal his life away. He couldn't break free, but he did manage to turn to look up at the contorted face of the man who held him there, eyes full of resentment and rage. It was the violent face of a killer, a man that he had seen before and of whom he now found himself the helpless victim.

The bleak waters of the bathtub washed away, leaving Aaron upright as he stood dripping at the threshold of a narrow set of stairs that led down into the basement. He blinked, staring down into the gloomy underbelly of the otherworldly house. The chill still remained, yet he found that he was able to breathe once more. It was then that a haunting voice addressed him from somewhere down below, yet the words were foreign. Aaron couldn't make sense of of what was being said, but he knew that he was meant to seek out its origin.

Beginning the descent, it was clear that the stairwell hadn't been used in some time as thick cobwebs hung from the ceiling, catching in Aaron's hair as he passed under them. As if that wasn't enough, he also noticed that the walls seemed to shift away from him as if they detected his presence. However they didn't move as a whole, instead skittering away in every direction as if they were made from a thousand insects. They seemed to swarm around him on all sides, infesting the entire place while still maintaining their distance.

Aaron tried to get a closer look at the insects, but they scattered, quickly disappearing between the cracks in the stairs. Even though he couldn't see them anymore, he could still hear thousands of tiny feet crawling around beneath him. As troubling as that was, they appeared to be as scared of him as he was of them.

Aaron couldn't shake the feeling that something was crawling on him, making its way down his neck and back. He kept stopping to check himself, but couldn't find anything on him at all. There was nothing he could do but ignore it, telling himself that he just had to get down to the basement floor. Quickening his pace, he took multiple steps at a time as he tried his best to shorten the trip. It wasn't much longer before he had made it to the bottom, trading the hard wood of the stairs for the softer floor of compact dirt.

Aaron's parents hadn't been aware of the basement when they bought the house, as it was hidden behind a secret door in the pantry and he had been the first to make the discovery. The spirit of the girl had originally led him to it and he now found himself there once more. There were no solid foundations or concrete down in the dark, just compressed soil and old beams that held up the structure above. The room itself was bare, with no furniture to fill its vast emptiness. It had likely been used for storage at some point, but had since been forgotten about and left to rot.

As barren as the room looked, there was something down

there that had been hidden away within the ground. Aaron wouldn't have even noticed it if it hadn't been for the mud that marked the spot, bubbling away in the furthest corner. For some reason the soil there was wet, as something seeped up from below.

As Aaron walked closer, the form of the girl shimmered in to view, her head lowered and facing away from him as she stared down at the patch on the floor. As disconcerting as that was, he sensed no malevolence from her. There was no evil intent. She may have been a spirit, but she was seemingly innocent and as much a victim as him. The ghost shuddered to life and pointed down at the mud, whimpering quietly to herself as it continued to bubble away. The knee length dress that she wore was saturated with the same dirt-drenched water from the bathtub upstairs and smelled rife with disease.

As Aaron grew closer, the girl slowly turned to face him. Her skin was pale and swollen, with blank eyes that stared directly in to his soul. "Are... are you okay?" He spoke timidly, not wanting to spook the little girl as he crept towards her.

Tilting her head to one side, the spirit opened her mouth to speak, and with each word a torrent of water spilled from her mouth as she cried for help. "Help... me..." She seemed to move with very little balance or control, shifting from one leg to the other as she waited for Aaron to approach.

Moving with caution, Aaron felt goosebumps break out across his body as an unnatural chill spread through the room, originating from where the girl was standing. He could see the breath escaping from between his lips as it turned to vapor in the icy air. His mouth was left feeling dry, as if all the moisture had been drawn from it by the freezing temperature.

"I want to help you... Tell me how!" Aaron genuinely wanted to help, speaking to the apparition through chapped lips, but the girl didn't answer. She just continued to cry softly as she stared downwards with blank eyes.

As he got within arms reach, mere steps away from the mucky pool, Aaron extended his hand towards the girl in an attempt to comfort her. However, his fingers touched nothing but air, his entire arm passing through her as if she wasn't there. Freezing on the spot, he realised that she didn't have a physical presence, but he could still see her as clear as day. As terrified as he was by her lack of substance, he wouldn't allow himself to leave. Aaron had to stay and help her in any way that he possibly could. The feeling of apprehension subsided after a few seconds, allowing him to move once more.

Aaron followed the girl's gaze, looking down towards the expanding puddle at which she continued to stare. "Is something down there?" He desperately tried to get an answer, but the spirit remained stubbornly silent. She didn't seem to be hearing anything that he said, as if she wasn't actually there and was just an old recording going through the motions. Perhaps the apparition didn't possess a consciousness and was merely an echo of the past.

Crouching in the dirt, knees just touching the edge of the puddle, Aaron began to dig at the ground with his fingers. He scooped up handfuls of mud that began to ooze out between his fingertips, dripping to the ground. With only a moment's hesitation, he tossed the mud to the side and began to dig up more. It wasn't long before a pile started forming where he had been discarding each handful with increasing speed, the ghost's constant sobbing causing him to work faster and faster. Whatever he found down there, he hoped that it would ease her pain. He would do anything just to help her and make her happy.

Aaron's fingertips hit something hard, his nails raking across its surface. The sensation seemed to harm the spirit, as her jaw opened wide releasing another torrent of water and an an ear piercing scream that penetrated his mind like needles through the brain. He panicked and pulled his hands out of the shallow hole, holding them to his ears as he tried to block out the sound. Raising his voice, he yelled over the noise, pleading with the girl for forgiveness. "I'm sorry! I didn't mean to hurt you!"

Almost as soon as Aaron had covered his ears, the screaming stopped and the girl closed her mouth tightly. It was as if nothing had even happened as her gaze was still fixated on the hole, drawing his attention back down too. "You want me to keep digging?" The ghost didn't respond and kept staring at the hole with dead eyes. "Okay, I promise I'll be more careful." There was still no response, and so Aaron decided to keep going, carefully brushing the mud away instead of clawing at it with his fingers. He was making slower progress now, but the apparition didn't seem too perturbed anymore.

The next layer of soil revealed a hard, pale object that was slightly smooth to the touch. As Aaron continued to excavate it, the spirit loomed over him and seemed to take an interest in his discovery. Feeling encouraged by her reaction, he continued to pull mud put if the hole until the rest of it had been revealed, not knowing what he would find there.

Aaron carefully removed the object from the surrounding dirt before gently taking it with both hands and lifting it out of the hole. He held it up to the ghost as some sort of offering without examining first, wanting to impress her for reasons that were unclear to him. It wasn't until he showed the item to the girl that he realised what it was. A skull, approximately the size of her head stared back at him with empty sockets and yet he no longer felt scared. As he looked at it in wonder, images were projected straight in to his mind. He had somehow opened a door to the girl's own broken memories, with the dark eyes of her skull acting as the key.

The girl. Her name was Emily. She was playing in her room, so many years ago. Aaron recognised it as his own bedroom within the same house. All seemed well until a man came home. Her stepfather. He was stressed and angry. Emily's mom had died that same year and he had become her sole guardian. She overheard him on the phone from upstairs. He had lost his job and couldn't afford to pay the bills. There was a chance that he would lose everything.

The man was pacing and tripped, injuring himself. He had fallen over one of Emily's dolls. Her stepfather had always hated looking after her and there was so much rage in his eyes. He was yelling as he climbed the stairs and entered her room. Emily had tried to hide, but he still found her and grabbed her by the neck. He wouldn't stop shouting abuse at her and she couldn't break free.

Emily's stepfather dragged her to the bathroom. He filled the bathtub to the brim and that's where he killed her. He held her under and she tried to scream, but she couldn't breathe. She knew that it was the end, but couldn't do anything to stop it. She was so alone and no-one was there to save her. If only her mommy was still there to protect her.

The slideshow of images faded as Emily's life was stolen from her. After that, Aaron could put together what had happened next. Guilt, or most likely self preservation, made the man bury the girl's body in the basement. He boarded up the stairs and built a pantry, trying to hide what he had done from the world. The man had tried to forget, but Emily wouldn't let him. She haunted him day and night. He couldn't sleep. It was too much for him to bear and so he sold the house. Where he went next, she couldn't follow. Emily was tethered to her body and to the house that surrounded it. She was doomed to spend the rest of eternity there, so alone in her grief. That was until Aaron came along.

It was strange, but a feeling of relief took over, as if Aaron had finally found what had disturbed him so much about the house. Standing still behind the skull that had been presented to her, the spirit's blank expression curved up into into smile and for just a second she took on the form of a normal little girl.

"Thank you." Emily said, with such innocence.

Aaron was so taken back that all he could do was simper in return. He knew the truth about what had happened there and she seemed pleased by it, but before he could pull himself together and form a sentence, the girl's face began to melt away. It wasn't like melting wax from a candle, more like water running down a window pane. Her entire body turned to a clear liquid as she was washed away, the water that had formed her body seeping into the soil until there was nothing left. Emily was finally free. At least until the next night when the nightmare would start all over again.

****

Aaron woke the same way that he did every night, drenched in sweat and lungs gasping for air. Sitting upright in his rickety, motel room bed, he tried to go through what he had seen, his heart pounding in his chest. He didn't understand why he still dreamed that same dream, night after night. However, this last one had been closer to his actual memories than his other nightmares. The basement and everything that occurred within it was real, it had happened when he was nine years old and he still remembered it like it was yesterday.

It was supposed to be over. Aaron thought that he had solved the mystery as a child, his first ever case at nine years of age. Perhaps it served as a reminder of where he had come from and why he made the choices that shaped who he was. He had found the truth, but the culprit had never faced justice. The police examined the corpse that had been buried under the house, but Emily's stepfather was long gone and they apparently couldn't find any sight nor sound of him. No-one seemed to believe how Aaron had found the body, not even his parents. It was difficult for anyone to put trust in the child's story, as he raved about how the ghost of the victim had revealed herself to him and that she had shown him what had actually happened that day.

Aaron would have likely forgotten about it all too if it hadn't been for the incessant nightmares. He knew that everyone had their demons, but not everyone had to live through them on a nightly basis. Everyone had their regrets, but some were much worse than others. Aaron knew that Tommy's biggest regret was that he wasn't able to protect Christie, and he had almost let that destroy him. Whereas Aaron's regret was the fact that Emily's stepfather had gotten away, managing to avoid any repercussions and he was still out there somewhere. He hoped that one day he would be able to finish the hunt by finding the murderer and confronting him, but he had no idea what would happen the day that he did. Killing a human was completely different than slaying a monster and he wasn't sure that he could live with the consequences of such an act.

Taking a few deep breaths to try and calm himself, Aaron lay back down. He tossed and turned for a few moments, beating his pillow with his hand to fluff it up and make himself comfortable. He had lost so many hours of sleep over the years due to his uncontrollable dreams, but he was still determined to get some rest if he could. It was likely that sleep would elude him, but that didn't mean that he would give up.

Aaron closed his eyes tightly and tried to clear his thoughts, hoping that he would soon be able to fall asleep. It took a while, but he eventually started to drift off. He would soon be dreaming again, but this time it would hopefully be about something more pleasant than his childhood experiences, as rare as that was.

Coming close to achieving some well needed rest, Aaron was interrupted by an overly familiar sound. Tommy's timing was impeccable as always as he began to snore loudly in the next bed over, disrupting any chance for him to have even the lightest of snoozes. It was typical that his snoring would start now of all times.

Groaning loudly, Aaron pulled the pillow out from under him and placed it over his head. He would either muffle the noise or smother himself in the process. Falling unconscious due to asphyxiation was a kind of rest, wasn't it? Either way, he would certainly make sure that his friend was aware of his transgressions in the morning. At least he wouldn't be dreaming about anything else tonight, good or bad.

CHAPTER SIX: THE LEARNING CURVE.

"Take care of yourself, Fitzpatrick. Oh, and tell that buddy of yours that he still owes me fifty bucks." The familiar baritone voice on the other end of the phone was comforting, leaving Aaron feeling homesick for the Northeastern States.

Aaron simply chuckled, not letting the oblivious Tommy know that they were talking about him. "I will. Make sure you look after yourself too, old man."

Aaron hung up, placing his cellphone back down on the side table next to his bed. It was good to hear the voice of someone other than his best friend, even though the guy had the annoying habit of calling him by his surname. He was just glad that there were others like him and Tommy out there, fighting the good fight. The conversation with Eric had been an enlightening one at that, and there was a promise of more details to come. The much older hunter had taken a shine to both Tommy and Aaron, teaching them everything he knew about supernatural beings and how to combat them. They still relied on his knowledge and experience from time to time, especially when they were struggling on a case like this.

Tommy shot an inquisitive look towards Aaron. "So? What's

he got?" He had made himself at home in the motel room, taking his spot on the ragged couch as he reclined and watched TV, a half empty six pack of beer resting on the carpet near his feet. He was just about to crack open his fourth can as he waited for an answer.

Aaron rubbed his weary eyes, still suffering from his severe lack of sleep. "He said that you still owe him money."

An unimpressed Tommy waved his hand dismissively. "The old guy's losin' it. I paid that son of a bitch back last month."

Aaron couldn't help but grin. "Sure you did, but that's between you and him. Anyway, he said that he'd encountered something similar before."

Tommy suddenly looked interested, turning down the volume on the old television that had been blaring loudly until then. "Same as the Mitchell kid? Fuckin' sweet! Well don't leave me hangin'!"

Aaron sat up on the side of his bed facing his friend, his legs dangling off the edge as he began to explain. "Get this... Eric said that he was hunting a guy a while back. The weird thing was that he had been dead for well over a year. After some digging, he came to the same conclusion as us. That he wasn't chasing a vampire, changeling or your regular walking cadaver, but something else entirely."

Tommy took a big gulp from his beer before gesturing for his friend to continue. "And? What the hell was it?"

Aaron sighed, shaking his head slowly. "He never found out... but he did track it down and ended it."

Tommy looked thrilled. He clapped his hands together,

spilling a little of his drink on the sofa. "Legit? So we can kill this fuckin' thing?"

Aaron simply nodded, making a face as he caught a whiff of stale beer. The smell of alcohol was strong in the room, either from the open containers or from however much beer had been spilt over the last couple of days. He wished that Tommy would keep a clear head, but he knew that his friend drank to ease the pain of his past. Each sip that he took made the world seem a little less bleak, but Aaron still didn't like seeing him this way. "Do you have to drink all the time? That stuff will kill you..."

Tommy raised his arms up, making an exaggerated shrugging motion with his beer can still in hand. "Seriously, dude? The shit we deal with on a daily basis and you're worried about my fuckin' liver? I'll be long dead before it gives in."

Aaron couldn't help but laugh at his comment. "True enough, I suppose."

There was a brief moment of quiet, with only the lowered volume of some Eighties action movie playing on the TV disturbing the silence, complete with explosions, gunfire and cheesy one liners. At least most of the other guests had left their rooms for the day. The things they had heard over the years through the thin walls of motels was enough to make even a seasoned hooker blush.

"So what else you got?" Taking another long sip of his beer as he moved to an upright position, it was easy to see that Tommy's interest had been peaked.

Trying to recall the rest of what Eric had told him, Aaron

prepared a mental list as he spoke. "Well we already know that he bites and drinks human blood, but he can't be a vampire as he was out during the day... Eric confirmed that what he hunted didn't have fangs either, just regular teeth."

Tommy nodded, still interested. "Which explains the messy bite, right? What else you got?"

Aaron pondered for a moment. "He's fast. Not much gets away from you."

A stupid grin spread across Tommy's face as he took another sip from his can. "Fact! He's also crazy fuckin' strong. The dude dug his way out of his own grave!" That much was true. It must have taken a great deal of strength and stamina to break through solid wood before digging up through six feet of heavy soil.

"Strong and fast..." Aaron pulled his laptop from out his backpack and opened it up, resting it on his lap. He then proceeded to compile a list of everything they had mentioned. "There. I'll put it in the case file and we can add to it when we know more."

Tommy lay back on the couch again, balancing his beer on his chest. He seemed to watch it rise and fall with his breathing, relaxing his body again. "Just tell me when and where to shoot." He never was much for research, but without him the team would be incomplete. They were two halves of a whole when it came to hunting and each of them needed the other.

Opening the Samuel Mitchell folder on his screen, Aaron began to read through everything that they had gathered so far. Tommy had already stopped paying attention and had turned the volume on the television back up in order to fully immerse himself in his action movie. It was a good thing that Aaron was used to filtering out the noise, as he was able to continue his work regardless. He loaded his web browser and began to cross reference keywords and any details he had on Sam with other sightings, reports or similar types of encounters. It was surprising what you could find out by reading through obscure forums, blogs and other such websites. The internet was used to hide a lot of useful information in plain view.

At a brief glance, Aaron could see that there were plenty of mentions of weird goings on, but nothing specific to Sam Mitchell or anything else like him. It could take a few hours to find anything of note, but at least Tommy was amusing himself. He would likely be fast asleep on the couch and snoring away again at some point within the next few hours. When he woke up from his slumber, they would likely feast upon the usual pizza, burgers or whatever fast and easy food that they could get their hands on. The usual brain food. It wasn't the healthiest lifestyle, but they usually kept themselves so active on a daily basis that gaining weight wasn't an issue and neither of them believed that they would live long enough to suffer from heart disease or diabetes.

"I've got it!" Aaron's outburst of excitement caused Tommy to almost jump out of his skin as his nap was disturbed prematurely. He was close to falling off the sofa and on to the floor, catching himself just in time as he sat up looking bewildered.

"What the fuck, man? I was having the best fuckin' dream...

This one girl was doing this weird thing with her..." His sentence was cut short by Aaron who was oblivious to how much he had scared his friend.

"Forsaken. It doesn't go into too much detail, but from what I've read... Sam Mitchell has to be one." He turned his laptop towards Tommy so he could see the wall of text that he had been reading though. It was doubtful that he would read it too, but that didn't seem to matter.

Tommy scratched his head, his hair standing on end where it had been pressed up against a cushion. "A what?"

Aaron continued. "A freak of nature that's extremely rare. No idea where they come from, but they're basically a poor man's vampire. They share some of the same strengths, but are generally much weaker. Apparently some can withstand sunlight for extended periods of time. And get this... some of them don't even grow fangs. Apparently it's some kind of deformity."

Cracking his neck, Tommy began to stretch as he slowly stood up from the couch, a pizza stain adorning his white tank top. "So... he's a weakling bloodsucker who can walk around in the day, but he's not so great at eating? Sounds like a shit life, but easy work for us, right? The usual then."

Aaron turned his laptop back towards himself, beginning to scan through the text on the screen again. "Yeah... Fire, maiming or decapitation. Maybe we can get through this without either of us being stabbed again."

Tommy looked down and noticed the stain on his shirt,

cursing under his breath. "Yeah, dude. Wait... I didn't get stabbed, that was you! And then there was the time you took that bullet right in your ass!" He laughed, clearly picturing the whole ordeal in his mind and Aaron couldn't help but join in the hysterics. It had been a horrible thing to experience at the time, with pain worse than he could have ever imagined, but in hindsight it was a hilarious location to get shot.

It took a minute for them both to regain their composure. Tommy eventually managed to stop laughing at his friend's past misfortune, but his usual grin was left plastered across his face. "So how we gonna find this kid?"

Aaron looked Tommy straight in the eye, his own expression taking on a more thoughtful state. "Now that's the tricky part..."

****

Sam had been running straight through the night and in to the early hours of the morning. Even when the sun had risen over the horizon, with its rays lighting up the sea with orange fire, he just kept on running. As his skin started to break out in a rash and it began to blister, he kept pushing onwards and kept his body moving. He no longer had a clue as to his whereabouts, eventually heading further inland and away from the ocean until high rise apartments and hotels gave way to rows of ramshackle housing, built way too close together to maintain any sense of privacy. Boarded windows and walls overrun with graffiti let him know that he had found his way in to one of the less reputable areas of town, whichever town or city that it was.

Tiring in the light of day, Sam's speed slowed to a brisk walk and after a few more miles even slower still. He pulled his hood down over his face, keeping the rank smelling fabric as low as possible in order to protect his eyes. Jamming red raw hands deep into his pockets, he tried to shelter himself from the sun as much as he could, but he still felt it slowly burning him through the very fabric itself.

Sam was glad that he had left his family behind for their own safety, but found that he wasn't able to simply forget about them. His parents were an integral part of his life after all, or rather they had been a central part of his old life and had to be spared from harm as he still loved them dearly. Whereas the poor alley cat that he had gotten his hands on in desperation hadn't been so lucky. Sam had left the cat's remains behind a pile of trash bags, its body cold and lifeless. The death of the small, defenseless animal made him feel terrible no matter how much he tried to defend his actions. His own survival was still high on his list of priorities, but he now started to feel the burden of remorse.

The feral feline had tasted foul and disease ridden, but some of the rush of feeding was still present as Sam bit in through the matted fur and drank deeply. It would take days for him to pluck the hairs out from between his bloody teeth, but at least this way he wasn't as likely to harm another human being. So far, he had been fortunate enough to avoid killing anyone, even when he lost control and attacked the people living in his old house. However that streak of luck would not last forever. There would come a time where he wouldn't be able to stop himself and no-one would be around to stop him either. It was a disaster waiting to happen and it was bound to happen sooner than later.

Struggling to keep moving, Sam stumbled around around the corner of a little bodega, trying to find some respite from the sun. He was suffering now, his body wracked with the pain of the pox as his flesh started to burn. His body felt like it was on fire and there was little he could do to relieve it. Cowering in the first spot of shade that he could find, he rested against the whitewashed wall of the alleyway. It wasn't much, but the temporary shelter would give him a moment to rest.

The shop owner had tried to cover up some recent graffiti, but the faint lines of black paint could still be seen beneath. Attempting to focus his mind, Sam tried to read it, but the words didn't seem to make much sense. Something about the Locos, whoever they were. Thinking nothing of it, he pushed himself along the wall, trying to get further into the shadows of the narrow alley and away from the bright open area of the main street. It hadn't occurred to him that he was wandering away from one danger and heading right into the next.

"You lost, man?" The heavily accented voice instantly

betrayed the Cuban origin of the man who stepped out from a doorway behind him. And from the sound of it he wasn't alone.

"He looks lost, don't he." Sam couldn't find the energy to turn and face them, instead resting his head against his hand as he used it to hold him upright against the wall. From the heavy footsteps, he could tell that the second man was much larger, yet his voice made him sound as though he was a similar age to the first. Both of them were likely in their mid to late twenties and they seemed as though they were ready for trouble. The reek of cigarette smoke stung Sam's nostrils, causing them to twitch as the men came closer.

"Too good to talk to us, eh?" The smaller man spat, now near enough to rest his own hand near Sam's head as he leaned in a little too close for comfort. His breath stank like he had been drinking cheap booze, and there was something else in the air. The smell of knock off aftershave and bargain deodorant. He clearly wasn't wealthy, but the gold rings that encircled each finger tried to say otherwise. "You okay, bro? Looks like you had a rough day."

Sam still felt weak and tried to formulate a response, not getting much further than a single word. "No..."

The man slapped his hand against the wall's surface a little closer to Sam's face than before. "No, what?"

All Sam could manage was the same word again. "No..."

The second man was right behind him now, cracking his knuckles as he spoke with a threatening tone. "You stupid or something, man? This is Loco turf."

Sam sighed loudly. He tried his best to push away from the

wall, but his muscles failed him.

The first man leaned in closer, his black goatee and nicotine stained teeth now visible. "Let's see what you got."

It took few seconds, but Sam managed another word. "...What?"

The man shoved Sam a little with his other hand. "Give us your money!"

Taking a brief moment to concentrate, Sam still struggled to form a sentence. "I... don't... have... anything."

Enraged by his answer, the bearded man grabbed Sam by the shoulder and shook him violently. "Give us your fucking money!"

It wasn't quite adrenaline pumping, but Sam began to feel his blood boil. He began to gain strength in response to the threat, as if his own body was fighting to protect him. "I really don't have any." His voice wavered. "Look at me... I'm a mess and don't even have any cash to look after myself."

The man almost growled at him through clenched teeth. "Yo, you giving me lip?"

Sam closed his eyes for a moment, the act of talking becoming a little easier now. "What? No, I..."

He was quickly interrupted by the confirmation of the larger man. "He's giving you lip, bro."

There was a metallic click and then Sam could see the reflection of something silver as it was moved into his field of view. It was a pocket knife, its sharp blade glinting in the low light of the alley. Tattooed knuckles gripped the handle tightly, holding it close to his throat. "You wanna get cut?"

Sam shook his head slowly, eyeing up the knife as a feeling of fear rose in him. "No. I just want to be left alone..."

That wasn't the answer the men were looking for. The larger of the pair rested his hands on Sam's arms, squeezing tightly as he yanked him away from the wall. He held him in his vice like grip, not relenting for even a second. "Stick him, Luca!"

Sam could see the first man properly now, the one called Luca, his eyes glaring in anger. His smooth, shaved head contrasted with the dark hair of his beard, giving him a menacing look. An oversized basketball jersey hung loosely from his skinny torso, with shorts, white sneakers and knee length socks beneath. He was holding his tattooed forearms out in front of him in a fighting stance as he brandished his weapon wildly. "Listen, you wanna die here?"

There was only one obvious answer. "No. I just want to leave." Sam tried to wrestle with his captor in an attempt to break free, but he found that he was still too weak to overpower him.

"You messed up, man. Tell Santa Muerte the Locos sent you." Still feeling sluggish, Sam barely had time to react as the cold steel of the blade found its way into his gut. It could have just been the shock, but for some reason it didn't hurt quite as much as he would have expected. There was a sharp pain of course, but it wasn't staggering. The effect of the sun's rays had been far worse.

The fact that Sam didn't fall to his knees, or even react much at all for that matter, left his attacker looking surprised. Luca hesitated for a brief moment before pulling the knife out and then jabbing it back in to Sam's stomach. The second stab was even less painful than the first, as if his body had adapted now he knew it was coming. A smile began to emerge on Sam's face as he stared the man down.

"What the...?" The man stabbed again and again, driving the knife in and out of Sam's chest this time.

"Luca? What you waiting for, man?" The curious brute holding Sam couldn't see what was happening and was still waiting for his friend to carry out the murder.

Luca's face was overrun with confusion as he kept on thrusting with the blade again and again. It must have been over a dozen times now, but Sam didn't falter. The realisation that the knife wasn't causing any real harm, other than flesh wounds that his victim didn't seem to suffer from, caused the man to drop the weapon as a look of abject fear washed over him. "El Diablo!" Luca yelled, with terror in his voice as he stepped back, with Sam's blood dripping from his hands. He turned to run out of the alley, so fast that he almost tripped over his own feet.

"Luca?!? What the hell man!" Came the concerned voice of the man who had now let go of Sam and was following his friend at a hurried pace. Sam could see him now, a large man who clearly liked food more than he liked exercise. He was trailing behind, holding his jeans up to stop them falling due to his lack of belt. The back of his white t-shirt had a trail of sweat leading from the buzzed haircut on his head, down to the top of his exposed boxer shorts.

Sam tried to laugh at the sight before him as both men ran

around the corner and out of sight, however the sound of laughter was instead replaced with a splattering of thick, red liquid that he coughed up in to his hands. Examining the fluid on his fingers, he recognised it for what it was. Blood. He was leaking from more places than he could count and the rush of the moment had gone, leaving him in a state of fragility that he hadn't felt before.

Trying to reach the wall again to steady himself, Sam staggered and lost his balance, crashing into a row of trash cans and knocking them over. He fell hard, landing in a pile of waste as plastic bags were dumped out, torn and their contents were spilled all over. The sudden aroma of rotting food smelled so bad that his sinuses burned with over stimulation while his mind tried to process a multitude of different stenches.

Sam rolled onto his side, trying his best to pick himself up but he no longer had the energy. "H... help..." His cry was far too quiet for anyone to hear. He could just about see people back on the main street walking by, but even if anyone found him there, it was unlikely that they would be a good Samaritan and lend a hand. Sam had inadvertently stumbled into gang territory and no-one would do anything to tempt their wrath, or risk calling the police who in places like this were often as bad as the gang members themselves. As usual, it was better for the locals to stay under the radar and avoid drawing any unwanted attention to themselves from either side.

It was impossible for Sam to stay conscious, no matter how much he tried to resist. The combination of being active during the day, his lack of sustenance and the heavy loss of bodily fluids through deep cuts in his abdomen was finally taking its toll. He tried to call for help again, but no words escaped his mouth. A trickle of blood left his lips and rolled down his cheek, dripping to the ground. He was surrounded now by what little vitae he had left in him, the open knife wounds no longer able to release any more.

Despite the the fact that his body was shutting down, Sam didn't feel as though he was dying. It was closer to falling into a deep sleep, his vision fading to black as he spiralled down in to the depths of his subconscious. He couldn't sense the world around him anymore. There was nothing for him to see, hear or touch. It was just him, his thoughts, his dreams and the hunger that screamed out for satisfaction. The craving for blood was now so strong that it took on a form of its own. It was a beast of sorts, snarling as it tried to claw its way out, but there was no escape for either of them. Not while the shell that they inhabited starved and withered. Sam was trapped with the beast. They were caged together somewhere inside himself, and he couldn't see a way out.

CHAPTER SEVEN: A HOME WITHIN THE CHAOS.

"Are ya sure 'e's not dead? 'E bloody looks it." The man's accent was thick and definitely foreign. From the sound of it, the voice belonged to someone who had spent most of their life growing up in the north of England and so they probably hadn't been in the United States for long.

Sam could hear everything, but found that he was unable to move a muscle or respond. He was trapped in his body and had no way of letting anyone know that he was conscious. He had no idea where he was, how he had gotten there or how long he had been out.

The woman who replied was a little more local and much easier to understand. "No. He's about as dead as I am." She enunciated her words, remaining clear and concise.

The Englishman raised his voice in frustration. "Oh fer fuck sake... You brought another one back 'ere? Don't ya remember what 'appened last time?"

Whoever she was, the woman seemed to be hurt by his words, as if she was full of regret. "Of course I remember... How can I forget if you keep bringing it up? I was more careful this time though. No-one saw me, I swear."

A second man raised his concerns, his Southern twang not as apparent as it had likely once been. "Right... If he's a vamper, then why ain't he healin'? He's got holes all over."

The woman snapped at him. "I don't know, do I? Something about him smells... different. Try giving him some blood."

A snicker from the Englishman signalled his disbelief. "No bloody way, ya daft bitch."

His loud opinion was closely mirrored by that of the other man, a little calmer than the first. "Don't look at me, En. You may be the lead, but you're not my damn boss."

A fourth voice, also male, signalled his own disapproval. His accent was Hispanic in origin, but relatively plain and easy to grasp. "No way, chica. Go look somewhere else, eh?"

The woman sighed loudly. "Fine... Some help you guys are. I'll do it myself. It'll be my own little pet project!"

The sound of footsteps walking away on a hardwood floor let Sam know that someone was leaving. The Englishman's vocalised exasperation was now being projected from the other side of the room. "Go play with yer blood doll then, yeah. Just fuckin' leave us outta it, alright?"

The woman called back to him, clearly unimpressed. "You're just jealous, Jack!"

He cackled in response. "You wish, mate! Come on, fellas... Let's leave 'er to it an' get set up." It sounded as though the other two men were following his lead, as more footsteps could be heard walking off in the same direction.

100

The Southern man replied with an air of calm as he trailed off. "Don't be takin' too long up here, En. Just holler if you need help."

The three men exited through a creaky door not all that far away, letting it slam behind them. As soon as they were gone, Sam could hear the woman turn back to him. She spoke quietly so as not to be overheard by anyone outside. "We'll show them, won't we? This won't be like the last time at all." He felt her lips press softly against his forehead, cold as his own skin as she kissed him lightly. "You're going to absolutely love it here."

Sam didn't recognise the woman's voice, but something about her reminded him of someone he once knew. Although she was trying to mask it with a positive attitude, her words sounded as though she had a heavy heart that was full of sorrow. In all honesty, she seemed as though she was lonely and just wanted some companionship, and it appeared that she had her sights set on him as someone that she could share her life with.

Sam had to admit that the thought of spending some time alone with the woman was pleasant, but he couldn't help but wonder what had happened to the last guy who she had brought home with her. Whatever had occurred, the other men were concerned about history repeating itself and the very thought of it terrified him.

****

The concept of time seemed alien to Sam as minutes, hours or possibly even days passed by, broken up with brief interludes of consciousness. It was impossible for him to know if it was even night or day, as he constantly felt as though his body had been drained of all energy. He did feel as though he was gradually gaining strength though, but it was not the rapid recovery that he desired. Far from it in fact.

After a near eternity of sleep, Sam's somewhat peaceful rest was disturbed by the muffled noise of loud instruments that could be heard belting out jarring tunes somewhere in the building nearby. A rhythmic drum beat and steady baseline penetrated through the poorly insulated walls, resonating through Sam's body as he began to wake from his slumber. Wherever he had been relocated to, the cacophony of sounds shook the place like an earthquake, sending tremors across the floor. The room itself seemed to move in time with the music, each note causing it to shift in unison.

Sam bolted upright, finally conscious and fully aware of his surroundings. His eyes darted around the room, still struggling as blurry shapes slowly began to focus into view. He could just about see that the bare brick walls of the windowless room were plastered with a collage of different band posters and flyers. The entire place was cluttered with cardboard boxes and the odd piece of mismatched furniture, the most prominent pieces being an old wardrobe, a powder table stacked with various makeups and beauty products, and a recliner that had been draped with several blankets and an assortment of cushions.

The final item that formed the centrepiece of the room was a well used mattress that Sam now found himself on, with plain white sheets that had been stained red with dried blood. The fabric smelled unusual, with the coppery scent of plasma combined with various different perfumes that permeated everything including the pillow cases. From the smell alone, Sam concluded that the makeshift bed likely belonged to a woman, but had since been repurposed for his own recovery.

Sam still felt weak, his head spinning as he tried to stand unsuccessfully. His arms struggled to hold him upright and his strength was failing him, but he still continued to push through with determination. It was then that he realised that he was no longer in his own clothes and was instead wrapped up in similarly blood saturated bandages that covered his chest and stomach, with nothing else but his boxer shorts to cover himself.

It took almost all his remaining might, but Sam eventually managed to push himself up by first rolling onto his knees and then placing his hands against the uneven springs of the mattress. Another moment passed before he could stand himself up straight, legs shaking under his own weight. His bare feet rested against the hard, wooden boards that made up the floor, as he swayed from side to side with nothing but sheer force of will keeping him from collapsing.

Taking some time to steady himself, Sam looked around for something to wear. He quickly realised that his best option was the wardrobe that he had spotted a little earlier and so he carefully made his way towards it. It wasn't long before he found himself stumbling over his own feet as he lost his balance. He grabbed at the handle in desperation, barely catching the metal between his fingers as he stopped himself from tumbling to the ground. Sam knew that if he had fallen he likely wouldn't have been able to pick himself up again, and one thing he hated more than most was feeling helpless.

Sam waited until he felt sturdy enough to move again before checking inside the wardrobe, wearily pulling the door open to see the rack full of clothing hanging within. He clumsily grabbed at a hanging t-shirt, not paying too much attention to the aesthetics as he pulled it over his head and squeezed in. The shirt felt a little tight, as its thin material stretched between his shoulders and pressed against his back. It was definitely on the small side and was very uncomfortable to wear, with little room left for him to to breathe. Fortunately for Sam, that was no longer an issue.

The distorted music continued to play, only now it was accompanied by the haunting melody of a woman's voice, the lyrics difficult to hear through the brickwork. It was a siren's song, calling out to Sam in a way that he found impossible to resist. Her vocals were undeniably alluring and before he knew it he was reaching for the door, unsure as to how he had gotten that far without toppling over. His weakness had somehow faded and he felt renewed vigor as if from nowhere. It seemed that her voice made him forget all about his pain as it reeled him in like a fish on a hook.

Exiting the confines of the makeshift bedroom, Sam found

himself on the metal grated floor of a walkway that overlooked a much more spacious room. It was a theatre of sorts, with a modest sized stage and an open floor plan filled with metal folding chairs. The music was clearer now, but it was so loud that it hurt his overly sensitive ears. He hadn't learned to filter out noise and any sudden sounds would almost leave him stunned.

It was from that vantage point above the lighting rigs on high that Sam could see the origin of the music. Lit up by purple tinged spotlights, a small band played their hearts out. They were unfamiliar to the country boy who had always been relatively conservative in taste when it came to music. It was always Alice that had loved alternative music more than him, but there was something about this particular group that Sam found mesmerising.

There were five members in the band, but one stood out amongst them all as she danced and sang in between the skinhead drummer, heavyset keyboard player, bearded bassist and a skinny guitarist thrashing away with his bright green mohawk. The lead singer was a young woman in her mid twenties, with black hair that seemed to glisten with purple highlights as she jumped around the stage enthusiastically, gyrating to the music.

The singer's fierce, in your face attitude and punk style took Sam by surprise. He had never seen someone quite like her before, at least not in person. City girls were so different to those that he was used to, especially in Florida, and this one in particular was on another level entirely. An array of different piercings decorated the woman's lips and nose, with studs bordering her ears. Her makeup was bright and wild, with matching tones to compliment the streaks of her hair. The singer was clearly trying to stand out from the crowd and from what Sam could see, she was succeeding.

There was something about the way that the woman moved that drew Sam's eye even more than her bold style. She had an elegance to her, with a gentle grace that drew him in, but there was also a hidden power that was waiting to be unleashed. She kept him on his toes by breaking her flow with quick, explosive movements that displayed her dominance. It was that self assured domination of the stage that left him feeling a little shaken. This was definitely someone that he shouldn't trifle with.

As he made his way quietly across the walkway and down the steel staircase that ran parallel, Sam found that he couldn't take his eyes off the singer, not even for a second. He was in awe of her talent. Not just because of her dancing and the way she controlled the space around her, but the fact that her voice was so powerful it almost drowned out everything else, filling the room with her mighty presence.

In contrast to her outgoing attitude, there was an underlying sadness that was apparent in the smallest of movements and within each note she belted out with forced confidence. It was then that Sam realised that it was the same woman who had nursed him as he slept. The same sorrowful person who had brought him in from the street and taken care of him when it had felt as though the whole world was against him. He owed her everything, and yet he still couldn't help but wonder what had happened to make her this way. Despite her outward appearance, she was clearly hurting and needed someone to help heal her own emotional wounds.

As Sam reached the last step, moving from metal to hard concrete, the woman's bright blue eyes met his from across the room and she let out a gasp, stopping dead in her tracks. The world around her seemed to peel away and Sam lost himself in her gaze. There was nothing else but him, her and the music that filled the hole where his heart used to beat. In that moment, he saw the singer for who she truly was. No makeup, no bright hair or piercings. Just a normal girl, angry at the world for everything that it had taken from her. She was a lonely soul, lost in the universe just like him. It was the first time that Sam had ever stared so deeply into someone's eyes, and it left him feeling spellbound.

"What the fuck, ya twat? Why'd ya stop?" The jarring English accent of the angry looking guitarist dragged Sam back down to earth, and suddenly he found himself back in the cold harshness of reality. The music had screeched to a halt, leaving the room in an uncomfortable silence.

"He... he's awake." The singer looked as though she couldn't believe her own eyes as Sam stood there in front of her, increasingly aware that the tables had turned and he had become the centre of attention.

"Um... Hey." Sam felt awkward as his voice seemed to echo around the room. The acoustics coming from the stage had seemed perfect, but he was almost sure that the physics had changed just to torment him.

The drummer placed his drumsticks down as quietly as possible before rubbing the top of his smooth head with a loud sigh. To his immediate right the darker skinned man at the keyboard looked over at the loud mouthed guitarist and shook his head slowly as if to tell him no, but it didn't stop words from spewing out of the Englishman's mouth. "Would ya look at that! The sleeping prick came ta grace us commoners with 'is royal presence."

"Jacko... That ain't cool, man." The large, Southern bassist tried to calm his friend, raising a hand out towards him as he ran the fingers of the other through his beard.

Looking a little red faced and flustered, the skinny man slid off his shoulder strap and slammed his guitar onto a nearby stand with a loud clang. "Nah, man. What 'ain't cool' is little miss princess stoppin' practice again for 'er own fuckin' selfish needs!"

The woman didn't seem to hear his harsh words as she stared at Sam, locking her eyes with his as she made her way down the wooden steps at the base of the stage. She seemed a little plainer now, her slim frame hidden under her baggy, sleeveless shirt and ripped jeans, her untamed hair and piercings less apparent than before. They were still there, but Sam could see the person beneath and from the look on her face, she could see him too.

Stopping just shy of Sam, a warm smile lit up the woman's face. She was a little shorter than him, but not by much, and beamed at him with a twinkle in her eye. Pausing for just a second, she wrapped her arms around him tightly and rested her head against his shoulder, speaking in a manner that depicted them as old friends. "Hey. How're you doing?"

Sam repressed a gulp and fought against a stutter as he replied nervously. "I'm okay, thanks."

She pulled her head back and looked up at his face again, her smile just as wide as before. "I knew you'd pull through."

Not knowing how to respond, Sam just smiled back. The woman suddenly seemed to realise how confused he must have been. "Oh, I'm sorry..." Letting go of him, she took a step back, tilting her head to one side as her pale skin seemed to light up the same colour as the highlights in her hair under the warmth of the spotlights. "I'm Entropy, but most people call me En."

Sam couldn't hold back his stutter any longer. "S... Sa... Sam."

Delighted by his answer, Entropy took Sam's hand and pulled him a few feet towards the stage. "Pleased to meet you, Sam." She stopped and looked at him in slight puzzlement, glancing down at his chest. "Wait... is that my shirt?"

Sam wasn't sure how to defend himself as he stood there in his skin tight top. He hadn't realised that it was a woman's t-shirt at the time, but it made sense now he thought about it. "Sorry, I..."

Entropy chuckled, smiling playfully. "Don't be. It looks cute on you."

Sam would have blushed if he could, but his face remained pale. He was standing there with a combination of her t-shirt and his own boxer shorts. What had he been thinking?

It was fortunate that Entropy didn't dwell on it for too long, and she continued as if nothing had happened. "Come and meet my band!" Pulling Sam forwards, she stopped him right in front of the stage. Entropy released her grip and held her arms out to each side as she introduced her group with fervour. "This is Entropy of the Heart!" She paused dramatically as if she was waiting for a round of applause and cheering that never came.

The only sound that followed was the audible resentment of the frustrated guitarist. "Oh fer fuck sake!" He threw his hands in the air and turned to storm off stage, slamming through a swinging door just to the left of the band's setup. The other three members just shrugged to each other and casually passed off his actions as if it was normal.

Entropy looked a little embarrassed, hiding a cringe behind her forced simper as she lowered her hands once more. "And that charmer was Jacko. Don't let his temperament fool you, he's a nice guy... sometimes."

The beer bellied man on the base cleared his throat, drawing Entropy's attention. She introduced him next. "This is our esteemed bassist, Mikey P."

The man continued to stroke his beard as he studied Sam for a few seconds before nodding his head in greeting. His deep voice boomed with an ever present, yet slight, Southern twang. "Hell with it. Just call me Mike."

Entropy looked relieved at her friend's surprising acceptance of Sam. She turned to the beefy man on the keyboard next, continuing the introductions with a refreshing flair. "And next on the keys is the Latin lover, Chavz!"

The man looked Sam up and down, giving him a once over. "'Sup, man."

The drummer was the next on the list. He had picked up his drumsticks again, proceeding to twirl one around his fingers as he passed the time. Entropy hopped back on the stage and made her way around the edge to stand behind her band member, resting her hands on his shoulders. "Last, but certainly not least... Skid!" She rubbed her arm on the drummer's bald head, pretending to polish it. He seemed unphased, as if the action was a common occurrence. Raising a hand to her mouth, she pretended to whisper to Sam, speaking loud enough for everyone to hear. "Just don't ask us how he got that name." Entropy grinned widely, with wildfire dancing in her eyes. To Sam's surprise, the drummer just smirked, not annoyed by his friend's jokes at all. He continued to spin his drumstick, aware of the conversation, but not really participating in it.

Sam felt himself beginning to grow frail again, but he did his best to ignore it, as he didn't want to appear weak in front of strangers. He pulled together the words and what was left of his quickly waning energy to respond politely. "It's good to meet you all..." He felt faint and his knees began to shake, close to giving way under the burden of his own weight. His body seemed to grow heavier, and it was getting harder and harder for him to remain standing.

A look of concern quickly replace the smile on Entropy's face. "Sam? Are you okay?"

Chavs stepped past his keyboard, nearing the edge of the stage. "He don't look so hot." He was right. As much as Sam fought to stay standing, and as much as he struggled, he had to accept that he was fighting a losing battle. His vision blurred once more and that's when he knew that he was about to drop.

"Sam?!? Sam!!!" Sam could hear Entropy's cries of panic and then he felt someone catch him before he could hit the floor. Their skin was cool to the touch, with a chill of the dead that matched his own, and then there was nothing. No music, no band and no Entropy. And yet, Sam couldn't seem to get her out of his mind until there was nothing left but the blackness of the void.

CHAPTER EIGHT: THE FORSAKEN ONE.

It was a full day before Sam recovered and was in a fit enough state to socialise. It seemed that Entropy had been watching over him as he slept, the entrancing beauty of her worried looking face the first thing he saw when he opened his eyes. She genuinely seemed to care about him, but Sam was left with a nervous feeling that he was there to fill a void that had been left by someone else.

With doubts and questions in his mind, Sam sat down with the band that night, around a circular table at the far end of the venue from the stage. Even Jacko had returned, seemingly getting over his outburst and acting as a somewhat functional human being, although most of his interactions were either crude, sarcastic or condescending. Entropy explained that Jacko found it hard to build trust and that he always took a while to warm up to new people. Sam found that difficult to believe, but had no choice but to take her word for it. It was the perfect time for him to get to know the people who had taken him in off the street during his time of need, despite some obvious objections.

The band had apparently found Sam's body in Loco territory after one of their gigs, as Skid stopped to take a quick leak in the same alley. The 79th Street Locos of Miami were infamous for fiercely defending their turf with extreme prejudice, and so the group knew that there had been some trouble. Sam had somehow run for miles down the coast after fleeing his parents house, all the way from Fort Lauderdale to the city of Miami, and had stumbled into the wrong part of town at the wrong time. He had been unaware how much ground he had actually traversed and had gotten lost within the streets of the huge metropolis soon after.

When the group had discovered Sam's body, they knew that it wasn't a simple mugging gone wrong and that they could be targeted too if they stuck around for too long. They honestly believed that he was dead until Entropy somehow managed to discover that he wasn't. How she realised the fact wasn't made so clear. The band had dragged the singer away from the scene, but she returned later on that same night to rescue him without their help. As to why she had taken him home instead of dropping him off at the hospital, Sam still wasn't sure.

Sam felt a little weird wearing someone else's clothing, but Entropy had provided some from a box that she had stashed in her room. He presumed that they belonged to a former boyfriend, or maybe the guy before him who he had heard so little about, as they were a little baggy in places. The plain, black t-shirt was one size too big and he had to tighten the belt to keep his well worn jeans up around his waist. The old, black, lace up boots were too large as well, but there wasn't exactly much to choose from. The style was simple, but it was still an upgrade from a torn burial suit and garbage soaked hoody.

Resting on a folding chair, Sam's elbows supported him against the round table that he was sitting by. He peered up towards the windows that lined the wall opposite the walkway. They had been sitting in the room for a while now, but he had only just realised that he couldn't see out of them. There was no moon or stars, and no flashing signs or street lights visible. At first he didn't know why that was, but Sam had now noticed that the windows were layered with a thick black paint that blocked the view of outside. It seemed a little odd, but he wasn't really sure what these types of places were meant to be like. Perhaps it was done to keep the sun out of the eyes of the performers. Or maybe there was another reason that wasn't yet clear to him.

"What are you? You smell dead and look dead, but something's not quite right... I can't seem to place it." Entropy's tone was one of curiosity as she probed Sam for answers. He still didn't have any to give, and what did she mean by him smelling dead?

"I don't know... I was kind of hoping to find someone that could tell me."

For some reason Jacko found Sam's ignorance to be hilarious. If it was any funnier he would have been doubled up with laughter. "Hah! Poor sod doesn't 'ave a clue!"

Entropy raised her eyebrows, catching Sam's gaze as usual. "You really don't know what you are?"

Jacko cackled, slapping the table hard with an open hand.

"Found 'nother smart one, didn't ya?"

Chavz, Skid and Mikey P didn't seem quite as amused as they sat around the table on folding chairs of their own. In fact Mike shot a harsh look over at Jacko with the goal of shutting him up, but it seemed like that was an impossible task.

No matter what Jacko said or what rude comments spewed from his mouth, Entropy appeared to be able to ignore him as if he wasn't even there. She was clearly well practiced at it as she focused all her attention on Sam and Sam alone. "When I heal, I'm as good as new. You... Well, you have multiple knife shaped scars, and those took a long time to get even that far."

Sam didn't understand what she meant. Was she like him in some way? Were they all like him? "Who are you people?"

Mike grunted, crossing his hairy arms in front of him as he leaned back in his chair. His thick, brown beard rested on his chest as he jumped into the conversation. "Our marketin' campaign clearly ain't all it's cracked up to be."

Jacko laughed wholeheartedly, but Entropy paid him no mind. She shuffled her chair closer to Sam, moving around the edge of the table until she was within arms reach. Placing a hand on Sam's knee, she looked him directly in the eyes. He couldn't help but admire the crystal blue colour of them as she spoke. "If you haven't guessed already, I'm a vampire."

Not entirely sure if she was being serious, Sam didn't react. He sat there straight faced as he asked his question. "You're a what?" The fact that Entropy wasn't smiling now and was as expressionless as him made him stop and think. Was she actually being earnest? "Are all of you vampires?"

Jacko guffawed, slamming the table with both hands before clapping them together slowly. "Bloody 'ell, we got ourselves a right thicko."

Entropy grimaced, not appreciating her friend's last comment but still refusing to give him the satisfaction of her exploding in anger. She instead continued to address Sam. "No, just me. These guys are all one hundred percent human. Well, except Jacko. The jury's still out on that one."

It was everyone else's turn to laugh now, with Jacko as the butt of the joke. He didn't find it as funny and Sam was too busy contemplating the existence of vampires to join in.

Alice had believed in the supernatural as a child, and Sam had seen things in his life that he couldn't explain since meeting her. And then there was the fact that he was back from the dead. That was too recent and far too crazy to deny. He didn't put much stock in rumours, but perhaps there was more to the world than the average human being was aware of. "So... am I a vampire too? Like you?" Sam really wasn't sure anymore. His existence had been turned on its head and he lacked a sense of direction.

Any potential answers were denied by Entropy's words as she tried her best to help Sam through his identity crisis. She squeezed his leg lightly and forced a half smile. "I honestly don't know. Something about you is different and I can't place it, but..."

She cut her own sentence short, causing Sam's interest to

peak. "But what?"

Entropy bit her lip before replying. "We have a friend who might know more, but we need to bring him a gift."

Chavz chimed in for the first time. "Guess I'm goin' shoppin', eh?"

Inclining her head to look at the bulky armed man, Entropy nodded her head with thanks. "I'll owe you one."

Sam was intrigued. "When can I meet them?"

She looked back at him, a real smile returning to her face this time. "Tonight! We'll go as soon as we have what we need."

Sam couldn't believe his luck. He had stumbled upon a group of people who could possibly give him the answers that he needed, or rather they had found him in an alleyway. By the end of the night he might have a real idea of who he was now and what he had become. It was now his turn to grin. "Great. I can't wait."

****

Sam hadn't realised what the gift was until Chavz returned with a small cage containing a couple of rats. He was now sitting in the darkness of a small room, staring at the rodents as they ran around behind bars under the unnatural glow of a large set of computer monitors. The rats were just as innocent as he had been on the way to the downtown apartment, unaware that they were being offered up as a sacrifice. Payment for services from an antisocial child who preferred to be left alone.

The child, who went by the name of Jonah, was apparently much older than he appeared, or so Entropy had claimed. However, Sam had a hard time seeing him as anything more than a six year old boy. It was more than a little creepy hearing the kid speak with a vocabulary beyond his years, the underdeveloped vocal cords still high pitched, his voice never having broken.

Sam didn't know what was more unnerving, the fact that the boy was older than him or the fact that the rats were going to be his dinner. He couldn't stop staring at them as they played with each other, innocent and ignorant of their ultimate fate. Jonah had barely acknowledged the rodents, as if the gift meant nothing to him but it had been Sam and Entropy's ticket into his domain. Whether you had an appointment or not, you didn't turn up at Jonah's place with questions unless you came bearing a gift.

All of the other band members had stayed at the club, not wanting to brave the streets at night as they had seen what the darkness of the city held. It was only Entropy that went out that late out of necessity, unless they had a concert that they all had to attend. The band wouldn't have even been in Loco territory or have found Sam at all if it hadn't been for the set they had played at a local bar that same night. It seemed that lady luck had well and truly been on his side. Who knows what would have happened if someone else had stumbled upon his lifeless corpse.

Entropy seemed to sense Sam's discomfort, placing a cool

hand on his arm as she watched from an office chair next to him. The entire place was spartan, with the only furniture in the room looking as though it had been stolen from an office supply store. Unsure about what else to expect, he remained pensively quiet, awaiting whatever information the kid could find.

Jonah was hunched over his keyboard, typing away in his executive chair with a high back that dwarfed his small frame. His computer setup was impressive to say the least, but Sam didn't understand why anyone would need four screens. One of the monitors was streaming videos and another flicked between security camera feeds of the exterior of the building. The other two appeared to be used for chat windows, emails and a confusing variety of different programs and browsers. He tabbed between them with ease, feeling at home at his desk. It was Jonah's fortress of solitude and Sam really felt as though he was intruding.

Entropy on the other hand was done waiting. "So you find anything?"

There was no answer from Jonah as he continued to type away. Other people were annoyances and he preferred to speak to them through the medium of the internet than in person.

Sam could feel Entropy's inquisitive gaze upon him. Finally pulling his attention away from the cage, he glanced over at her. There was something odd about her eyes and the way they seemed to shimmer in the dark, not from the light of the monitors, but from something inside of her. He still struggled to believe that his companion was an undead creature of the night, as she seemed far too kind to be the sort that preyed upon the living, but maybe there was some truth to the tale. After all, he didn't want to hurt anyone either, it was just something he had done out of necessity.

The childlike voice of Jonah broke Sam's train of thought, drawing both his and Entropy's eyes to the screens. "According to the hierarchy, you're what they consider to be an undesirable in vampire society."

Sam couldn't quite grasp what he was hearing. "A what? I'm a vampire too?"

A little annoyed by Sam's interruption, Jonah turned to glare at him. From what Entropy had explained, it was highly possible that further distractions could lead to a tantrum and so Sam decided to keep his mouth shut from then on. "As I was trying to say... You're not quite one of us and not quite human either. They call people like you the Forsaken, and other vampires in high standing and positions of power will actively hunt you down if they're able. It's best that they don't discover your existence, for your own sake, not mine."

The very thought of being hunted and killed by vampires was terrifying. Sam wondered if the men at his parents house had known what he was, and that was the reason they were after him. They couldn't have been vampires themselves, could they? He remembered that they hadn't been affected by the sunlight at all, so from his limited knowledge on the subject he was fairly sure that couldn't be the case.

Jonah continued. "Your maker likely thought that they had failed to turn you, or they simply abandoned you when they realised what you would become. It's a social stigma to make one such as yourself, however rare the cases may be." Turning back to his computer, he began to work away. It seemed that he had nothing else to add, but Sam dared not disturb him until he was sure.

Entropy on the other hand wasn't quite so worried as she leaned over Jonah, her head just to his right as she tried to read the screen. The boy was obviously bothered by her close proximity, his hands balling into fists as his extremely short fuse was close to burning out. It didn't take much to anger him, just an invasion of his personal space such as this one. "Get back! Get back I tell you! This is my area, not yours! Mine, mine, mine!!!" Jonah's face had screwed up into a little ball of rage as red streams began to run from his eyes. Sam hadn't expected that reaction or for blood to fall like tears, and he was understandably freaked out by the whole situation. He sat back in his chair, distancing himself from the desk. What the hell was going on?

Taking it all within her stride, Entropy stood up straight and grabbed the arm of Jonah's chair with both hands. With one swift pull, she whipped the boy around and away from his workspace, facing him out towards where both her and Sam had been sitting. However, she didn't yell at Jonah or berate him for how he was acting, instead sitting back down in her chair where she calmly placed her hands into her lap.

With a forced smile, Entropy addressed the boy in the way you would calm a small child. "How would a few more rats make you feel? If you're good and tell us more about my friend Sam here, I'll come back with all you can possibly eat."

Her tactic miraculously worked, with Jonah calming down almost instantly. He sniffled, smearing crimson streaks of blood across his cheeks with a brush from his hands. "Really? You mean it?"

Entropy nodded. "Of course. Have I ever let you down?"

Jonah shook his head, sniffling again as he turned himself back towards his monitors. Sam on the other hand was still feeling tense after the kid exploded at them and so he sat motionless on his chair.

It took a little while for Jonah to bring up more information, continuing with his explanation. "As I said, it's a rare case, but the actual symptoms seem to vary between subjects. Most age like humans and have some resistance to sunlight, but they aren't fully immune to its effects. You'll have to work out what your own strengths and limitations are in your own time."

From what he had experienced, Sam already knew about some of his own weaknesses, but he now found himself wondering about his body aging. Did vampires not change at all? Was he going to grow old, while others like Entropy and Jonah stayed the same? He was concerned about what that would mean for him in the long run. What if his body became frail and he was unable to die? He would be trapped within his body again, yet this time there would be no hope of regaining his independence. It was a horrible thought that he likely wouldn't be able to purge from his mind.

Jonah didn't have time to ease Sam's worries, nor did he

realise that there were any. "All the Forsaken are still cursed with the thirst, but you mentioned something about the issues you had when feeding. It seems that in your case you don't grow fangs, which sounds very inconvenient. That's most unfortunate for you."

Sam definitely didn't feel at ease as his fingers dug into the fabric of his chair. This was an awful lot for him to take in, but that didn't stop Jonah from blurting out more unwelcome facts. "Three things can occur during the creation process. Ideally, the deceased is reborn as a fully fledged vampire, but in many cases, inexperienced members of our kind end up killing the person permanently. The rarest cases of all are when the process appears to have failed and the maker abandons the body. However, the potential vampire isn't actually dead and is merely dormant as the process hasn't been fully completed. In those few situations they may return after some time as an unfinished sort of half vampire. Incomplete. Those few are destined to wander the world, shunned by vampires and mortals alike."

That was it. Sam couldn't handle it anymore, he was in full on panic mode as he jumped to his feet, knocking his chair over in the process. He didn't even stop to see how the others reacted as he bolted towards the door and ran full pelt down the hallway that led to the exit. That was always Sam's reaction to situations that he couldn't cope with. He had run away from home to escape his feelings for Alice, he had fled his parents house when he saw those men and now he was running away to escape a situation that he just couldn't comprehend.

As Sam scrambled to turn the locks on the door, slide the deadbolt and unhook the chain, he could hear Entropy's calling his name. "Sam! Sam come back!" He fumbled at the door, unable to unlock it fast enough in his current state. As he struggled with the final lock, he felt someone's arms wrap around him tightly from behind, their face burying itself into the fabric of his t-shirt.

"It's okay, Sam. You're not alone. We can work through this together." It was Entropy, the combination of her comforting voice, exotic perfume and reassuring touch enveloping him like a safety blanket. She was somehow able to take his fear and shrink it down in size, allowing rationality to take over more. Perhaps he wasn't alone after all. Perhaps they could get through this together. Her very touch eased Sam's suffering and left him wondering how he had ever coped without her. Whatever he was, he knew that Entropy would be there for him.

****

It was getting late now, and the sun would likely be up soon, but Sam wanted to enjoy the rest of his night with Entropy while he could. Even though it had been a rough few hours, he somehow felt better about it now. They had been talking things over for a while and it wouldn't be long before they had to hide inside and sleep away the day. The pair sat on an air duct on top of the club, a couple of storeys above the street below. The light breeze was warm, with the hum of the nearby air-conditioner creating a soundtrack of white noise. The world around them seemed strangely peaceful, as the average people of Miami began to wake and go about their normal lives. But now Sam's life was anything but normal.

Leaning in to be close to Entropy, Sam had his arm around her with his hand resting against the small of her back. He felt comfortable there and it seemed that she did too, as she placed the side of her head against his shoulder. His other hand held hers gently, her skin cool and soft to the touch. He didn't want to ever move from that spot, but he knew that they would have to vacate the roof in the not too distant future. The sun's rays wouldn't be forgiving.

Entropy's voice was soothing as she spoke, with Sam still content enough to just listen to her words. "So what if your scars don't heal? Scars are cool." Sam just smiled, letting her continue. "And I wouldn't worry about being hunted by other vampires either. Jonah doesn't talk to many people and Miami is a huge city. The funny thing about Florida is that most big shot vamps don't want to live in the Sunshine State. They don't like to get tans!" Entropy chuckled infectiously, causing Sam to join in. He wasn't sure if she was right, but that didn't matter. The important thing was that she had made everything seem like less of a burden.

Sam rested his cheek against the top of Entropy's head. "Thanks."

She looked up at him, her big, blue eyes shimmering in what

was left of the moonlight. "For what?"

Unable to resist, he kissed her lightly on the forehead. "For being you."

Entropy really wasn't like anyone that Sam had ever met before, not even close. She reminded him of other people in some ways, his mother and Alice to some extent, but she was still so different that she kept him on his toes. She had a fiery personality, an undeniable charm and the biggest heart of anyone that he had ever met. She was so full of life for someone who claimed to be dead, and yet there was still something that bothered him. A nagging feeling in the back of his mind. Sam never was one to get close to people, and yet he was falling for Entropy faster than he ever thought possible. It just wasn't like him to act this way.

Nuzzling Sam's neck, Entropy groaned. "We should get inside. I'm not in the mood for baking to death." She slowly sat up straight, stretching her arms and legs out in front of her.

Sam observed for a moment, the black and purple strands of Entropy's hair falling over her narrow shoulders, one of which had been exposed as her shirt hung loosely from it. Her skin glistened under the fading light of the moon, as the sky behind her began its slow change from black to a blazing, fiery orange. He couldn't help but think how perfect she was, the bright purple of her lipstick a contrast to the world around her.

Mimicking Entropy's groan, Sam prepared himself to stand. "The nights here are way too short."

Entropy turned her head to peer at him, her teeth visible as she smiled happily. "There's always another." She hopped to her feet, twirling to face Sam with her hand outstretched towards him. "Come on, let's go before I burst into flames. Not all of us can bask in the sun."

 Sam took Entropy's hand and she dragged him over towards the metal ladder that led down to the fire escape. She was surprisingly strong and had no trouble trailing him behind. As they reached the edge of the roof, she released her grip to step over the knee high wall, grabbing hold of the ladder on the other side.

 Sam took a moment to peer back towards the horizon, where the sky had been filled with various hues of red that merged with the bright oranges as they swept behind a loose scattering of white clouds. It was a truly breathtaking sight to behold as it lingered over the city like a colourful oil painting, but he was left feeling a little saddened. Sam couldn't watch the sun rise or set with Entropy by his side. She was bound to the night and didn't have quite as much freedom as he did. It occurred to him that he might not have drawn the short straw after all. His new existence wasn't quite as hellish as he had originally believed.

CHAPTER NINE: THAT SINKING FEELING.

Aaron hit the ground hard, sliding on his back in the thick mud of the swamp. The impact stunned him, leaving him sprawled out and defenseless as the large figure they had been hunting towered over him. The hunt had started well and they had managed to take the creature by surprise, but it had since proven to be quite resilient and extremely hard to kill.

Staring down at him with hollow eyes that wept green slime, a thick ooze dripped from the open maw of the creature's toothless mouth. It was the shell of a human, with real flesh worn as an ill fitting suit. However the skin didn't sit right, hanging loosely in some places while stretched tight in others, looking anything but human. As if that wasn't disturbing enough, something shifted just beneath the skin's surface, constantly moving and changing shape.

It looked as though the skin-suit had once belonged to a man, his balding head and rough stubble still visible. The irregular facial features were asymmetrical, with no bone or cartilage to support them. Grease covered overalls suggested that the man had once been a mechanic in town, yet it would be impossible for him to blend in now as his inhuman appearance oozed from every orifice. This wolf in sheep's clothing had to live out in the wilderness, preying on those who were stupid enough to brave the swamplands of Florida alone. There was no way that it could ever have survived within the city, not looking like the way it did.

Tommy and Aaron had already discovered the body of the man that the skin had once belonged to, or what little was left of him, hidden away within a supposedly abandoned cabin out in the middle of nowhere. They had been following reports of people going missing along a particularly rough stretch of dirt road, and after several days of hunting through the swamp, they had stumbled upon the creature's lair.

The building's interior was swarming with flies and the overpowering stench of rot was unbearable. It wasn't long before the pair had found the source of the smell, left out in the open within the dusty living room. Partially digested body parts were strewn around the place, with a sticky mucus that covered the walls and floor. There amongst the mass of limbs, organs and sinew lay the perfect specimen of a corpse, devoid of skin as it was preserved in a gelatinous substance.

Aaron would never forget what he had seen in the cabin, the sight of the gore-filled room etched into his mind, nor the acidic smell of bile that had been burned into his nostrils. It was one of the worst things that he had ever witnessed in his life, or at least somewhere in the 'top five' according to Tommy. Even the taste of his own vomit couldn't purge the memory of what had happened to those poor people. Aaron's only hope was that the victims had died quickly and that they hadn't been eaten alive. Unfortunately the clues were pointing to that being the slow and agonising horror of the truth.

Tommy was made of much sturdier stuff than Aaron and had a stronger constitution when it came to that kind of thing, his stomach seemingly lined with steel. He had dragged his friend outside, giving him room to breathe while formulating a plan to capture and kill the monster who had abducted those poor people. As sound as his ideas had been, building traps and selecting the right weapons for the job, they were based around the creature thinking and acting like a human being, and it was anything but human.

The oozing, flesh creature shifted its weight, raising enlarged fists high into the air as it prepared to bring them crashing down upon Aaron's head. Its arms stretched out unnaturally, pulling skin further than it was meant to go. The strain that the creature put on its suit placed it dangerously close to tearing open and spilling out the slimy contents inside. In some areas, the flesh itself was stretched so thin that the green ooze was now visible through it, flowing just beneath the surface like a river rife with disease.

Aaron tried his best to scramble out of the way, but the thick muck wasn't letting him off easy and it had left him in a vulnerable position. He struggled to stand up in the mud, mere seconds away from being crushed by the creature's immense strength. The sheer power it possessed was something that he had already experienced, as he had been tossed across the clearing like a rag doll just a few moments before. This wasn't quite how Aaron had pictured going out, but he wouldn't give it the satisfaction of hearing him scream before he died. He had accepted death as an integral part of his life a long time ago, and that acceptance had helped him to overcome his own fear of dying.

This day wasn't destined to be the final one of Aaron's life, however. Not if Tommy had anything to say about it. The tip of a blade slid out from between the monster's weeping eyes, the other end of the weapon brandished by a determined looking partner that Aaron was proud to call his friend. Trust was important in their line of work, and they were both fortunate enough to have someone that they trusted, watching their backs without fail. A lone hunter would die alone, yet a close knit team like theirs could live to fight another day.

"Knife to meet you, ya big ugly fuck!" Tommy's wit was as sharp as his blade. He had succeeded at distracting the creature long enough for Aaron to recover. "Get up, dude! This party ain't over!"

The thing began to whip its arms around defensively as it made an awful gurgling sound, giving Aaron just enough time to roll to his feet and reach for his own machete that had been dropped in the mud.

As soon as he saw that his friend was free, Tommy yanked the hilt of his weapon backwards, pulling out with it a mess of sludge and slime that clinged to the edge of his blade. "Oh, come on! You got shit all over Bethany, asshole!" Yes, Tommy was the sort of guy who named pretty much everything. The truck, his knife and even his favourite shotgun all had pet names. Female names of course.

Re-entering the fray, Aaron brought down his machete on the creature's shoulder in a swift hacking motion. The cold steel sliced through the skin suit with ease, with the soft interior offering little to no resistance. Removing it on the other hand was another matter entirely, as the green ooze seemed to try and ingest the hard edge of the blade, making it difficult to pull free. The more he tried to pull at the handle, the harder the task became, until he gave up and decided to abandon his weapon altogether, narrowly avoiding a vicious backhand from the creature who was becoming increasingly riled up. The arms of the suit flailed around wildly, the gurgling sounds replaced with that of a low bellow that reverberated throughout the swamp, sending flocks of birds scattering in all directions.

Witnessing his partner's misfortune, Tommy quickly changed tactics, swapping his deep cuts and thrusts for shallow slices and jabs that were designed to inflict less damage, but still keep their quarry on its toes. It seemed to be working, as stretched limbs struck out in every direction. Both hunters dodged, sidestepped and jumped with practiced timing, trying their best to avoid being knocked senseless. The blows were inaccurate, but the power behind was them undeniable. Branches were broken and splintered, with a rock getting dislodged from the mud and sent hurtling towards the wooden walls of the cabin where it left a similarly sized hole.

Aaron knew that they could keep up that same dance of death for a while, but he had the feeling that whatever this thing was it could likely go for longer. If they were lucky, they could maybe tire it out and then Tommy could deliver the killing blow, but luck hadn't been on their side that much in the past however many weeks. Besides, the creature was a glutton for punishment and all their knives seemed to do was anger it further, only harming the suit of flesh that it wore. Nothing they had done within the last ten minutes or so had managed to physically harm whatever lay beneath.

Wracking his brain as he tried his best to think outside the box, Aaron came to realise that their traditional armaments were useless in this situation. Fortunately for them, he had an idea. "Tommy, give me your lighter!"

Tommy ducked under another deadly swing, shooting Aaron a look of confusion. "Seriously? Now's not the time to start taking up my bad habits, man!"

Aaron rolled his eyes, rummaging around in his jean pockets, past his wallet and phone. He had to stop what he was doing a moment to hop out of the way of another savage strike. "I need you to shut up and trust me!"

Still hacking away with his slime covered blade, Tommy slid a small silver object out of his back pocket and tossed it over. It sailed through the air, just past the sagging head of the enraged creature, with Aaron only just managing to catch it. Now it was time for him to put his new plan into action.

Ever since they had arrived in Florida, Aaron had been sweating profusely due to the humidity. To counter the potential stench caused by his perspiration, and to prevent the smell from scaring off the much wanted attention of women, he had purchased a travel sized deodorant spray from an overpriced convenience store. Since then he had been spraying it at regular intervals to try and keep himself smelling fresh. There was only three quarters of the can left now, but he hoped that it would be enough to do the trick.

With a flick of his wrist, Aaron opened up the lighter's lid and proceeded to use the flint inside to spark up a flame. With his other hand, he managed to locate the small canister at the base of his pocket, fishing it out with two fingers. He popped the cap off with his thumb and let it fall to the floor as he moved the spray nozzle up behind the lighter, aiming both in the direction of his target. A split second later and the space between them was lit up by a scolding cone of burning chemicals, the air around it rippling from the heat.

Tommy dropped to the ground to avoid the jet of flames, whereas the lumbering creature had been too distracted by trying to whip its arms at them to move out of the way. It squealed horrendously as its suit was engulfed in fire, the oozing substance inside beginning to bubble out through the openings. It was starting to boil, growing in mass until it caused the singed flesh to expand like a balloon.

The thing was barely holding together as Aaron continued to exhaust the entire contents of his can, refusing to stop right up until it ran out of fuel and the flame died with a splutter. He thought that would be the end of it, but the creature continued to grow, stretching skin until it was no longer recognisable. It was just a thin membrane holding back the insurmountable pressure that was building inside.

"It's gonna blow!" Yelled Tommy, burying his head in the dirt as he sheltered it under his arms.

Aaron was about to drop to the deck and follow suit, but he didn't have enough time to move before the skin-suit exploded with an earth shattering bang. The shockwave of hot slime catapulted him backwards again as the creature detonated with unbridled force, his body landing back in the mud that he had only just managed to escape.

Almost sure that his ear drums had blown, Aaron could hear only the ringing sound of a tone he would likely never be able to hear again. The wind had been knocked out of him and he knew that it would take a minute or two to recover. The damp, murky stench of the swamp had been replaced with the potent smell of melting flesh and burnt hair, and he could feel that he was covered from head to toe in what was left of the creature. He didn't want to think about the debris of mucus and thick slime that had painted him green, nor the wretched scent that came with it.

The sky was a bright blue, with the bare branches of dead trees swaying somewhere above Aaron's head. He sighed loudly, managing to recover his breath with a cough to clear his throat. The sight before him was somewhat peaceful despite what they had just been through, and it helped him to clear his mind if only for a second. Finally able to gather enough strength to right himself, he raised his head to look around at the aftermath. Aaron could see a small crater where their quarry had once stood, with vivid shades of green and brown splattered outwards in all directions. The monster was definitely dead, but his concern grew for his friend who was still lying there just shy of the other side of the hole, face down in the mud.

Aaron's voice was crackly and surprisingly loud inside his own head as his ears struggled to recover. "Tommy? Are you dead?"

There was an uncomfortably long silence that followed, the ringing in Aaron's ears eventually beginning to subside. From where he sat resting back on his elbows, he couldn't see if Tommy was even breathing. Any sense of victory had been trumped by an overwhelming sense of worry. The loss of any friend was bad enough, but these two were inseparable.

A grunt, followed by a pained groan let Aaron know that Tommy was still alive after all. His voice was muffled as he spoke down towards the ground. "Yeah. A little more heads up next time, ya fuckin' pyro…" Aaron felt instant guilt for almost killing his friend, but true to form, Tommy raised his head to display the largest grin spreading from cheek to cheek. "Fire's supposed to be my thing, d-bag!" He began to laugh, cackling as he rolled onto his back and proceeded to make a mud angel.

The laughing was contagious, as Aaron, weary from the fight, couldn't help but join in. A good few minutes passed as they rolled around, slinging muck and other unidentifiable objects at each other. It was a disgusting kind of fun, but they were already completely filthy, and it was good to blow off a little steam.

****

It had been far too long since Aaron and Tommy had taken a break from work. They still struggled to find leads on Samuel Mitchell, having lost him somewhere just north of Miami. It had become necessary for them to take on the odd job to get by, working low end jobs for cash under the table during daylight hours. It wasn't meant to be fun or uplifting, but they had to have some source of income to keep going. At night they conducted their investigations, carried out research and followed an endless amount of leads that often took them nowhere. It was extremely frustrating, but neither of them were ready to give up the hunt. They had dedicated their lives to a cause and were determined to see it through to the bitter end. That end being their retirement, or more likely their untimely deaths.

Some leads had helped the two of them locate and take out other dangers like the monster in the swamps. Sure, they technically didn't save anyone this time, but their work meant that others wouldn't fall prey to such a fiend. It was more of a preventative task than anything. Monsters needed food too, and they fed on people more often than not. Cities and their outlying areas were hives of activity for the supernatural world, like a watering hole that they needed to sustain them. Where there were humans, monsters were sure to be nearby, lurking in the shadows as they waited for an opportunity to strike.

There were other hunters like Aaron and Tommy that the duo would run into them from time to time, however every hunter had their own methods and some of them were questionable at best. Not everyone would get along, and such meetings could sometimes lead to violent scuffles between those who should be working towards a common goal, not fighting between themselves. Everyone had their reasons for leading the life, some were similar, yet no two were ever exactly the same. The pair had more than their fair share of run ins with psychopaths that claimed to be hunting for the greater good, but they just turned out to be sadistic madmen looking to cause some pain. Collateral damage was just a statistic to those kinds of people and they didn't care who got hurt as long as they achieved their own personal goals. Civilians were just a means to an end and their well being was of little consequence.

Not everyone was bad though, and there was such a thing as pleasant hunters too. Kind souls who had lost someone close to them, or had witnessed something and refused to just stand aside and let it continue. Aaron was proud to call many of those people friends, and his phone was full of numbers that he had collected over the last decade or so. They were loyal people that he could call for help if they ever needed some backup. Tommy had his own share of contacts too, some of which happened to live in Florida. He had asked them to keep an eye out for any signs of Sam Mitchell and report on anything that they found. Tommy trusted those men and women almost as much as he trusted Aaron, and he could rely on them to call with updates should they see or hear anything. The bonds of like minded hunters were very strong indeed.

Aaron and Tommy's goofing around in the swamp had ended a little while ago, the friends now lying in the mud as they stared up at the clouds, taking advantage of some rare free time to relax. They had already grown to accept the rancid smell of their own clothing as part of their current state, but it was nothing a long shower and a ceremonious burning of said clothes wouldn't fix.

The now placid swamp was disrupted by an electronic ringing that originated from Tommy's jeans. Aaron was surprised to hear that the phone even worked after what they had been through, his own having succumbed to the ravages of swamp water.

Tommy was surprisingly quick to answer. "What you got?" As he listened, Aaron hoped that the call was finally the lead they were looking for and not another saying that they had been fired from another job. "Legit? Alright, I'll tell him." It seemed that his prayers had been answered. "Later, Murphy."

Aaron waited until Tommy had hung up before he jumped in on the conversation, his curiosity reaching its climax. "Okay, spill. Do we finally have a solid lead?"

Sitting up straight, Tommy flipped his phone shut and used his forearm to wipe slop from his brow. He was almost glowing with pride, which only served to increase Aaron's level of anticipation. "Hell yeah! I told you my buddies would find somethin' first. Looks like we're headin' downtown."

Aaron sat himself up too, his spirits uplifted by the positive news. "Finally. I want to finish this and then go somewhere much, much colder."

Tommy chuckled, sliding the dirt caked phone back into a similarly messy pocket. "You and me both, man! Let's get the fuck outta this swamphole!"

CHAPTER TEN: THE HAND THAT FEEDS.

Sam couldn't remember why he had agreed to be an accomplice in a robbery, let alone the getaway driver, but something about Entropy made him want to please her in any way that he could. She had tried to protest against involving him at first, but Jacko claimed that Sam owed them for the group taking him in and she reluctantly agreed after a heated discussion. So there Sam was with the engine still running, the wheelman in some sort of heist, waiting in a side street by whatever unposted building the group had decided to rob.

The others had been inside for almost ten minutes now, but it seemed like it had been a great deal longer. Sam had been checking the clock the whole time as he peered around nervously for police cars or cops on the beat. He looked immensely suspicious, dressed in black with a hat pulled down low to cover his face and he almost couldn't bear the anxiety that it caused. There was no reason for him to be idling there, other than to cause trouble or just generally being up to no good.

The car that had been provided was a generic sedan, with four doors and nothing much inside other than the old radio that

Sam hadn't even checked to see if it still worked. Beaded chair covers made his back feel uncomfortable, not that he could have made himself all that cozy, with muscles so tense that they felt like they might just pop at any second. As time went on he began to feel as though he was being set up, but for what reason he didn't know. The thought had occurred to him that he could just drive away, leave town and never return, but he couldn't do that to Entropy. He never wanted to leave her and hated the fact that she had gone inside without him.

It pained Sam when they were apart, not just emotionally, but there were physical symptoms too. His body began to tingle and there was an inkling of pain, with the promise of more. He absolutely had to be near Entropy at all times or at least whenever possible, but he couldn't disobey her when she asked him to stay. It had been a request, not a command, but he couldn't do anything to break her trust.

The pair of them had grown closer over the weeks and months, or however long it had been. Sam couldn't remember. Time was no longer of consequence when he was with Entropy. He was staying in her room at the club full time and had the pleasure of being there as she slept. It was odd to him, as she felt cold and lifeless during the day. The first time it happened he had freaked out, not knowing what to do, but she woke that very night as if nothing had happened. It was another step in what had been a big adjustment for him.

Sam loved sharing a bed with Entropy, but his body didn't

share the same desires as his mind. The necessary parts no longer seemed to work, or at least he didn't know how to make them work anymore. Whereas she didn't seem to mind at all and was just happy to be held, not ever expressing any wishes for anything further. It was something that Sam had learned to accept, not that he had much choice.

The other members of the band didn't stay at the club, instead returning to their own homes for much needed sleep before their alarms woke them and they had to work their day jobs. Music was more of a distraction for them, but for Entropy it was everything. There was a reason that the band had been named after her, or maybe she had named herself after the band. Sam didn't know which order it had occurred in as she wasn't big on sharing her past or her inner thoughts, instead putting on a mask that she would hide behind. There had only been a few occasions when he saw through it, getting to know the real woman underneath, and it was those brief moments that he treasured the most.

One of the most convenient parts of their living arrangement was that Sam never had to go out to feed, and he never had to hurt anyone to get what he required. Instead, Entropy would go out for for him, making him promise to stay behind where it was safe. Upon her return, she would share her own blood with him by making an incision in her wrist and allowing him to drink deeply from it. Every time he licked blood from her self inflicted wound, he felt a rush much greater than anything he could remember. At least anything since the night that he had died, but that was just a fading memory.

Each and every sip strengthened Sam's bond with Entropy and made him love her even more. He had realised that he was growing too dependent on his supposed savior and he had always hated losing his independence, but he couldn't resist her charms. His entire existence revolved around her, and it had reached a point where he couldn't imagine things being any other way.

Attempting to keep her true nature hidden, Entropy never showed her fangs to Sam, nor did she tell him how her wrist healed so quickly. He wasn't a prisoner in the club, but she also didn't want him to leave it without her. Most nights would be spent inside, with the occasional foray outdoors under her escort. She seemed to want to protect Sam from the darker parts of herself, but he was keen to know everything and at least her blood kept his hunger at bay, for now.

A loud bang caused Sam to nearly leap out his skin, his eyes darting over to where the sound had come from. The emergency exit on the far end of the building had burst open, and a gang of five people wearing ski masks came charging out through the small opening. They were a rough looking crew, wielding shotguns, six shooters and one even held a baseball bat, but Sam already knew who they were.

The masked figures sprinted for the car, the loudest among them yelling in an English accent for him to get ready, with a few added profanities for good measure. It didn't take them long to close the gap, piling into a car too small to fit them all. They stuffed into what little space was available, out of breath with shoulders pressed together as they slammed the doors shut behind them.

The masked Englishman yelled at the top of his voice. "What are ya waitin' for, ya twat? Just fuckin' drive!"

Sam smoked the tires, the wheels spinning until they found traction and the car raced towards the main street. The woman in the front passenger seat pulled the mask from her head, her purple hair wild and untamed. She was the only one who didn't seem to be gasping for air as she placed a hand on his arm. "You did good, Sam! I'm proud of you!" Entropy's smile helped calm him down a little, but his hands were still braced for a white knuckle ride. He focused on his driving, staying silent as the others talked.

Jacko wasn't best pleased, sandwiched between two larger men, with a skinnier man almost sitting on his knee. He removed his mask too, his mohawk pressed flat against his skull. "Fuck, fuck, fuck!"

The familiar voice of Chavz in the back seat questioned Jacko's agitation. "'Sup, man?"

Jacko had blown a gasket. "We're so fucked! I know that fella! E's gonna bleedin' kill us!"

Chavz was confused. "Which guy?"

"Big bollocks in't suit!" Jacko gestured wildly.

Entropy looked at them in the rear view mirror. "So... who was he?"

Jacko looked as though he was ready to tear his own hair out. "'E's one o' TJ's top men!"

It was Mike who spoke next. "You sure? Don't go rilin' us up if you ain't sure."

The punk haired Englishman couldn't contain his anxiety. "Don't be a bloody wanker, Mikey! I'm fuckin' sure, alright?"

It was Entropy who managed to hold it together as everyone else started to panic, while Sam tried his best to stay on the road. "If that's true, then we need to pay TJ everything we owe him and more, before he finds out who did it..."

Mike nodded. "You need to get us some shows, girl."

Finally getting a handle on his driving, Sam couldn't help but ask the question that was begging to be asked. "Who's TJ?"

Everyone but Jacko fell into silence, the crude man laughing hysterically. "Is 'e takin' the piss?"

It took a few seconds for Entropy to answer. "Trust me, you don't want to know..."

****

It took some prying to find out who TJ was, but Sam finally got Entropy to include him after some persuasion. She told him that the man was a loan shark, a businessman of sorts and a self-made entrepreneur who also dealt in the arcane. He wasn't particularly gifted with magic himself, but he had learned a few minor incantations that he had dabbled in over the years. He also had the odd trick up his sleeve, which he often used to get one up on his rivals.

Entropy wouldn't have even known who TJ was if it wasn't for the accidental death of the vampire who had turned her. Unbeknownst to her, the two of them had been close friends, although she had never been introduced until after she had branched out on her own. She admitted that she had been stupid after that, borrowing money from the dangerous man in order to finance her band's expensive equipment. At the time it had given them the boost that they needed to start making a name for themselves, but it turned out that their music wasn't quite worth the price that they had to pay for it.

Constant threats and increasing interest rates meant that it was impossible to ever pay TJ's loan off, and so the group had resorted to more extreme methods of making money, such as holding up convenience stores and the like. And then there was the robbery from the other night involving one of TJ's own places, meaning things were going to get much, much worse. He would now be searching for the culprits, and if he ever found out it was them, the payback would be severe.

That wasn't even the worst part, as Sam was told why Skid had never said a word to him. A late payment meant there had been serious repercussions and an example had been made. Skid's tongue was viciously removed by TJ's bodyguard, Akoni, with the rest of the band being forced to watch. The ordeal had left the poor drummer mute, a punishment for being in the wrong place at the wrong time and speaking out of turn. The fact that someone could commit such an atrocious act was something that Sam found appalling, and his faith in humanity took yet another blow.

Since explaining the situation to Sam, Entropy became a little distant. She went out most nights, looking for places for the band to play with the hope that they could make some quick cash. She managed to score a couple of gigs at smaller venues, but was struggling to find anything that was really worth their time. That was until one particular night when she returned without so much as a word, carrying dozens of shopping bags. Entropy rushed right up to her room, refusing to let Sam in to see what was going on. He promised to wait, as it was going to be a surprise that he didn't want to miss. So he stood by the closed door like a lost puppy, not moving from that spot until she emerged.

Sam gawked at Entropy as she stepped out from her room, her makeover now complete. If he had passed her in the street he might not have recognized her, as she no longer looked like the same woman that he had come to know. She had gone through a metamorphosis of sorts and was drastically different, with the long purple highlights of her hair having been replaced with a bright pink that stopped just shy of her shoulders. Black lipstick and eyeliner seemed to change the shape of her features, with dark eyeshadow that made her eyes positively glow.

Leaning against the metal railing of the walkway, Entropy turned to face Sam who stood completely still next to the door that she had just exited. She seemed to be taller than him now, with buckled, knee high boots adding several inches to her height. A black, laced corset and skinny jeans hugged her figure, a far cry from the baggy and unflattering clothes that she usually wore. To tie the look together, she had added an open waistcoat, giving the style a sophisticated depth of formality.

Entropy gave Sam a twirl, her arms out by her sides as she awaited his judgement. There were rows of bracelets, bangles and wristbands that now hid the writing across her forearms that Sam had committed to memory, but somehow still didn't quite understand. 'Remember me so I don't disappear, within the darkness of my own fear'. He presumed that they were lyrics from one of her songs, but never thought to ask.

After a couple of full rotations, Entropy stopped to try and gauge Sam's reaction. "So, what do you think? You like it?"

Sam's reply wasn't exactly smooth. "It's different..."

She pouted, dropping her hands to her hips. "You hate it..."

Shifting awkwardly on the spot, Sam tried his best to recover from his mistake. "No! I'm just not used to it yet. It's like you're a different person..."

Her spirits seemed to raise again as she took a step forwards, face beaming with joy. "Well that's the point!"

Sam wasn't sure if he actually liked Entropy's new image or not, but he didn't want to upset her. It would take some getting used to, but he secretly hoped that it wouldn't be a permanent change. He liked her old look, but she definitely looked the part of a rock star now, which he guessed was the general idea. Sam wasn't convinced that the new style was really her and thought that Entropy should change back to how she was before, but he would never say that to her face. Those types of comments were best kept to himself, locked away with all his doubts in the cage of his own mind.

Unable to control her excitement, Entropy began to bounce with enthusiasm. "Come on! Let's see what the others think of their new things!"

Sam raised his eyebrows in surprise. "Wait, you bought stuff for them too? Even Jacko?"

Entropy nodded with increased vivacity. "Of course! We all need to match for the big show!"

"What big show?" She had totally lost him now.

Clapping her hands together and almost squealing with elation, Entropy was proud to share her big announcement with him. "This is it, our big shot at making a name for ourselves! We're going to Canada!"

****

Sam kept quiet as the band tried on their new clothes in the main hall, feeling slightly left out as he watched them put on a miniature fashion show. They were all standing up there together, joking around having gathered in front of a full length mirror that

Entropy had placed centre stage. The matching outfits of plain white tees, open vests and black jeans were representative of a group that was still trying to discover their true identity. However, Sam had to admit that it did make them look less like a ragtag band suited to playing in a garage and more like the rock icons that they sorely wanted to be.

Wishing that he could join in, Sam knew that he couldn't play an instrument or even hold a tune. In fact, he wasn't really a part of the band at all. He was closer to being their mascot or groupie than a fellow musician, so he just sat down on a chair at the bottom of the steps, observing from a distance as he was left feeling like an outsider.

Chavz was a little too big for his clothes, having done his best to squeeze into them. It seemed that Entropy had underestimated the denseness of his bulky muscles, the result of years of exercise, supplements and a high protein diet. The short sleeves of his white shirt were stretched thin around the bulging biceps of his arms, revealing a tapestry of different designs across his dark skin, detailed with crucifixes and other religious iconography.

Adopting the stance of a man who clearly wasn't impressed, Chavz ran a hand through his short black hair as he chewed on the thin gold chain that he wore around his neck. "You gotta be jokin', chica..."

Jacko cackled loudly, checking out his pale self in the mirror. "I 'ope not. I'm lookin' suave as fuck. Nice one, En!" His enthusiasm actually seemed to be genuine as he spiked his green mohawk, grinning widely with nicotine stained teeth while he continued to admire his reflection.

Jacko's tattoos were a little less tasteful than his Latino friend, complete with curse words, odd looking cartoon characters and badly drawn symbols that were likely the result of many drunken nights and even more poor choices. He wasn't the type to regret his decisions however, if his array of piercings were anything to go by. Silver rings protruded from his nose, lips and eyebrows, with rubber plugs that stretched the lobes of his ears to impossible proportions.

The skinhead drummer, Skid, appeared to be pleased with his outfit too as he carefully adjusted his vest. He was the polar opposite to Chavz, seeming way too thin for the shirt and waistcoat. Unlike the others, he had no visible tattoos. However the dark circles under his eyes, scars up his arms and the pasty whiteness of his skin made him look as though he was someone who had struggled with addiction in the past. He nodded at Entropy with a smile, signalling his approval.

Mike didn't seem to mind Entropy's choice of clothing either, the fat of his belly shaking as he laughed heartily. "Not bad, En. We might actually look the part."

Sam noticed some markings on the bassist's tanned forearm that looked like some sort of military logo, possibly for the US Marines, although he didn't know enough about it to be sure. His long greasy hair and matching beard didn't seem like they belonged to an ex-soldier, nor did the smell of cheap whiskey and beer, but that didn't mean that it wasn't true.

Entropy paraded around the stage, still wearing her own ensemble as she drew Sam's gaze away from the others. "So now we have our look, we should really start packing. It's a long drive and the show is only a week away!"

Mike was already planning the details of the trip, seeming to daydream as he did so. "We'll take my van and bring some road sodas. Nothin' like a cold one on the open road."

Chavz nodded in the direction of Sam, who was too busy watching Entropy to pay attention. "What about lover boy?"

Jacko dismissed him with a wave of his hand. "Fuckin' leave 'im."

A nightmarish scowl flashed over Entropy's face for a split second, betraying the beast inside of her as it caused even the loud mouthed Jacko to stop chattering. "Sam's coming with us!" She turned to look fondly at Sam, who had only just realised that they were even talking about him. He suddenly felt paranoid that he had been staring a little too much, however Entropy didn't seem to mind being the centre of attention. "He can be our roadie!" She winked at him, a sly, yet friendly smile on her face.

Sam didn't know what to say, but he was pleased that she wanted him to travel with them. He would have struggled if left to his own devices for too long and may have even wasted away from abandonment. Now all he had to do was ignore any snide comments from Jacko and ride out the long days in the back of a windowless van. He would volunteer for some of the night shifts if he could and help to drive at least some of the way.

Sam couldn't be happier with how things had turned out. He was going to explore more of the world with someone who he adored, even though he would likely feel like a spare part at times. It was time to leave Miami, if only for a while, and venture into the far northwest, up mountain roads and through pine forests like he had never seen before. The whole trip wasn't just going to be a new experience for him, it was going to be an adventure.

****

"All clear!" The signal echoed throughout the empty brick hall, the limited furnishings offering little to dampen the sound of Tommy's voice.

The entire place had been left in darkness, with long drapes framing the tall windows that had been coated with a thick paint, preventing any light from entering. They had tried to locate the breakers, but had so far been unsuccessful, deciding to instead proceed by flashlight.

The pair had broken in through the rear entrance, the front door having been chained shut. Aaron had led the way, with Tommy following close behind, his gun trained on the shadows as if he was waiting for them to leap out at him. After pushing their way through what appeared to be a stockroom piled high with boxes and other junk, the pair entered the main venue through a door in the back. Once inside, they had begun to explore further, each of them taking their own route around the interior of the building.

Shining his flashlight around, Aaron examined the folding chairs that were spread throughout the room in loose formations that were more like staggered lines than actual rows. In the far corner, surrounded by the same flyers and posters that decorated much of the rest of the room, he could see a round, wooden table that had been littered with cardboard coasters, a few half empty beer bottles and an ashtray full to overflowing. He moved the beam of light across to his right to view the small stage that was central to the room's layout, with empty stands where instruments had once been. All other equipment had been removed, the only evidence of which was the dust free spots on the wooden floor. From what he could work out, the occupants of this place had left not all that long ago, but there was no telling if or when they would return.

"Aaron, you've got to see this shit!" Tommy's voice boomed from somewhere up above, causing Aaron to crane his neck to look upwards. Sure enough, the eager hunter peered down from over the edge of a walkway on high. "Come on, man! They could be back any second!" He was right. They needed to find out as much as they could in the shortest possible time, and nothing was better than surprising someone from high ground.

"I'm coming!" Aaron called back, making his way to the bottom of the metal steps that led up to where his friend was waiting. The metallic clang of his footsteps bounced off the walls and were reflected back at him, making it sound almost as if someone was following him up. However when Aaron stopped to check over his shoulder, he could see that no-one was there.

A short ascent later and Aaron was face to face with Tommy, who was standing ready next to the open door of a brightly lit room beyond. The light was harsh on the eyes after spending so much time in the dark, but they were already beginning to adjust. "What did you find?"

Tommy stepped through the doorway, forming a silhouette in the entranceway for a brief moment before disappearing around the corner. "Come check it out!"

Blinking a few times, Aaron followed Tommy through and began to look around the veritable treasure trove of information and potential leads. There wasn't much to the room itself, with only a mattress as a made up bed and various other pieces of furniture stashed around the area. But the interest Tommy had in the room had nothing to do with what filled it, rather with what covered the walls.

There were more posters of a band that went by the name Entropy of the Heart, the one that they had been told played in this so called club. They were crudely drawn and clearly made by an amateur, but it gave the impression of a group that was proud of their music. The band were trying their damnedest to make it in the business, wanting nothing more than to share their songs with the world. Around the posters and taking up space in between were handwritten lyrics on paper, music sheets and a multitude of photographs that were either pinned to the wall or held there by tack. The pictures seemed to be of the band members and their times together, with the occasional fan selfies thrown in for good measure.

As Tommy put his nose up to some of the notes to read the lyrics contained on their pages, Aaron matched up photographs of people with the band members on the poster, using the information they had been given by Murphy to fill in the blanks. "Miguel Chavez... Chavz on the keyboards."

Tommy chuckled. "And one hell of a bro, huh? Check out those guns!"

Aaron continued, moving along to the next band member, a skinny little man with a bald head and a big lip ring. "Skid. AKA Skinny Pete, the Skidster."

It was difficult to ignore the smirk on Tommy's face as he came to stand nearby. "Shoulda called him shit stain."

Aaron shot his friend a glance. "Not nice, Tommy."

The white pearls of Tommy's teeth were clearly visible. "Neither's the smell."

Clearing his throat, Aaron moved onto another picture. This time it was of a large man who looked as though he belonged in a biker gang. "Mike Peterson. Extreme bassist and all round badass." It was surprising that Tommy had nothing to say to that, instead letting Aaron continue. "Jacko. Jack Olsen, the axeman."

It seemed that Tommy's silence wouldn't keep up for that long after all. "Now that guy just looks like an asshole, am I right?"

Aaron nodded once. "Yeah, sure... Now for the interesting one. The singer only known as Entropy. Murphy said that there was no real name on record. In fact, he couldn't find anything about her at all."

He looked up and down the wall, looking for a purple haired woman that matched the one drawn on the poster. However, Tommy beat him to the punch, plucking one particular photo off the wall as he stared at it in disbelief, his jaw wide open. "What the...?"

Aaron moved over to take a look, his friend's hand almost shaking as he gripped the picture so tight that it crumpled in the middle. "Tommy? What's up?" There was no answer as he seemed to be stunned by whatever he had seen in the photograph.

The man in the image was unmistakable and easy to recognise as the one they had been after him for some time. It was Samuel Mitchell, his hair past his ears and looking like he needed a haircut. His dark eyes looked tired, but his smile was genuine. It seemed that he had found happiness there in Miami, but that wasn't something that Aaron wanted to dwell on. Sam Mitchell was a monster that had already harmed people and he was a danger to anyone around him.

From his own past experiences, Aaron knew that supernatural creatures had to be kept in check or they could run rampant and innocents would be hurt in the process. He couldn't afford to see a monster as anything other than what it was, a threat to humankind. To humanise them would take him a step closer to losing his will to hunt, and that in turn could run the risk of more lives being lost. That risk was simply unacceptable.

Aaron didn't understand why Tommy had been so shocked by the photo until he looked over at the woman in the picture. She was caught in an embrace with Sam Mitchell, her own happiness more than apparent. It was the same person from the poster, with purple streaked hair and a variety of piercings, but there was something about her that seemed familiar. She looked like someone who he used to know, but that was impossible.

"Christie..." Tommy's words caught Aaron by surprise. It wasn't his eyes playing tricks on him, the girl looked exactly like Tommy's girlfriend and his old friend, Christie Reece, albeit with an updated image.

"Tommy, that can't be her... Christie's dead." He reached out to place a comforting hand on his friend's shoulder, only to have it batted away in anger.

Tommy wasn't going to take no for an answer, grim determination set on his face as he shoved the photograph in front of Aaron's nose. "Take a fuckin' look, Aaron, it's her! She's alive! My girl is alive!"

CHAPTER ELEVEN: OUT OF THE WOODS.

It had been a long trip across North America, with countless stops to fill up the gas tank, obtain snacks, or for those with functioning bladders to take regular bathroom breaks. The journey had been slow going through Texas after Skid had eaten some bad Mexican food, with Sam wishing that his nose couldn't pick out specific scents within the consistent waves of flatulence. It didn't help that he could literally taste the gaseous stench of the burrito and whatever else had been digesting in the man's gut. Entropy apparently had an easier time at filtering out smells and didn't seem quite as grossed out. That or she had survived through a similar situation before. Whereas Skid seemed to think that the entire situation was extremely hilarious and didn't show any sign of suffering at all.

The van was a little cramped when loaded up with six people, their bags and all their instruments, but they somehow managed to cope. The mattress in the back found heavy use, with Sam and Entropy using it through the day under the cover of thick blankets and the other three taking turns throughout the night. It wasn't pleasant resting in the drool and sweat of the other guys, with perspiration being a big problem in the warmer states, but there wasn't much choice. After all, Sam was the only one who didn't need to be there and so he didn't have the right to complain. Of course, Jacko couldn't help but remind him of the fact, with tagalong, waste of space and other more colourful terms fast becoming part of his repertoire.

However unpleasant the drive had been, it was finally coming to an end, with Sam taking on the last leg of the journey. The border crossing had been stressful for everyone as he didn't have a passport or any other identification so to speak, so the others had hidden him under the drum set. Thankfully the Canada Border Service Agency wasn't quite as strict as the US side, which was something they wouldn't need to concern themselves with until they were heading home. That was a bridge that they would have to cross when it came to it.

The open ranges of the prairies with their shallow, rolling hills would occasionally give way to clusters of trees and small wooded areas as they passed by towns not too far away from their final destination. The city of Calgary was in their sights and the lights could already be seen on the horizon, with the mountainous backdrop of the Canadian Rockies just beyond. The white peaks glistened under the light of the moon, making them stand out amongst the stars in the clear night sky. Although the city was an impressive sight to behold, it wasn't anywhere near the size of overpopulated Miami and Sam was thankful for that. After all, he had come from a small town in the middle of nowhere and had been out if his depth ever since. Sure, Calgary wasn't anywhere near being a small town, but it was at least a little more manageable. The smaller population, with much less overcrowding, wouldn't overwhelm his senses quite so much.

As Sam carefully drove the van down a particularly straight stretch of road, he slouched backwards in his chair, leaving one hand on the wheel as he tried his best to relax. The nights driving had been uneventful so far, with Entropy in the front passenger seat in her tank top and sweatpants, listening to her favourite tracks on her phone with her eyes closed. The wailing of a guitar could be heard blaring out from her earphones as she tried to drown out Mike's heavy snoring coming from the back. Unfortunately there was no such escape for Sam, and he had to listen to each and every deep, rattling breath. He envied her ability to tune out the world around her as she lost herself in the music, which was a skill that he had never managed to acquire.

Boredom had taken over and Sam couldn't carry on without some sort of mental stimulation, so he nudged Entropy in order to grab her attention. Her eyes popped open and she bolted upright, looking around to see what had happened. "Huh? What's up?" She almost yelled at him, not able to hear the volume of her own voice over the music. The sudden noise caused someone to stir in the back, but they quickly drifted back to sleep with a disgruntled murmur.

Entropy pulled her earphones out, looking at Sam with her eyes wide. "Is everything okay?"

Sam chuckled, both of his hands back on the wheel. "Yeah, just bored."

The surprise faded from her face as she settled back into her chair, smiling wryly. "Oh. What you wanna talk about?"

He hadn't thought that far ahead and shrugged his shoulders. "I don't know... Just something. Anything."

Entropy pondered for a moment or two, looking out the windshield. "Okay. I never did ask... Why were you in that area of Miami the night we found you? You said you went to see your parents in Fort Lauderdale, but that's miles away."

Sam stared at the road, taking time to respond. "These men were at my parent's house, looking for me. They chased after me, and I just kept on running."

Entropy looked over at Sam, her eyebrows raised. "You ran all that way? Holy crap!"

He glanced back at her, tilting his head to one side. "I was scared... I think they were trying to kill me."

A look of dread crossed Entropy's face. She stared directly at him, a serious tone in her voice. "Jesus. Those sound like hunters, Sam... You were lucky to make it out alive."

Sam was left feeling bewildered. He couldn't believe that there were people that hunted down others like that. After all he was still a person, wasn't he? Despite any physical changes that he had gone through, he still had feelings, thoughts and emotions. "That's a thing now? They hunt down what? People like us? What did we do to deserve that?" He had plenty more questions where those had come from, but Entropy didn't seem to have any answers.

"I don't know... But that's one of the many reasons that we need to be careful. You more than most."

Sam's grip on the steering wheel had tightened. "Do you think they're still after me? It's been months."

Entropy frowned, speaking through gritted teeth. "I won't let them touch you."

The pair fell into silence, both lost in their own thoughts. As Sam continued to concentrate on the road, Entropy sat there with her body turned towards him. She just watched him without a word, as if she was studying his face. He appreciated how protective she was of him, but he hoped that the danger had passed and that those men would never find him. It had been so long now they that had to have given up the chase. No-one could be that persistent.

The van reached a section of road where the foliage was so thick that the trees blocked out the natural moonlight, leaving the vehicle's headlights as the sole source of light. It was so dark outside that the beams seemed to struggle, barely penetrating through the clouds of fog that swept across the tarmac. The mist seemed to appear out of nowhere, obstructing the view of the road, bringing with it an eerie feeling that they were being watched.

Sam slowed the vehicle to a crawl, not wanting to run off the side of the road or hit anything that may have fallen in their path. There was something primal deep inside that caused him to tense up in fear, and from the look of it Entropy was experiencing the same petrifying sensation. Neither of them could find the words to express how terrified they were feeling, jaws locked tight as teeth ground together.

"We there or somethin'?" Chavz yelled from the back, the sudden break in speed disturbing his slumber. He popped his head out through the door in the divider and into the cab at the front, looking out from between Sam and Entropy's seats. Neither of them could bring themselves to answer as they stared out into the woods.

"Wha's goin' on?" Chavs rubbed his eyes sleepily.

It was Sam who finally pulled himself together enough to vaguely answer the question. "Something's out there…"

Entropy stayed quiet, her eyes scanning what little she could see of the treeline through the fog.

"We stoppin'?" It was Mike this time, squeezing into the opening next to Chavz who took it upon himself to reply.

"Nah, man. They said they seen somethin'."

Mike joined in the search, looking out the windshield for whatever might be out there. "Well alright then. Been some time since I last played 'I spy'."

A frustrated groan from Jacko in the rear let them know that he was awake. "Some of us are tryin' ta get some bloody sleep!" A few seconds later and he too had squeezed in through the same opening, his head poking out over both Chavz' and Mike's. "What the fucks goin' on?"

Mike was the one to answer this time, holding back a yawn. "They said somethin' was blockin' the road."

Sam shook his head, still scanning for movement as he slowly pushed forwards through the fog. "No. I said that something's out there. We haven't seen anything yet."

Jacko grumbled. "So ya pissed yerself for no reason? Don't be soft."

For a split second, Sam could swear that he saw something move between the trees in the corner of his eye, but when he turned his head to look there was nothing there. "I swear it's out there, whatever it is."

Jacko cackled, the foul smell of old cigarettes on his breath. "Calm ya tits, fella. There's nowt there."

As if on queue, a ferocious howl echoed out from somewhere in the darkness. Sam felt as though he almost ripped the steering wheel from the column as he jumped out of fright. Entropy had dug her nails into the dashboard with a yelp, while the others were stunned into silence, other than Mike who proceeded to bark an order. "Keep drivin', Sam. Don't be stoppin' for nothin'." He didn't have to tell Sam twice, as the van picked up a little speed, the driver still struggling to see the road.

Sam caught a glimpse of something moving again, although this time he could see something similar in shape to a wolf, but much larger. Its head was oversized, with a powerful jaw and huge teeth that could easily shatter bone. The beasts matted fur looked grey in the dark and its sinister eyes almost glowed a deep red. It looked as though it was on the prowl, hunting for its next meal, but hopefully they were not part of the main course.

167

As Sam tried to get a better look, the giant wolf skulked off into the bushes, disappearing off into the night. Beginning to wonder if he was the only one who saw it, he turned his head to see that he wasn't alone at all. Even Skid had joined the group now, with both him and everyone else sharing the same look of abject horror. They had all seen the the beast in the woods and were not sure if they could believe their eyes.

Entropy's voice quivered as she spoke. "Sam, you heard Mike. Keep driving and don't stop until we reach civilisation."

As beautiful as the landscape was, there was a darkness that lurked there in the wilderness. It wasn't safe to linger in the woods or walk alone across the prairies, for dangerous creatures wandered at night. There was safety in numbers, but only the foolish would stop to look around. The best thing for them to do was to make it to the next populated area and wait out the darkness, which was easier to do when you weren't deathly allergic to sunlight.

****

It was getting dangerously close to dawn when the van rolled into the parking lot of the Whispering Pines Motel, a small place at the edge of the city's limits. It wasn't a pretty sight, with a flickering sign and poor upkeep, but it was going to be their accommodation for the next few nights until it was time to head back home. The band couldn't afford luxuries and had to stay at whatever cockroach infested place that they could afford, and this motel more than fit the bill.

As the others unloaded their bags from the van and argued over who had which room, Sam and Entropy sat on the hood of the vehicle enjoying each others company. Sunrise was about twenty or so minutes away, so they just wanted to relish what little was left of the night before they had to lock themselves indoors. Entropy leaned in to Sam, her body pressing up against his as they watched the horizon. The bright lights of the city were somewhere behind them as they looked back out towards the endless fields.

Sam's voice was weary, his body beginning to tire. "What do you think it was? It was bigger than any wolf I ever saw."

Kicking her legs back and forth as they dangled over the bumper, Entropy took a moment to consider. "I'm not sure, but you know it won't be the only danger here, right?"

He looked down at her face, trying to understand what she meant. "There's something worse than big bad wolves?"

Entropy nodded. "It's not like Florida. There are older vampires here and they have rules. If they find out what you are…"

Sam finished her sentence. "…They'll kill me."

She buried her face in his arm. "I won't be able to stop them, I'm not strong enough. It was selfish of me to bring you here…"

Placing a hand under Entropy's chin, Sam gently lifted her face until their eyes met. Her pupils dilated as he stared deep into the crystal blue of her eyes, brushing a strand of bright pink hair from her face. "I wanted to come. You didn't drag me here against my will."

Entropy bit her lip, looking away from him and back towards the prairie lands. She didn't say another word, lying her head against his chest until it was time to head inside.

The thought of meeting ancient vampires and having to hide himself from them in plain sight was a frightening prospect, but Sam wanted to be there to support Entropy and the band as he felt that he owed them. He knew that he would be on edge during their entire stay, but he was there already and was determined to enjoy himself as much as possible. It was his first time in another country and he wanted to make the most of it. All he could do in the meantime was take each night as it came, and tomorrow was bound to be full of new experiences and endless possibilities. The journey was over, but the adventure was just beginning.

****

The immense tower stretched up into the sky, a silent sentinel grandly lit with red and white hues as it stood still against the dark backdrop of night. Bright lights atop the saucer shaped rotunda seemed to block out the stars, its awe inspiring pinnacle far out of reach of the city streets below. There were taller buildings in Calgary, but none quite so impressive, with their flat glass sides that were comparatively dull in design. The Calgary Tower was a symbol of a more prosperous time, when oil prices were high and business was booming. The city itself was far from rundown, but it was a shadow of its former glory, struggling just as much as the rest of the world following the economic crash. It was a matter of pride that the building be kept well maintained, with a great deal of care going into its preservation.

Sam had wanted to take Entropy up to the observation deck above the revolving restaurant to show her a view of the city that she deserved, but he couldn't afford the high price of entry. "I'm sorry... I thought it'd be a fun idea." Sam spoke with a tone of sadness in his voice, upset that he couldn't pay for the tickets. He wanted to take Entropy out on a date, but his empty wallet had made things difficult.

Thankfully there wasn't a hint of disappointment in Entropy's voice as she took Sam's hand, gently turning him to look into her eyes. "One day we'll be able to go anywhere and do anything we want, I promise."

Sam managed a half smile, but he couldn't help but feel as though he had let her down. He existed to make her happy and failure to do so wasn't an option. "I should be the one making promises..."

Entropy kissed Sam lightly on the cheek, her gaze lingering for a moment before she began to wander down the street with him in tow. Gently squeezing hands, the pair slowly strolled along the sidewalk, taking in the cool, late evening breeze.

This was the Entropy that Sam wanted to know. A regular

girl in normal clothing, not someone who was pretending to be someone else. Although she insisted on going by her stage name and kept her true identity hidden from him, he believed that he was getting close to the real person inside. Entropy had removed most of her makeup and tied her pink hair back to reveal the natural beauty of her face. There was no need for her to hide behind false pretenses or put on a show while she was with him. In that moment, she was just the woman that Sam had found himself falling inexplicably head over heels for.

    The streets had been bustling with activity just a short while earlier, but it was as if the city had emptied out soon after rush hour. It seemed that all the people that worked within the city centre couldn't afford to live there, so as soon as work hours were over they vacated to the suburbs and left downtown Calgary eerily quiet. There were a few people hanging out around bars and pubs, but it was nothing compared to the nightlife in Miami. Sam felt a little saddened that a place with so much potential could seem so neglected, as although it was clean and well kept, the city seemed to be lacking in spirit.

    In contrast to the grand metropolis whose golden years had long gone by, Sam was sporting a new look that made him feel better about himself than he had felt in a long time. Entropy had used some of her limited funds to take him around some thrift stores, his newly acquired hoodie and baggy jeans fitting nicely, unlike the hand me downs that he had been dwarfed by up until now. He even had a pair of second hand skate shoes that were in his own size, instead of the oversized boots that he had almost tripped over time and again.

A short and stylish haircut made Sam feel like a new man, with a clean shaven face that took years off instead of adding them on. The style brought with it a new found confidence and self esteem that he felt he owed to his doting benefactor. Pretty much everyone had complemented Sam on his appearance since, which was a change from how people usually viewed him. He had always been an awkward boy growing up, not feeling like he fit in his own body, but now he truly felt as though he belonged in his skin. Perhaps that's what it felt like to be a man instead of a boy, after all he was still aging. It wouldn't be long until he had surpassed Entropy in physical years and then he would be her elder in all but actual age.

It was only Jacko who had poked fun at Sam for how he looked, comparing him to a doll that Entropy could play with and dress how she wanted. His comments were unfair, but they did leave Sam wondering if there was some truth to it. He dared not question her on the subject, but that didn't mean that he couldn't enquire about the guitarists attitude towards him.

Sam cleared his throat, mentally preparing his words before he delivered them. "Why does Jacko despise me so much? Did I do something to upset him?"

Entropy looked straight ahead, as if she was avoiding looking directly at him. "No. I wouldn't worry about it too much."

The brief answer spurred Sam onwards. "Then what's his problem?"

Her eyes stayed straight as the two of them continued to

wander along the sparsely populated streets. "Jacko really isn't as bad as he seems."

Sam frowned. "Really? Because he seems pretty terrible."

A sigh followed. Entropy kept up the steady pace, still refusing to look over at Sam as she spoke. "He's just overprotective. You see, we used to have a thing."

Sam raised his eyebrows in surprise. "You were a couple?" From what he had witnessed, the two of them didn't seem like they had ever been that close. Entropy tended to ignore both the guitarist and the snide remarks that spewed from his mouth. It was difficult to imagine them being anything more than bandmates or friends, as she was kind and he was just unpleasant.

Entropy shook her head. "Not exactly, no. Whatever it was, it didn't work out."

Sam felt his curiosity rising. The way Jacko acted towards him was starting to make sense. "So that's why he's a jerk to me?"

She nodded half heartedly. "Yes, and no..."

There had to be more to the story, but she wasn't being overly forthcoming. He needed to know more. "So what happened then?"

The pace of the stroll slowed to a crawl, Entropy chewing her lip in thought. "There was another guy."

That much was clear, as Sam was fairly sure he had been wearing the man's clothes. There had also been the odd comment or two alluding to the fact. "I heard Jacko mention him. Who was he?"

Stopping on the spot, Entropy let go of Sam's hand and pulled away. It was obvious that she didn't feel comfortable with his line of questioning which caused guilt to well up inside of him, but he had gone too far now to turn back. She crossed her arms in front of her chest, her hands resting on the sleeves of her leather jacket, almost comforting herself in a self embrace. "He wasn't like you. Frank was a full on vampire, but he had... issues."

Entropy still wouldn't make eye contact, which caused Sam to feel concern as he hadn't seen her looking so vulnerable before. This wasn't the wild entertainer that she strived to be, but rather who she truly was inside. The outer layers were slowly being peeled back to reveal the real girl beneath the mask. He pushed on, speaking as softly as he could to try and ease the process. "What kind of issues?"

Entropy appeared to shiver, which was particularly odd as like him she didn't feel the cold. "He became obsessed with me and... and it took a turn for the worst. When I tried to leave him, he kidnapped me and tried to kill us both. He said that we could 'be together forever'." A single tear of crimson rolled down her cheek.

Sam felt awful. He didn't understand why anyone could treat someone so precious that way. How dare someone hurt her! The very thought of it infuriated him and left him fuming, but he pushed down his anger to play the part of the shoulder to cry on. "That's awful..." He stepped forward, testing the waters while Entropy stayed put, continuing to hug herself with arms wrapped tightly.

Entropy smudged the tear across her cheek with her hand. "Yeah... If Jacko hadn't tailed him and brought the others along, I would be dead too..."

Sam couldn't resist a moment longer. He closed the gap and placed his own arms around the quivering wreck, trying his best to steal her pain away. He whispered softly in her ear. "I hope you know that I'm not like that. I'd never hurt you..."

Entropy's body went limp as she buried her face in his neck, tears of blood leaving the collar of his hood feeling damp. "I do. I wouldn't make that mistake twice. But that's why Jacko has trust issues, especially with other guys..."

Sam felt bad for smiling. He was just glad that she had finally shared something personal with him, even if it had been hard for her. They had never been so intimate as they were in that very moment. "Well that makes sense, I guess. I'll try my best to get along with him."

Entropy's arms snaked around Sam's waist as she made herself at home. "Thanks, Sam."

He rested his head against hers. "Don't mention it."

Sam felt happy there, out in the open, locked in an embrace. It was as if he belonged in that place with Entropy and that they should never leave. He had felt that way with her before, but this time his feelings had grown in intensity. He would lay his life down for this woman if he could, he would offer it up gladly. He would die a thousand times over if it meant that she would be safe. Compared to her life, his own meant nothing.

CHAPTER TWELVE: THE PERFORMANCE OF A LIFETIME.

"They call people like you the Forsaken, and other vampires in high standing and positions of power will actively hunt you down if they're able." The words of Jonah, the rat hungry hacker, rang true. It was all Sam could think about as he meandered through crowds of well dressed people, not really knowing who was human and who was a vampire that might rip him to shreds should he give himself away. It was impossible for him to tell them apart, and for all he knew he could be completely surrounded.

Sam's entire body was on alert, tensing up as he struggled to act normally. His increasingly delusional mind had him convinced that everyone was on to him and that he could find himself at their mercy at any moment. The bloodthirsty predators would surely kill him if they discovered what he was. A freak and an outcast of both human and vampire society alike. Intense paranoia had set in, leaving him feeling flustered and trapped, but at least he didn't perspire anymore, as that would have certainly given him away. Then again, Entropy had mentioned that he smelled a little odd. Sam began to wonder if anyone else could pick up on his strange scent too. All he could hope was that they were too preoccupied with their social games of power mongering to notice him amongst them.

'Don't make eye contact. Don't stare at them. Just keep moving.' Sam's inner monologue had kicked in again, screaming orders at him as his survival instincts played havoc with his rational mind. He had to concentrate just to prevent himself from fleeing in terror. Why didn't he just stay in the dressing room with Entropy and the others? Sure, it was a little dull waiting there as they prepared for their set and Jacko was being his usual rude self, but the risk of death was far less than it was out here.

Even in his distracted state, Sam noted that whoever had decorated the lobby had done an excellent job. Sheets of red velvet were draped over the walls, lending a certain elegance to the proceedings that was accentuated further by grandiose tapestries that bridged the gaps between wooden panels. Delicate crystal chandeliers hung from the ceiling, their prisms refracting rainbows of light over the polished brass railings of the stairs that led to the upper levels. However, the true focal point within the lobby was the luxurious water feature, which consisted of a sculpted fountain in the shape of a maiden holding a large pitcher that poured water into a shallow pool lined with smooth pebbles.

Nervously surveying the theatre lobby as he made his way across the red carpet, Sam kept an eye out for anyone paying particularly close attention to him. Fashionably dressed people in their tailored suits and expensive dresses were grouped up in their various cliques around the room, fully engrossed in their conversations as they seemingly enjoyed each other's company. It was supposed to be the soirée of the year, with everyone who was anyone in attendance, and there was Sam, severely underdressed in his secondhand shirt and slacks. He seemed to be the only person in the room who looked out of place, and he was not having a good time at all.

The main entrance to the theatre swung wide open, causing everyone in the place to turn their heads to look in its direction. They all wanted to see who was making such a grand entrance, the groups shuffling closer together to make a large crowd as they gossiped among themselves. Sam was relieved that the focus was being placed on someone else, the feeling of being watched finally fading. He was tempted to make his escape, moving in the direction of the door that led back to the main stage, but something inside pulled against him, dragging him back towards the gathering crowd. He felt as though he was being drawn towards the entryway, his curiosity crying out to know more.

Peering through the narrow gaps that people had left between themselves while they stared on in awe, Sam could just about see what all the commotion was about. A tall woman strode past the crowd with confidence, knowing full well that she was the topic of conversation. A long, emerald dress hugged the curves of her hourglass figure, overlapped at the back by the brown curls of her hair that fell down her neck and over her shoulders like waterfalls. Her diamond necklace sparkled in the light, giving a sense of wealth and regality to her appearance. Whoever the woman was, she was certainly someone of high standing within the city and Sam presumed that meant she was also a member of the vampire elite.

As interesting as the woman in green was, her companion peaked Sam's interest further. He only got a glance of her red dress and blonde hair before his view was obscured, but he could have sworn it was a girl that he hadn't seen for a few years now. Someone who had once meant the world to him before he pushed her away. She looked an awful lot like Alice Delaney, his best friend and the one person who knew him better than anyone else, Entropy included.

Sam shook his head, trying to come to his senses. It couldn't be her, not here. Alice should have been down in Kansas or with his parents in Florida. Why would she be up in the middle of Canada, far from everything and everyone she had ever known? Then it occurred to him, why was he there? She could have her own reasons for being in Calgary, the same as him. If it was Alice, then she had to have her reasons for being there, and it was a hell of a coincidence. Or maybe fate had brought them together. Then again, it could have just been a case of mistaken identity. Maybe it wasn't Alice at all, as it could have been someone else entirely. He had only caught a glimpse of her as she walked by, not nearly long enough to confirm who it was.

Trying to move around the edge of the crowd to get a better look, Sam was quickly overrun by masses of people as they began to disperse, returning to their own smaller groups. He had forgotten all about his reasons for trying to hide amongst them, ignoring the fact that he was still in danger of being discovered. For some reason he couldn't find the girl in the red dress, rudely pushing past anyone who got in his way as he searched the entire room for another sighting of her.

Sam clumsily tripped over someone's foot, stumbling a few steps as he tried to regain his balance. He didn't recover fast enough to stop his body from slamming into another guest's arm, knocking a full glass from their hand that was sent crashing to the floor. The liquid contents began to soak into the carpet, with countless shards catching in the fibres like clear, jagged jewels. The sound of breaking glass and the gasps that came with it caught the attention of the majority of patrons in the place, their disgust over Sam's actions apparent as they silently passed their judgement.

Completely embarrassed and quickly realising that he had overstepped his bounds, Sam ducked behind the closest gathering, trying his best to hide from their scrutiny. Fortunately for him, it wasn't long before the social faux pas was forgotten and the atmosphere in the room had returned to how it was before. Even the grumbling man who had lost his drink decided to ignore what had occurred as soon as he obtained more champagne from a passing waitress.

Something about how quickly the moment had passed seemed odd to Sam, as if everyone had been programmed to forgo any drama. None of them seemed to pay him any mind as he took a step back, beginning to look around for any signs of Alice once more. Perhaps their indifference meant that they wouldn't sniff him out and that his secret was safe at least for now. No-one would be trying to kill him if they couldn't even be bothered to investigate further, the thought of which he found strangely comforting.

Stepping out from behind the group in which he had taken refuge, Sam caught sight of the bright red and green fabrics in the corner of his eye. He could see the two women with their backs to him, the contrasting colours of their dresses standing out at a distance. He still couldn't tell if the woman in red was his friend from that far off as she faced away from him, her hair tied up in a complex design of interwoven braids. The pair were exiting the room through another set of doors at the far end of the room, just out of earshot of Sam who tried to call to them, his words drowned out in an ocean of voices.

Sam rushed to towards the doorway with surprising speed, not realising that he had somehow quickened his muscles, propelling his body faster than he could normally move. However, even with his burst of speed, he couldn't reach the door in time before it was closed tight in front of him. He would have opened it and gone after them, but two burly guards barred the way, standing tall in their black suits. They stepped into Sam's path, huge bodies blocking the door as they denied him entry. He would have argued his case, but the intimidating size of the guards and their steely gaze made him think twice. It seemed that whatever lay on the other side was intended for special invites only, and a private guest of the entertainment didn't qualify.

The shortest of the two guards peered over the frames of his sunglasses at Sam, his nose twitching as if he smelled that something was off. An arching eyebrow acted as a warning that made Sam realise that it was time to leave. He took a few steps backwards, smiling sheepishly as he excused himself and quickly turned to make himself scarce.

The confirmation of whether the girl was his estranged friend or not would have to wait, with his own continued survival taking precedence over pointed curiosity. For now, he would retreat to the relative safety of the band's dressing room, hiding out among those who he considered to be his friends, with the odd exception. They would likely need his help setting up their equipment anyway. Perhaps he would have the chance to make another attempt at finding the girl in the red dress after the show, as he certainly wasn't ready to give up the search quite yet.

****

It was showtime in the main auditorium and that meant it was Entropy of the Heart's time to shine. They were already halfway into their set, the band's performance invoking a sense of wonder as their music rang out for all to hear. Each and every member was playing their part to perfection, blending the sounds of their instruments seamlessly into a musical masterpiece of alternative rock. Despite their professionalism, Sam still felt pity for the band members as they placed their very hearts and souls on display, putting everything they had into the performance of a lifetime.

The audience in the theatre was surprisingly small, especially for a place that could seat thousands, with only a few people drifting in from the party that was still going on outside. At least the money was good, even though the band hadn't drawn in the crowds and prestige that they had hoped for, but that didn't stop them from trying their hardest to put on the show to end all shows.

Sam could see almost everything from where he stood behind the side curtain, watching in reverence as the band made full use of the stage. It was much larger than the one they practiced on, but that didn't stop them from dancing around and performing with flourishes designed to capture the crowd's interest and draw them into the performance. They were lit up by their trademark purple spotlights, making it impossible to see the faces of anyone watching, with only their outlines visible like shadowy figures listening in silent awe. For an amateur band who were yet to hit the big time, the group could have easily fooled anyone into believing that they were stars. Entropy's powerful voice filled the entire place in a way that she couldn't have achieved in their practice venue, with just the right acoustics and equipment setup to project her lyrics to every corner of the theatre.

Whatever Sam thought about Jacko, he couldn't deny the guitarists obvious talent as he shredded away at his strings with a level of skill befitting a true master of the art. Chavz hammered at the black and white keys, while Skid kept the drum rhythm going with arms and legs that seemed to move independently of his body.

Mikey P wasn't one to let the side down either, setting the pace of the music with a bassline that would have whipped a larger crowd into a frenzy. It was a mystery why the band hadn't managed to snap up the ever elusive record deal that could have put them on the mainstream stage, where fans far and wide would shower them with adoration. Sam honestly believed that they deserved that much, but they sadly weren't getting the recognition.

After the final notes of the last song had been played, the house lights lit up the rest of the theatre to let everyone in the audience know that the show was over. The band began to gather their equipment and pack up their things, getting themselves ready to leave the stage. There was no encore, as they had already played all the songs that they had ever written and Entropy wasn't too keen on covering the work of other bands.

Sam could see the rest of the theatre now in all its glory, with three floors of seating, complete with balconies and box seats, separated by brass railings and all connected together by grand staircases. The beige decor was broken up by wooden panels and alcoves packed with soundproofing. Massive speakers and lighting rigs scaled the walls nearest to the stage, ending at the ceiling where they branched out with walkways that reminded Sam a little of the one back at the club. The few people that had stayed to enjoy the entire show began to filter out through the doors at the back, heading out to join the rest of the partygoers. Preparing for the next act, the stage crew began set up the space for a ten piece orchestra, fronted by an eccentric opera singer.

All but one person in the audience had exited the auditorium, and Sam was surprised that he hadn't noticed them before. He stared at the girl who had seated herself a few rows from the front, oblivious to the fact that the band had collected their instruments and were leaving the stage. He couldn't hear Jacko's smart-alec complaints about him not helping out, instead gawking at the blonde female in her red dress. She was gazing hypnotically at the stage, her eyes glazed over as if she was in some sort of trance.

Sam realised that he hadn't imagined anything at all. Alice Delaney was indeed in Calgary and she was sitting there just a short distance away from him. She looked almost exactly the same as he remembered, having seemingly aged very little since he had seen her years before. He hadn't laid eyes on her since they were teenagers, and the only thing that had really changed was how she presented herself.

Alice's style of dress suited someone who was much more confident and self assured than the girl Sam had known. Her long hair was something that she had once hidden behind, yet now it was tied up and out of the way of her face. She also wasn't one for wearing makeup and yet here she was looking as though it had been done by a professional. Whatever had happened to Alice, it had seemingly changed her for the better and Sam couldn't have been happier for her, yet he also felt saddened that he hadn't played any part in that transformation. He couldn't help but feel that he had somehow been holding her back and that any previous lack of positive development had been his fault.

Sam continued to watch Alice from the sidelines, noticing that she still hadn't moved. Her eyes were locked on the stage where the band had previously been and she showed no sign of getting up from her chair any time soon. He was so distracted by her that he hadn't noticed Entropy standing next to him, her head so close to his as she leaned in, cool lips almost touching his ear as she whispered. "Who is she?"

Sam almost leapt out of his skin, surprised by the close proximity of her voice amplified by his sensitive hearing. "What the...?!?"

Entropy chuckled, wrapping her arms around his waist as she rested her chin on his shoulder. "It was just a question. Do you know her?" There was no apparent jealousy in her voice, but she was certainly interested in who the other girl was.

Sam nodded slowly, his own voice monotone and devoid of emotion. "I used to..."

It was surprising that Alice hadn't heard his yell of fright, as she still sat motionless in her dreamlike state. Entropy didn't seem to be too concerned by it at all. "An old friend?"

It took a moment for Sam to respond, but he nodded again. "My best friend."

Entropy took a step back, releasing her grip on Sam. She beamed at him, tugging his sleeve in the direction of where Alice was sitting. "Come on then. Let's go and see her!"

Sam resisted, not budging from his spot. "No... I can't. Not like this."

Her face changed from a look of joy to one of concern. "What's wrong, Sam? You can tell me."

Sam sighed, not taking his eyes off his friend for a second. "We didn't part on the best of terms. It was my fault really..."

Running her fingers down Sam's arm, Entropy clasped both her hands around his. She tried to look into his eyes, but he was far too focused on Alice for that. It was unusual as not long ago he would have done anything to simply stare into hers. Somehow Sam's feelings for her were somehow being overridden by how he felt about Alice.

Entropy spoke softly, not wanting to startle Sam a second time. "Maybe it's time to reconcile?"

He pondered for a little while before nodding, not sounding too sure in his reply. "I guess so."

As Sam took a step forward, egged on by Entropy who was being as supportive as possible, he felt a large hand pull him back. "Easy there, chief." It was Mike. Sam peered back at him, not quite sure as to why the bassist had stopped him.

Entropy wasn't too impressed by the interruption either as she frowned at him disapprovingly. "What, Mikey?!? What's up now?!?" She didn't mean to snap, but it was just something that happened occasionally. It seemed that the bloodlust of vampires could sometimes result in short tempers.

Mike raised his hands up in defense, not wanting to start a fight with someone who could likely overpower him. Not that he would have done so intentionally, as he wouldn't lift a finger against a friend either. "Easy, En. It's just that girl's darn close with one of the big shots here. She has major connections. Don't want 'em gettin' a load of your boy."

Sam was confused. What did Alice have to do with vampires? Unless... It dawned on him. There was a reason that she hadn't aged as much as he had expected. Like him, Alice was dead, except she was likely a fully fledged vampire and not some sort of freak like him. It was upsetting to know that his friend was as cold and lifeless as he was. His mind began to wander. Did his parents know about what had happened to her? No, they couldn't have. There was no way that she would have dragged them in to her problems as she cared about them almost as much as he did. At least Alice didn't seem to be alone in her existence, as there was the brunette in the green dress, and from the sound of it there could be others too. She was safe there amongst the timeless predators, as strange as that seemed.

The look of concern on Mike's face was surprising as Sam didn't know that the man cared, yet there it was. Perhaps he had more friends than he thought. Sam raised his eyebrows, realising that what the man had said was right. Miami may have been lacking any truly powerful vampires, but apparently Calgary was crawling with ancient beings who could destroy him with a mere glance. If he contacted Alice, there was a high chance of being discovered and he didn't want to die. There was also a risk of them going after Entropy and the others just for being associated with him, and he wanted to keep them safe.

Sam turned back to look at Entropy who had a similar expression of worry as she spoke. "If Mike's right, then you shouldn't risk talking to her... I'm really sorry, Sam."

There was no question in Sam's mind, he knew that she was right. Both of them were. As much as he would love to rekindle his relationship with Alice, it wasn't worth the consequences of such a selfish act. "At least she's protected. I won't destroy what she's built for herself here." Sam had muttered just loud enough for the others to hear. His voice wavered, but his words were sincere.

Entropy stepped in, embracing him tightly as she tried to comfort him. "Come on. Let's get you out of here and go home. There's no point hanging around any longer than we need to."

Mike turned to leave, making his way to the back entrance of the theatre that the other band members had already gone through. He tried to sound cheerful, joking half heartedly as he walked. "Jacko's gonna kick up a fuss if we don't help pack. It won't be pretty, but that goes without sayin'."

Linking arms with Sam, Entropy moved to follow but he was still resistant. He had turned his attention back to Alice, wanting to see his friend one last time. It was difficult, but he had to convince himself that like his parents, she was better off without him.

Entropy let Sam savour the moment, holding off for a minute before speaking to him in a soft tone. "Don't worry, Sam. She didn't see you and wouldn't remember if she had."

Sam didn't understand. It seemed that his companion knew

more about Alice's trance than she had been letting on. "Did you do something to her?"

Entropy smiled lightly. "I just gave you the time you needed. It's a gift." She began to walk in the direction that Mike had left, sauntering towards the exit.

"How did you know that I needed it?" Sam questioned her with curiosity.

Entropy stretched her arms out to the sides, flicking her hair back as she did so. "Women's intuition."

The way that Entropy moved her hips drew Sam in. He was intrigued by her many hidden talents and the powers that she had not yet shared with him. Maybe this gift was something that she could teach him in time. His feet beginning to move in a slow pursuit, he couldn't resist watching her go, enjoying the show as he followed close behind. Sam felt as though he had been bewitched, unable to look away as any thoughts of Alice were lost somewhere in the back of his mind. In that moment he decided that there was nothing in the world more important to him than Entropy. Nothing at all.

CHAPTER THIRTEEN: A SUDDEN REVERSAL OF FATE.

Sam didn't believe in miracles, but the band had somehow smuggled him back across the border without any trouble from customs and immigration. The tense atmosphere within the van had since been replaced with one of calm that had lasted for the remainder of the journey back home. The group had almost driven across the entire country, making various stops along the way, and they were already halfway down Florida when they had to make yet another stop to fill up the gas tank.

Sam had been driving throughout the night, and it was finally time for someone else to take over. The sun would soon be peeking over the horizon and it wouldn't be safe for him to stay behind the wheel, so Skid had signalled that he would take the next shift. Sam didn't care who took his place as long as he could rest, the daylight leaving his body weak and vulnerable. They would be back in Miami by the time he woke and then he would be able to settle into his new routine, at least until the next road trip.

It had been a slow trip southwards along the massive turnpike that spanned a large portion of the state, but the journey was relatively easy going, with few vehicles occupying the multi-laned highway and dry weather allowing them to move unhindered. As dull as things had been at times, Sam felt that he preferred the boredom over constantly fearing for his life. The dangers of Calgary and the elder vampires that occupied the city were far behind them, so he could instead focus on building a future with Entropy and her aspirations of being a world renowned rock star.

There was something that bothered Sam about his time in the north, but he couldn't quite remember the reason why he felt that way. It was as if a small fragment of his mind had gone missing and the memories stored within were lost, yet he had no chance of recovering them without any clue as to what had been stored within. Perhaps it was for the best that the memories had been lost and that they stayed that way. After all, there had to be a reason that he had purged them from his brain.

Sitting alone in the driver's seat of the van, Sam waited patiently for the others to return, as most of them had wandered over to the convenience store that sat adjacent to the gas station. They had likely gone to use the bathroom, obtain some snacks or stock up on the cigarettes that had already permeated his clothing with the smell of smoke. Mike was the only one to remain outside, leaving the passenger door of the van wide open as he manned the pump and filled up the tank with unleaded.

A warm breeze drifted in from outside, along with the pungent scent of gasoline that seemed to overpower most other smells. The light in the cab had been left on, its warm glow illuminating the mess of empty beer cans that were liberally spread out across the dashboard. It hadn't been a particularly pleasant experience travelling in the van, as crowded as it was with everyone crammed inside like sardines in a can. The entire vehicle had that lived in feeling, with crumbs decorating the sticky floor and trash lying around in small piles that gravitated towards the corners over time. The band had a tendency to act like slobs, but they would eventually clear up after themselves once the dirt and grime became unbearable. Unfortunately, that was a fairly uncommon occurrence that didn't happen quite as often as Sam would have liked.

At least Skid had avoided Mexican food this time around, and Jacko had been unusually quiet almost the entire way. Chavz kept to himself, while Mike was just entertaining to be around as he was full of over-exaggerated stories of times gone by. Each of them had their quirks, matched closely by their varied driving styles, with some a little more erratic than others. Sam just prayed that they kept their eyes on the road and always hoped that they would consume a little less alcohol, not that he had any control over what any of them wanted to do at any given time.

The main thing that all the members of the band had in common was that they were free spirits who had a problem with authority figures and those in positions of power. They weren't afraid to show their feelings towards those people either which had caused some issues in the past, with TJ being just one person in a long list. Perhaps that intolerance of authority was one of the main reasons that they still hadn't landed a record deal, and it was doubtful that the situation would change any time soon unless they had a sudden change of heart.

"Y'alright, lad?" To Sam's surprise, Jacko was the first band member to hop back into the van and the strangest part was that he was unusually cheerful. The punk's yellow toothed grin was as unsettling as it was wide, his spiked mohawk brushing across the fabric of the ceiling as he made himself at home in the passenger chair.

Sam smiled weakly, already starting to feel weak as the night began to give way to morning. "Hey, what's up?"

He fully expected Jacko to lash out at him with a sarcastic response, but that wasn't what followed. "Cheers for 'elpin' out. We got enough dosh fer payin' TJ an' fer gettin' a few sound upgrades. It's gonna be plain sailin' from now on."

Sam was almost speechless. These were the nicest words that the guitarist had ever slung in his direction and it had been completely unexpected. "You're welcome, I guess?" It was all a little confusing, but he had to take what he could get.

Jacko punched Sam in the arm, a quick wink letting him know that it was done in jest. "Yer not so bad, but don't go tellin' tales. I got a rep to protect, so don't be a wanker an go' messin' that up fer me."

The friendlier tone was a pleasant change that Sam could get used to, but he didn't want to presume that it was permanent. Jacko could switch back to his usual self at any moment, so he just had to accept it for what it was. A rare moment of uncharacteristic comradery.

Sam nodded politely, his words as sincere as ever. "Don't mention it. I'm just happy to help out whenever I can."

It was the gaunt face of Skid that showed up next, his skinny frame barely filling the open doorway. He inclined his head with respect to Sam with a warm and welcoming smile.

Jacko chuckled to himself. "Would ya look at that, Stinkboy is back! Clean yer arsehole this time?" As he said, he had a reputation to protect and it didn't take long for him to resort to insults, even if they weren't directed at Sam this time.

Skid just rolled his eyes and shrugged it off as another typically unpleasant conversation with his bandmate. He hopped into the van, squeezed past Jacko who put up a fuss about him invading his personal space and then disappeared between the chairs into the back.

It was the much larger body of Mike that darkened the doorway next, the grease in his beard glistening under the fluorescent lighting outside. "Looks like we're gonna be headin' straight to TJ to get this over an' done with."

Chavs pushed in next to him, his own bulk blocking the rest of the opening. "Then we gonna celebrate!"

"Hey." The familiar voice of Entropy through the driver's side window startled Sam as she tapped on the glass. He quickly recovered and wound down the window, allowing her to talk freely. "Chavs is right. With no debts left, we'll be free to live the way we choose. There are big changes coming for Entropy of the Heart. This is our time to shine!"

Entropy beamed at them, displaying her teeth between pale lips. Sam caught a brief glimpse of her fangs as they retracted, leaving behind a set of normal looking canines. He had only seen them for a split second, but something about the sharp points made her seem ferocious, a look that quickly faded as they were hidden away. A single drop of blood ran down from the corner of her mouth, leaving a crimson trail as it slowed to a halt just shy of her chin.

Mike alerted Entropy to the remnants of her most recent meal as he pointed to the same spot on his own face. "En, hon... You got a lil' somethin'."

"Oh, thanks..." She appeared to be a little embarrassed as she dabbed the blood with a tissue that she had pulled from her jacket pocket.

Sam wasn't sure, but he could have sworn that he saw Jacko scratching at his neck, his nails irritating the skin around a particularly juicy looking vein. There was no apparent wound, but he had seen Entropy heal her bite marks before and he knew that she left little to no trace of any sort of puncture wounds. But she wouldn't feed from her own friends, would she?

Entropy focused her attention on Sam now, her eyes flickering with her usual fiery spirit. "You look a little hungry."

She wasn't wrong. Sam could feel the beast inside of him starting to stir with his ravenous appetite. "Yeah, it's been a long night." He knew what was coming as he looked at Entropy, his eyes full of longing. There was nothing more pleasurable to him than drinking straight from the source.

Jacko couldn't help himself. "Getta bloody room!"

His laugh was closely mimicked by Entropy who carefully opened the driver's side door. "The sun will be up soon. Come on, Sam, let Skid drive. It's his turn anyway."

Sam nodded, the hunger rising as his body grew weaker. Making their way into the back of the van, he couldn't take his eyes off Entropy as anticipation set in for the sweet, coppery liquid that he would soon consume. He couldn't help but feel glad, as although his situation was far from ideal, the group was beginning to accept him as one of their own. With Entropy's help, he was slowly making friends with them and would soon become a part of their dysfunctional family.

Sam couldn't wait to find new ways to pitch in and pull his own weight. There was nothing worse than being the weak link in the chain and he wanted that all to change. There had to be something he could do other than drive and help move equipment around. Maybe he could be their sound technician, but he still had a lot to learn. He might even be able to help promote the band and find them some gigs. Either way, he had found a place where he was given the opportunity to fit in and he couldn't remember the last time that he felt that way. He had finally found a place to belong and wouldn't give it up for anything. Unfortunately for Sam, good things don't often last.

****

"Drive, Sam! Drive!!!" Entropy jumped into the van through the passenger door, startling the already nervous Sam into action with her cries of panic. He shifted gear and jammed his foot down on the gas pedal, pulling out into the road in a hurry. The tires squealed as rubber struggled to grip the road's surface, causing the vehicle to suddenly lurch forwards the second it gained traction.

Speeding away from the curb at an accelerated rate, Sam glanced at Entropy for a split second to see her in shock. She wasn't usually scared of much, so to see her this way was more than a little unnerving. "Where are the others?" Sam demanded an answer, struggling to keep his eyes on the road as he gripped the wheel tightly with both hands, knuckles white from the strain.

He couldn't see the expression on her face anymore, but he knew from her shaky voice that things had taken a turn for the worse. "They're dead... They're all dead..."

"What?!?" The response wasn't what he had wanted to hear.

Entropy continued her explanation, sounding as though she was almost petrified with fear as she forced herself to speak. "TJ did it... he... he killed them!"

The van drifted wildly around a corner, clipping an overflowing trash can as it mounted the sidewalk, sending its contents spilling out over the pavement. Sam gasped, struggling to maintain control of the wheel. Sure, he could drive, but he had never driven this fast through crowded city streets before. He quickly discovered that it was a lot more difficult than it looked and he didn't have enough experience to keep up that kind of speed for long, not without causing a major accident. Continuing to weave in and out of cars that obstructed their route, Sam could hear the engine roaring under the strain as they sped by other vehicles that were honking their horns in frustration. It was late at night, but a city as large and bustling as Miami was never completely free of traffic.

Sam's mind was racing almost as fast as the van that he was driving, his thoughts whirling around in his head, making it difficult to focus. "What happened in there? I thought we were all set!"

A bump in the road caused the back of the van to fishtail, with Sam only just managing to regain his composure before having to swerve to avoid a taxi that was double parked. He could see in the corner of his eye that Entropy was looking even paler than usual, trying her best to find the right words. "The deal... It went sideways, Sam. TJ knew that we stole from him and said we still owed him... He was so fucking mad!"

Sam furrowed his brow, annoyed by how bad things had gotten in such a short space of time. "How did he know that it was us?" Charging straight through a red light and narrowly missing a crossing pedestrian, he did his best to listen to the answer, but found the task to be increasingly difficult as he tried to not get them or anyone else killed.

Entropy ran fingers through her hair, nails digging in to her scalp as she played the events back through her mind. "I don't know, but Jacko was a damn fool! He tried to make a bargain... Things escalated..."

As if on cue, a black truck rammed into the back of the van, appearing out of nowhere. Temporarily losing control of the rear wheels, Sam did his best to turn out of a spin as the vehicle spiralled across the street, smashing sideways into a parked car. "Shit!" He exclaimed with renewed fear in his voice. "Things are still escalating!" That wasn't even the half of it. He didn't have the time to think about the pain that he felt from the crash, as the windows of the truck lowered and guns opened fire from inside.

Entropy ducked down in her chair. She seemed to be shouting something, but her voice was barely audible over the sound of gunshots and shattering glass as it rained down on them from freshly broken windows. Sam dropped down low too, covering his head with his hands to shelter it from the splintered shards.

An eternity seemed to pass as bullets riddled holes in the van's door. Sam had positioned his body between the gunmen and Entropy in order to protect her, and when the shooting was finally over, he was surprised to find that neither of them had been hit. It was about time that he had some sort of luck, and not getting shot was pretty high on his list of priorities.

Once the ringing in his ears began to die down, Sam could finally make out what Entropy had been yelling at him the whole time. "What the hell are you doing, Sam? Step on it!" He didn't hesitate, stomping his foot down hard as he pushed the pedal to the metal.

The van's bodywork cracked and sheared, leaving the back bumper somewhere in the middle of the road. There was no doubt that the vehicle was damaged beyond repair, with scratches, dents and several missing parts, but as long as the frame held together and the engine still ran, Sam didn't care if it meant that the van would be completely totalled. As they began to gain speed once more, he could feel the vehicle pulling to the right, and so he adjusted his hands on the wheel to compensate. In the remnants of the rear view mirror, he could see the same black truck giving chase, with its own front bumper crumpled from the impact.

Entropy turned her body in her chair, twisting her neck to follow Sam's gaze. "It's TJ's crew… We're screwed!"

A second car, closely matching the truck with its blacked out windows and midnight paint job, sped out of a side alley before skidding into the street to join the high speed pursuit. It took point, leading the chase with the truck not far behind.

"What do they want with us now?!?" Sam exclaimed as the steering wheel began to shake from the engine strain, or possibly from the fact that one of the wheels was close to falling off its axle.

He didn't appreciate the answer that followed. "TJ's put a price on our heads. He wants us all dead…"

The black vehicles were gaining ground, or their van was starting to lose it. Sam wasn't sure, but he kept pushing the motor as hard as it could possibly go. "Why the hell would he want us dead too?" He was feeling both confused and angry at the same time, and was beginning to wonder how he had gotten into this mess in the first place.

Entropy yelled over the engine's roar. "Maybe because he wants to use us as an example? I don't know! What do you want from me?!?"

The pair both fell into silence, neither wanting to keep the argument going. Sam took another sharp left as he tried to head out of downtown Miami and into the more open areas of the city. They crossed over a narrow bridge, squeezing in between passing cars before bearing sharply right.

As they took another turn, Entropy seemed to perk up, apparently coming up with an idea of what they could do to escape their imminent deaths. "Take forty-one straight out through Westchester!"

Sam frowned, knowing exactly where she intended for them to go. It was the same part of the city that she had found him in with knife wounds in his gut. "To seventy-ninth street? Are you out of your mind? That's Loco territory!"

Entropy simply nodded, looking towards the vehicles that were chasing them once more. "We don't have a choice, they're gaining on us! It's do or die!"

Sam was giving it all he could, but the van now refused to go over sixty, gradually losing power as they flew down the road. "The Loco's will kill us, En... They won't appreciate us speeding through their territory unannounced!"

One of the passengers in the black car was hanging out of the rear window, taking pot shots at them with his handgun. Entropy ducked down again, hiding from the gunman's sights. She shrieked at the top of her lungs. "TJ's crew are going to kill us!"

Sam tried to keep the other drivers guessing as he continued to weave in and out of traffic. Over the rough roar of the engine, he could just about make out the electronic wailing of police sirens approaching from somewhere in the distance. They had clearly heard all the commotion and were coming to intercept. A loud clunk, followed by smoke rising from the hood, let him know that the engine was overheating and that the van didn't have much left in it. To add to that stress, the metallic sounds of bullets echoed as they ricocheted off the van's heavily dented body.

"We can make it out of the city!" Sam yelled his opinion, but Entropy didn't seem to agree.

"Are you high? The old girl is barely holding together! We wouldn't even get close!" He knew that she was right, but he still didn't like her plan one bit. Entropy interjected before Sam could even try to think of another argument. "Hear me out! The Locos hate TJ's crew... They'll let us through just for a chance to kill some of them!"

A stray bullet hit the driver's side mirror, taking it out completely. "Fine! It's not like I have much of a choice!" Sam yelled, his voice as tense as his body. "What else have we got to lose?"

He tried to wedge the accelerator down further, but it was already down as far as it could go and the van still wasn't gaining speed. That wasn't the worst of it either, as smoke continued to rise from underneath the hood and the motor began to splutter.

"Keep going, Sam!" Entropy had poked her head back up and was now peering over the dashboard. "Ten more blocks and we're there!"

Sam decided to count the city blocks in his head as they went by, trying to use them as a way to calm himself down, but the counting only served to intensify his fear.

Ten.

Both vehicles were closing in, appearing in full view of the remaining two mirrors as they seemed to grow larger in size.

Nine.

A bullet clipped Sam's shoulder, tearing his shirt sleeve open as it grazed the skin beneath. It hurt like hell, but he had already experienced much worse. He grimaced from the pain, only just managing to keep both hands on the wheel. Clenching his jaw, Sam ground his teeth together and pushed through the agony.

Eight.

Veering left to avoid an open manhole cover that had been cordoned off with cones, Sam closely skirted past the utility vehicle on the opposite side. He used the truck to temporarily block the shots of their pursuers, but it only gave them a moment's peace.

Seven.

The black truck was almost upon them now, with the car moving to flank from the right. The gunman in the back seat began to aim for Entropy who didn't have room to move out of the firing line.

Six.

Just before the man could fire his shot, Sam swerved in the

cars direction, causing both vehicles to collide at high speed. The gun still went off, but the bullet hit air as the driver fought to stay on the road. The desperate maneuver didn't stop the chase, but it did buy Sam and Entropy a few more precious moments. Perhaps enough time for them to survive the ordeal.

Five.

The car backed off, adopting a different method of attack, which included the truck that was now close enough to smash into the back of Sam's van again. The truck's bumper buckled from the impact, locking frames with the van as they grappled for control.

Four.

Sam continued to battle against the truck's driver as he tried his best to shake free of them, but that turned out to be a seemingly impossible task. All three vehicles blitzed through another red light, continuing to travel at dangerously high speeds down the confined city streets. The gunman in the black car began to fire again as his vehicle pulled up alongside them once more.

Three.

Sam's vehicle was falling apart, but he managed to wrestle it away from the truck that almost ran itself off the road due to losing the weight of its hood ornament.

Entropy clawed at her seatbelt, buckling herself in securely as she fully expected a crash at any second. "We're almost there, Sam! Brace yourself!"

Two.

They were so close to their destination, but neither the truck nor the car showed any sign of backing away. Their pursuers were apparently too engrossed in the thrill of the chase to realise which part of town they had stumbled into. Sam used their distraction to his advantage, pushing his van harder and further than it was ever designed to go. The back left tyre blew, causing the vehicle to swerve uncontrollably as he struggled to reign it back in.

One.

Sam focused on the finish line. 79th street was milliseconds away, and it would hopefully be the end of their daring escape. The truck was coming in for another blow and was just about to hit when they were stopped in their tracks by a hail of bullets that penetrated both glass and bodywork with ease. The driver was hit, letting go of the wheel as he collided head on with a lamppost.

Zero.

Sam glanced back at the chaos, just in time to see the car launching over a newsstand. It hurtled through the air until steel met an immovable object in the form of the concrete wall of a nearby building. The front end seemed to disintegrate, leaving little left of the vehicle as it crashed back down to the pavement.

Entropy was right, the 79th Street Locos wouldn't tolerate another gang in their territory, but that was a lot to have gambled their lives on. The van's engine shuddered, sounding as though it was close to dying as Sam slowed to a crawl, otherwise moving relatively unhindered. He didn't have a second to relax though as the worried voice of Entropy chimed in. "Keep driving, Sam. They might change their minds and come for us too…"

The ever increasing crescendo of sirens were growing nearer and if the Locos didn't catch them, the cops surely would. Sam continued to putter along in what was left of the van, moving as quickly as it would allow. He could feel his hands shaking, not from the vibrations of the steering wheel this time, but from whatever was flowing through his dead veins these days. The reckless drive through the city had taken as much of a toll on his nerves as it had their vehicle and all he wanted to do now was get somewhere safe.

Both Sam and Entropy stared straight forwards at the road, trying their best not to make eye contact with any of the gun toting gang members that lurked in the shadows of doorways and alleyways. They had already drawn too much attention to themselves and it wasn't wise to outstay their 'welcome'. The Locos were known for their cruel and unusual treatment of outsiders who wandered into their territory at night, so it was wise to get out of there as soon as possible.

As soon as they were far enough away from 79th street, they would have to dump their vehicle somewhere and torch it to remove any evidence of who it belonged to. After all, they didn't want the cops to trace it back to them, as burning in the sunlight of a Miami jail cell wouldn't be a pleasant way to go. However, dying at the hands of TJ didn't sound appealing either. It was clear that Sam and Entropy needed to find allies of some sort, and they needed to find them sooner rather than later.

CHAPTER FOURTEEN: THE SHOW MUST GO ON.

It was a dangerous move, returning to the club when TJ's men were after them, but Entropy and Sam needed to gather a few supplies before going off the grid. The plan was to stuff as much as they could into a duffle bag as quickly as possible and then vanish into the night before anyone came looking. It likely wouldn't be long before they had company and moving too slowly could spell the difference between their own demise and escaping to start over somewhere new.

Creeping through the back door of the club, the pair kept the lights off as they made their way through the storeroom and out into the main hall. The place was eerily quiet, like a graveyard at night, and Sam was haunted by the ghosts of the recently departed. They hadn't had time to recover from losing the other members of the band, their friends who were now deceased and who they would never get a chance to see again. They couldn't even bury the bodies and there had been no time to grieve or mourn their loss. All of that and more had been stolen away from them by TJ and his goons. It had all been lost in just a matter of moments.

The venue seemed larger in the dark as Sam's eyes adjusted

to compensate for the lack of light. The place was exactly how they had left it, an unorganised mess of folding furniture with the smell of stale beer and old cigarette butts, both reminders of those who were gone and memories now passed. Sam couldn't imagine how awful Entropy was feeling, as he himself was overwhelmed by sadness and he had only known them for a fraction of the time. She needed to work through her grief in her own way, but he would be there by her side for as long as it would take to get through it.

Hidden amongst the usual smells, there was something else that Sam's nose picked out as he peered at the empty chairs around the table in the far corner. The new scent wasn't quite as familiar as the others in the room, but he had gotten a whiff of it once before. It was some kind of cheap perfume, with overbearing chemicals that burned the senses. No, not a perfume at all, a sports deodorant that had been over applied to disguise body odour. It seemed that they weren't alone inside the club and that someone else was there too.

Sam glanced back at Entropy who was so close to him that they were almost touching as they crept across the hardwood floor. He whispered to her, trying not to alert the intruders. "Do you smell that?"

From the worried look on her face he could already see that she sensed it too. "Yes. And I hear them breathing..." She replied quietly as her eyes scanned the edge of the room for any signs of movement.

Sam realised that he could hear the breathing too, but he couldn't pinpoint where it was coming from. There were at least two men, and one of them was definitely a mouth breather. Whoever they were, they were hiding somewhere nearby and would likely attempt an ambush soon. Mentally preparing himself to repel an attack, Sam tried to think things over logically. Had TJ's crew beaten them there? They couldn't have recovered from what the Loco's had done to them, could they? Several of their number were dead as they had been shot in the street. They couldn't have recovered that quickly, unless there was more to the gang than he knew. Entropy had mentioned that the loan shark dabbled in arcane powers, but did he have the power to control life and death?

Sam suddenly remembered where he had encountered the smell before. It had been a while, but he recalled that the last time he had caught that particular scent on the wind was the day that he was chased from his parent's house in Fort Lauderdale. It was the very same day that he had run for his life and ended up in Miami, and that could only mean one thing. It meant that the hunters who were there that day had followed him here. They had apparently never given up the chase, spending months tracking him down and after all that time they had finally found him.

As if on cue, a spotlight from somewhere up above flooded the immediate area with a blinding white light. Sam temporarily lost use of his eyes as they struggled to compensate for the sudden change in environment. His vision was rendered useless and he knew that Entropy had been similarly stunned as she grabbed at his arm to make sure that he was still there with her.

"Don't fuckin' move!" The harsh, deep tone of a man's voice

echoed out from somewhere on high. Sam's first reaction was to attempt to dash for cover, but Entropy had frozen still, the sheer strength of her grasp holding him in place.

A second, commanding voice boomed out from somewhere behind them, a darkened silhouette of a man stepping out from somewhere behind the stage. "I would listen to him if I were you. He's a really good shot."

Sam's eyes were slowly getting used to the light, as he could now see the blurred look of panic on Entropy's face as she spoke. "Sam, I know those voices…"

The man on the walkway seemed to be aggravated by her words. "Yeah? I was startin' to think you forgot about us, Christie."

Christie? Sam wondered if that actually was her real name, the realisation that he still didn't know much about her kicking in. Unable to see the faces of the men, he stared straight at his companion as if he was waiting for an explanation, yet it was hardly the time for one as the men's weapons were trained on them. Sam believed that he could survive a few gunshots, but he wasn't willing to test the theory as his shoulder still hurt from where it had been grazed by a bullet already.

Her voice bursting with conflicting emotions, Entropy looked up at the walkway, slowly releasing her grip on Sam's arm. "Tommy…" She didn't just know who the men were, she knew at least one of them on a first name basis. Sam found himself wondering how on earth a vampire could be friends with those who actively hunted her kind. Who were these men to her?

****

Watching from his vantage point upon the stage, Aaron kept the barrel of his shotgun aimed towards his quarry. Samuel Mitchell was in his sights and he wasn't about to let him get away. He tried to ignore the fact that his friend Christie Reece, and Tommy's ex-girlfriend, was standing there too, as she was supposed to be dead. She had died years ago and he remembered her funeral like it was yesterday. It should have been impossible for her to be standing there and yet there she was, as clear as day.

Staying put, Aaron tried to focus his mind, taking a few deep breaths to calm himself as he let Tommy take charge of the situation. There was a lump stuck in his throat as he observed in silence, having promised his friend that he could take the lead. This odd turn of events could possibly offer Tommy the closure that he had sought for years. After all, it's not every day that you can confront the person that you were accused of murdering, despite there being a severe lack of evidence to actually prove it.

The air was thick with tension, Aaron's lungs struggling to maintain a regular breathing pattern as Tommy began to pace on the metal walkway that was suspended high above the room. The anger in his voice was apparent as he almost snarled at the two people who had been caught in the spotlight within the centre of the room.

"Couldn't take the time to let us know you weren't fuckin' dead? How about lettin' the cops know? Or was that too much to ask?"

Christie's distress was obvious as she replied weakly. "I... I didn't mean for you to get hurt." Both her and Sam were lit up for all to see, yet from their squinting, Aaron could tell that he was still obscured by shadows.

Tommy slammed his hands down on the railing, his own gun slung over his shoulder by a strap. The metallic clang rang out like a gong that echoed throughout the entire hall. "They locked me away! Do you even know what that's like? We all thought you were dead and I was the number one fuckin' suspect!"

Hanging her head in shame, Christie lowered her voice until it could only just be heard. "I'm sorry, Tommy. I didn't know..."

Aaron noticed that Sam was trying to edge out of the spotlight, and so he cocked his shotgun in response. "Don't even think about it, dumbass!"

"Okay! Just please don't shoot..." Sam's startled words were as weak as they were pathetic, making Aaron feel sorry for him. He didn't even need to see Tommy's face to sense the scowl of disdain. It had taken all of his friend's willpower to not shoot Sam Mitchell where he stood, but he knew that if he did the conversation would be over and chaos would ensue.

"Did you even think to check?" All Tommy wanted now was some answers to the questions that had eaten away at him for years. He spoke with purpose as he ignored Sam completely, treating him as nothing more than a distraction that was no longer worth his time.

Christie glanced at Sam and then back up to Tommy who she couldn't look at for long without turning away with guilt. "I didn't think that..."

"No, you didn't think! You never fuckin' do!" Tommy yelled at the top of his lungs, his pent up anger on display.

Scarlet pools began to form in the corners of Christie's eyes, the red liquid glistening under the bright light. The sight of it set off alarm bells in Aaron's head, as they let him know what she had become and how she had managed to return from beyond the grave.

"I thought you'd be better off without me." Christie suppressed a sob, trying to hold back her floods of tears.

Tommy hadn't noticed the odd colour in her eyes as he was too swept up in his own anger. "Yeah? Nothin' I love more than being a cop's goddamn punchin' bag! You have no idea what I went through after you went missin'!"

Christie was struggling with her words, the red pools close to overflowing. "I went through a lot too..."

Aaron tried to get his friend's attention by calling out to him, his gun now aimed at Christie instead of Sam. "Tommy, look at her eyes!"

Unfortunately Tommy was on a roll and remained oblivious to the fact that his ex-girlfriend wasn't exactly human. "Well boo hoo! Cry me a fuckin' river!" His harsh words set off a reaction that he hadn't anticipated. Christie's tears formed crimson streams that flooded down her cheeks. It was then that he realised that she wasn't all that she appeared to be. Plucking his rifle from his shoulder, Tommy took aim at her head as years of hunting experience took over and muscle memory placed him into a combat ready stance. "It figures you'd become a damn bloodsucker!"

His reaction left Christie speechless, turning her into a quivering wreck which forced Sam to come to her defense. "Leave her alone! It's me you came for!"

He spoke with such vigor that it took Aaron by surprise, but Tommy remained unphased by it. "Shut the fuck up, Mitchell! This doesn't concern you!" Sam's temporary burst of confidence was knocked from him by the power in Tommy's voice. Whereas Tommy himself had already forgotten about it, as he was far too busy catching up with events that had up until now been a complete mystery to him. "It was Frank, wasn't it? He did this to you. I'll kill that son of a bitch!"

****

Frank. Sam knew the name. He was the one who had become obsessed with Entropy and had tried to kill her. Christie, not Entropy. He was still getting used to the idea of knowing her true identity and was no longer sure what to call her. Had Frank been the one to turn her into a vampire too? The pieces, however jumbled, were beginning to fall into place. He looked over at Christie, wanting nothing more than to come to her rescue, but any sudden moves could result in their untimely demise. There was no way of telling how trigger happy this Tommy and his friend were or what their intentions were for her. Sam didn't care if his own life was forfeit, he just wanted to make sure that she wouldn't come to harm.

Blood still streaming from her eyes, Christie tried to plead with her accuser. "Frank's dead, Tommy... It's over. Please put the gun down, I don't want to hurt you or Aaron."

It was clear that Tommy and Christie had some serious history that Sam didn't want to get involved with, but what he shared with her was special too, wasn't it? He fought his own silent battle against the doubts that plagued his mind.

Tommy grumbled from up high, the barrel of his rifle lowering a little as he spoke. "Yeah, he's a walkin' corpse and I'm gonna stick 'im."

Still struggling for words, Christie only just managed to pull herself together to form another sentence. "No. I mean he's dead dead. He won't be coming back."

Sam eyed up the second, shorter man on the stage, the shotgun moving back and forth between him and Christie. He wondered if he could move fast enough to block any shots that were intended for her, but it would be impossible to defend her against fire from both firearms simultaneously. Either both of them had to run at the same time, or they had to talk their way out. He severely doubted that they would emerge victorious if it came down to a fight.

****

Tommy seemed to be taking a minute to think things over, which made Aaron wonder if his friend was losing what little was left of his composure. He had been waiting for him to take the lead, but the conversation with Christie seemed to be taking its toll. It was now time to take point and deal with the situation before things spiralled out of control. Aaron knew that Tommy wouldn't forgive him if he took Christie down, as if anyone ended her existence, it had to be him. However, Samuel Mitchell was still fair game and was still his primary target. If Sam died, then there would be one less monster in the world, and one less monster meant that fewer innocents would suffer. It was his one purpose in life and he could never forget that.

Aiming his shotgun for a blast to Sam's head that would be lethal for a human and enough to stun even a vampire, Aaron's clear shot was quickly blocked by Christie who had noticed his intent and stepped into the line of fire. She glared at him with blood red eyes, flashing fangs that protruded from where her canines should be. In that moment he knew that he had caused her true form to reveal itself from behind the mask of his long dead friend. "Step away from him, Christie."

She dismissed his instruction with a vicious snarl. "Put the gun down, Aaron! This is your only warning!"

He could see in the corner of his eye that Tommy had raised his own gun again and was aiming it straight at Christie. A look of disgust had crossed his face now he had seen her for what she was, his instincts taking charge once more. "Don't even think about it, bitch!"

Tommy's words cut deep like a knife, causing Christie to instantly retract her fangs and resume her desperate pleading. "Please don't let it come to this, Tommy. I love you, but this won't work out the way you planned."

He grimaced at her, ready to fire his rifle at a moment's notice. "You're right about that. Besides, I don't date corpses... You're fuckin' dead to me!"

****

There was no time for Sam to react as Tommy's finger pulled back on the trigger. Fortunately for him, Christie's response time was much faster. She released a scream that caused the space between them to shudder, the sound sending ripples through the air until they collided with Tommy. Caught completely off guard, the hunter's body was thrown backwards into the wall with such force that the rifle was knocked from his hands.

The shoulder strap that held the gun in place was torn from its mounting as the rifle fell from the walkway, hanging in the air for a short while as time itself seemed to slow down around them. It crashed against the floorboards, the fall setting off the weapon and causing the chambered bullet to ricochet off the wall with an ear piercing bang.

****

The unexpected gunshot caused Aaron to flinch as he watched Tommy slam helplessly against the brickwork upstairs, his body slumping down against the metal grates of the walkway. Distracted for no more than a second, he fired his own gun, the spread of pellets spraying out in a narrow cone across the room. The shot had been meant for Christie, but it instead met the pale flesh of Sam who had foolishly thrown himself into its trajectory.

As Sam took the brunt of the blast, he dropped to the floor, showing no sign of recovering any time soon. This gave Aaron the opportunity to take Christie down on an even footing with only the two of them left standing, but she was so much faster than he could have ever anticipated. With a savage roar, she began to run towards him at full pelt, her face twisted with bestial rage. Before he could even fire another shot, Christie was already within point blank range, dodging past the barrel is of his gun to wrap her long fingers around his throat. It seemed effortless for her to pick him up by the neck, the crystal blue of her eyes lined with red as she stared directly into his soul, fangs bared and ready to strike.

"Drop it." The command was firm, yet simple, and Aaron found it impossible to resist. He was compelled to loosen his grip on the shotgun, letting it fall to the floor. Suspended from Christie's arm, he began to choke as her immeasurable strength lifted his feet off the stage and into the air. As much as he wanted to break free, he soon found that his limbs wouldn't respond and that he had been left completely defenseless.

"Now sleep." Unable to look away from Christie's hypnotic gaze, Aaron felt dizzy. The world around him started to spin, causing his head to feel like dead weight. He was so tired that it became impossible for him to keep his eyes open, the world around him fading to black as his body went limp. There was no fighting it, as much as he tried and all Aaron could do was give in to the call of his deepest, darkest nightmares. The hunt was over and he had lost.

CHAPTER FIFTEEN: A PAIN LONG PAST.

Christie Reece had been a part of Aaron's life for longer than anyone else, Tommy included. In fact, Aaron had even been the one to introduce the two of them to each other in the first place, and that was the reason he blamed himself for all the bad things that had befallen them since. Perhaps if they had never met, then they would never have been irrevocably damaged by an intense, yet toxic relationship that had somehow spiralled out of control.

Even after all these years, Aaron could still remember how Christie had been as a child, so innocent and full of hope for a world that sorely lacked it. She was a timid girl, with mousy brown hair and crystal blue eyes that were almost angelic, a far cry from the woman that she had become. A great deal had changed since then, as the harsh realities of life had screwed Christie over time and again, leaving only small traces of the little girl that she had once been.

At one time, Aaron and Christie had been the best of friends and were almost inseparable, playing together at every possible opportunity. Aaron had a few other friends too, that he played with almost as often, but there were none that he had grown attached to as much as her. The Fitzpatrick and Reece families had been neighbours for years and she had been the girl next door for longer than he could remember. The two of them had been so close as children that they made a promise to each other to be friends forever and vowed that they would never be apart, but fate often has a way of changing such plans.

The heartbreak that Aaron felt as his parents broke the news was still as clear in his mind now as it was on the day it happened. His father's new career prospects and a drastic increase in salary meant that they had to leave their home in Michigan and move east to the smaller state of New Hampshire. Aaron didn't know much about that state or the area called New England in which it was located, but he already hated it with a passion.

However bad he felt at the time, Aaron's sadness was nothing compared to the look on Christie's face as they said their goodbyes and went their separate ways. The two of them made another promise that they would keep in touch and that they would see each other over each and every school vacation, but it never did work out the way they planned.

As Aaron's family moved away from the only home that he had ever known to plant new roots in the small town of Edison Heights, Christie followed a completely separate path. While he was haunted by ghosts and became a witness to things that shouldn't be seen by the eyes of children, she had to deal with an entirely different sort of trauma.

Christie's parents had their own issues that they struggled to work through, and which resulted in their eventual separation and a messy divorce. She had never gone into specifics, but there was some mention of an affair of some sort that set events in to motion, changing her life forever. All Christie wanted was her best friend to comfort her, but Aaron was so far away and far too busy with his new life to remember the girl that he had left behind.

Completely alone in her grief, Christie was dragged down to Florida by her angry mother who had obtained full custody, denying her ex-husband any visitation rights. The aftermath of the divorce was a huge mess that lasted for years and was never fully resolved, with far too much money being spent on lawyers and legal proceedings. Aaron didn't know much about what happened, other than what he overheard from conversations that his parents had in private. After that, there was no sight nor sound of Christie for almost ten years. In that time, Aaron became distracted by the existence of supernatural beings and his new friendship with Tommy, almost completely forgetting about the girl who used to live next door.

The eventual rise of social media allowed Christie to track Aaron down, letting her get in contact after so many years had passed. She was a rebel now, nineteen years old and as tough as they came. The natural brown of her hair was dyed as black as night and she had begun to amass a collection of different piercings. But however she looked on the outside, Christie was still pretty much the same girl beneath. Her wild exterior masked the kind and caring person that she still was inside, even though she tried to deny it. A passion for music had helped her survive her teenage years, however she hadn't made it through entirely unscathed.

Christie told Aaron about her life growing up and how she had almost destroyed herself through addiction at an unbelievably young age. Florida was far from the best place to raise children, and she wasn't the only kid to fall victim to drugs and alcohol. She had managed to clean up her act since, but not before she had been roughed up by a string of abusive boyfriends. Aaron found everything about Christie's unfortunate tale upsetting, but he could still see the hope that she held in her heart. She was battered, bruised and scarred, but far from broken. It was plain to see that Christie Reece was a fighter and above all, a survivor.

Aaron felt bad that he couldn't really share much about his own life in return. He wasn't sure that Christie would believe what he had witnessed or that she would understand his choice of vocation. However, he did share the fact that he had left New Hampshire to pursue his own goals in life. He told Christie about his friend Tommy and how they had both left town to rescue him from his dead end life in the trailer park. What he couldn't say was that it was only a small part of the entire reason, as he didn't think that the story of the Witchwood Shrine they had found deep within an old bunker, or the secrets it held, would go down so well.

After so many years apart, Aaron and Christie finally met face to face while he was passing through the south of Georgia 'on business'. She had taken a few days off work to focus on her songwriting and their timing just seemed to work. It was also the first time that she had met Tommy, which to Aaron's surprise led on to something that he never expected.

The pair really hit it off despite their differences, and they continued to stay in contact throughout the months that followed. More than once, Aaron caught his friend up late at night, talking to Christie on the phone. It was something that turned into a regular occurrence, with Tommy making excuses to see her at every opportunity, which was unusual for someone who hated the hot climate in the Southern States. He told her everything about himself, which was a privilege shared by few except Aaron. His life was an open book for her to read, including his dad's alcoholism and the beatings that often followed, his mother's neglect and the acting out that led to countless run-ins with the police.

The sharing didn't stop there, with Tommy telling Christie everything about his encounters with supernatural creatures and his choice to become a hunter too. However she wasn't scared off by his honesty and actually believed every word of it, becoming fascinated with their experiences and everything that they had seen over the years.

Abandoning what she described as her stagnant life, Christie travelled with Aaron and Tommy for a while, learning everything that she could from them about what they did and the dark world they lived in. A world where monsters lurked in the shadows and only those with open minds could see the truth. And for a time, everything seemed to work out well, until the day that Tommy and

Christie began to argue about how to spend their lives together.

It was surprisingly Tommy that decided that he wanted to settle down and start afresh somewhere quiet, but Christie wanted to continue their life of action and exploration. She loved to help other people and wasn't ready to stop, yet he had begun to tire of it. There was a time when all he wanted to do was hunt monsters, yet his opinion had gradually shifted over the years. He wanted out, and Aaron wasn't about to stop him, but Christie had a different opinion. She wanted them to all keep hunting together and was far from ready to give up.

Everything changed the day Christie disappeared during a routine missing persons case out in the Midwest. A week long search turned up very little, with Tommy barely sleeping as he became obsessed with finding her alive. It was that sheer determination, backed up with Aaron's investigative skills that eventually got them the clues that they needed to track her down to an old farmhouse in the middle of the countryside. It seemed that she had become the most recent victim in a string of kidnappings that the police had yet to solve, and no-one ever suspected the kindly old farmer who had lived amongst the townsfolk for years.

Aaron could still remember the unwritten melody of wind chimes as their sound was carried across the open fields by a gentle spring breeze. He could still picture the farmer in his overalls facing him in a standoff, yelling with words that weren't his own. It was unexpected at the time, but it turned out that the man had been a victim too. The farmer had somehow been possessed by the ghost of his dead wife, who had been so overcome with jealousy towards other women that she forced him to abduct them from town and carry them back to the storm cellar at the farm.

It was strange to watch a man argue with himself, with two separate personalities at war with each other, the unstable situation resolving itself in a way that Aaron had wanted to avoid. He was left in shock, watching helplessly as the innocent man died, the bullet Tommy put in his brain releasing the woman's spirit as she lost the only thing tethering her to the land of the living. As he charged into the open cellar door to find his beloved, Aaron was left kneeling over the farmer's lifeless body, feeling sick to his stomach about how events had unfolded.

There was no stopping Tommy when someone he cared for was in danger, and Christie was the only woman in his life that he had ever loved, which turned him into a nigh unstoppable force. He vanished down into the storm cellar for quite some time before emerging with her held tightly in his arms, her naked body wrapped up in a thick woolen blanket, hair matted with dirt. Both of them remained silent, with neither of them ever mentioning what had gone on down there. Whatever had happened, Tommy refused to leave the farm until the place was in flames, standing watch over the inferno until he was sure that the house would be nothing more than a smouldering pile of ash.

Despite what had occurred at the farmhouse, Aaron still believed that Tommy and Christie belonged together and he was sure that they would be even closer now. However, something about what happened that dreadful day caused them to get into fights more than ever before. Tommy just wanted to protect Christie, but she was adamant that she didn't need his protection. A split started to form between the two of them and their relationship took a turn for the worse.

The constant arguments eventually became too much for Christie to bear and she left Tommy to head back to Florida where she could work on her music, deciding that it was for the best that they went their separate ways. She had apparently lost the taste for hunting, which was the polar opposite of Tommy who had now become more driven than ever before. He became single minded in purpose, pushing Aaron to find more work and more cases to solve. Any thoughts of settling down had seemingly been wiped from his head as he began to smoke like a chimney and drank the days away.

A couple more years passed by and Aaron could see that Tommy was feeling lonely, despite his many flings and one night stands. Nothing seemed to fill the void that Christie's departure had left within him. It was actually Aaron's suggestion that they should go and visit her in Florida, with the hope that his friends would be able to rekindle their relationship and pick up where they left off. It was that misguided notion that set into motion the events that would result in Christie's death and leave Tommy a broken man. A poor judgement that still weighed Aaron down with guilt.

Tommy decided to leave Aaron behind at their motel room,

heading to talk with Christie alone. Unfortunately, his plan to win her back quickly backfired, largely due to his pride and hot headedness. According to him, Christie had fallen in with a bad crowd and he was convinced that she was using again. His clumsy attempts at trying to help her only served to cause more strife, the conversation blowing up into one of their worst arguments ever. The usual harsh words were exchanged, with neither of them truly meaning the things that were said, but that didn't matter. The fight ended with Tommy storming off, leaving Christie with her bandmates and their manager, a man that introduced himself as Frank. The argument itself would have been inconsequential if it wasn't for what happened afterwards.

It was early the next day when Tommy was violently dragged from his motel room by police officers who presented a warrant for his arrest. Aaron could still recall the devastation that he felt as they informed him of Christie's death. The three of them had been through so much together that he struggled to accept that it could end so suddenly. According to the police reports, she had died from a drug overdose under suspicious circumstances. They believed that there had been foul play and that her death was actually a murder that had been made to look like an accident. It seemed that there were several eyewitnesses too, each reporting that Tommy's fight with Christie had escalated, which came as no real surprise due to it occurring in a public place.

The biggest shock was that Tommy was the prime suspect in the supposed murder, despite the obvious lack of proof and the fact that he had been drinking at a bar across town when she died. Of course, it didn't help that Aaron couldn't be his alibi, as he hadn't been with him at the time, and no one else came forward to confirm that they had seen him there.

Tommy's harsh treatment in jail never made the news, nor did it result in any official action being taken, as he didn't want to dwell on the events any longer than he had to. Police brutality was putting it mildly, as he was eventually released with broken ribs and bruises in places that could be hidden away from prying eyes. The officers involved had been careful to avoid his face, as any obvious injuries would have resulted in an enquiry, but the physical scars were nothing compared to the mental torture that he had endured. Their cruelty had done more to Tommy than he would ever care to admit and he left jail a changed man.

It took the detectives investigating the case far too long to work out that they didn't have enough evidence to hold Tommy any longer. They begrudgingly released him as the investigation continued, but made sure to keep a close eye on his movements. In the end, none of it seemed to matter to the detectives in charge, as Christie's death soon became just another unsolved case.

The body was eventually released from the morgue, with Christie's family holding a funeral soon after. It was a closed casket affair, as Mrs Reece wanted to remember her daughter the way she had been instead of seeing her for what she had become. Christie's mother made sure to make Tommy feel as though his presence was unwanted and even went as far to scream at him during the wake.

Surprisingly, he stayed silent and didn't have any comebacks or witty retorts, just taking the full brunt of the woman's anger as he hung his head in shame.

Aaron knew that his friend loved Christie more than anyone else he had ever known. He was extremely passionate, but didn't have it in him to kill her. Something else had to be going on and Aaron was pretty sure that Frank was to blame, but any proof was impossible to come by due to what Aaron claimed to be a professional cover-up. Someone or something was watching out for him and cleaning up after him too, but Tommy no longer seemed to care. He just wanted to bury the past along with Christie and didn't feel the need to dredge up old memories that he had tried so hard to forget.

Until their recent encounter with Christie and the discovery of her true fate, Tommy had never spoken to Aaron about his feelings, even though he knew that his friend was there to help him work through it in whatever way he could. He was a private person who kept to himself, which meant that the best way for Aaron to help was by simply being there. He did his best to keep his friend occupied with work, so that the beer and cigarettes wouldn't take over completely. The broken man had a habit of drowning his sorrows in the bottom of a glass and at the rate he drank, it would surely be the end of him.

The pain that Tommy felt over Christie's loss soon turned into anger. Realising that he had a problem, he worked hard to channel that aggression into his training, harnessing the rage and using it to hone his skills to better himself as a hunter. The ability to turn such negative energy into something positive was a talent that Aaron envied, but he was more than happy to give his friend targets to set his sights on and goals for him to achieve.

Aaron found it difficult to digest the fact that Christie had become a vampire, one of the very monsters that she had once hunted alongside them. He had convinced himself that the friend that he had once known was dead after all and that whatever was occupying her body was something else entirely.

Tommy on the other hand seemed to believe that there was some way of saving Christie's soul and perhaps winning back the heart of the woman he loved. Unfortunately, his short temper, combined with the betrayal that he felt over her secrecy, had once again changed the outcome. The rage that he had tried to keep locked away had been unleashed and had led to a different ending, with Christie overpowering both of them in seconds. It was a stupid sort of mistake that could get them both killed, if it hadn't already.

CHAPTER SIXTEEN: THE HUNT GOES ON.

"Aaron! You okay, man?" Tommy's voice woke Aaron from his deep slumber, his body feeling slow and groggy as he began to stir. His memory of what had happened was a little fuzzy, but he knew that Christie had done something to him. She had somehow put him to sleep through the power of suggestion, using nothing but her voice. The after effects seemed to linger, making him feel like he had been drugged, but he knew there was nothing in his system. Whatever had been done to him had only happened to his mind, with his body left untouched, except for what would likely be finger shaped bruises around his neck from where she had grabbed him.

"Come on, dude. Wake up!"

It took Aaron a moment to open his eyes as Tommy shook him by the shoulders, attempting to break him out of his daze. "I'm awake! Quit shaking me!"

Tommy let go, a look relief spreading across his face. "Damn it, Aaron! You scared the hell outta me! You good now?"

It required a great deal of effort, but Aaron managed to sit himself up straight, taking a moment to check himself over before answering his concerned friend. "Yeah, I think so. What happened?"

Tommy frowned, his anger over what had happened still apparent. He had already retrieved his rifle, the strap hanging loosely from his shoulder as he crouched nearby. "Christie happened... She took us out so quickly it was a fuckin' embarrassment." He stood up straight, holding his hand out to Aaron in order to help him stand. "I thought I was ready to face her... but I wasn't even close. She threw me off my game and I couldn't pull the trigger in time."

Aaron accepted Tommy's offer of help and took his hand, both of them working together to pull him up on shaky legs. Still recovering from whatever Christie had done to his brain, he tried to smile encouragingly but managed something closer to an awkward grimace. "Well now we know what she can do and what we're dealing with. We just need to find her and Mitchell too, before it's too late and they give us the slip. Then we can do things the right way."

Tommy waved his hand dismissively. "Screw the Mitchell kid... It's all about Christie now. She's a goddamn bloodsucker and needs to be put down like the rest of them."

Aaron raised his eyebrows, a little taken back by his friend's response. He wondered if Tommy's words were born of the anger he felt at being outmatched, or from Christie choosing Samuel Mitchell over him. Either way, he felt as though he understood, at least a little bit. "I thought you wanted to try and save her. I'm guessing that's changed now?"

Tommy snarled, slamming a fist into his own open palm. "That's before I knew what that freak Frank had turned her in to!

She's not the same girl I loved, she's something else!"

Aaron leaned down to pick up his shotgun from where it lay on the stage, taking a moment to check it over for damage before holding it down by his side. "Alright then. What's the plan?"

Tommy seemed to mull things over for a minute, beginning to pace a little as he formulated his response. "We do what we do best, we hunt monsters. So let's pick up their trail, track them down and then I'll kill the bitch myself!"

Feeling a little hesitant, Aaron knew that Tommy was right and that vampires were a danger to humans wherever they were found, however this was Christie that they were talking about. The same girl who at one time had been one of the best friends that he had ever had. He wasn't sure that he could bring himself to harm someone that he still cared so much about, and yet he had a job to do. He couldn't just stand by and do nothing as innocents were hurt, even if the monster hurting them inhabited the body of a once dear friend.

Aaron replied, his voice quietened by his inner turmoil and self doubt. "Are you sure you can do it? Can you really kill her?"

Tommy removed the rifle from his shoulder, lifting the gun up in front of his face to check the sights. His voice was monotone and lacked every part of his usual dry humour, letting Aaron know that he was truly sincere in his words and that he meant serious business. "Sure as shit! You just take the Mitchell kid and leave the rest to me."

****

Sam lay on his stomach, his shirt lying next to him on the floor as he spread himself out on the blood stained rug. Christie knelt over him, carefully picking at his back with makeshift tweezers that she had made from a bent piece of scrap metal.

"Could you please lie still?" She sounded annoyed, but Sam couldn't help but squirm as the painful process caused his muscles to flinch. It was slow going as Christie plucked out dozens of tiny pellets that had embedded themselves deep within his flesh, leaving them in a small pile next to her.

Sam cringed, replying through gritted teeth. "I'm trying..." He had so many questions about what had happened, but had been holding them back as he let Christie play the part of his dutiful nurse. They had somehow escaped from the hunters at the club and had fled across town, breaking into an apartment that smelled like it had once belonged to Jacko, the poor fool. Sam still had trouble believing that all of the band were dead, but it was a cold, hard truth that he would have to learn to accept.

The entire place was littered with beer bottles, old pizza boxes and an almost impressive amount of used skin mags, all accompanied by a disgusting mix of smells that Sam was glad that he couldn't identify. His nose was pressed up against the filthy rug, the fibres covered in cigarette ash and what looked like shredded strands of dried cannabis leaves, both of which were now being drenched by the steady stream of blood that was leaking from the holes in his back.

Sam was starting to feel impatient, with the pain causing the beast inside of him to stir. "Who were those guys?" He couldn't see Christie's face, but he could sense that his question had caused her discomfort.

"Just some people I used to know. It doesn't matter." She pulled another sliver from underneath Sam's skin, repaying his inquisitiveness with a sharp stabbing pain.

Whether it was an accident or on purpose, it didn't stop Sam from continuing. "It does matter as they were trying to kill us! It seemed like they were a little more than acquaintances too... Who's Tommy?" He didn't mean to sound so agitated, but the pain wasn't helping.

Christie sighed, pulling at another pellet as she tried to dislodge it "Tommy Hughes. We were close... but... it's complicated. He helped me when I needed it most. Can we please just drop it?"

Sam wanted to know more, but he didn't want to upset her. He cared about Christie too much for that. "Okay. I'll drop it for now, but you'll eventually have to tell me something."

Remaining silent for a while after, Christie continued to work at removing the last few pieces of metal, taking her time so as to not cause any further damage. Once she was satisfied that she had successfully removed all the foreign objects from Sam's back, she sat back and carefully placed the tweezers down on the rug. "There, I just need to wrap it up so you can finish healing. You're going to have an awful lot of scars..."

Sam turned his head to look back at her, allowing him to see the solemn look upon Christie's face as she sat there staring at the bloodied fabric of his crumpled t-shirt and torn hoody. She noticed his gaze lingering on her and forced a weary smile. "We also need to get you some new clothes. I'll see what's here."

As Christie started to stand, Sam pushed himself into a sitting position and reached out to stop her from leaving. He placed his hand on her forearm, her skin still as cold to the touch as ever. "Relax. We can find something in a while."

For a second it looked as though Christie was going to pull away, but she stopped herself and slumped back to the floor right next to him. As much as she tried, she couldn't bring herself to make eye contact. Sam moved his hand from Christie's arm to her chin, placing his fingers there gently as he turned her head to look at him. Her eyes lacked their usual sparkle, instead appearing a much duller shade of blue. She was clearly upset by what had happened that night and couldn't bare to look at him for long, pulling away once more.

All Sam wanted was to ease Christie's pain, but he was instead left feeling useless. Unsure as how to proceed, he fell back on a familiar line of questioning. "What happened in there? What did you do to the other guy?"

Christie bit her lip, idly scratching at her arms with chipped nails as she spoke. "I made him sleep..."

Sam adjusted his posture, his back still more than a little uncomfortable after being probed. "Yes, but how?"

The enquiry seemed to take Christie's mind off the hunters for a little while at least. She looked over at Sam from the corner of her eye, her head still facing away. "It's a gift. I can plant suggestions in people's heads, or dominate their mind for a short time, but it takes a great deal of concentration."

Something occurred to Sam that he hadn't really thought about before. He didn't want to believe it, but it dawned on him that Christie could easily control him if she wanted to. "Did you ever use it on me?"

The very suggestion seemed to offend Christie, as she turned her head to stare at him in disbelief. Her response was more than a little defensive in tone, the hurt obvious in her voice. "No! I'd never do that to you, Sam!" It was easy to see that she was upset by the question and Sam felt sorry that he had even asked. She continued, running the red tipped fingers of her hands through her jumbled mess of pink hair. "What we have runs deeper than simple mind tricks. It's in our shared blood."

The answer confused Sam. "What do you mean?"

Christie settled down, perceptibly at ease as she began to explain. "We're bound by blood. You feed from me and that level of intimacy makes our bond special."

It all sort of made sense in Sam's head. After all, Christie had been feeding him her blood since before he had even laid eyes upon her, which might explain why he had fallen for her in an instant. If

240

the life essence of vampires held that much power, then it was possible that all his feelings towards Christie had been distorted by that bond with her. Whatever the reason, he couldn't change how he felt about her now and he certainly didn't have the willpower to turn her down if she offered up her wrist.

Sitting there within arms reach, Christie seemed to silently study him. Sam could still see the red smears down her cheeks where she had tried to wipe away her tears, emotions having run high more than once within the last few hours. It had been a rough night for both of them and neither knew what to do next, but returning to the club definitely wasn't an option.

It was Christie that spoke first, sounding as though she had been contemplating the meaning of her own existence. "I should be almost thirty... but I still look like I'm twenty three. People often say that immortality is a blessing, but right now it feels like a curse. I envy the fact that you can still grow old. The years will pass us by, you'll eventually die and I'll be left all alone."

Sam didn't know what to say, simply moving in to wrap his arms around her in a tight embrace. He hadn't really considered the possibility of someone who was as strong and sure of themselves as Christie having such striking vulnerabilities. It may have been the blood flowing through his veins that originally drew him in like a moth to a flame, but he couldn't imagine not carrying a torch for a woman as tough and independent as her. Despite that independence and ability to do everything for herself, she still required companionship, and Sam was certain that he could fill the role.

****

Over the course of the next few hours, Sam worked hard at prying more information out of Christie about her past with varying degrees of success, however she still refused to go into any details about her past relationship with Tommy Hughes or her friend, Aaron Fitzpatrick. The topic of old friends was a sensitive matter that she did her best to avoid, changing subject each and every time their names were mentioned in conversation.

What Christie didn't mind discussing so much was her connection to the man who went by the name of Frank. In fact she was generally open about the person who Sam had previously presumed was nothing more than a former boyfriend turned psychopath. It seemed that he had been a larger part of her life than previously mentioned, playing a pivotal role in what she would become.

Frank had done so much more than carry out a kidnapping with an attempt at premeditated murder. The truth of the matter was that his botched attempt wasn't such a failure after all, as not only was he the man who had killed Christie, he was also the one who had brought her back into the world as a vampire. Sam had already heard about how Jacko had rescued Christie from Frank the night he abducted her, however what she had neglected to mention was that her bandmates had turned up far too late to actually prevent her death.

The group hadn't been aware of Frank's true nature when they found him battered and bruised in an alleyway. The conman claimed to be in the music business and they agreed for him to be their manager, with false promises of turning them all into stars. They were also unaware of his growing obsession with their lead singer and the dangers that brought with it. It was that blind ignorance of who and what Frank was that would drastically change their lives, with the realisation of what had truly occurred coming far too late. Christie's body had already been drained of blood when Jacko arrived with the others in tow, with Frank hunched over her lifeless corpse as he waited for her to rise again as a creature of the night.

For Sam, the most shocking revelation was the discovery of Frank's ultimate fate. He had apparently stalked Christie for weeks after her official death, watching closely as she redesigned her image and began calling herself Entropy. He obsessed over her as if she was an object that belonged to him and refused to let go. Jacko, Mike and the others tried their best to chase him off on several occasions, but it proved impossible to scare someone who could quite easily overpower them. The situation eventually proved too much for her to bear as she confronted him and lost herself in a frenzy, ripping him to shreds while he stood there and refused to fight back. It was safe to say that he didn't survive the ordeal, as there wasn't much of him left.

Unknown to Christie and the rest of the band at the time, Frank was close friends with a career criminal named TJ, a man who they already owed a great deal of money to due to the small print on their contract that everyone had neglected to read. TJ's cash had paid for their instruments and also the venue that they practiced in, but they had all presumed up until that point that everything had belonged to Frank.

The untimely death of Christie's maker placed the group even deeper into the shady businessman's pockets, and so they had to resort to crime to make even the smallest dent in the loan. Almost everyone who owed TJ money was in for the long haul, especially as his interest rates would skyrocket more often than not. The concert in Calgary was supposed to provide the band with enough to pay the loan shark back for good, but things hadn't quite worked out the way they had planned. Of course it didn't help that they had stolen from TJ just a couple of weeks earlier.

Ever since the night of her rebirth, Christie had tried her utmost to keep the darker side of herself hidden from others, especially those for whom she cared for the most. Sam had only ever had a brief glimpse of the beast that was caged inside her, but he hadn't seen the full extent of her rage. Like all vampires, she had an insatiable lust for blood and a killer instinct with which she constantly battled for control.

Sam understood that death was part of Christie's existence as much as it was his and knew that violence was in her nature, but he loved that she didn't let that define her. Despite everything she had been through and all that she had lost, she was still a prime example of what he could become if he put his mind to it, and he wanted to be like her more than anything.

****

The street outside was unusually quiet for a Thursday night in Miami, and Sam was unable to see any signs of life from his perch up on the window ledge. Reflections of the mess of a living room behind him acted as an overlay for the world outside, the furniture seeming to hover in the air as if suspended by strings. He could see Christie in the bedroom, packing up some things in a satchel, likely clothing that they could use as disguises if needed. Whatever she could find to help them blend in with a crowd.

Taking a moment to examine his own appearance, Sam used the glass as a mirror. His face was pale and eyes strained, his hair spiked with moisture after his shower. The clothes he wore made him look like a pale imitation of Jacko, with a leather jacket decorated with metal studs and worn jeans, with torn knees that some would pay good money for, even though this pair had achieved their look from daily wear and tear. Of course nothing fit, with the sleeves too long and the waist of his pants cutting into him, but at least he could still wear his own sneakers. They may have been a poor match for the rest of the outfit, but at least they were the right size, and that was a small comfort.

Sam actually missed the crude, sarcastic guitarist who had once owned the clothes on his back, despite how poorly he had been treated by him in the past. It was far too quiet now Jacko was no longer yelling in the thick accent that sometimes made him hard to understand. It was also weird not having Mike around, or Chavz, and even Skid had made his impression. Sam missed them all, and he could tell that Christie did too, but she was tired of crying and feeling sorry for herself. Now all she wanted to do was survive and so she was preparing to go on the run, with the hope that TJ would lose track of them and give up the chase somewhere along the way.

It didn't help that there were two separate parties after them now, what with Tommy and Aaron thrown into the mix. Granted they were after Sam first, but they had been a distant memory until their most recent encounter. Both TJ and the hunter duo wanted them dead, the question being who would make them suffer the most beforehand. Sam was convinced that TJ would put the most hurt on them, but he really didn't want to end up in a position where he could find out.

As Sam pondered the possibility of his own demise, a black car rolled into the street, slowly coasting to a stop just outside the apartment building where he was currently residing. The back end of the expensive looking vehicle was left halfway in the road, the driver parking crooked with the nose of the car barely over the edge of the curb. If that wasn't odd enough, the headlights were left on with the engine still running as the door opened and someone stepped out from inside.

Watching from his safe place on high, Sam observed as a large, smartly dressed man in a pristine suit emerged, adjusting his tie as he looked around. The dark skin of his shaven head seemed to glisten under the street light, his black goatee trimmed to perfection. The man clearly took pride in his appearance as he straightened his jacket to make sure that it was sitting straight on his shoulders. It was odd to see someone so well dressed in that part of the city, the atmosphere doused with suspicion. A feeling of unease crept in, leaving Sam frozen stiff, his face pressed up against the glass to get a better look. That feeling was only intensified as the man craned his neck to look upwards, his midnight eyes catching a glimpse of the awkward looking gawker on the window sill.

Sam found it impossible to look away as their eyes locked, fear rising up from deep within. Even the beast inside him wanted to cower and hide, letting him know that whoever this person was, he was a force to be reckoned with. The way Sam felt only seemed to escalate as he stared helplessly into dark orbs that seemed to draw him in like black holes.

Calling out with panic in his voice, Sam summoned his companion to the window. "Christie! Someone's here!" At least he hadn't lost the ability to speak, but he still couldn't turn his head to look away. His neck refused to move an inch and his eyelids wouldn't even blink, let alone close altogether.

It didn't take long for Christie to reach Sam, the palms of her hands flat against the glass as she leaned over him and tried to see down into the street. "Grab whatever you can, we need to go now!" The sheer terror in her words was enough to let him know that they were in serious trouble.

Sam desperately tried to move again, but he was still left paralysed. There was no chance of him moving on his own as long as the man in the suit maintained eye contact. Fortunately for him, Christie was there to solve that particular problem. Grabbing him by the shoulders, she used her might to pull his body away from the glass. As soon as Sam lost sight of the man's face, he found that he had regained full control of his body as she pulled him in so close that their noses were almost touching.

Mouthing her words so Sam could read her lips, Christie spoke loud and clear enough for all to hear. "Sam! We need to go! Now!!!" She hadn't realised that he had been stuck there like a fly caught in spider's web and was just trying to make sure that he understood the urgency of the situation.

Sam blinked a few times, clearing his head as he prepared himself for a quick exit. "Who is that?"

Christie barely had time to respond as she grabbed Sam's hand in her vice like grip and yanked him towards the door. "A battle we can't win! He's way out of our league!"

They had only made it a few steps when the front door exploded in a shower of wood chips and splinters, as it was completely decimated by an unstoppable force. Shielding his face with his free hand, Sam could see the massive silhouette of someone in the hallway blocking the way out. It only took a second for him to realise that it was the same well dressed man from outside, his flawless skin as black as night as he glared at the pair of them with bloodshot eyes.

Before the debris even settled, Christie had pushed Sam towards the closest window, yelling at the top of her lungs in obvious terror. "Run, Sam! Run!!!" She didn't need to tell him twice as he barreled towards the opening, moving as fast as his legs would take him.

Sam hoped that Christie was close behind as he threw himself at the window pane without breaking his stride. The leap of faith sent him crashing through the thin sheet of glass and out into the open air beyond. Time slowed to a crawl, causing glass shards to hang in the air like floating diamonds, giving him the feeling that he was flying for just a second. That brief taste of freedom was soon interrupted by the inevitable fall, as his momentum ran short and his trajectory changed to send him plummeting down to the hard concrete below.

Acting on instinct, Sam shifted his body weight so his feet would hit the ground first as he tried to maximize his chances of survival. He was certain that the impact would hurt, but he would still make it to the street and start running in whatever direction his legs carried him. All he knew was that he had to escape, and he prayed to God that his companion was with him. After all, he wasn't sure how to survive without her. Without Christie by his side, he would surely be lost.

CHAPTER SEVENTEEN: A MOST SECRET MEETING.

Ducking under the police tape, Aaron could see the damage that had been wrought by whatever destructive force had broken into the apartment. The door had been torn from its hinges and shattered into a million pieces of splintered wood, with nothing left to show of what it had once been. He struggled to picture the type of being that had the strength to achieve such a feat, but imagined that they were truly a terrifying sight to behold.

The entire place looked as though it had been ransacked, the overturned coffee table and broken dishes telling only part of the tale. Discarded bottles and empty pizza boxes littered the floor, and the air itself was filled with the stench of old cigarettes and stale beer. It was hard to see whether or not there had been a struggle or if things had been stolen afterwards, as the living room already looked like a crack den. It left Aaron wondering what type of person could stomach living in such squalor without much care for personal hygiene or anything else for that matter. Jack Olsen was likely someone who had made more than his fair share of poor life choices.

Snapping the tape in half as he followed closely through the entryway, Tommy made sure that his presence was known. "Oh shit!

What the fuck happened to the door?"

Feeling nervous in unfamiliar surroundings, Aaron spoke quietly, sounding distracted as he began to peer around the room. "I don't know, but there's not much of it left..."

In the corner of his eye, Aaron noticed the fluttering pages of a faded magazine that had been left on the floor, the glossy paper moving in a breeze that originated from the living room window. Making his way across the room, he could see that the glass of the window had been broken, as if something large had been thrown through it. The lack of shards on the blood stained rug showed that the window had been smashed outwards in the direction of the street and hadn't resulted from something coming in from outside.

As judgemental as always, Tommy shared his disgust of the living conditions as he proceeded with his own investigation, beginning a search of the far side of the room. "Either somethin' went down here, or this dude was a real fuckin' slob."

Aaron nodded his head slowly, agreeing with his friend wholeheartedly. "I'd say a little of both."

It was good to see Tommy acting more like himself again, but Aaron was still nervous about what would happen once they caught up with Christie. He was concerned that another face to face meeting could result in a mental breakdown, or that an error in judgement that could lead to his friend's demise. It was a valid concern after what had happened during their last encounter, but he wasn't sure that he could do anything to prevent it.

The pair of them had already scoped out several apartments that belonged to the other band members of Entropy of the Heart, finding no leads as to Christie's whereabouts, or any sign of the band members themselves. They had been notably absent at the club too, which made Aaron wonder if they had skipped town or if something had gone awry.

Jack Olsen was the final name on the list, and the patrol car waiting outside the front door of his building let them know that they had the right place, with someone having tipped the police off to some sort of disruption that had occurred earlier that same night. It hadn't been much of a challenge to sneak inside, as Aaron and Tommy had become quite adept at breaking and entering. A crowbar and a simple lesson in physics were more than enough to best the low end security offered by the back entrance located next to the dumpsters. After that it wasn't difficult at all to find the right place, with the missing door and yellow tape making it obvious which apartment had been occupied by the guitarist.

"Check this out, dude. It looks like it hurt." Tommy crouched down low, reaching over with an open hand to dip his fingers into a large pool of blood that had been partially soaked up by the carpet.

The shape of the puddle was too neat to have resulted from a struggle, which meant that someone had suffered from some severe injuries and had been close to bleeding out. At least that would have been the case if they were human, but both Sam Mitchell and Christie Reece were anything but. A vampire low on blood would be ravenous and extremely dangerous, even more so than usual.

After pausing for a few seconds, Tommy lifted red fingertips up to his face in order to examine them closer, soon confirming his suspicions with a satisfied nod. "Blood's still wet... Looks like they pissed someone off. That or you managed to clip Mitchell at the club."

Aaron moved over to the broken window, sticking his head through the opening in order to look down at the street below. He could see the shards of glass on the pavement, liberally scattered over the concrete slabs that made up the uneven sidewalk. "It looks like they made a speedy get away, which means that someone or something other than us was after them. Something powerful enough to turn solid wood into sawdust."

Annoyed by another missed opportunity, Tommy kicked over a nearby bottle, the contents of beer soaked cigarette butts spilling out over the floor. "Fuck! We're always one step behind!"

Aaron moved back from the window and turned to face his frustrated friend, the palms of his hands held out to try and soothe him. "Calm down, man, they can't have gotten that far. At least we know that they're still in the city."

The scowl on Tommy's face let Aaron know that his words hadn't achieved the desired effect. "For now, but we need to pick up the damn pace if we're not the only ones chasing them... I can't lose her again!"

Aaron agreed, but he was a little more level headed than his friend and Tommy's choice of words weighed heavily on his mind. "We should go before the cops return. Don't worry though, we can still track them down first if we're smart about it. They can't run from us forever."

Tommy was still flustered, but he seemed to be somewhat reassured by the promise of finding their quarry. "Let's go before the trail gets cold. We have competition now and I fuckin' hate losing!"

With so little left of the night, Aaron knew that Christie and Sam would have to find somewhere to lie low for the day, which gave him and Tommy an advantage that they couldn't afford to waste. However, that meant that whatever else was following them could take advantage of that temporary vulnerability too. Despite the additional pressure that had been applied by another party being thrown into the mix, he felt a renewed sense of hope due to the possibility of ending the hunt and finally getting out of the wretched hellhole that was Miami. Still, he couldn't help but wonder if there was anything left of his former friend.

Was it really true that Christie was gone and only the monster remained? Aaron found that he was starting to doubt himself, although he wouldn't admit it out loud. The line between his work and personal life had blurred and it was becoming increasingly difficult to differentiate between the two. Unfortunately for him, such uncertainty could spell the difference between life and death.

****

Sam wasn't entirely sure where Christie had taken him, but perhaps that was for the best. If he didn't know where they were, then perhaps the man chasing them wouldn't know either. They had fled from Jacko's apartment, running halfway across town until they ended up in what he could only describe as the industrial district of the city.

The pair of them were hiding out in a dusty old warehouse, cowering behind some wooden crates that they had turned into a makeshift haven of sorts. Christie had found a thick, white tarp that she had pulled over the crates to act as a shelter from any sun rays that poked their way through the dirt caked windows. It wouldn't be comfortable, but at least they could get some much needed rest. The shelter wouldn't be enough to protect them indefinitely, but perhaps their little hideout could buy them enough time to make it through the harsh light of day and back into the night.

Resting his back against the side of one of the crates, Sam had sat himself on the floor across from Christie, his arms hugging his knees. He watched his companion in silence as she typed away on her phone, the light from the screen illuminating her face and allowing him the opportunity to admire her. Her hair was a mess and her makeup had long faded, but this is how he preferred to see her, in all her natural beauty.

Christie furrowed her brow as she concentrated on what she was writing, her nose scrunching up as she thought hard about what to say. All she had told him was that she might have a way to get them out of their current predicament by contacting a dear friend.

Whoever they were, she claimed that they might be able to help them out, but she refused to go into specifics.

It wasn't until Christie had finished her message that she noticed Sam staring, managing a weak smile as she too felt drained by the daylight hours. He had been waiting patiently for her to finish, biding his time until he could ask the question that had been burning a hole in his head. "Who was that guy? I've never felt anything like it."

Her faint smile was wiped from her face and replaced by the grim expression of defeat. "Akoni. He's TJ's right hand man and if he's after us, we're really screwed. I hear they call him the Huntsman... and if his reputation is anything to go by, they call him that for a reason."

The name sounded foreign, but Sam couldn't place its origin. He remembered Christie mentioning him once before, so the sobering look that she gave him as she slid her phone back into her pocket only served to boost his curiosity. "What is he though? Is he a vampire like us?"

She shook her head slowly, maintaining eye contact. "I don't know... I've only seen him once before when he took Skid's tongue, but I've heard stories of what he's capable of. All I know for sure is that he's extremely dangerous."

Sam pondered for a moment, leaning back further to place his head against the hard surface behind him. He tried to think of ways to escape the city, but all of them were impossible without the cover of night. He didn't like feeling like a sitting duck, left vulnerable and waiting to be killed, but he had to wait until it was safe enough for Christie to go outside. He knew that he could survive out there for a time, but he couldn't leave her behind and wouldn't risk her going up in flames.

It was Sam who eventually spoke, turning his head to look back at Christie again. "So what should we do next?"

Christie idly rested a hand on the outline of the phone in her pocket. "We wait for a reply, or failing that we find some transport and a way out of here. How do you feel about California?"

Sam realised that he didn't really have an opinion of the far Western State, having never thought about actually venturing that far before. He shrugged his shoulders, expressing neither excitement nor apathy for the suggestion. "Sure, what's a little more sunshine... What else is out there for us?"

It seemed that she didn't really have an answer herself, replying with a question instead. "A fresh start?"

A smirk flashed across Sam's face. "It's been a while since I had one of those."

Christie returned a similar look, the corners of her mouth curling into a wild grin the likes of which he hadn't seen since the drive back from Canada. It was good to see her smiling again, without it being forced. "Thanks, Sam."

Reaching over from where he sat, Sam placed a hand on Christie's leg. "Don't mention it. I'm always here when you need me."

No more words were exchanged between the two while they enjoyed the peace and quiet of each other's company. It was a pleasant change to simply exist for a little while, without being chased or having to fight for their lives. The last couple of nights had been hectic to say the least, with the promise of more to come. For now, they would need to build their strength, taking turns to keep watch as the other rested. There was no telling how long it would take for either the human hunters or the Huntsman known as Akoni to find them, but Sam at least hoped to have a few more hours of down time first. Just a few more hours before they would have to face death once more. It wasn't too much to ask for, was it?

****

Aaron knew that Tommy would be furious with him, but he couldn't help but go in his friend's place when he caught sight of the mysterious text message. His phone had gone off while he was taking a shower and Aaron had glanced at the screen to see if it was something urgent, but what he saw instead was a cryptic text that instantly raised his suspicions. Neither him nor Tommy had changed their phone numbers in years, so the message could have been from almost anyone, but the way the sentences were formed reminded Aaron of someone who he used to know. The fact that she was contacting Tommy while they were actively hunting her was more than a little confusing.

After carefully deleting the message and removing all trace of it, Aaron made the excuse that he was going on a supply run and left the motel alone, driving off into the night while feeling guilty about lying to Tommy's face. In his defense, all he wanted to do was protect his friend. It was an act born out of love for Tommy, not malice, however he knew that his deception could come back to bite him if he didn't proceed with care. They weren't usually the sort to lie to each other, so it was highly likely that Tommy could end up feeling betrayed and that was the last thing on Aaron's mind. He knew that he wouldn't be able to stand the look of heartbreak on his friend's face should his deceit be discovered, but it was a risk that he had to take.

Although he understood the need for secrecy, especially when one was being hunted, Aaron wished that the chosen meeting place was somewhere a little more public. The underside of a bridge adjacent to a disused rail yard was inconspicuous enough, but it was also a place where a dead body could be dumped and left undiscovered for any number of days. It was that very thought that made him start to consider the fact that he may have stumbled into a trap. Perhaps the message was designed to lure Tommy out so that he could be killed without Aaron being there to watch his back, or maybe it was just another bout of paranoia kicking in.

The street lights high on the bridge above did little to fend off the shadows beneath it, leaving Aaron in encompassing darkness as he waited in the driver's seat of the truck. He had already turned the engine off, leaving the key in the ignition as he grounded himself in silence, with no headlights to illuminate the area in front of him and no hope of a quick escape. His eyes scanned every nook and cranny, staying peeled in the hope of spotting anyone approaching before they could get the drop on him. He wasn't willing to allow anyone the chance to sneak up, feeling a sense of unease as he idly toyed with the machete that rested next to him on the passenger's side of the cab.

Aaron's due diligence soon paid off as he caught sight of a shadowy figure cautiously approaching from the opposite side of the bridge's arch, the slim outline of their figure and the familiar walk letting him know that his suspicions had not been unfounded. Christie had tried to organise a secret meeting with Tommy, most likely with the goal of manipulating him to her cause. He knew that when it came to Christie Reece, his friend had trouble thinking clearly, and it was a pattern that had repeated itself on more than one occasion. Her plan to sway him may have succeeded too, had Aaron not intercepted the text and gone in Tommy's stead.

As Christie grew nearer, Aaron could see her pace slow to a crawl as she began to sense that something was amiss. Before she could have second thoughts about the meeting and flee from the scene, Aaron opened the truck door and stepped out to reveal himself, watching intently as his old friend visibly tensed her muscles in surprise. "Aaron!" He could see her nervously eyeing up the blade in his hand as he held it by his side, but she made no attempt to run, instead waiting for him to make the first move. "Please, don't..."

Aaron was feeling tense himself, remembering that she was more than capable of taking him down should she wish it. She was only a few feet away and was a bigger threat to him than he was to her. Regardless of the fact, he spoke to her as calmly as possible, trying his best to purge any signs of fear or weakness from his voice. "Were you expecting someone else?"

Christie was clearly saddened by the sudden turn of events, still unsure as to what to make of the situation as it unfolded. "Tommy isn't coming, is he?" Her disappointment was clear, but he tried not to take it personally.

Aaron shook his head slowly, tapping the flat side of his weapon against his leg. "No, he isn't. He doesn't need to deal with your bullshit." He wasn't usually one for swearing and she knew it, but he wanted to get his point across.

"Get out of my way, Aaron. I don't want to fight you again..." Christie's face was still obscured by shadow, her expression difficult to see in the blackness.

Aaron sighed loudly. He tired of the chase, but he wasn't sure that he could go through with it now she was within his reach. "I don't want to kill you either, but you know that I can't let a monster like you go free. There are people that need my protection."

He didn't need to see the look on Christie's face to know that she was starting to get agitated. "You already made it clear how you feel about me, Aaron... I'm an evil monster that you need to put down. You always did see things in black and white."

Christie was both right and wrong at the same time. Aaron

knew that he had a job to do, but he still struggled to believe that she was inherently evil. Perhaps there was another way to resolve the issue, meaning that things didn't need to escalate further. He tried his best to compromise. "It's not that simple and you know it... Let's make this easy. Hand over Sam Mitchell and I'll let you go. I won't even tell Tommy that I met you here."

Christie snarled, her hands balling into fists as she made a sound that wasn't quite human. "I won't hand Sam over to you! He doesn't deserve to be marched to his death, and being an accomplice to that would make me a bigger monster than even you think I am!"

There was a long pause as both of them stared each other down, neither quite knowing what to say to ease the situation. Eventually, Aaron decided to speak up, still unsure of how to break the standstill. "Then how do you suggest we proceed?"

Christie shifted on the spot, seemingly unnerved by the possibility of another full on confrontation. "That's what I was hoping to speak with Tommy about. He'd be a little more open to..."

Aaron snapped, cutting her sentence short. "You've hurt him enough! He doesn't need to see you! Not now, not ever!"

Christie sighed with resignation, which seemed odd to Aaron as he had already noted her unnatural lack of breathing; one of the telltale signs that he was dealing with an undead creature and not a living human being. Doing his best to avoid eye contact, he remembered how she had dominated his mind the last time they had met. She had clearly noticed his blatant attempt at avoiding her gaze, but didn't respond right away, seeming to mull things over before hitting him with a question that came straight out of left field. "Do you remember how things were back in Michigan? Life was so simple and full of joy. We were happy there. If only things hadn't changed. I just wish... I wish you hadn't left me behind."

Caught completely off guard, Aaron hadn't been prepared to talk about his childhood with Christie. He wasn't sure if she intended to stagger him with memories of days gone by or whether she was just feeling strangely nostalgic. Either way, he didn't back down from the conversation, the handle of his machete still grasped firmly in his hand. "Of course I remember, but I can't change the past. What's done is done."

The way she looked at him made it seem as though she was contemplating their childhood and genuinely regretted the way that everything had ended between them. Those apparent intentions were mirrored closely by the sincerity of her words. "I know... but then Tommy would never have met me and he could have lived a normal life. We'd all have been happier for it."

Aaron shrugged his shoulders, not really caring for what might have been when history had already been written and former events set in stone. "Maybe, but it didn't work out that way, did it? Besides, it wasn't all bad."

Christie had to admit that he was right about that. "No, it wasn't. You introduced me to him when I needed it the most, and he helped me turn my life around. Those were the best days of my entire life, and as bad as things have gotten since then, I still remember them fondly."

Aaron's patience was starting to wear thin, but he wanted to see where the conversation would take them. "Me too, but that doesn't matter now."

The end result was far more important than reminiscing about old times. However, Christie didn't seem to agree with his lack of sentiment. "It matters to me... We've been friends our entire lives, Aaron. It was hard for me to forgive you when you left me behind, but I did. I never forgot how it felt to be alone, but I forgave you for that and for everything that happened to me after."

It made Aaron feel uncomfortable that she had once harboured such resentment towards him, but he also felt anger at her words. "You can't blame me for that... It wasn't my fault."

Christie nodded her agreement. "I know, but that's how it felt." There was another slight pause as she carefully phrased her request. "Let me go, Aaron. Both me and Sam. He's all I have left and we're no threat to you."

She should have known better than to ask something so impossible of him. Past experiences had made Aaron resolute in his belief that monsters were a danger to humankind and that they were a menace that had to be wiped out. He had seen too much pain and destruction to have his opinion changed so easily. "You're a vampire, Christie. You drink the blood of innocents and that means you're a threat to everyone, including me. I can't let you live!"

The harsh response didn't stop Christie from pleading. "Please, Aaron. Just let us go. Forget we ever existed and you'll never hear from us again."

Lifting his machete to bridge the gap between them, Aaron pointed it directly at Christie's face. Her eyes widened in shock as the razor sharp edge stopped barely six inches from her nose. "No. Tommy needs his closure. You can leave for now, but don't try to contact him again. We'll see you soon enough and you can count on it being your final night." He needed to let her know that he meant business and that he wasn't there to bargain. This meeting was meant to act as a warning and a promise of things to come. As soon as he was certain that she had gotten the message, he placed the machete back down at his side.

Christie lowered her head, looking down at the ground between them. "I see... So that's how it's going to be. I hate that things had to go this way. Goodbye, Aaron. I hope that you don't take it too personally when I fight tooth and nail for my survival."

They both knew that there was no hope of reconciliation or a friendly embrace. The rift in their relationship had grown too wide and it was way beyond mending. As Christie turned to leave from where she came, Aaron made sure that he got the final word. "It's nothing personal... It's just what has to be done." He stood there, weapon still at the ready as his old friend disappeared back into the dark.

Remaining motionless until he was certain that Christie had gone, Aaron began to breathe heavily, his body now suffering from the stress that he had felt throughout the entire meeting. He was no longer sure why he had decided to go alone, as he could have simply deleted the message and purged it from his mind. Perhaps it was because a face to face meeting could provide the finality that he needed to make the necessary decision to end her existence once and for all.

As much as Aaron had once loved Christie, she was dead to him and he had put that ghost to rest a long time ago. He was now prepared for the final hunt and would be ready to deal the killing blow when the time came. There was no doubt that Tommy wouldn't be able to finish her off, and so he would have to do it for him. After all, a vampire was still a vampire. An evil being that stalked the night and preyed on those who couldn't defend themselves. There was no place in the world for something so unnatural. Christie Reece had to die, and Sam Mitchell along with her.

CHAPTER EIGHTEEN: NOWHERE TO RUN.

It had been three nights since Sam and Christie had camped out in the warehouse, and her secretive meeting with an old friend that had refused to bear any fruit. Their stay had been interrupted that same night by the tireless Huntsman who had somehow tracked them down, with another desperate getaway resulting in them expending more blood than they should. The resulting hunger had barely been satiated in time, with both of them coming dangerously close to losing control to the beast inside. It was that unrelenting hunger that led to them feeding together for the first time, as Christie carefully guided him through the process.

Sam hadn't tried to draw blood from a living, breathing human in a long time, his botched attempt in Birchfield resulting from his own lack of fangs. The very thought of it made him feel anxious, but Christie had a way of putting him at ease, turning the act into a surprisingly intimate experience. She undertook the majority of the work herself as she punctured the man's neck with the points of her teeth and crimson streams began to flow from the open wound.

Sam's revulsion lasted barely a second, his mind screaming

out for him to drink from the font of vitae as it was offered up to him as a sacrifice. Although less potent than the blood he regularly drained from his companion, the intoxicating solution was as delicious and satisfying as he could have hoped for. It was like the finest of wines, if wine was necessary for your continued survival and you were an alcoholic with an incurable thirst for it.

    Once the deed was done, Christie had lapped up the final drops from the man's bare flesh, sealing the wound with her tongue as she left him with enough blood to live, although he would feel extremely weak and nauseous in the morning. Leaving the body safely tucked up in a doorway, Sam peered into Christie's eyes and could see the same beast still raging within her that he had deep inside of him. There was no doubt that she had killed before, either on purpose or by accident, but now she was trying to be someone different. Someone better. She wasn't the type to revel in death and didn't enjoy being the cause of it either, but Sam was sure there were many like them that wouldn't even bat an eye at the thought of taking a life.

    Ever since that night, Akoni the Huntsman had turned up out of the blue on more than one occasion, causing Sam to conclude that he was tracking them via the GPS on their unsecured cell phones. The only option left was for them to ditch their phones and forgo the conveniences of modern technology, something that had become easier over time. The longer the pair were without their phones, the less they felt that they needed them, with the withdrawal symptoms soon beginning to fade. A lack of search engines, email access and other similar applications became a strangely liberating experience for them both, allowing them to enjoy whatever time they had left together without distractions.

With no sign of the Huntsman for a while afterwards, Sam was convinced that his plan had succeeded. He felt as though he could rest easier, however Christie was still on edge. She wasn't so sure that they were out of danger yet and was starting to believe that they would never be able to leave the city. Of course she was right, and it didn't take long for TJ's right hand man to find them again. However he was tracking them, it wasn't through the use of technology, and now they were left without a way to call anyone for help.

They had tried to leave Miami by bus, but Akoni was waiting for them at the depot. The train station hadn't been safe either, with the Huntsman already standing on the platform when they arrived. Even the car they had stolen had been smashed to pieces when they made a last ditch attempt at driving away, but neither Sam nor Christie had been injured in the attack. Everywhere they went, the Huntsman was somehow already there. It would have been easy for him to kill them both, but it seemed that he took pleasure in toying with them and watching them squirm. The man clearly enjoyed the thrill of the chase and wanted to draw it out for as long as possible.

Sam felt drained, the result of struggling for his survival without hope of respite. The psychological effects of running night after night were starting to take their toll, with him becoming convinced that he was developing a nervous tick. He jumped at every sound, expecting the door to burst in at any moment. He wasn't sure how much longer he could keep it up, beginning to wonder if he should just surrender and accept his fate.

The modest sized apartment they had broken into was posted for rent, with no furniture or belongings inside. A little more upmarket and far more luxurious than their recent string of accommodation, the entire place had been left spotless. It seemed that the owner had cleaned it for potential viewings, with the aim of getting a new tenant as soon as possible. However, the lack of curtains and threat of people showing up meant that they couldn't shelter there for the day, but it gave them a place to rest for a moment before the inevitable chase.

Christie had locked herself in the bathroom so she could freshen up, and Sam could hear the shower running, the light shining out from beneath the door as he paced back and forth in the dark. He had already changed out of Jacko's old clothes and into the ones that they had 'acquired' hanging from a line down the street. The polo neck shirt and jeans fit surprisingly well, a pleasant change from what he had been wearing for the past few days, but he still didn't feel like himself. It felt as though he was trying to be someone else entirely and that he hadn't been Samuel Mitchell for quite some time now.

As the sound of running water ceased, Sam couldn't help but peer out the windows for any sign of Akoni, the threat of Christie's old hunter friends now a distant memory. As terrifying as it had been to face them, they were nothing compared to what he had seen since. The Huntsman had been there at every turn, seeming to appear from nowhere. It was almost as if the well dressed man could be everywhere at once, with little effort expended on his part. Christie had called it omnipotence, but Sam didn't believe that such a thing was possible. Fortunately, the street was currently clear and there was no sign at all of Akoni or his car, at least for now.

Every part of Sam's body ached and he found himself wishing that the hollow shell of a living space contained furniture. After sleeping on hard floors, exerting himself by running for miles and barely having a minute to relax, he desperately wanted to sit down in comfort, even if it was just for a little while. He had hoped that becoming a vampire, even a shadow of one like he was, would mean that he wouldn't need to deal with aches and pains anymore, but that hadn't been the case at all. Sam was more resilient than ever and could sprint for miles if he had to, but he didn't have a boundless supply of energy. Even if he drew on his blood stores to push himself further and keep his body moving, he would still eventually run out of steam. He knew that Christie had a much easier time than he did, but even she could exhaust herself when pushed to the limit.

The scars on Sam's back had finally stopped itching, the wound left by the shotgun pellets having mostly healed. He hadn't seen the markings himself, but Christie said it was an impressive amount of scar tissue. She hadn't been disgusted by them at all, instead smiling warmly as she looked him dead in the eye. "Chicks dig scars." Those were the very words that Christie had chosen to ease Sam's worry that he was going to end up as a scarred up freak, with a tapestry of old cuts and holes that might eventually cover every inch of his body. She assured him that her feelings wouldn't change just because of some minor physical defects. What they had together ran deeper than mere flesh. It was in their blood.

    The door to the bathroom creaked open, a cloud of steam and moisture bellowing out into the empty space that was destined to become the master bedroom. Sam turned from the window to see the bright light from the room beyond stretching out across the floorboards, broken up by Christie's long shadow as she stood in the doorway. She flicked the light switch, leaving the place in darkness once more as she made her way from the bathroom and out towards where Sam had been waiting.

    As his eyes grew accustomed to the dark again, Sam saw that Christie had undergone yet another transformation. Her hair was no longer a bright pink, instead replaced with a jet black that hid any sign of the once vibrant colour. She no longer looked the part of the lead singer of a band; not that she had a band to back her up anymore, with simple clothing in the form of jeans that were a little less worn than those she would usually wear, and a plain blue tank top that was far from her typical wild style.

    Christie was now as Sam had seen her in his mind the very first time they had met, like it had all been some strange vision of the future that they were just now living through. She had removed all jewelry, including her piercings, with no makeup left to cover up her natural beauty. The only identifiable markings left behind were the tattoos on her forearms that she could still cover up if needed. This was her idea of going incognito, disguising herself as a 'normal' person without her usual eccentricities, and if Sam was perfectly honest, he was more attracted to her now than ever before.

Unable to hide the fact that he was awestruck, Sam struggled to piece together the words to express himself. "You... you look fantastic."

Christie tilted her head to one side, her eyes fixed on Sam's face as if she was judging him by his reaction. "You really think so?"

Sam nodded. "Yes... Really."

She looked him up and down, giving his new outfit the once over. "You're not so bad yourself." Pulling at her top to try and make it sit right, Christie didn't look so convinced by her own appearance. "I don't know... I don't feel like me."

It was almost as if they were operating on the same wavelength, as Sam still had doubts about his own clothing. "I know exactly what you mean..."

Christie half smiled at him, looking as though she was uncomfortable in her own skin. "I guess that's the point. We're not meant to look like ourselves... Maybe we'll get used to it?"

Sam adjusted the waist of his pants, taking a moment to look down at what he was wearing before peering over at Christie once more. "Don't worry, it won't be forever." At least he hoped that it wouldn't be.

****

Over an hour had passed since Sam and Christie had vacated the apartment, leaving behind no trace of their passing. They had gathered what little belongings and supplies they had left, stuffing them back into the satchel that she had procured from Jacko's place. It must have been somewhere after four, as the early risers were already beginning to make their way to work with the hope of missing the morning rush.

Trying to keep out of sight, Christie led Sam off the main streets and into a stretch of park that ran parallel to the boardwalk and the white sands of the beach beyond. They ignored the sign stating that the area was off limits during the hours of night, a law that had been put in place to keep vagrants off park benches. The palm trees that bordered the paved path swayed in the ocean breeze, with the high tide sending waves crashing against the sand not too far away. It would surely have been as serene a setting as any if it weren't for the dreadful sense of foreboding that Sam felt deep within his gut.

"Can you feel that?" Sam's instincts were on fire, alerting him to the presence of another, more powerful predator nearby. He could tell by the look of apprehension plastered across Christie's face that she felt it too. It was a feeling he hadn't experienced since...

"The Huntsman!" Christie's yell of fright attested to the fact that a vampire's instincts weren't often wrong.

Straight ahead of them, standing tall under the fluorescent light of a lamppost, stood the unforgettable and imposing shape of a man who simply refused to give in. His dark skin seemed to blend with his suit, turning him into a hulking, shadow of a man that stared through them both with sunken, black holes for eyes. He adjusted his cufflinks as he began his long walk towards them, his great strides covering more ground than Sam ever thought possible.

Preparing himself for another daring bid for freedom, Sam watched in horror as the gap between them closed. "How does he keep finding us?"

Christie's voice was as equally panicked, and she was fast running out of ideas. "Magic, maybe? TJ dabbles in it, but I don't know! He just keeps coming!"

It had reached a point where Sam was sure that he had never met someone quite as tenacious and determined as the Huntsman. The man seemed to be single minded in purpose, leaving no prospects for escape. Wherever Sam and Christie went, he was sure to be in close pursuit. It didn't matter what they did or where they went, he would be there waiting. Circumventing their fate seemed almost impossible, and Sam had begun to lose hope of the unyielding Huntsman ever giving up the chase. They seemed to be doomed to run from him for all eternity, with salvation acting as a mirage to tempt them with false promises of freedom.

"Is there no end to this?" Sam's mind may have gradually been broken down over the last few nights, but his spirit was still strong. He decided to stand his ground as Akoni continued to approach, resisting his companion's pull as she tried to drag him away. Christie was ready to keep moving, but Sam had grown tired of it. He wasn't sure if he was being brave or stupid, but he was absolutely sick of running away. It was time for him to take a stand and possibly buy enough time for her to get away. "Go! I'll slow him down!"

Unfortunately for Sam, Christie wasn't in a cooperative mood. She turned back to face him as the Huntsman stopped mere steps away, his black eyes staring with intensity. "Seriously?!? This is how you want to play it? I'm not leaving you, Sam!"

Sam tried to step between the Huntsman and Christie, wanting nothing more than to protect her. He would rather she lived on without him than they die there together. "Don't be stubborn! Get out of here!"

The ever headstrong Christie pulled Sam backwards and over to her side, wrapping her fingers tightly around his hand, with no intention of letting go. "I'm stubborn? Well you're being stupid and reckless! Two can play at that game!" She tilted her head to look up at Akoni who towered at least a foot over them, his straight face betraying no emotion as he stopped a short reach from his quarry. He didn't move a muscle, continuing to stare with unwavering eyes that Sam felt were peering through him as if he wasn't even there.

"I've had enough! Let's end this stupid charade!" Even Sam's yelling at the Huntsman didn't get a reaction as the man resolved to stand there, unresponsive and unblinking.

A ball of unheralded aggression began to form somewhere deep inside Sam, fueled by the beast that lurked within him and a lust for blood that he had not yet fully explored. He wasn't the sort to feel such unbridled rage, and yet it was growing in size, expanding outwards until it filled every limb and corrupted his mind. He had had enough of being downtrodden and had expended every option bar one. Violence. The only way out of this desperate situation was by going through the Huntsman, for he could see no other way out.

Sam leapt towards Akoni without warning, much to the horror of Christie who couldn't move fast enough to stop him. Completely unphased by the attempt, the much larger man barely moved to defend himself, easily plucking the foolish attacker from the air with hands that could crush bone. He didn't do anything to harm Sam however, instead discarding him like a piece of trash as he tossed him to the ground. The clumsy attempt at putting up a fight seemed to amuse the Huntsman, as a cold, heartless smile crossed his face. A smile that only served to fan the flames of Sam's rage.

"Leave him alone!" Christie jumped to Sam's defense with a shout as he picked himself off the floor. She entered the skirmish without a second thought, but she was smarter and knew that they were outmatched in a straight up scuffle, deciding to use her cunning and guile instead of mindless brute force.

Christie dashed to the edge of the path and thrust her hand into the ground, digging her fingers into a pile of sand. With one swift motion, she rose to her feet, flinging a handful of it into the Huntsman's face in an attempt to stagger him. The grains caught him straight in the eyes, but he didn't even flinch, instead staring on as if nothing had even happened. Following up her maneuver with a feint to the left, Christie changed her footing and moved to strike the Huntsman in the throat with her balled up fist.

To Christie's dismay, the man raised his arm to block the punch, his eyes looking straight ahead as if they were fixated on something out of sight. Despite the supernatural strength behind her blow, he still didn't falter. Akoni the Huntsman stood tall and proud before her, as solid as a rock.

Looking up at their opponent's face, both Sam and Christie noticed that Akoni's gaze never seemed to fall upon them and the sand in his eyes hadn't even caused him to wince. It seemed that he didn't feel pain, nor did he use his eyes to see. "He's blind!" Christie exclaimed, backing away as she prepared herself for another round.

It appeared that whoever or whatever the Huntsman was, he didn't see the world the same way as everyone else. He didn't use eyesight to navigate around the city or to track his targets, instead relying on some other form of detection that was cloaked in mystery. The cold smile upon his face slowly changed into a wide grin, yet he still remained deathly quiet. That silence was beginning to leave Sam feeling more unsettled than any taunting ever had, dampening his anger until all that remained was a chilling fear.

Sam dusted himself off, looking at Christie with a new found sense of dread. "What should we do? Can you try your mind tricks?"

She turned her head to peer at him with a look of sheer terror that matched his own. "No, it won't work if he can't see me…

It's not too late to run!"

The pair of them were startled by the thick accented reply of a man whose home was in a land so far away. "Yes. It is far too late." The Huntsman's direct, yet simple use of language was not difficult to understand, nor was the veiled threat behind his words lost on them either. A deep throated laugh bellowed from his mouth, causing Sam's instincts to flare up. His bestial side no longer wanted to brawl, instead begging him to flee in whatever direction the Huntsman wasn't in. The sound of laughter left him feeling frightened beyond belief, yet his legs ignored the pleas of a demoralised mind.

"I am death, come to claim your souls." Akoni continued, the power clear in his gravelly voice. "A debt must be paid." He rubbed his neck with a large hand before stretching his arms out in front of him and cracking his knuckles loudly. It was obvious that he was preparing himself to strike, and the sense of impending doom was inescapable.

What happened next was a blur that even Sam's enhanced senses failed to take in. In the blink of an eye, the Huntsman had set upon them, seeming to flicker in and out of existence as he moved at impossible speeds. It barely took a second for him to incapacitate Christie, pounding her into the ground with such force that the concrete slab beneath her fractured.

The feeling of helplessness that Sam felt as in that moment didn't last long as Akoni turned on him without so much as a pause. He realised in that brief moment that the only reason the chase had gone on so long was because the Huntsman had willed it. The thrill of the hunt was something that the man seemed to prize above all else, and he appeared to take some form of sinister pleasure out of playing with his prey before moving in for the kill.

Sam raised his hands up, pathetically trying to protect himself from an assault that he was powerless to stop. He had felt defenseless before, but this was something else entirely. Trying to fight back was futile, and so he tried to endure instead. The Huntsman had found his mark and wasn't about to let them escape his grasp. They were at his mercy, their continued existence depending on the orders that he had been given by the master holding the leash.

CHAPTER NINETEEN: JUDGE, JURY AND EXECUTIONER.

Even though they had practically been living there for the past few months, Aaron still couldn't comprehend how the traffic in Miami could get so bad. It was after ten at night, and there had been total gridlock for the past hour, with the truck only managing to make it a few city blocks. There had been some sort of sports game on, and the streets were crowded with cheering fans, mixed with the usual bar patrons who were just out to enjoy their weekend.

Tommy had been strangely silent at the wheel, focusing on the cars in front without so much as a sound, and he was only ever that quiet when something was eating away at him. Curiosity taking over, Aaron couldn't help but pry. "What's wrong?"

Tommy's hands gripped the wheel tightly in response to the question, but his poker face revealed no emotion as he verbally replied. "Nothing…" That settled it, something was definitely bothering him. He wouldn't have been acting this way if that wasn't the case.

Aaron pushed further. "Come on, spill."

Aggravated by his friend, Tommy's fingers tensed, coiling

around the steering wheel as if it were a small animal and he was wringing its neck. He inclined his head, glaring at Aaron with a fury normally reserved for those that they hunted. "I'm not fuckin' stupid, dude... I know you went to see her without me!"

Despite his anger, Aaron could hear the obvious hurt in Tommy's voice. He had clearly been wounded by the discovery that his best friend had been sneaking around behind his back. Aaron didn't know how he had found out, but that didn't matter. They weren't the sort to go around lying to each other, and that somehow made the situation worse.

There was almost an entire minute of silence before Aaron managed to speak up, the guilt he felt from his deception choking his words. "I don't think you're stupid."

Tommy grumbled, now sounding more depressed than outraged. "Come on, man... You know people call you the smart one. I'm just the dumbass who follows you around."

Lying to his friend had apparently done more damage than Aaron realised, and he was worried that the wounds might be irreversible this time. He could keep blaming Christie all he wanted, but that wouldn't change the fact that he was the one that had deleted the text message and had attended the meeting alone.

"Tommy, you're not a dumbass, okay? I learn from you every single day. I've always believed that you're clever, you just don't believe it yourself." Aaron meant every word he said, but he wasn't sure if his friend was convinced by them.

Seemingly frustrated by the direction that the conversation

had taken, Tommy slammed his fists down upon the wheel, raising his voice until he was almost shouting. "Then why the fuck did you hide it from me?!? You went to meet Christie and you fuckin' lied to my face!"

Aaron kept his own voice low, knowing that Tommy was well within his rights to yell at him. "I'm sorry. I didn't think that...."

Tommy didn't give him the chance to finish his sentence. "You didn't think I could handle seeing her, did you? I'm ready for this, dude... I know she's dangerous and needs to be taken out. I can follow through."

Aaron shifted in his seat, feeling disgraced by his own actions. The only excuse for his behaviour was that he was trying to protect Tommy, but perhaps that wasn't enough. "Are you sure? Christie's not the same person anymore. She isn't even a person."

Tommy nodded, looking Aaron directly in the eye with a glimmer of determination. "Trust me, I can do this."

There was a moment of silence when the pair stared at each other, the bond of trust seemingly still present. Perhaps it wasn't so easy to destroy a friendship that had taken so many years to build, and it would take a great deal more than one incident such as this to drive a wedge between them. Aaron and Tommy were still brothers in arms, and closer than any siblings could be.

The car in front moved up a little, drawing Tommy's attention back to the road as proceeded to inch the truck forwards. He was a little calmer now, his arms relaxing as he reclined in his seat. "So, where to next?"

Aaron felt relieved that the situation had resolved itself, but couldn't help but feel ashamed. He didn't believe that he deserved forgiveness, but was glad that Tommy didn't hold a grudge. Working through his mental checklist, he tried to push any negative thoughts out of his head. It was time to get back to work and that required focus. They had been to several different locations already, hoping to find the place where Christie and Sam Mitchell might be hiding, or at least a clue as to where to search next. "A small apartment downtown. Christie apparently had a friend there who might have an idea where she is. With any luck, he'll give us something useful."

Tommy placed the truck back into park, resigning to the fact that they wouldn't be moving again any time soon. "We'll never find them like this…" He punched the horn out of frustration, causing it to sound loudly as he started a wave of similar behaviour. It wasn't long before road rage swept through the line of traffic.

Aaron chuckled lightly at his friend's antics. "Feeling any better?" There was no reply from Tommy, but the question had been rhetorical anyway. With a loud sigh, Aaron made himself as comfortable as possible. With cabin fever beginning to set in, boredom was sure to follow.

Without warning, Tommy wound down his window and stuck his head outside to yell at the other drivers. "Come on, let's fuckin' move!"

An impressively quick reply came from a loud mouthed man caught somewhere behind them in the line. "Shut your pie hole, jackass!"

It was the type of aggressive social situation that Tommy revelled in, his own response spilling from his mouth without a second thought. "Right back at ya, douchebag!" He pulled his head back in, shaking his head with a slight grin. "Goddamn city traffic..."

Aaron felt relieved as it looked like everything was back to normal for now, or at least what passed for normal in the daily life of a hunter. He wasn't sure that events would go so smoothly once Christie was thrown back into the mix, but he would cross that bridge when it came to it. For now, he would just be content with getting out of the truck.

****

"Did you believe that you could get away from me?" The strong, Caribbean accent caught Sam off guard, but the man's words were not difficult to understand. Sitting upon a carved wooden chair as if it was some sort of grand throne, he made sure to enunciate his words so that they were clear to those whom he was addressing. The message behind them was a thinly veiled threat, with a promise of dreadful things to come.

Christie didn't hesitate to plead with their captor, her hands pressed against the floor as she looked up from where she was kneeling. "Please, TJ... Sam has nothing to do with this. Let him g..."

Her attempt at reasoning with the man only served to anger

him further, causing him to stand as he slammed a fist into his open palm. "Silence! I will be the one to decide who is involved and who is not! You have no say in the matter!"

Christie fell silent, not wanting to bring TJ's wrath down upon them. Cowering close by her side, Sam recalled what she had said in regards to what had happened to Jacko the last time she was here and he immediately understood her concerns. Their captor's fit of rage seemed to pass quickly as he paused for a moment before lowering himself back into his chair, his large fur coat draping over the arms and making it appear as though he was floating. The coat's fabric was made up of various different animals, both domestic and exotic, all stitched together to make a patchwork of death that he seemed to pride himself on.

An orange glow, originating from the burning embers within twin braziers that sat adjacent to each side of the throne, accentuated the shape of TJ's face, giving him a sinister appearance that filled Sam with fear. Thick dreadlocks framed his gaunt and bony features, with a wicked grin beneath that was constructed more from gold than anything else. "I own you both now. You cannot leave Miami without my permission."

The man underneath the massive coat fancied himself a lord of sorts, his bare chest adorned with a circular, gold medallion that had been encrusted with an impressive array of sparkling rubies. Similarly styled rings encircled each finger, some of them displaying different jewels such as emeralds and black diamonds. From what Sam could see, he didn't appear to be carrying any weapons, but judging by the number of armed men outside, TJ felt that he didn't need to protect himself as he had so many others to do it for him.

Pointing at Christie with a long, skeletal finger, the man spoke in a tone that was full of accusation. "You stole from me... I cannot abide that. The debt was paid in part by the death of your friends, but you still owe me so much more."

Sam couldn't bring himself to look up at TJ as he prepared to pass judgement on them, his eyes instead darting around the room as he took in his surroundings and desperately tried to find a way out. The room itself wasn't quite as grand as he had imagined for someone who held himself in such high regard, with a smooth, concrete floor and minimal decorations. The flames from the braziers were so bright that they hurt his eyes in the dark, making it difficult to see the outlying walls. He suspected that the place was kept bare in order to make cleanups easier, as he had noticed the floor sloping down towards a rusted grate that lay central to the room. Whatever his surroundings lacked in grandeur, TJ's appearance and demeanor had more than made up for it.

The carved throne rested on a wooden platform barely higher than a foot, with an assortment of skulls bordering the edge of it in a gruesome display. Amongst the collection of bone, there were some that were easily identifiable as human in origin, while others seemed to belong to beasts that Sam had never laid eyes on before. His attention was drawn towards one of the larger skulls that looked to be canine in appearance, but it was far too large to belong to any dog, wolf or coyote that he had ever seen, its empty eye sockets staring at him with a hunger that persisted from beyond the grave.

Sam's mind flashed back to the creature he had seen in the woods outside of Calgary, the enlarged head and red eyes peering at him from the dark. Perhaps he had actually seen a wolf big enough to own such a skull after all, but it was difficult to believe that a beast so large could actually exist, even though he had witnessed it with his own two eyes.

TJ's continued monologue dragged Sam's attention back to where he was sitting, the outline of his shape seeming to shift unnaturally under the flickering light of the flames. "I should have expected such betrayal from you, 'Entropy'. After all, you killed your own maker and my good friend. I should have ended your pitiful existence right then and there. You have been living on borrowed time."

TJ wasn't a tall man, nor was he heavy in weight or very muscular at all. In fact, he was noticeably scrawny in build, with his ribs visible as they poked out from underneath his dark skin. Despite his surprisingly small stature, he had an imposing presence that made him seem larger than life, with piercing eyes that were wide and full of madness.

Waiting somewhere just out of sight, hidden just behind where Sam and Christie were kneeling, the Huntsman remained close by. His massive form towered over them as he stood motionless like a statue, awaiting a signal from his master. He was so quiet that Sam wouldn't have known he was there if it hadn't been for the fact that he was the one who had brought them before TJ to face judgement. Akoni had forced them both to their knees with a strength so immense that it was impossible to resist, and he remained ready to carry out whatever order came next.

TJ leaned forwards to get a better look at the pair of them, resting his forearms on his knees for support. "Now, what should I do with you?" He sat there in silence for a moment longer, seeming to weigh up options as he assessed the situation.

Overcome with a fear so intense that it left him feeling desperate, Sam couldn't hold back any longer. He spoke out of turn as he raised his voice and tried his best to bargain for their lives. "You already took our money and our friends from us... We have nothing more to give you!"

TJ glared at Sam, but stayed silent, allowing him to continue with feigned interest. Becoming increasingly frustrated with his own helplessness, Sam felt as though he had nothing to lose, as both him and Christie had been doomed the moment they had been marched through the door. "You have everything we own... We have to be even now. Please, just let us go!"

A simple nod from the man upon the throne was all the signal Akoni needed to place his oversized foot on Sam's back. The sheer force behind it took Sam by surprise and caused him to release a pained grunt as he was pushed down into the concrete. TJ broke out into hysterics, laughing hard as he seemed to take a perverse pleasure in watching them suffer. He rose to his feet, approaching the edge of the platform to look down upon the two poor souls who had been dragged before him.

TJ pointed at Christie and Sam in turn with a finger so thin that it was a wonder that the gold ring on it stayed put. "No, there is still more for me to take. Do not ever presume that I cannot strip more from you for as long as the flesh is still upon your bones."

Sam felt physically inferior and weak under the sole of the Huntsman's shoe, but his willful mind hadn't given up yet. Despite the terror that he felt at being left powerless, he hadn't yet given up hope. He struggled to tilt his head to look up at TJ, channeling his terror into a defiance that burned like a fire in his eyes. "You have nothing to gain from keeping us here... Just let us go!"

The Huntsman's foot pressed down like a lead weight on Sam's back, his ribs in danger of cracking under the pressure. He tried his best to keep his composure, not wanting to give them the satisfaction of him crying out in agony.

The look of amusement on TJ's face faded and was replaced with one of contempt. "You have no authority here, boy! My word, and my word alone, is law!"

Christie looked horrified as she watched helplessly from where she was still kneeling. Sam could hear her whispering to him, begging for him to keep his mouth shut, but he had already gone too far to stop now. "Well your word isn't worth much is it? You murdered our friends in cold blood!"

To Sam's surprise, TJ didn't come back with a retort, instead turning away to return to his throne, the fur of his long coat trailing behind him. A dismissive wave of his hand came with a final command as he placed himself back down upon his throne. His eyes stared directly at the Huntsman, ignoring Sam entirely, the loudmouthed captive no longer worth his precious time. "Akoni, take them to the pit. They decided their fate the moment they betrayed me."

The pit. Something about the name evoked a sense of mystery and foreboding. The fear of the unknown was something that TJ seemed to use to his advantage.

As soon as Sam felt the weight lifting from his back he began to struggle, refusing to make the Huntsman's job easy. He tried to push himself up, getting ready to face TJ on his feet instead of from where he lay the ground. "Take me, but let Christie go! I'll stay in her place!" He took a brave, yet foolhardy step towards the platform, a move that caused Christie to call out to him in a panic.

"Sam, don't! You'll only make it worse!" It was far too late for her warning. Before Sam could gain another inch, the Huntsman had moved on him. The last thing that he felt was a dull pressure on the back of his neck before he was plunged into darkness. He was caught unaware, unable to bear witness to whatever happened next. It seemed that things had gotten much worse.

CHAPTER TWENTY: WAITING FOR THE DAWN.

Never in his entire life, nor his existence since, had Sam wondered what it would feel like to have his neck broken. However, now he knew without a doubt that it hurt like hell and was an unpleasant sensation to say the least. Fortunately for him, such a fracture was only temporary, and although it still ached, he wasn't going to suffer any permanent damage. Or at least that's what he hoped. Waking up from a particularly deep slumber, he felt the same dull sensation in his neck that he had felt when he lost consciousness, but this time it was accompanied by shooting pains in his head and throughout his entire body.

"Ow…" Sam sat himself up, resting his back against a hard surface behind him as he found himself slumped down upon a solid slab of concrete that made up the floor.

"Sam! Are you okay? I was worried… The Huntsman almost crushed your spine." The soothing tone of Christie's voice was a welcome sound, but he could clearly tell that she was distressed and had been concerned for his well being.

Rubbing his temples, Sam felt as though he had been hit by a bus. "I think so… I was kind of hoping that splitting headaches were a thing of the past. A human thing, you know?"

Christie chuckled softly. "No, we still feel pain."

Sam took a few seconds to look around in the darkness of the concrete walled room to see that he was in some sort of cell, with an open air ceiling blocked by a heavy, rebar cage. He could see the stars in the night sky beyond, partially obstructed by passing clouds.

Sam didn't need a mirror to know that his expression was one of puzzlement as he replied. "I noticed..." Making an attempt to stand, he found that his body wouldn't respond to his commands without being afflicted by incapacitating spasms of agony.

Christie gasped. "Don't try to move! You'll just end up hurting yourself more." Her voice rang out, echoing around the cell as if she was right next to him, yet she was nowhere to be seen. Wherever she was, she was close enough to be heard, but she sounded odd, as if her voice had been altered by some seriously strange acoustics.

A thin hand, covered in thick, grey dust, almost startled Sam as it poked out of a small hole in the wall, barely large enough to fit an arm. The chipped nails were mere inches from his face and yet he didn't feel threatened as he quickly recognised the tattooed forearm. Gently taking Christie's hand, he felt a reassuring squeeze that let him know that whatever he was going through, she was right there with him. As bad as things had gotten, they were still together and there was always the chance that they could still get out of this. The touch of her soft, cold skin gave him a sense of renewed hope.

Sam smiled softly, his face still twisted as he was wracked with pain. "Where are we?"

Christie's hand gently squeezed once more before releasing its comforting grasp and disappearing back into the hole. "TJ called it the pit... His description seems pretty accurate. My guess is it's part of an old construction site. A basement maybe?"

Slowly turning his head to examine his surroundings, Sam concluded that Christie had been right in her assumption. The unfinished walls and exposed rebar definitely gave off the impression that the place was an unfinished basement or maybe even the foundation of a building that had barely been started before a lack of funding or maybe something else entirely had forced the work to stop.

Checking his pockets, Sam discovered that they had been emptied of all belongings, leaving nothing but lint behind. Feeling disgruntled, his gaze followed the high walls back up to the rebar cage above, the silver glow of moonlight shining through and letting him know that freedom was just beyond his reach. "Did you try calling for help?"

Christie's response took the tone of someone who had almost given up hope. "Yes, but I don't think anyone could hear me. Wherever we are, there's no one around."

Sam tried to brainstorm some other ideas. "Do you think we can climb out?"

There was a short pause before Christie responded, but he could hear her pacing over hard concrete. "I already tried... I can get up there, I just can't get out."

Sam rested a hand against the rough surface of the wall.

"Then we break out? The walls might have weak points."

Christie's footsteps ceased and she forced a sigh. "I tried that too... They're reinforced with steel. There's a reason TJ put us down here."

Attempting to shift himself closer to the hole, Sam's body screamed out in agony, begging for him to stop. He continued to push through the physical discomfort until he was in position, but was again left feeling vulnerable and useless. He waited for the bout of pain to end before prefacing his next sentence with a grimace. "There has to be a way out of here!"

Sam could see through the hole now, his forehead resting against the wall just above the opening for support. He could see Christie standing in the centre of her own cell, her hands hanging loosely by her sides as she stared down a fist sized crater in the wall. The concrete around it had been pounded to a fine dust that exposed the steel rods lining the cell walls, the same powder covering both her arms and clothing.

Sam muttered to himself, realising that his companion had already tried her best to escape and had failed miserably. "So we're stuck here... Great. We may as well be in Alcatraz."

Tilting her head upwards to look out at the sky, Sam watched as Christie basked in the light of the moon. It had already started to fade, an early sign that the night was coming to an end and that dawn would soon be upon them. As she closed her eyes, Sam remained silent, observing as her pale skin seemed to glow, a striking contrast with the pitch black of her dyed hair.

Christie looked different somehow. Weaker. She was delicate and fragile, a far cry from her usual self and Sam could tell that she had expended too much blood trying to find a way out. He could sense Christie's weakness, the predator inside him coiling up, ready to strike. It must have been how she felt when he lay there unconscious and she too began to starve. His own hunger was starting to get the best of him, and he thirsted for blood, her blood. Whatever she had left inside her.

Before Sam could say or do anything, Christie opened her eyes and turned to face him with a faint smile overrun by a sadness that left him feeling guilty for the thoughts that his instincts had placed in his head. Her voice wavered, lips quivering as she spoke with sorrow. "Sam... I'm so sorry..."

Confused by her words, Sam raised his eyebrows. "Sorry? For what?"

Christie slowly approached, taking her time to respond as he peered at her through the hole in the concrete. "I'm sorry for getting you into this mess... You're here because of me. A direct consequence of my actions." She sat herself down on the other side, leaning against the wall as she positioned her head next to the opening.

Sam could only just see Christie's shoulder and the side of her head as she faced away from him. He couldn't see her face, but he knew that she was crying. Squeezing his hand through the gap, he tried his utmost to reassure her. "You have nothing to be sorry about. I'm here because I chose to be here. I wouldn't trade our time together for the world."

Soft fingers wrapped around Sam's hand as Christie accepted his offer of support. Her grip was unusually limp and frail as she spoke without much more than a murmur. "I'm weak, Sam. We've barely fed for days, and what's worse... The sun will be rising soon..."

Sam frowned, keeping hold of her hand as he felt her strength waning. The sun would deplete the last of her energy, and that wasn't even the worst of it. "How long have we got?"

Christie took a moment to think before speaking. "I don't know... Maybe an hour until dawn? A few hours after that and the sun will be high enough to flood the entire pit."

It was a grim outlook indeed. They were trapped and powerless, with nothing left but each other. Unfortunately, time wasn't on their side and Sam knew that Christie wouldn't make it through to see the next night. He wasn't even sure if he would survive in the sunlight for that long, nor did he want to find out. Yet in his current state, battered and broken, he was unable to do anything about it. They were both going to burn.

****

Sam didn't know how much time had passed, but he had spent every minute of it talking to Christie. He still felt anxious about their hopeless situation, his mind desperately trying to work out a plan as their conversation continued. Leaning his back against the wall as he looked out into the middle of the cell, he stretched his legs, trying to make himself as comfortable as possible against the uneven floor.

"So TJ's not been around for that long?" Sam was genuinely curious, but only kept the questions going as a means to distract Christie from what was to come. He wanted what could be her final moments of existence to be as pleasant as possible, even though it would be as unpleasant as he could possibly imagine. Admittedly, asking questions about their captor probably wasn't the best way to go about it, but he had already expended most other topics.

Christie worked on imparting what knowledge she had of TJ as Sam checked his injuries, her voice echoing out through the hole in the wall that was somewhere near his head. "TJ only became a major player in the last decade, no one had even heard of him before that. He came out of nowhere, took over one of the Jamaican gangs and turned them into his own crew."

Sam tried to stand again, but the pain was still too much to bear. The sooner he was able to get up and move around, the sooner he could find a way out. If only his damaged body would cooperate. A pained grunt prefaced his next question. "And now he's the boss of one of the most powerful gangs in Miami?"

Christie continued, seemingly oblivious to his struggle. "Exactly. Now TJ controls a modest sized chunk of the city, which doesn't do any favours for the Cuban gangs. They all hate him for it."

"Like the Locos do?" Sam let himself rest for a few seconds, preparing his weakened muscles for another push, but it was no good. His arms and legs weren't responding and he needed more time to recover, but time was one thing that they just didn't have. All he could do was enjoy the company of Christie as she continued to converse with him.

"One and the same. They're not the only rival gang, but they're one of the biggest and certainly the most aggressive. They weren't exactly pleased with TJ's grab for power, but because of the Huntsman, they were powerless to stop him."

Sam interjected. "But they push back when they can. I saw that first hand." The car chase through the streets seemed so long ago, but he could still remember the bullets flying.

"Yeah. It's not as often as they'd like though, and innocent people get hurt in the crossfire." Christie sighed.

Sam wondered if there was a chance, however slim, of the Locos turning up out of the blue and getting them out of this mess. It was wishful thinking though, especially as his only encounters with them had ended in violence and one of those instants resulted in a knife in the gut. There was no reason for the Cuban gang to help them, not without some sort of reward, and getting word out to them was impossible anyway.

Sam forced an unnatural sigh to match Christie's, listening intently as she began to regale him with tales of her own run ins with the 79th Street Locos. Surprisingly, not all of them were quite as standoffish as he had expected, as the gang had an appreciation for musicians and music in general. As much as he enjoyed the sound of her voice, he longed to be somewhere else. Anywhere but trapped within the pit. Of course, wherever he was, he would want her by his side, but he hated knowing that this could be the end of everything they had experienced together.

Sam had once worried that he would age and that Christie would grow bored of him, yet that worry had now been replaced with the thought of aging without her. He might live for a hundred years, all alone as his decrepit body rots away. An invalid, with no means to take care of himself, his flesh decaying and limbs slowly succumbing to atrophy. As awful an existence as that would be, he imagined that it wouldn't even come close to the suffering that he would feel due to losing the love of his life. Sam knew that at least part of his feelings were due to the blood that they shared, but he still couldn't help himself. Christie Reece was everything to him. She was everything that he desired.

Sam had died before, but this was going to be something far worse. He would have to witness the death of the woman he loved, and he couldn't bear the thought of it. Christie had been his rock for quite some time, and he couldn't imagine a world without her in it. Not one that he would want to be a part of anyway. Without Christie, he was nothing. Without her, he may as well be dead.

****

Sam and Christie waited in the pit for hours, talking about

anything and everything that came to mind as the great, fiery ball of the sun began its long ascent into the sky. As the light pushed back the shadows, a line of death encroaching on them, Sam did his best to distract his companion as they both huddled next to the hole in the concrete wall. Unfortunately, his body had refused to heal fast enough, and their limited time together was coming to an end all too quickly.

It seemed that the hole had been perfectly placed in the wall, allowing the pair to converse as they watched the sunbeams approach, both expecting to die. Christie was even paler than usual and Sam could see the terror in her eyes, but she still managed a faint smile as she looked at his face. The sunlight was barely a few inches from their feet and impossible to ignore, but that didn't mean that they wouldn't try to make the most of their final moments together.

Christie's voice was barely strong enough to carry her words as far as Sam's ears, his head pressed up against the hole in the concrete so he could hear every syllable. "Sam, promise me something."

Sam was fighting to stay awake, the fear of sunlight the only thing keeping him conscious. "Anything…"

Christie struggled to speak, each and every word becoming a chore. "Promise me… promise me that if you make it through today, you'll go on without me… Don't let this destroy you. I've seen your potential and I… I don't want you to waste it."

Sam didn't believe that he could make such a promise,

speaking up as he tried to object. "Christie, I..."

She cut him short. "Promise me!" The power behind those words seemed to come from nowhere, as Christie raised her voice with all the remaining strength that she could muster. There was no arguing with her, even now. Christie Reece was as insistent and sure of herself as ever, even when her body was left drained and close to death.

"Okay... I promise." Sam tried to believe that he meant it, but he couldn't even manage to convince himself of that. He didn't want to let Christie down, but he wasn't as strong as she was. He was just an immature kid from a small town in Kansas who had been out of his depth for a long time now, and she was the only thing keeping him afloat in a sea of chaos.

"Sam, I'm scared..." Christie's words shocked Sam. He wasn't used to her being the vulnerable one in their relationship, as he had claimed that role a while back. She didn't sound like the same independent woman that he knew. Then again, when faced with certain death, he didn't believe that anyone wouldn't feel some form of fear. Shifting his position to reach through the gap, Sam felt Christie's weak hand take his. Her touch was even colder than before and frail beyond belief. Her body was wasting away and her physical strength waning. The end was inevitable and it was just a matter of time before the sun would claim her.

"I'm here, Christie. I'm here with you." Sam didn't know what else to say. He tried his best to support her, but he wasn't feeling particularly sturdy himself. She deserved better, and he regretted not being able to stay resolute when faced with his own mortality. Vampires weren't truly immortal, they were just living on borrowed time. One could live for a thousand years and still eventually meet their demise. Everything had to come to an end.

It happened all too fast as the sun breached what was left of the darkness and flooded the entire cell with its scalding bright light. Sam found that he wasn't prepared for it at all, nor could he have ever been, ignoring his own physical discomfort as he watched in horror through a hole barely a few inches in diameter. As terrible a sight it was to lay eyes upon, Sam found that he couldn't look away as everything he loved was stripped and taken from him in a fiery blaze.

It was tormenting to witness Christie's abhorrent death as her bare flesh was burned to ash. Even as he closed his eyes, Sam could still hear her banshee like screams of agony as she writhed in pain, begging for the release that he was unable to provide. They were screams that he knew would haunt him for eternity. To watch such perfection being destroyed in the inferno of her own body would leave deeper scars on his soul than any he had obtained through his short, but miserable life.

As if the sight and sound of the ghastly ordeal hadn't brought with it enough anguish, the stench had been just as horrific. It lingered in Sam's nostrils, filling his lifeless lungs with a toxic smoke that would have caused him to choke had he needed air. He had once pictured what it would be like to die such a horrific manner, as it had once been described to him as the most terrible way to go, but experiencing it happening to someone first hand was somehow so much worse.

Sam was in a state of shock once nothing was left of Christie but a few cinders and a mess of smouldering remains. He didn't believe that she was really gone, even though he had witnessed it with his own eyes. He recalled the moment that she had pulled her hand away from him, the grim realisation setting in that she didn't want him to burn too. The level of devastation that he felt at her loss was insurmountable, and Sam wasn't sure that he would ever recover, nor was he sure that he would even want to. Their last conversation, the final words the two of them would ever exchange, had taken its toll on his emotions too. He was left feeling not only physically drained, but mentally exhausted too.

"I love you, Christie. I love you more than anything." Sam couldn't help but offer his heart up to her, a gift of his eternal and undying affection.

"I... I love you too..." Christie could barely speak the words through cracked lips mere moments before she crumbled to ash.

It was far too late for her to hear what Sam said next as he muttered the words so quietly that they were barely even a whisper. "I'll never forget you..."

As his own flesh began to itch and redden, Sam prayed that he would be taken too. With nothing else to live for, all he wanted was to be wiped from the face of the earth. He had nothing left but the promise that he had made to Christie shortly before she had been taken from him. A promise that he would keep going and that he wouldn't let the loss of his love destroy him. For the sake of that promise, he had to find the strength move on. He had to find a way to survive.

CHAPTER TWENTY ONE: AN ARMY OF ME.

The raw images of Christie's burning face were still fresh in Sam's mind. He knew that he would never forget the way she had looked at him, her crystal blue eyes engulfed in flame and ash. He would never forget the abject horror that he felt watching someone he loved die in the worst possible way. The sight, sound and god awful smell of it would haunt him forever. It had changed him. His grief and fear had turned into anger and hatred. A hatred of the man who sat before him now, wrapped in his fur coat upon his false throne of carved wood. However, now was not the time for vengeance. After all, revenge was a dish best served cold.

"How did you survive?" Sam stayed silent as TJ watched him with strange curiosity. "What are you?"

Sam's body was covered from head to toe with third degree burns, but despite his injuries, he was still alive. It had been the worst day in his entire existence, but he had somehow survived through it all. He knew that he had to keep going for Christie's sake, and for the final promise that he had made to her.

It was Akoni the Huntsman who replied after a few moments of awkward silence, standing somewhere close, yet out of sight. "I have heard of ones like him before. Freak, creeper, fangless, undesirable... Forsaken."

TJ stroked his chin, clearly intrigued by this new development. His eyes had widened further, a sly smile stretching across his face as he stared at the burnt wretch in front of him.

Sam's body had been ravaged by sunlight as a result of the pox and his thoughts were clouded by the beast inside of him as it screamed for blood. Once again, he had been forced to kneel, but he refused to show any weakness, fighting against his base instincts to hunt and feed. A voice inside his head wanted him to slaughter everyone in the room, but what little remained of his sanity held him back. There was no way that he could stand up to the Huntsman alone, he would need help.

Thick dreadlocks fell around TJ's shoulders as he leaned forwards, a sly smile upon his face. "Yes, you will be useful to me... There are so many possibilities. You work for me now."

The look in the man's eyes betrayed his overconfidence and the belief behind it that he was the victor. The egotistical megalomaniac was actually convinced that he had won. Sam would let him believe whatever he wanted. For now he would continue to play the part of the broken man, obedient and scared, but the time would come when he would get the upper hand and destroy TJ. He would watch the man burn, along with the Huntsman, his crew and the empire he had built for himself along the way. It would all come crashing down.

Sam refused to make eye contact with TJ, looking

everywhere but in his direction. It wasn't because he was scared, no, the fear had left him the moment that Christie had died. It was because he no longer felt as though he had anything to lose, as he had lost everything already. He couldn't look the man in the eye as he knew that he wouldn't be able to control himself. The stabbing hunger in his gut meant that he couldn't think straight, and he wasn't sure that he could hold back if he laid eyes upon the man who had sent them to the pit to die.

It seemed that the same man on the throne had noticed Sam's obvious avoidance, his smile growing into a wicked grin. "Not so talkative now, are you? What's the matter? Sun burn your tongue?" He let out a cackle that penetrated Sam's ears, the beast inside trying to claw its way to the surface, but he couldn't let it. Not now. Closing his eyes tightly, Sam did his best to act the coward, a part that he had played so well for so long. There was no one left to protect him, so that all had to change and he made a silent vow to himself that it would.

With a casual wave of his hand, TJ gave his command, sliding back to relax in his chair. "Toss him into the street. We will bring him in when I have need of his... innate talents."

Sam felt the sheer strength of the Huntsman's arms as he was yanked to his feet. He managed to keep his eyes averted from the man on the throne, not wanting to risk unleashing the beast that he was barely able to keep caged.

As he was roughly escorted from the room, Sam heard TJ's heavy accent calling out to him. "And remember... If you ever think of betraying me, you already know the consequences of such an act!"

Sam knew the consequences all too well, but he didn't care. As soon as he was strong enough, he would seek out allies and strike back with reckless abandon. Failure wasn't an option and TJ would rue the day that he took Christie from the world. The day that he had taken her from him. TJ would regret everything that he had done and would only have one chance to beg for his life before it was snuffed out once and for all. These were his final days. This was the beginning of his end.

****

Sam edged closer to the flames, the beast inside of him recoiling with fear. It was a primal fear, an instinct born from ancient knowledge. The same knowledge that a destructive force such as fire could burn a vampire's body to ash. He stared deep into the fire's core, the lingering screams of his lost love still tormenting him as it had every night since. It was a reminder of what he had barely survived through and everything that he had lost along the way.

Sam couldn't remember how long it had been since he had found himself trapped within the pit, the endless days bleeding into weeks, but every time the sun set he would come to this same place. The same dank alleyway, lit only by the orange glow of a burning trash barrel. It was a place where Sam barely existed, waiting to die a slow and withering death. He was wasting away to nothing, his hunger eating away at his body and driving his mind to the brink of madness.

The sickness from denying himself basic sustenance had quickly become intolerable, the withdrawal symptoms making Sam's body feel as though it was tearing itself apart. However awful he was feeling, the self imposed starvation was just a means to an end. He wasn't trying to torture himself despite the guilt that he felt over Christie's death. It was just a way for him to test himself and he was determined to see it through. This was the first step along the road to overcoming his limitations and becoming something else entirely. Something more than he had once been. Something greater.

The homeless people that often gathered in that dark place, mere mortals struggling to survive, seemed to avoid Sam like the plague, but that didn't bother him one bit. He just needed room to think and wasn't seeking their company any time soon. To make things worse, the blood flowing just beneath their flesh was a temptation so strong that he had to fight against himself to resist its pull. It would be so little effort for him to slaughter them all and feed upon the spilt vitae, but he refused to give himself the satisfaction. He didn't deserve the ecstasy that came from quenching his thirst, and would sooner leap into the fire than harm someone who didn't deserve it.

Each and every night that Sam had come to this alleyway, he had moved a little closer to the flames. He had become fixated on them, testing himself with every inch of ground that he gained and pushing himself that little bit further. Where he had once stood across the alley from the burning barrel, he was now within a couple of feet and could feel the intense heat emanating from within. Turning to run away would be the easy way out, but he simply refused. His sheer willpower was all that stood between him and escape.

As he watched the flames dance within their circular, steel prison, Sam swore that he could see Christie's face within the embers as her skin cracked and crumbled to dust. As horrifying as that was, and as much as he missed her, he realised that his feelings towards her weren't quite as strong as they had once been. Sure, he still loved her and likely always would, but he was no longer overcome with the same level of intense emotions that had turned him into her willing slave. She hadn't ever treated him as such, but he would have given himself over to her wholeheartedly if she had only asked it. As the effects of drinking Christie's blood gradually faded, so too did Sam's unwavering loyalty. He could see now that she hadn't been perfect, far from it in fact, but that didn't matter to him. Her life had been unfairly stolen and it was a debt that he had to repay in kind.

TJ was yet to call upon Sam, but that didn't mean that he wasn't still being watched. The man's goons were never far away, and he was sure that someone had been spying on him. The gangster's eyes were seemingly everywhere, but the thought of that no longer seemed to phase him at all.

Taking another step towards the fire, Sam reached towards it with an outstretched hand, his fingers so close that he could feel their tips burning. He ignored the pain, pushing through it as he concentrated on what the future would hold. All that was left now was him and the flames, with the only thoughts in his head those of revenge. He would watch TJ burn and stand amongst the smouldering remains until there was nothing left but ash. Despite Sam's current bout of apathy, he hadn't actually given up. No, he still sought vengeance, but he was preparing himself for what was to come.

A passing breeze caused the fire to waver, breaking Sam's focus as he saw something else moving within the burning refuse. Another girl's face emerged from the embers, the shape of it shifting as smoke swirled around like a thick fog. There was something about it that seemed familiar as long, billowing hair surrounded a face that he had somehow forgotten. The kind smile of a long lost friend warmed his soul in a way that the flames never could. The girl had once been his closest friend, so how could he have forgotten her? How could he have forgotten Alice?

An image flashed in Sam's mind, the extravagant theatre in Calgary, the last place that he had seen her. Alice had been sitting in the audience as the band played, unaware of his presence there. He couldn't fathom how such an important factor could have slipped his mind and wondered what had happened to him over the last few months to make him that way. Had Christie somehow wiped his memory? Had he asked her to? It was a distinct possibility that seeing Alice had caused him emotional pain of some degree and that he had wanted to forget, but Sam couldn't be sure of what happened afterwards. The details were sketchy at best and he wasn't sure if he would ever be able to accurately recall what had actually occurred. He might be able to piece events together given time, but there was no guarantee that they hadn't been altered in his brain somehow.

It had never really occurred to Sam before, but he couldn't work out what had drawn Christie to him in the first place. Had she simply felt sorry for him and how pathetic he was in his vulnerable state? It was difficult for him to accept that someone like her could ever fall for someone like him. He wasn't a competent or particularly manly person, in fact he was more of an incoherent mess than anything else. Perhaps she had considered him to be an innocent in need of protection from a harsh world that he was in no way prepared to face. Whether her feelings had been genuine or not, Christie had at least given Sam the illusion of being loved if nothing else. The doubt that he felt was just another insecurity in a list so long that he couldn't keep track of every item written down on it.

Paranoia set in, causing Sam's brain to brew up all sorts of wild conspiracy theories, with no proof as to any of them actually being true. He was reluctant to believe that Christie had meant him harm, so anything that she had done to him had to have been for his own protection. Whatever her intentions, it was unsettling to think of how his mind could be controlled and his memories changed. Sam wanted to know how Christie had achieved what she did, but most of all he wanted to know why. Unfortunately, there was no chance of him ever discovering the truth now, not with her having crumbled to dust.

As Sam continued to dwell on past events that he was powerless to change, a rogue idea popped into his head. It was an idea born of a hidden cunning that he didn't even know that he possessed, instead of his usual panicked desperation that he based most of his split second decisions off. He vaguely remembered his discovery of how Alice had met a similar fate and had become a creature of the night like him, albeit without the same flawed blood that had left him cursed as one of the Forsaken. Unlike Sam however, she seemed to actually have influence within vampire politics and likely had powerful friends in even higher places. She had resources at her disposal that he couldn't ever hope to match, and if he could somehow get in contact with her, then perhaps he could sway her to his cause. He could rekindle their lost friendship with a genuine request for help and Alice would have to bring out the big guns for the sake of the friend who she thought to be dead. TJ wouldn't stand a chance.

Sam realised that he only knew one person in the entire world who could help him to contact his old friend. Trekking up to Calgary alone would be borderline suicide, so his best option was to call her by phone. However, with no actual number to reach her on, he had run out of other options. The old soul trapped within a child's body, introduced to Sam only by the name of Jonah, was the best lead that he had to go on and would be one of the first steps in his campaign for revenge. But that could wait until tomorrow night, as for now he would have to test himself further.

There was another idea that came to mind alongside the first, one that was riskier, but could prove to be just as fruitful. Sam knew that without taking risks, there would be no reward and his victory would be denied. He had to explore every option, no matter how dangerous they might prove to be. Potential allies could be found where he least expected it, and that is what he was hoping to come to pass.

Another step towards the burning barrel and Sam could really feel the intensity of the heat. If he got any closer the hairs on his arms would be singed by the flame. The beast inside roared at him to get back, but he stubbornly refused and stood his ground. He had to master himself, to overcome his fears and the most basic of instincts. If he was destined to be a deadly predator stalking its prey in the night, then he wanted to be the one in control, not the one who was under control. Sam would allow himself to feed in time, but he would be the one to decide when that would be. His willpower would win the fight, it had to. If he couldn't overcome his own demons, then he wouldn't be able to claim victory over the man who had taken everything from him.

****

'The enemy of my enemy is my friend.' It was an age old saying, but as relevant now as it had been whenever it had first been spoken. If Sam wanted to take the fight to TJ, then he needed all the help that he could get, and who else to form an alliance with than the man's biggest rivals. The 79th Street Locos would be a hard sell, with their members having no reason to trust a nobody like him, but their assistance could prove to be invaluable. He would need their numbers to go up against TJ's crew, and no one else had the man power or the same level of motivation as they did.

While Sam was trapped within the pit, it had crossed his mind that no one else hated TJ more than the gang that he had stolen territory from. Sure, any encounter with them or request for parlay could end in violence, but that didn't mean that they weren't his best and only option. He knew that it was a longshot to even make an attempt at opening a dialogue with the gang, but he had to try. He had to risk making contact, even if it could all end in disaster.

It didn't take long for Sam to stumble across one of the Loco's members, the coincidence being that he was the man who had stabbed him within the same alley that he now found himself in once again. The sun was still high in the sky and the pox was already starting to irritate Sam's heavily scarred skin in the mid afternoon light. He didn't have long before it would really start to burn, but he would make the most of the limited time that he had.

The skinny Cuban man, with his white tank top and poorly scrawled tattoos, looked like a deer caught in headlights as he was startled by Sam's sudden appearance. "Oh shit!" He tripped over his feet, stumbling backwards onto the floor where he looked up at him with eyes full of fear. Making the sign of the cross over his chest with trembling hands, he cried out with a panicked prayer. "En el nombre del Padre, y del Hijo, y del Espíritu Santo!"

Sam couldn't believe how frightened the man was, especially as he was the one who had been wielding the knife the first time they had met. Perhaps he had changed a little after all. "I'm not here for you! I just need your help..."

He tried to speak calmly, but the man still tried to scramble away a little before raising his hands defensively. "You're fuckin' crazy, man! I don't want no trouble!"

Sam sighed, taking a step forward that caused the skinny gangster to flinch. "I'm serious... It's about TJ."

The name seemed to inspire almost as much fear as his own appearance. "TJ?!? Man, don't go sayin' that name 'round here!" Spittle stuck in the man's goatee, matching the glint of the beads of sweat that covered his bald head.

As Sam stood over the quivering wretch, he could smell the fear emanating from within and the sweet scent of blood in his veins. Despite the temptation offered up to him on a plate, he maintained his composure as his ravenous appetite screamed for sustenance. "I want to make a deal. Where's your boss?"

Panicked confusion overwrote fear as the gangster trembled at his mercy. "...What?"

Sam smiled with as much warmth as he could muster, not realising that the look he pulled off was more sinister than friendly, the whites of his teeth put on display. "I'm going to burn TJ's empire to the ground... and you're going to help me do it."

CHAPTER TWENTY TWO: THE LAIR OF THE DEAD.

It hadn't been easy, but Sam had somehow managed to obtain the support of the Locos. He had promised them more than he was sure that he could deliver, but was determined to do whatever it would take to raise the army that he required. Now the sun had finally set, he moved on to the next part of his plan, returning to a place that he hadn't visited in quite some time. Not since his first night with Christie.

Sam had only been to the apartment once before, but everything about that night had been ingrained into his brain and so he found it surprisingly easy to retrace their steps. The building itself was as run down and gloomy as he remembered, but that didn't bother him as much as it had when Christie had taken him there. He found himself wondering if Jonah would remember him or even let him through the front door, as one brief meeting was barely a mark in the life of someone who could be decades, if not centuries old.

For someone who seemed to prize his security, it was more than a little unusual to find that the place had been left unlocked. Sam tried the handle, the door opening with unnerving ease as he peered into the darkened hallway. It could just be that Jonah had witnessed his approach on the security cameras and had preemptively removed the safety chain, deadbolt and countless other locks, but from what little Sam knew of the him that seemed extremely unlikely. Someone else had to have been there already and they might still be somewhere inside, lying in wait.

Unsure as to what to expect, Sam should have turned to leave, but he was far too determined to contact Alice and wasn't about to let his fear of the unknown prevent him from achieving his goal. He drew upon whatever courage he could muster and stepped through the threshold, his shoes causing the floorboards to creak in a way that would have caused his hair to stand on end had he still been mortal.

"Hello?" The curiosity in Sam's tone seemed to hide his jitters, the self confidence that he felt by the burning barrel all but fading as he made his way towards the room at the far end of the hall. "Jonah? Are you in here?" There was no answer from anywhere in the apartment. If there was someone hiding within, they weren't willing or able to reply.

A cold, blue light stretched out from the open doorway, causing the shadow of Jonah's chair to appear larger than life against the far wall. The constant hum and whir of cooling fans could be heard from around the corner, with Sam unable to pick out any other sounds in the dark. The white noise wasn't enough to distract him from something much more sinister however, as it lingered in the air around him like a toxic cloud.

Sam's nose caught a scent of something that caused the

ravenous beast inside of him to stir. The coppery aroma caused pain to stab at his muscles as his stomach ached for the sweet sustenance that it could provide. Blood. It wasn't unusual to smell it within the lair of a creature that fed on it for survival, but something was distinctly off about the way it tasted in the air. He realised that the blood smelled similar to Christie's, but something about it was much older. This particular vintage was seemingly ancient and a great deal more potent than anything that Sam had picked up before. The odd thing was that it still smelled fresh, as if it had only just been spilled. It was the palpable stench of a fresh kill.

Despite the obvious signs that something terrible had recently gone down in the apartment, Sam still didn't give in to the thoughts in the back of his mind that begged for him to run. The beast inside him was drawn to the spilt blood, but that wasn't the reason for his refusal to flee. He had to find out what had happened there, but most of all he needed to find a way to contact his friend. Any worries in his mind had been overshadowed by his desire to see this through to the bitter end. Neither his nagging self doubts, nor the instincts that plagued him, were enough to stop him from wandering further into the lair of the dead.

The room itself didn't look out of the ordinary, at least compared to how Sam had seen it during his previous visit. The silhouette of a large, padded chair sat in front of the collection of monitors that had just resumed their screensavers due to sitting idle for too long. From where he stood in the entryway, he was unable to see if anyone was still sitting at the desk, but the lack of movement suggested that either it was empty or the occupant was resting there quietly. The stench of blood was much stronger in there than it had been within the hall, but that didn't stop him from acting foolishly and making his approach.

Sam crept across the floor, keeping his eyes on the chair as he closed the gap, his arm outstretched towards it. He wrapped his fingers around the headrest, his hand gripping the leather as he braced himself for what he might discover there. It finally crossed his mind that he could still turn back and leave that place before he delved any deeper, but he attributed those thoughts to a cowardice that he was still trying his best to overcome. With one swift movement, he span the chair to face him, but as its motion came to a stop he found that he still wasn't prepared for what he saw.

Sam's eyes widened as he caught sight of a small, lifeless body, lying motionless as it was cradled by the padded leather of the chair. It was slumped up against the curvature of the backrest, the pale skin starting to blacken as it slowly caved in upon itself. The wrinkled fabric of unwashed clothing was falling off the skeletal frame, due to there being little left to support it. Raw flesh had begun to decay at an unnatural rate, resulting in a stench that quickly overwhelmed the senses. However, the smell wasn't nearly as unsettling as the fact that there wasn't a head resting upon the bloody stump that sat empty between narrow shoulders.

Although the corpse was impossible to identify, Sam was fairly certain that it was Jonah lying there. After all, who else could it be? Before he could question things further, something large and wet hit the ground behind him, rolling across the wooden floor until it came to a halt by his feet. As he looked down to investigate, he was horrified to discover that the object was the severed head that he had just been searching for, in a state that made it just as difficult to identify as the rest of the body.

"Friend of yours?" The voice startled Sam, but he instantly recognised the man that it belonged to. It was the taller, more athletic hunter. The one he knew as Christie's ex-boyfriend, Tommy.

Turning to look the smug sounding aggressor straight in the eye, Sam's gaze was met with a grin that made his blood boil. He couldn't believe that he had allowed them to get the drop on him yet again. More than anything, he was angry at himself for not turning back when he had doubted the situation in the first place. Sam had knowingly stumbled into a trap with no care for himself or the consequences that came with it. He had foolishly allowed himself to be caught yet again and now there was no one else to blame for his current predicament but himself.

Tommy's arms were covered up to the elbows in blood. The same blood that dripped from the machete that he was now pointing towards Sam. "Looks like someone's been working on his tan lines. Who ordered their bloodsucker extra crispy?"

Sam simply gawked at the man, ignoring the whispers in the back of his mind that called for him to feed. "What did you do?"

Tommy was joined in the doorway by his shorter companion, Aaron, his stern voice filled with suspicion and hate. "We ended yet another of your kind before they could do any more harm."

The unwelcome, yet oddly familiar sight of the hunters had come as a surprise, but Sam began to wonder if they could be of use. If he could diffuse the situation, then perhaps the pair would join him in his quest for vengeance. He tried to calm his mind, biding his time by questioning the hunters in an attempt to humanise himself. "Is that all we are to you?" Sam could tell by the look on Aaron's face that he had not expected the question and that gave him the opportunity to knock the pair off balance.

The hunter lifted his own blade, using it to gesture towards the corpse. "You're all monsters and murderers. There's nothing else to it."

Sam couldn't help but frown at their closed mindedness. He knew that he had to twist the situation in his favour in order to challenge their borderline zealous beliefs and make them question their view of reality. "From where I'm standing, you look like the murderers. Who else would break into someone's home to do something like this?"

Aaron shook his head slowly, pointing his machete back towards Sam. "You're already dead. We're just restoring the natural order of things." Something about the hunter's choice of words sent a chill up Sam's spine. He actually believed everything that was coming out of his own mouth. Perhaps convincing them not to kill him would prove to be a harder task than he originally thought, let alone trying to sway them to his cause.

Sam sighed, keeping his arms by his side as to not alarm the men or force them into action. "This isn't how I want things to go... I don't want to fight you."

Aaron slashed the air with his weapon before taking on a combat stance that was designed to be as imposing as it was practical. He spoke through gritted teeth, the aggression in his voice more apparent than ever. "You don't want to fight? Then don't!"

Barely finishing his words before making a move, the hunter lunged towards Sam, who for some reason decided to stand his ground. He didn't even attempt to raise his hands in self defense. If he was destined to die there, he refused to cower and beg for his life. It was time to follow Christie's lead and show strength even when he felt as though he had none left. Closing his eyes as he awaited imminent death, Sam felt as though he was as ready as he would ever be. He didn't want to die, but he would rather face the end now than run from it.

A loud clang of metal striking metal rang out and there was no pain that followed, only the surprised gasp of the man who attacked him, followed by the sincere questioning of a companion who realised something was amiss. "Aaron, hold up! Something's wrong... Where the hell is she?"

There was a short pause, allowing Sam the time to open his eyes once more. The momentum of Aaron's machete had been halted by Tommy's own blade, mere inches from his nose. A sense of relief swept through him as he realised that he had been a millisecond away from having his skull cleft in two. If he could survive through this encounter, then perhaps there was hope for him yet.

A confused expression crossed Tommy's face as he pushed the weapons off to one side, giving Sam the space to move. He seemed to peer around the room, taking a moment to glance back over his shoulder before turning back to fire his next question. "Where the fuck is Christie?!?"

"She's dead..." Sam felt a lump form in his throat as he pushed himself to answer. Tommy had as much a right to know about her death as anyone, despite his previous intentions to kill her himself, but he felt sick just saying the words out loud.

The look of heartbreak in Tommy's eyes seemed to mirror Sam's own as he tried to buffer his emotions with denial. "I don't fuckin' believe you... Where the fuck is she?" His tone was threatening, but it only served to cover the blatant feeling of grief that had crept in on his face.

Tommy's choice of vocabulary left a lot to be desired, but this was a man who was hurting and Sam knew in that moment that they shared a common ground. "Christie's dead, I swear. I saw it happen..."

As Tommy stared deep into his eyes to discern the truth, Sam couldn't help but feel guilt. Her death had been his fault, he could have prevented it somehow. If only he hadn't spoken out against TJ, then they might still be together. Then again, he hadn't been present when things had gone south before, that was all Jacko's doing, and he wasn't the one who had owed the man money in the first place. Sam knew that he wouldn't have even been involved with TJ if it wasn't for Christie's meddling, but he couldn't be mad at her for that either.

After all, she had rescued him from certain death in that filthy alleyway. The worst part was that he hadn't repaid the favour. He wasn't strong enough to rescue her from the pit, and now she was gone forever.

Tommy continued to stare at Sam as if he was reading his innermost thoughts. "For real...?" The range of emotions that he was feeling seemed to spiral away from sorrow and remorse, quickly changing into red faced anger. "Shit! It wasn't meant to be this way... That stupid fuckin' bitch!"

The hunter's face kept changing with whatever was running through his head, with rage changing back to confusion that was jumbled together with an immense sadness that Sam almost felt as his own. Neither of them had realised it before, but they had a lot more in common than either would ever care to admit. There was a reason that Christie had chosen them, as she had seen something good and honest inside that neither had been able to see themselves. Perhaps they weren't quite as different as they had originally thought.

Before either Sam or Tommy could say another word, Aaron stepped in and threw a shadow of doubt on the situation. "We've believed that Christie was dead before, Tommy. This might just be another..."

A red faced Tommy span around to confront his friend, a fire in his eyes that reminded Sam of the look that he had seen from Christie before. "No! She's dead, dude. Give it a goddamn rest for just one second and look at the kids face... He isn't fuckin' lyin'!"

Aaron seemed to study Sam from a distance before raising his hands in the air. "Whatever, Tommy. You've got the lead on this." He seemed to give up, stepping back to stand in the doorway where he glared at Sam with skepticism.

As Tommy looked back towards Sam, he could tell that the news had shaken the hunter to his very core. It was that same feeling of guilt for the death of Christie that Sam was feeling himself. Tommy had lived through the grief of loss before, only to experience it all a second time around. Sam couldn't imagine how it would feel to lose Christie twice, as once was already more than he could take.

The gruff voice of a broken man was all that Tommy could muster as he let his arms hang loosely by his sides, the bloodied blade of his machete leaving stains on the denim of his blue jeans. "I just wanted a second chance… Is that too much to ask?" His usual crude choice of words had seemingly vanished from his repertoire, at least for the time being. He seemed to be a different person now, no longer a toughened hunter, but someone who had been wounded and left vulnerable by the loss of a loved one.

Sam knew that he had somehow gotten through to the man. They were equals and no longer enemies, but all that could change in an instant. However, that wouldn't stop him from using it to his advantage while the opportunity lasted. "She loved you, I know it. She never told me that in so many words, but I could tell. I know that she hated being at odds with you." He did his best to sound earnest, but wasn't actually sure if he spoke the truth or if he was lying for the sake of survival.

Tommy frowned, gripping the handle of the machete so tight that his knuckles turned white. "Yeah? Well it's too fuckin' late now, isn't it?"

Aaron took a step forwards to place a hand on his friend's shoulder, a brief look of sympathy protruding through the hostility that he still aimed towards Sam. "I'm sorry, Tommy. Let's just finish him and get out of here once and for all. We can go somewhere else and never have to come back to Miami ever again."

Swallowing loudly, Tommy shook Aaron's hand free from his shoulder, rejecting any form of comfort that he had been offered by his friend. "How did it happen...? How did she die?"

Sam mimicked Tommy's reaction with a gulp of his own. He knew that he would struggle to explain and that they might have a difficult time to understanding, but he had to try. "She... she burned in the daylight."

Tommy snapped at him. "What? How?!? She wasn't that stupid!"

Both hunters locked eyes at Sam, waiting impatiently for him to answer. "She had gotten on the bad side of a gang and owed their leader a lot of money. He decided to make an example of us..." Sam hoped that his pathetic excuse for an explanation sounded better out loud than it had in his mind.

Aaron didn't look quite so convinced as he silently scrutinized Sam from where he was standing. Tommy on the other hand lowered his head to stare down at the floor, ignoring the quickly decomposing flesh that was still pumping out the noxious fumes of decay. A few seconds passed before he raised his head once more. He seemed to look Sam over with a sudden realisation of what he had been through. "Shit, that's why you look so messed up... Who the fuck is this guy?"

Sam still hadn't moved an inch, observing the hunters as one paced in the doorway and the other probed him for more information. He tried his best to explain, but knew that any explanation he gave would sound either exaggerated or implausible. Fortunately for him, he was dealing with people who had likely seen more of the world than he ever had. "His name is TJ... I'll tell you all you want to know and more, but first I need your help. I'm planning on trying to take him down and maybe you..."

It didn't take long for Aaron to interject as he strode back into the room. "Uh uh. No way! We're not getting involved in this!" He stepped between the two of them, pointing his machete back at Sam as he confronted his companion. "Tommy, no... Let's just end this and go!"

The quiet tone of Tommy's voice soon followed as he tried to get his friend to see reason. Sam could no longer tell what was happening from where he stood as his view had been obstructed. "Aaron... He killed Christie. If anyone was meant to do that, it was me. But you're right, I couldn't fuckin' do it... and I didn't want you to either."

Sam noticed a throbbing vein on Aaron's neck as the pair kept on conversing between themselves. "I know, but you can do this. Finish Mitchell and let's get out of here!" He knew they were talking about him, but he couldn't help but hone in on the blood flowing just beneath Aaron's partially sunburnt skin. It smelled so delicious. So fresh.

Tommy raised his voice, still standing somewhere just beyond Sam's field of view. "God dammit, dude! He killed my girl! I don't care what she was... I know who she was. We're going for a team up."

Sam knew that it was the perfect time to strike. He could catch the pair off guard as they argued with each other and deprive them of their precious life essence. He could satisfy all his cravings by finally feasting upon that which he most desired and then two of his biggest problems could be easily dealt with in one swift strike. The hunted would become the hunter.

Aaron groaned loudly, the skin of his neck quivering with the sound of his voice. "You've got to be joking..."

Sam took a step forwards. He flexed his fingers as he slowly raised his hands towards his prey while Tommy responded with renewed fervour. "Not this time, I'm serious. Let's take down this scumbag!"

Side stepping around his resistant companion, Tommy's sudden attention upon Sam snapped him back under control. He crammed the beast back down inside, blocking all temptation from his mind as he dropped his arms back by his waist, pretending as if nothing had been going on at all.

Aaron followed suit and rotated himself to face Sam once more, his face twisted in annoyance. "A gang leader you say? We'll need others on our side..."

Despite almost sabotaging his own negotiations by nearly giving into his hunger, Sam had somehow formed a tentative alliance with two hunters who still wanted him dead. It seemed that they would put aside their differences for now in order to tackle a larger and more dangerous foe. It would be rough going, but the road to revenge was never meant to be easy.

Barely maintaining his self control, Sam idly chewed on his lip in a way that reminded him of Christie. "That's why I came here. I have another idea..."

Aaron raised his eyebrows quizzically as Tommy sheathed his machete in his belt, both of them letting Sam speak as he started to describe his plan in detail. The thought of teaming up with those who had pursued him for months had never crossed his mind before tonight, but this new development would open up even more opportunities that could give them the edge in the coming battle.

****

Sam felt extremely nervous as the phone began to ring, his mind racing with all sorts of thoughts about what he should say. To mention that he was feeling stressed was to put things lightly as he held the microphone tightly against his mouth. What if Alice didn't recognise him? What if she did recognise him but she didn't want to talk? What if she refused to help? What if she didn't even answer? There were so many possibilities and Sam had no idea what to expect.

It had been surprisingly easy to track down Alice and obtain her phone number, with Jonah's computers making the process quick and simple. Sam knew that contacting her was a risk, as if her new friends discovered what he was they would likely come for him, but it was a risk that he was willing to take. The thought of being discovered no longer seemed to terrify him, as he was far too focused on his goals to find fear in something that may or may not even happen.

As the phone rang a seventh time, Sam was almost convinced that it was going to go through to voicemail, but to his astonishment someone finally answered. "Hello?" He instantly recognised the sound of Alice's voice and was almost lost for words, pausing a moment as he worked hard to stop himself from stuttering.

"Alice? I need your help." Sam felt exhausted and knew that he was sounding a little off, his intense hunger still tearing away at his insides. The quality of the line itself was poor too, with the crackling of static affecting the call. It was one of many reasons that Alice didn't realise who was speaking, as well as the fact that he was supposed to be dead.

"I'm sorry, but who is this?" She sounded a little distracted and distant as she spoke, so Sam tried again, having less trouble talking this time around.

"It's me, Alice." He attempted to speak clear and concisely, but knew that exhaustion wasn't helping his case.

"Who?"

Alice still didn't seem to know who he was, so it was time to make his identity plainly obvious. "It's Sam."

For a moment Sam thought that the call had ended, but he could still hear noise in the background. It seemed that Alice had been struck speechless, which was understandable considering the massive bombshell that he had just dropped on her. He let the news soak in, not pushing the subject as he waited for her to process it all.

When she finally spoke, Alice sounded much perkier than she had before. She was seemingly elated to hear from him as she replied enthusiastically. "Sam, I've missed you so much. I thought you were dead... How did you get this number?"

Sam felt a renewed sense of energy himself, talking to Alice as if they had never been apart. "It's a long story, and most of it you won't believe." He had genuinely missed her and longed to see his friend again in person. Something about talking to her made him feel calm and relaxed.

Alice chuckled quietly. "Sam... You have no idea..." She seemed a little distracted now as a car engine could be heard running in the background, only just discernible over the continued static. "Sam, please stay on the line. I'm going to grab a quick bite to eat."

Sam understood exactly what that meant, as he too needed to feed. He knew what Alice was and felt the same hunger. However, she likely didn't starve herself in the same way that he did and could feed normally without the need for implements or breaking flesh. After all, her blood was thicker than his, so she hadn't been cursed with a lack of fangs. Unlike him, she didn't suffer from the thin blood of the Forsaken.

CHAPTER TWENTY THREE: A FRIEND IN NEED.

Aaron and Tommy were back at the same dusty, old motel room that had started to feel as though it was becoming their permanent home. They had been living there for far longer than they had stayed anywhere else in years and the state the place was in just showed that the pair of them weren't used to leading normal lives. Aaron had actually managed to unpack his luggage and filled the drawers in an attempt to make himself comfortable, whereas Tommy liked to live out of his bag so that he could leave at a moments notice. Neither of them liked feeling as though they were trapped, but they dealt with it in their own separate ways.

Recently Aaron began to notice that the place reminded him of Jack Olsen's apartment. They had stacked up numerous pizza boxes and empty beer bottles, with neither of them wanting to take out the trash. Suspicious of people snooping through their belongings, the pair had denied the maid entry to the room despite her protests and repeated complaints to the manager. Fortunately for them, the man in charge didn't care as long as they kept up their payments. However, it was a task that was proving to be increasingly difficult due to their cash reserves getting low.

Tommy sat across from Aaron at the small table they had placed adjacent to the window. They kept the shade down to avoid the prying eyes of passers by as they loaded bullets into empty magazines. Their guns had been dismantled for cleaning, with each part laid out professionally and with more care than they gave to their other belongings. Eric, their old friend and mentor, had always taught them to respect their weapons and it was a lesson that they had never forgotten.

Aaron finished loading his magazine and placed it carefully on the table, looking up at his friend with quiet curiosity. There had been something eating away at him since their meeting with Sam Mitchell and it was about time that he ended the awkward silence between them. "Do you trust him?"

Tommy smirked in response, moving on from loading bullets to sliding the parts of his handgun back together. "Hell no!"

Aaron furrowed his brow in annoyance. "Then why did you agree to help him?" He had been reluctant to leave Sam Mitchell alive, and it had taken a great deal of convincing from Tommy to leave the apartment. He didn't want to compromise who he was, nor break the promise that he had made to himself years ago.

Tommy placed his half-finished gun down and leaned back in his chair where he crossed his arms across his chest and smiled wryly. "It's simple, man... They killed Christie. There's no way in hell that I'd ever let them get away with that. Mitchell is just a tool to get the job done."

Aaron felt comforted by his friend's words, relieved that he hadn't completely lost his mind. "So we let him live for the time being... and then?"

A quick shrug of the shoulders let Aaron know that Tommy didn't really care. "After it's over, you can do whatever the fuck you want with him. Just don't expect me to help."

Tommy shifted his weight forwards, picking up his pistol as he proceeded to finish the task of assembling it, leaving Aaron wondering if there was more to left to say between them. "Is that all? We go after this TJ, I kill Sam Mitchell and then we finally get out of here?"

Aaron waited for a reply that came a little slower than he would have liked as Tommy put together the final pieces of his gun, quickly inspecting the slide and chamber to make sure that everything worked as it should. "Dude, you know me. I realise the kid is a little to blame for her death and I can't ever forgive him for that, but... I can't kill someone she loved, even if it was another guy. That's like destroying a piece of her. I just can't fuckin' do it."

Aaron finally understood. Everything was about Christie Reece and it always had been. Her legacy was one of music and misery, and joining Sam Mitchell's quest for revenge was just part of Tommy's grieving process. "Alright then. I won't force you to do it, just don't get in my way when the time comes."

Tommy nodded slowly to signify his agreement, laying his completed handgun back on the table. He glanced over at the parts lying in front of Aaron and grinned widely. "I'm still faster. Hurry the

337

fuck up, dude!"

Aaron looked down at the table and chuckled. He had been so distracted by the conversation that he had forgotten what he was doing. "Okay, Tommy... You're still number one."

It was good to see that Tommy still had a lighter side to him, even after everything that had happened. He jumped up from his chair, raising his arms into the air as part of his victory celebration. "And the crowd goes wild! Tommy Hughes takes the gold!" Tommy pretended to pick up a microphone as he simulated the sounds of a large crowd cheering for him. "I'd like to thank my fans for their support and my awesomeness for making it all possible!"

Aaron groaned loudly, covering his face with his hands. "Please make it stop..."

Unfortunately, the celebrations would likely continue for at least an hour, but Aaron wouldn't do anything to stop it. It was good to maintain his friend's high spirits for as long as possible, as there was no telling what the next few nights would hold. Hopefully the morning's inevitable hangover wouldn't be too punishing.

****

Sam waited patiently at the bus depot, having sat himself down on a bench outside. He was still feeling completely drained and couldn't find the energy to stand for long. He also couldn't remember when he had last fed, his body wracked with pain that came in waves. Even the undead needed to feed, although he wouldn't die from starvation. Without blood, he would simply fall into a deep slumber, with no way of waking up from it without the assistance of another. Sam didn't know how close he was to the precipice, but he suspected that he was nearing its edge.

It had been almost a week since Sam had spoken to Alice and requested her aid, and the hunters were already getting restless. They didn't seem to understand that Calgary was hundreds of miles away and that she could only move by cover of night. Alice would be travelling as fast as she could, with only her vulnerability to sunlight slowing her down. Sam knew that Aaron and Tommy didn't trust him, but that was fine as long as they stayed put and didn't try to do anything stupid.

Leaning back against the concrete wall behind him for support, Sam felt nervous with the anticipation of Alice's arrival and still wasn't sure what to expect. He knew that he had changed and that he wasn't the same person he had been when he knew her, but he also had no idea of knowing who she was anymore either. He had only seen her at a distance and that had only been a brief glance. If she was truly part of the vampire elite, it was possible that she would revile him due to what he had become. Sam recalled the fear that he had felt within the theatre in Calgary and silently prayed that their friendship was more important to her than any discriminatory beliefs.

The depot had been unusually quiet, with only a few buses

pulling up to drop off passengers, although the usual traffic still passed by in the street at the far end of the complex. Cars and taxis were cutting each other off in typical fashion while beeping their horns in frustration. Sam didn't know which bus Alice was arriving on with her entourage, but she had sent him a text message to say that they would be arriving shortly. He kept an eye on the screen hanging just above his head, checking the time at a regular basis as if it would make any difference at all.

The loud roar of an engine snapped Sam to attention, causing him to sit up straight as he looked around for where it was coming from. The deafening sounds originated from a large motorcycle that slowed to a stop by the curb a dozen or so feet from where he was sitting. The rider was a large and mean looking man dressed in military style clothing, who looked him up and down as he planted his boots on the ground and lowered the kick stand. The noise soon ceased as the the man turned off the motor, his intense stare locking on to Sam who found himself unable to turn away.

The unwavering gaze of the biker's dark eyes made Sam feel unwelcome there, although he had been the one to claim that spot first. Even with his new found confidence, he didn't feel as though he was ready to stand up to a man who exuded power and strength on a level that almost matched the Huntsman's. As he stood up straight and dismounted his vehicle, Sam saw that the man towered over him in height, his lean and muscular figure only adding to his already high level of intimidation.

The tall man strode forward with purpose, his body language

signalling that he wasn't someone to be trifled with. A long, faded scar across his forehead cut deep into the dark hair of his buzz cut, with a five o'clock shadow beneath that clashed with ghostly white skin. It was the rugged appearance of a no nonsense type of man, who for some reason had focused his attention on Sam and was closing the gap between them at record speed.

Sam braced himself for a fight, quickly standing up from the bench so that he could better defend himself. He shifted his weight so that he was ready to move at the drop of a hat, but the large biker stopped in his tracks just out of arm's reach. There was a moment of eerie silence that confused him to no end. It was a feeling that was only added to when the man stepped aside, allowing a clear view of the motorcycle behind him and the much smaller passenger who hadn't been noticable at all until now.

It took Sam a little while to recognise the woman clad in her white t-shirt and jeans. She was still straddling the leather seat, her slender form having previously been hidden behind the biker. She looked at him through blonde, windswept hair, her smile widening as she studied his face. "Sam!" Alice called out with glee in an accent that reminded him of everything that he had once loved about his home back in Kansas. She hopped down from her perch and rushed over to him at pace much faster than should have been possible.

Sam didn't have time to react before Alice slammed into him with surprising force and her thin arms wrapped around him. She buried her face into his shoulder as she gave him a tight squeeze. "I've dreamt of this moment for so long." She sounded genuinely happy to see him, but her sudden appearance had caught him off guard, leaving him somewhat speechless.

Sam's attention was drawn back to the man who still stared at him with distrust, a look that was becoming increasingly familiar to him these days. Whoever he was, he didn't appear to approve of the whole situation and clearly wasn't impressed with them meeting at a bus depot. He crossed his arms in front of his chest, not taking his eyes off them for even a second.

After another minute of holding Sam in her arms, Alice let go and took a step back to get a better look at him. She still stood a little taller than he did, which was made even more obvious by the way she now carried herself, so full of grace. The edges of her lips curled upwards as she beamed widely, the blue of her eyes slightly tainted by pools of crimson that began to form around the edges.

Alice was still the same girl that Sam had known growing up to a certain extent, but she was still different somehow. Like him, she had grown up from the skinny kid that she had once been and had gained a great deal of confidence along the way. A confidence that they had both been lacking. She was no longer the same shy child, but that wasn't the biggest change that he had noticed. There was a glint in her eyes of something darker, something feral that was trying to break out. Sam had seen that look before, but this time it actually scared him. He would rather face the Huntsman or the mysterious biker than cross the girl who had at one time been his best friend.

A hand reached out to carefully rest soft, cold fingers against Sam's cheek and with it Alice's smile faded as it was replaced with a look of concern. "Oh Sam, your face..." She traced the lines of his burns and scar tissue with her fingertips as she fought back tears of sorrow. "You've been through so much... I'm sorry that I wasn't there for you."

Sam tried to smile at her, but he simply couldn't find the energy. "It's fine. You thought I was dead, and for a while I kind of was."

Alice's nose appeared to twitch in response as she sniffed the air, her eyes narrowing to slits as she studied him further. "You smell a little weird... It's strange though, I can't place it."

Sam had an idea of what it was, but he didn't know how to say it. Fortunately, or unfortunately for him, Alice's intimidating companion knew exactly what was going on. "I know the scent, I've smelled it before." The man spoke slowly but surely, catching her attention.

"What is it, Matty? What's wrong?" She peered back at him, awaiting an answer that Sam wasn't sure he wanted to come.

Matty took a step towards them, large fangs protruding from his mouth as he bared them aggressively. "Your friend is cursed. That smell... It's the blood of the Forsaken."

****

"I'm sorry, but I don't quite understand." The puzzled look on

Alice's face made it clear to Sam that she didn't have a clue what her companion had meant by him having the blood of the Forsaken.

The trio had migrated from the bus depot to a relatively quiet bar just a few streets over. The place was quaint to say the least, with a small seating area that housed a few tables and a couple of booths that could fit at least four people each. Sam and Alice had made themselves comfortable at the booth in the furthest corner from the bored looking bartender and his single patron. They had ordered drinks to maintain their cover as normal humans who were just catching up, with no intention of drinking a single drop.

The brooding man, who Alice introduced as Matty, kept his voice low as he squeezed into place next to her, his knees and elbows taking up more space than was necessary. He was less than friendly when speaking to Sam, insisting that he be addressed as Matthew instead. He appeared to have a soft spot for Alice, which bothered Sam no end as they both kept an eye on each other from a safe distance.

Matthew rubbed his rough chin with his knuckles, his brow knitting together in annoyance as he continued to eye up Sam who had sat directly across from him. "He isn't quite like us, he's broken. Some say cursed." It was difficult to pin down where Matthew's accent hailed from, but Sam suspected that he was from somewhere along the east coast. "His blood is weaker, making him something else. His kind aren't welcome in most cities and in others, they're hunted to extinction."

Sam grumbled, raising his voice in annoyance. "My name is

Sam!"

Shushing him to keep from drawing unwanted attention, Alice reached across the table to place a hand upon Sam's arm, a move noticed by Matthew who instantly scowled. "It's okay, Sam. He doesn't mean any harm. Do you, Matty?"

The tall man huffed loudly, an act which she chose to ignore. It was clear that Alice cared for him a great deal, a fact that she seemed to be trying not to flaunt in Sam's face. After all, their friendship had sadly fallen apart following the awkwardness that had arisen from Sam declaring his feelings for her.

After a brief silence, Alice turned her attention back to Sam as she tried to gleam some more information from him. "You both keep saying that Sam's different, but what does that actually mean?"

Sam looked down at Alice's hand, his gaze lingering on it for a moment before he began to play with the full glass of beer that he hadn't touched. "I age slowly, but I will still grow old, or so I've been told... I can go out in sunlight for a time, but I'll never fully heal from it." He gestured to the burn marks on his face before continuing. "But that's not even the worst part. I don't have fangs like you, so I can't feed without ripping or cutting flesh. That's why I starve myself... I can't bear to hear the screams, so I let myself go hungry."

Alice squeezed Sam's arm gently, causing him to look up at her blue eyes full of sorrow. They weren't quite as bright as Christie's, but they were just as beautiful to behold. "I'm really sorry, Sam. I can't imagine what that must be like. Perhaps we can help you somehow..." She peered back at Matthew who simply shrugged his shoulders in response, saying nothing until he received a sharp nudge from her elbow.

"We'll come up with something..." There was a darker note in Matthew's tone that made Sam feel uneasy, but he didn't know him well enough to judge whether it had been a veiled threat or not. The glint in the man's eye as he spoke the words was unsettling, and it seemed that the lack of trust ran both ways.

Neither Alice, nor Matthew truly understood what Sam had been through, but he was sure that they had survived through trials of their own too. What he wasn't sure of was what Alice had meant by helping him. If she offered him her own blood in the way that Christie once had, he would have to deny the offer as he wasn't about to bind himself to another vampire any time soon. He had only just come to his senses, but it wouldn't seem right to be so close and intimate with anyone else either. It would feel like cheating. Like he was being unfaithful to the one he had lost.

Sam was surprised when Matthew spoke again, not expecting much from the man who had so far said so little. "I know the Forsaken. I once counted a few of them as friends, but we live in a world that doesn't accept those who are different." A sense of guilt seemed to take over, causing Matthew to avert his gaze and stare down at an empty spot of the table as if he was remembering something that he had tried to forget.

Alice appeared to notice the distant look in her companion's eye and looked up at his face with concern. "What happened to them?"

Sam didn't say a word as the man began to dredge up old memories, his voice solemn and yet stern at the same time. "I fought my way to the top of the food chain, but did some things along the way that I'm not proud of..." He spoke slowly and in a strained manner that suggested that the words didn't come easy to him. "The path to becoming an enforcer of the king's will isn't an easy one. You have to make sacrifices for your city... and mine involved the extermination of all Forsaken who lived in Baltimore."

Sam had no idea that kings even existed, let alone what an enforcer did. The mysteries of the upper echelons of vampire society were still a mystery to him. Matthew continued his story, still refusing to make eye contact with either him or Alice as he spoke. "I regret what I did, and I'll never forget the faces of those I killed... The night I carried out my king's command was the same night I decided I was done with that city."

From how he sat, it was plain to see that Matthew's actions weighed heavily on his shoulders. He clenched his fists where they rested on the table, one of which was soon held by Alice who had moved her hand off Sam's arm to do so. "And that's when you came to Calgary." She smiled at him encouragingly, letting the man know that she didn't harbour any ill will for the things that he had done before they met. In return, Matthew nodded slowly, lifting his gaze up to meet hers with a slight smile pushing through his serious expression.

Sam didn't really want to know how the two had met, a feeling of jealousy bubbling up inside of him. He didn't know if it was because he was jealous of Matthew's relationship with Alice or because he no longer had one of his own, but however he felt it didn't stop her from elaborating further. "We're from the same bloodline. We both have different makers who were created by the same elder vampire. One who called all her surviving descendants to her side."

Sam wondered if that meant that they were actually related as cousins of some sort, or if there was something more complicated going on. He felt confused by the meaning behind their words and what familial ties meant to immortal beings who had been reborn as creatures of the night. Had they forgotten their old lives and their families, or had they simply decided to move on? At least Alice still remembered him, if no one else did.

Sam looked back and forth between the pair as they silently enjoyed each other's company. "So why did you leave Calgary? When I spoke to you before you said that you were already heading south."

Both of them seemed to tense up at the question, with only Alice giving a response that came as barely more than a whisper. "We have our reasons, but it's best not to discuss them right now. Let's just say that events could have gone a little smoother. Besides, we came here to help you, so we should really focus on that."

Matthew shook his head at Sam who was still feeling clueless. "It looks like someone doesn't watch the news."

Sam was baffled by that particular comment, wondering why anything related to vampires would be on the news anyway. Their existence wasn't exactly public knowledge, as they liked to keep any mention of their kind out of the media as much as possible. It was a simple task, as vampires were rumoured to be in control of all forms of news coverage, which meant that they could alter it as they saw fit. To be discovered by mortals would be to put vampire kind in a most precarious situation. They would end up in as much danger as Sam would be in if other vampires ever discovered his existence.

Alice raised her eyebrows inquisitively, turning her attention back to Sam. "Do you know who made you this way?"

Sam thought about it for a moment before he came to the realisation that he didn't have a clue, nor had he thought about it for a long time. "Not really. I remember a voice and the way that she smelled, and then I woke up in the ground." He had been far too distracted by current events to think about what had happened before it all and how he came to be.

A sudden realisation hit Alice, causing her jaw to drop in horror. "Oh, Sam! I didn't know. I wouldn't have left if I had known..."

Sam didn't blame Alice for what had happened to him, especially the part when he had to dig his way out of his own grave. It was ultimately his fault that his life had ended in the manner that it did. After all, he had set out that fateful night with the intention of committing suicide. He nodded wearily. "I know, and it's fine. No one knew, but that's in the past now anyway." Sam hadn't told them much about what had happened to him since, especially the part when he had seen Alice at a distance in Calgary. It didn't seem that important to him now, and the thought of explaining it all was exhausting.

Matthew leaned forwards, his elbows resting on the table as the light hanging above the booth left strange looking shadows across his face. "Alice took a big risk coming here to see you." He wasn't really one for using big words and was seemingly limited in vocabulary. "You should have told us what you are. Just being here puts her at risk and she has had enough trouble already."

Alice frowned, her thick, yet defined eyebrows exaggerating her response. "I can speak for myself, Matty. Sam is my friend and we're here to help him." Her much larger companion grumbled to himself and sat back in his seat without another word. Sam had never seen Alice this sure of herself before and had to admit that whatever had occurred in Calgary, the changes that she had gone through since he had last seen her were most impressive.

Still nursing his full beer glass, Sam smiled lightly at Alice, finding it difficult to replicate the same expression for Matthew. "We should get out of here. I have a place where we can stay, but I can't promise luxury accommodation."

Alice returned the smile. "That sounds great. Let's go."

Sam pushed the glass away from himself, spilling some of the liquid in the process. In the corner of his eye he could see the bartender looking over with interest as three of his patrons prepared to leave without having drunk a single drop. The disheveled looking man picked up a fresh cup, poured some beer from the tap and sniffed it suspiciously. As the trio stood up and made their way to the exit, he shrugged and downed the golden liquid, apparently confounded by the behaviour of the peculiar visitors in his establishment.

CHAPTER TWENTY FOUR: A MEETING OF MINDS.

The club was almost exactly as Sam and Christie had left it, other than the graffiti that now covered a couple of walls and the added aroma of urine. Now the hunters weren't actively tracking him down, Sam presumed that it should be safe enough to stay there again. The place should have been abandoned since their confrontation with Aaron and Tommy, but it had apparently been used as a local hangout for vagrants ever since. He wouldn't have been surprised if he found used needles amongst the scattered pieces of trash, but he didn't care enough to check.

"This is it?" Matthew said with obvious disapproval in his voice. "When you said you had a place to stay, I didn't expect you to bring us to a crack den."

The tone in his voice annoyed Sam to no end, but he didn't have time to think of a suitably sarcastic response before Alice stepped in. "It may need a little work, but I like it. Thanks for letting us stay."

The club was at one time Sam's home, and a place that he shared so many memories with Christie. Sure, it was a bit of a fixer upper, but that didn't make the building any less special for him. At least Alice seemed to understand how he felt, but it would take a lot more to convince Matthew who was still complaining. "The locks are busted... I'll need to barricade the doors and secure the windows. For the record, I still don't think it's a safe place to hide out." It didn't seem as though anything would impress him as he continued to criticise pretty much everything about the club.

Sam couldn't think of anything pleasant to say, so he bit his tongue and said nothing at all. He turned his back to Matthew and started to walk towards the stairs that led up to the walkway. As he reached the bottom step, he quietly hoped that he wouldn't find anyone unconscious upstairs, even though it would provide a tempting and easy meal. Stabbing pains shot through his body as he was reminded of the hunger that he had denied for far too long.

Sam grabbed at the railing by the stairs for support as his legs began to fail him. The fact that he was feeling faint let him know that his self imposed starvation was finally taking its toll. His body was starting to shut down piece by piece and without the blood that he needed to survive, the possibility of a deep and eternal sleep was a threat that he could no longer ignore.

Before Sam had even realised what was going on, Alice caught him in her arms, stopping his head from hitting the floor. He had somehow lost his balance and fallen over, but her quick reactions saved him at the last moment. "Matty! Find him some blood as fast as you can!" The panic in her voice overwrote any other emotions as she called for help. "Sam, stay with me!"

Sam would have stayed conscious if he could, but he had

been running on empty for far longer than should have been possible and he had nothing left to keep himself going. He tried to speak, but couldn't manage more than an incomprehensible mumble. Alice would get him the sustenance that he required, so he likely wouldn't be out for long, however Sam still hated feeling vulnerable. He hated having to rely on others to survive and this was no exception. There was still so much to be done and so many preparations to be made, but even the dead need to rest.

****

When Sam came to, he found himself in a room that he recognised instantly. Christie's sanctuary had seen better days, with spray paint covering most of the posters and flyers that decorated the walls, but it still felt good to be home. An awful stench threatened to spoil his homecoming, but Sam refused to let it ruin the moment. Wherever it was coming from, it was an unpleasant mix of scents that he tried not to identify.

Once again, Sam found himself lying on the old mattress that made up the bed, although the soiled sheets had been stripped and tossed into the far corner, the sweat stains clearly visible. It seemed that the origin of the disgusting smell had been easier to locate than he expected as it drifted over from the very same corner. He found himself increasingly curious about what had gone on in there, but thought that it was best not to question it.

Carefully sitting himself up straight, Sam saw that Christie's wardrobe doors were wide open, with half of her clothing spread across the floor boards and the rest missing altogether. It angered him that her memory could be disrespected that way and he wanted nothing more than to start tidying up the place. Unfortunately, he still lacked the energy to stand and wasn't yet ready to test his limits by cleaning.

Amongst the scattered clothing lay three empty blood bags, the sides of which had been slashed open with a sharp object and drained before being discarded. There was very little left inside them other than a few small red drops here and there. Just beyond them stood Alice, her back turned towards Sam as she closely studied one of the larger band posters. Either she hadn't noticed that he had awoken from his slumber or she didn't want to crowd him, and was keeping her distance for however long that he needed.

The answer arrived a few seconds later as Alice began to talk softly just before Sam could open his mouth. "The place was in this state when we brought you up here. It seems that someone else has been sleeping in your bed. I was about to clean up a little, but you weren't out for quite as long as I expected." She turned to face him, her hair hanging loosely around her shoulders as she smiled. "I'm glad you're okay. How are you feeling?"

Sam still felt groggy, but he was no longer in pain and the agony of starvation had finally passed. He remained seated as he rubbed the top of his head weakly. "I think I'll be fine... Where did you get these?" He raised his other hand and pointed towards the empty plastic bags.

Alice walked over to the bed and carefully sat herself down on the edge of the mattress near Sam's feet. "Matty came back with a few, but didn't want me to ask how he had obtained them. There are some more in the fridge downstairs if you're still hungry."

Sam couldn't remember ingesting the blood, but there was a stale taste on his lips. It clearly hadn't been as satisfying as drinking it fresh from the source, but he was in no position to complain and at least this way no one had gotten hurt, or so he hoped. "Thanks, Alice." There was a brief silence as he managed a thankful smile and Alice reached out to gently squeeze his leg in response. Her hair had fallen over her face in a similar manner to how she used to wear it as a child, giving him the chance to see that she really was the same girl that he had once known.

Sam admitted that Alice was still pretty, but he wasn't really sure why he had pined after her for so long. Perhaps he had finally gotten over his feelings for her after all these years and they could just get back to being friends. Perhaps any feelings of jealousy that he had felt could be purged from his system. Sam's perspective on the world had changed a great deal and he was glad that he didn't revert back to his old ways when faced with the biggest aspect of his childhood. It made him proud to see that Alice had found her own stride too, as she was no longer the little girl who ran to hide in the woods after being bullied at school. No longer would he have to comfort her as she cried herself to sleep or play pretend as she escaped into her own imaginary worlds. Alice Delaney was no longer a child and had become a woman in her own right.

Although Sam wanted to tell Alice how happy he was for her, he couldn't bring himself to say the words. Instead he managed an entirely different subject altogether. "What's Matthew up to now?" He would have kicked himself if he had the strength to do so, but he would have to just make do with a mental scolding. Another blood bag or two and Sam would be up to full strength, then he could beat himself up all he wanted. He wondered if it took this long for 'normal' vampires to recover as he didn't remember Christie ever struggling like he did. Of course she had never starved herself either.

Alice glanced over at the door which was currently shut tight, likely to give Sam some privacy as he slept. "Matty's downstairs. He said something about securing the building and keeping watch."

Sam inclined his head inquisitively. "So you and him are…?"

It looked as though Alice would have blushed if she could, but her cheeks remained as pasty white as ever. "Still working things out. It's a little complicated, but we've been through so much together."

"Okay, I won't pry." Sam couldn't help but grin, feeling stronger by the second.

It was obvious that Alice didn't want to discuss it further, especially when she quickly changed topic. "I think I can help you find some of the answers you've been seeking, if you want to that is. We may be able to discover the identity of the woman who gave you new life."

New life. It was an interesting way of describing his state of existence, but Sam wasn't sure that he agreed with the terminology. "I guess so. It's been a while since I even thought about it."

Alice shuffled herself up the mattress and moved herself into a kneeling position before reaching out towards Sam's face with both hands. "May I?"

Sam nodded his agreement, allowing her to place her cold, delicate hands on each temple. The feeling that followed was strange to say the least as he found himself being plunged into the depths of his own mind in an instant. The world around him vanished completely and was replaced with near endless corridors of memories, some as clear as day and others shrouded by the mists of time.

The act of delving into his own mind was a strange experience and one that Sam found to be surprisingly enlightening as he waded through his memories with Alice in tow. She was bound to him like a spirit and could only go where he wanted her to, but it still felt unusual to let someone else in, especially as he was usually so closed off. However, if there was anyone left that he would trust enough to let down his defenses, it was her.

It wasn't long before the pair stumbled across the core of Sam's mind and the memories that occupied his thoughts throughout the long nights of his tormented existence. Every one of them shared something in common and had been linked together by the appearance of a single person, Christie Reece.

Christie had once been a mystery to Sam, introducing herself to him by the name Entropy, but he had grown so close to her since the first time they had met. At one point he couldn't have imagined his life without her and yet that devastating reality had since been thrust upon him. Waiting somewhere within the center of his mind, an incorporeal wraith stood amongst the wreckage of shattered dreams and waking nightmares. Its shapeless form wore Christie's face like a mask, it's features contorted in a permanent expression of terror.

"Is that her?" Alice's voice whispered to Sam as he approached the ghost, his hands reaching out towards her as he tried to ease her pain.

"It's her." He replied with overwhelming sadness at seeing his lost love in pain. "This is the last moment before she died…"

Sam couldn't bear to see Christie that way and closed his eyes to block it out. A few seconds passed before he dared to open them again, coming face to face with a happier memory of their night exploring the city of Calgary. Christie was standing beneath the base of Calgary tower, her crystal blue eyes sparkling under the streetlights as she laughed with glee. This was how Sam wanted to remember her, but he struggled to get those final moments out of his head. Those awful memories were scars in his mind and he was trapped within them as if they were a cage that he would never be able to escape.

Alice's words carried on the air, brushing past Sam's ear as he took the time to admire the contours of Christie's face. "I saw her picture on the posters in your room, but they didn't do her justice. She's so pretty."

Sam nodded his agreement, but choked on his words as Christie's bright pink hair shifted in the breeze. He realised that he missed everything about her. The way she moved and how she spoke, the wild look that she would get in her eyes when she was up to no good and even the way that she smelled. If only they had been able to spend more time together, but that too wouldn't have been enough to satisfy his needs.

There was a brief pause before Alice spoke again. "When were you were in Calgary?"

Sam didn't take his eyes off Christie as he idly replied. "Christie's band played at a theatre there."

He could almost hear something click as Alice pieced the puzzle together. "Entropy of the Heart? I knew that I recognised her! The theatre, the posters here... I had only seen them play the once, but their performance left a lasting impression." There was another slight pause. "Sam... Did you see me there?"

The question broke Sam's concentration, causing him to look away for just a second, but that was all it took for the memory to be lost amongst the chaos once more, leaving nothing but blackness in its wake. It hurt him to lose sight of Christie again, but he understood his friend's curiosity. "Yes I did, but only at a distance. I was backstage during the performance."

"Then why wouldn't you come and speak to me?" Alice sounded a little hurt as she replied.

The answer didn't come easy, but he knew that he owed her an explanation. "It was dangerous for me there... If I was discovered, I could have been killed. As Matthew said, the Forsaken aren't exactly welcomed by most vampires. They see people like me as mistakes that need to be wiped out." It wasn't much of a reason but it was the truth, if only just part of it.

"It's okay. I understand..." Sam could hear the disappointment in her voice, even though she had tried to mask it.

He continued. "I was scared... Not just because of that, but because I hadn't seen you for so long and didn't know how you'd react." That was the true reason that he had kept hidden from even himself. Samuel Isaac Mitchell was still a coward at heart, despite everything that he had tried to overcome his basic nature.

"You're my best friend, Sam. I would have just been happy to see you." Part of him had always known that Alice would have welcomed him with open arms and her words had just confirmed that. It had always been his feelings of rejection that had gotten in the way of his friendship with her and had driven a wedge between them, not the fact that she hadn't wanted to risk their relationship by pursuing romantic interests.

"I know and I'm sorry..." Sam wasn't lying. He felt guilty for pushing Alice away and for sending himself down a dark path that resulted in his death. His own foolish actions had been the catalyst for his own demise.

"It's fine, Sam. We're together again now and that's all that matters." There was no trace of contempt in Alice's voice, but that didn't change the past or prevent Sam from screwing things up in the first place. However, despite everything that had happened, the only friend that he had left in the entire world was there to help him and she wasn't asking for anything in return. That was true friendship in its purest form. He couldn't ask for a better friend than Alice Delaney.

There was another voice in the dark that spoke softly with masked intent. A familiar one that he hadn't heard since the fateful night that had changed his entire existence forever. "I can show you all the wonders of the world." The woman's words were saturated by false promises and lies. She had never wanted to show him the world and had only ever wanted to use him. Her voice was distorted, making her sound different to what Sam had previously remembered. His thoughts were corrupted and unclear as he struggled to conjure up a clear image of his maker.

It was Alice's whisper that followed, guiding Sam through his own memories as if she had the map that he had been lacking all this time. "Focus on her voice. Let an image form in your mind. Don't chase after her memory, let it come to you."

Sam could see the woman's lips, red with blood as she mouthed the words, but he still found it difficult to recall the rest of her face, as if it had been purposely blocked from his mind. "This isn't the end. It's the beginning of something much greater." The words were clearer this time, but were rife with yet more lies. Everything she had told him had been a lie. A means to an end.

Whoever the woman was, her voice seemed to trigger

something in Alice that filled her with fear. "Sam, I know that voice…" It appeared that the woman was someone that Alice knew quite well. It was someone that she was familiar enough with that she could recognise them from their voice alone, and from her fearful tone, that wasn't exactly a good thing.

Sam concentrated as a face began to form around the dripping, ruby lips and his lost memory began to surface. It wasn't long before her other features began to take shape, the narrow and defined nose of a regent, hazel eyes full of the wisdom of someone who had witnessed indescribable acts of horror, and smooth skin that was as pale as moonlight. Dark, brown hair bordered the elegant bone structure of a woman of timeless beauty, her cordial smile hiding a malevolence that chilled Sam to the bones.

"Sam, wake up! Wake up now!" Alice's terrified plea wasn't enough to break Sam free as he was enveloped in the woman's arms. What began as a gentle embrace soon escalated into a vice like grip that threatened to crush bone as her sheer strength overpowered him. He could feel the curves of her body pressing up against him, her hands poking through his skin like daggers between his ribs as she refused to let go. The more he squirmed and struggled against his captor, the stronger she seemed to get and the wider her smile grew until he could see the points of her fangs protruding from her mouth. An elongated tongue poked out from between her reddened lips, licking every drop of blood from them as her pupils dilated with frenzied intoxication.

"What's happening?!?" Sam called out to Alice in panic, the

feeling of helplessness fast becoming more than he could handle.

"It's not just a memory, Sam, it's actually her. I don't know how she's doing it, but she can sense your presence, which means that she may be able to track you down too." Alice's words offered no comfort even though she tried her best to speak in a calm and reassuring manner. Her fake confidence wasn't enough to mask the trepidation that she clearly felt.

The woman's tongue seemed to taste the air, picking up the scent of Sam's blood before she slowly moved her head down towards his neck. She pressed cold lips against his bare skin and proceeded to devour the precious liquid as it flowed from a freshly opened wound. Her fangs had torn open his jugular, letting her suckle his life directly from his veins like the sweet nectar that it was. Sam knew the feeling all too well and the high that came from consuming his fill, but he had never been the one who was being consumed, or at least he had forgotten about it until now. He wondered what it was like to cut with the precision of a scalpel instead of rending flesh with teeth ill suited to the task.

"I don't... I don't understand..." Sam was beginning to have trouble speaking as the woman's limbs entwined around him like vines, squeezing the very life out of him. Her body was changing, her shape transforming as if she was becoming something else entirely. Something powerful and primal.

Disembodied and unable to directly intervene, Alice still tried to lend some aid. "You can do it, Sam, just open your eyes! You really don't want her to find you, trust me..."

The woman continued to lap up Sam's vitae as he began to disappear under a mass of flesh like vines. This wasn't part of his lost memory, it was something else entirely. It was as if someone else other than Alice had forcibly entered his mind and was wrestling for control, with no care as to what state it would be left in afterwards.

Sam cried out in terror. "This is just in my head. None of it's real. She can't be this bad, can she?" The woman's fangs began to multiply, their points elongating until the maw of her mouth had been filled with several rows of razor sharp needles. To his horror, her jaw opened unnaturally wide and then wider still as she prepared to consume him whole.

Alice's voice was quieter now as she was being systematically shut out by a creature of considerable strength. "She's worse than this... She drains you of your free will without you realising it. You don't even know that it's happening until it's far too late."

Sam wanted to fight back, but he couldn't move a muscle. He was trapped and would soon become a meal for someone who he didn't know that well at all. Why would the woman create him only to snuff him out? None of it made sense. This wasn't the same person that he remembered at all. Just like everything else, it had all been a lie.

Wait a second... This couldn't be real. Sam realised that all of it was in his head and that he wasn't a prisoner there. It wasn't his physical body getting crushed, just a representation of it. Alice couldn't do anything to save him from the woman's grasp, only he could to save himself. He had to break free of her tendrils and reclaim his mind from those who had invaded it, guests both invited and uninvited.

Alice had helped Sam to locate his maker, but in doing so had inadvertently put him in jeopardy. He was thankful for his friend's assistance and had been more than willing for the intrusion when it was offered, but it was now time for her to leave. It was time to free his consciousness from all outside influences.

"Get out of my head!!!" Sam yelled as loud as he could, projecting his command throughout the misted corridors of his memories and out to every corner of his mind.

The horrific form the woman had taken pulled away from his neck and glared at him with bloodshot eyes. "I will come for you, my child." Her eyes darted up to where Alice's spirit still floated nearby, her wicked grin of pointed teeth gnashing together as she spoke. "I will come for you all!" And with those final words, she slipped away like a serpent in the darkness, leaving no trace of anyone having been there at all.

Still feeling stunned by what had happened, Sam peered up at Alice, who's form was now little more than a cloud of fog with a human face as it began to dissipate. He could tell by her expression that she was terrified and if what he had just seen was anything to go by, she had every right to be. As the last vestiges of her form faded from view and became one with the mist that surrounded it, she whispered to him in the most soothing of tones as her voice was carried off into the void. "Open your eyes, Sam. It's time to wake up."

With those final words, Sam was whisked off his feet and

sent spiralling back from where he came. He caught glimpses of old memories as he passed them by, some full of joy and others drenched in misery. He could see his parents and their baby girl, Entropy of the Heart performing on stage, the hunters who had become tentative allies and the blonde haired girl who he had grown up alongside, as well as the intimidating companion that she had brought to Miami with her. These were just some of the events that had forged the man who he was today, for better or for worse.

The last face that Sam saw as he was pushed back into the real world was that of Christie. Her features were no longer contorted and twisted in pain, as she instead smiled with a warmth that he was still so fond of. The wild spark of mischief was still present in her eyes as she looked back at him with pure affection. This was the way that she had always looked at him, pushing any doubts of how she had felt about him aside. Whoever she was or whatever she had done, Christie's feelings for him had never been a lie. Sam could see it clearer now than he ever had, knowing full well that it hadn't just been their blood that had brought them together, it had been a force much more powerful. Love.

Sam tried to take a moment to observe every aspect of Christie's face, but the image had already begun to disappear. Her beautiful features were soon replaced with those that belonged to another familiar sight, the slightly plainer appearance of a girl who's look of concern was easy to read. "Alice…"

Alice's nose was just a few inches away from Sam's as she leaned in to check on him. "I'm really sorry… I had no idea."

Sam's mind felt numb from exertion. He had fought off someone far stronger than him, with a level of mental discipline that he had never seen before. She had dominated him with ease and it had taken every ounce of his being to resist her. "Who was that? The things she could do..." He couldn't find the words to describe the state that his head had been left in. It felt as though his brain matter had been tossed in a blender before whatever was left was crammed back into his skull.

Alice was so frightened that her pupils were dilated as she spoke. "Katherine. Katherine Louviere..."

The fact that the woman inspired so much dread in those that knew her caused Sam to wonder just who his maker actually was. It couldn't be a coincidence that Alice knew who she was. "And what is she to you? How do you actually know her?"

He awaited her response, studying her closely as she moved back to where she had been sitting at the edge of the mattress. "We share the same blood. She was my mentor and I'm her grandchild, so to speak."

Sam was a little confused, still coming to terms with vampires and how they traced their convoluted bloodlines. "So that means that your maker is her child?"

Alice nodded solemnly. "Yes. It can get a little complicated after that, but that's the basic idea."

Sam scrunched up his face in mock disgust as he tried to lighten the mood. "Does that mean that Matthew and I share the same blood too?"

Alice chuckled wearily. "I'm afraid so, but that's not a bad thing. You're both very special to me."

There was a lot for Sam to think about, but his brain just couldn't process it right away. His body had only just recovered from starvation, but now his mind needed to rest. He smiled lightly at Alice, showing her his appreciation. "I'll really try to get along with him then." He paused a moment, tiredness hitting him once again. "Thanks, Alice."

She returned his smile, her concern still apparent. "You're welcome. I'll let you get some rest. If you need anything, anything at all, we'll be downstairs." Alice reached out to gently pat Sam's leg before standing up and heading towards the doorway. She paused a second to look back at him, a forced smile still upon her face as she made her exit and closed the door carefully behind her.

Sam breathed a sigh of relief. He was thankful for Alice's help in identifying his maker, but he wasn't sure how to process the information that had been forced onto him. He would try to rest if he could, but was sure that sleep would evade him. For now it was just good to be alone. It was a welcome change of pace to just have a few minutes to himself without any pressure of what to do or say. He didn't have anyone that he needed to impress and could just be himself. Sam's mind was his own again. Perhaps tomorrow night he would try to make sense of everything.

CHAPTER TWENTY FIVE: THE CALM BEFORE THE STORM.

"Is it always like that?" Sam queried as he sat across the circular, wooden table from Alice.

She shook her head slowly, resting her hands upon the table's surface as she did her best to answer any questions that he had for her. "No, it's different almost every time. It really depends on the person and how much they open themselves to you."

There was a brief pause as Sam contemplated her response. Matthew had placed himself in the chair next to Alice, quietly studying him with apparent suspicion. The club seemed eerily devoid of life as the other seats were left depressingly empty. The laughter and casual banter of the band members as they joked around with each other was sadly no more, and Sam had almost forgotten about them on more than one occasion. The guys had finally accepted him as part of their group and then they were all gone in an instant. He soon found that he struggled to recall what they even looked like, with only Christie's memory still fresh in his mind. The fact that he could forget them all so easily was deeply saddening and only added to the guilt that he already felt.

Sam's train of thought was interrupted by Alice, who was still trying to piece together a puzzle that she didn't have all the parts for. "Katherine must have wanted to use you to get to me..." So he was nothing but bait to lure her in? Sam felt empty, as if something had been ripped out from inside him when he realised how inconsequential his existence was in the eyes of his maker.

Matthew seemed to be thinking along the same lines too. "She would have given up on that plan when you didn't turn right away. She probably thought she had failed." He leaned forward and rested the elbows of his large arms upon the table before propping his chin upon a closed fist.

Sam still didn't enjoy being the center of attention, but the revelation that all three of them were of the same bloodline had been enough to peak his curiosity. He turned his attention to Alice, his own questions burning holes in his head. "Why did she want you so badly? You're just a country girl from Kansas, aren't you?"

Alice brushed blonde locks behind her ears, trying to keep the strands from falling upon her face. "Remember my overly active imagination as a child?"

Sam nodded once, remembering his youth. It had been a part of his life when he had actually been happy. "How could I forget? It was how we had so many adventures together. It became so real for both of us."

A warm smile crossed Alice's face as she too recalled those days with a certain fondness. However, the expression was soon replaced with the serious look of someone who had been forced to grow up too fast. She wasn't a child anymore. "Well it wasn't just my imagination... I had a gift that allowed me to see things that others couldn't and could also see glimpses of the future." She looked momentarily puzzled as she seemed to examine Sam's features with care. "I helped Katherine track down members of her bloodline using that gift, but for some reason I didn't see you."

Sam admitted that it sounded a little odd, but he had been dead for much longer than she had anticipated. "Maybe whatever link we had was severed somehow?"

Alice inclined her head thoughtfully. "Perhaps. Or maybe it never developed in the first place."

Matthew interjected. "Katherine wanted Alice's power for herself, but she had to settle for controlling her."

"And she did for a time, but her greed and lust for power pulled me to my senses." The face that Alice made was one of regret and Sam could tell that she had done things that she wasn't proud of. They were the type of things that ate away at her on a nightly basis.

However unimportant he was, Sam was glad that he didn't have to carry such a burden. It was funny how fast a gift could turn into a curse. "So that's why she was after you?"

Alice nodded once more. "Exactly. She wanted to turn me herself, but her own child beat her to it. I didn't actually meet Katherine until much later. Just before everything took a turn for the worse..."

It was obvious that there was more to the story, but she wasn't yet ready to share all of the gory details. Sam understood how she felt as he too had difficulty telling his own tale. It didn't matter what had happened along the way or who had done what to get this far, as all of it was mere speculation. Without any solid facts or the word of Katherine herself, there was no way of working out what her plan had actually been. Whatever she had been up to, both her methods and motives were still a complete mystery.

Alice peered over at Sam, her blue eyes full of guilt as she spoke. "I know that I keep saying it, but I really am sorry for everything that you've been through. It wasn't just my actions that caused you pain, but who I am and what others wanted from me too. It was never my intention for you to get hurt."

Sam found it impossible to maintain eye contact with her and looked off to the side as he replied. "It's fine..." It really wasn't, but he didn't want Alice to punish herself for something that had been out of her control. He didn't blame her for anything that had happened, so she shouldn't blame herself either. "I was reckless... and I was going to end up dead either way. At least this way I had another chance."

Shifting awkwardly in his chair, Matthew decided to change the direction of the conversation. "So what do we do about this TJ? I'm prepared to fight if we need to."

"Well you're in luck as there's no other way that this can go." Sam wasn't big on confrontations, but Matthew's whole existence seemed to revolve around fighting, or at least that's how it appeared to an outside observer. He didn't share the same connection with Sam that Alice did, and the only thing they seemed to have in common with each other was a shared lineage. It was as if the pair were polar opposites and Sam struggled to see what Alice saw in the man, but he couldn't be all that bad if she confided in him like she did. Perhaps he just needed to break the ice.

Alice observed in silence as the two of them conversed, her face seeming to lack emotion as Matthew responded. "Okay. What's the plan of action?"

He was definitely the straight to business type, and Sam couldn't help but crack a smile at that. "You're eager, aren't you? I have a few calls to make first. We have an army to put together."

It pleased Sam to see that his words took Matthew by surprise. "What kind of army?"

"Oh, you'll see soon enough." With vampires, hunters and gang bangers, it was more of a band of misfits than an actual army, but Sam disliked the term. He was just glad that he wasn't as predictable as Matthew had likely presumed. He felt a sly grin spread across his face as he looked upon his companions. He wouldn't have been surprised if his eyes had the glint of wild mischief that Christie used to get and he supposed that in some ways she still lived on through him. He was her legacy.

****

Aaron felt increasingly apprehensive as they entered the club through the same back door that they had previously broken in through, but this time it was left unlocked as they were expected. He didn't feel comfortable there in that place, especially due to the fact that Samuel Mitchell had summoned them. Who did he think he was? He didn't have the right to call them up and demand their attendance at some sort of mystery meeting.

"He thinks he can just call for us on a whim? This better be important..." Aaron wouldn't have even considered turning up if Tommy hadn't practically blackmailed him to do so. He couldn't let his friend walk into the lion's den alone, and that's exactly what he had threatened to do. From his point of view it was foolhardy to trust a vampire or any creature of the night at all, but it seemed that he didn't have much choice this time. He would just have to stay alert and be prepared for an ambush. In his experience, backstabbing and betrayal were just some of the key traits of the walking dead.

Tommy stopped just shy of the doorway that led into the main hall and turned to face Aaron, his nose scrunching up as it picked up the stench of something foul. "Oh man, this place fuckin' stinks!" He wasn't joking. Something was indeed off, and he wasn't just talking about the smell of feces and rot. The whole situation stank, not just literally, but figuratively and metaphorically too.

Aaron didn't have the words to describe the level of aggravation that he felt as he pushed past Tommy and slammed open the door. The loud bang caused by wood striking against crumbling plaster drew the attention of the gathering of misfits that were waiting around the circular table at the opposite end of the room. All chattering ceased as the group stopped to stare at the newcomers, some gawking and others eyeing them with distrust. It was a limited attendance of five people in addition to themselves, but not few enough to put Aaron's mind at ease. Was this the army that they had been promised? If it was, it was more than a little underwhelming.

The central figure at the table was an awkward, scarred wretch clad in mismatched clothing. No one else but Samuel Mitchell would look that out of place amongst the rest of the group, his new found confidence not nearly enough to counter his scruffy appearance. He looked as though he had been put through the ringer and was sorely in need of rest. It was hard to believe that he was the same person who had brought this group together, no matter how small it was.

To the far left was a tall, brooding, mercenary type who looked as though he had seen more than his fair share of fighting and could easily carve a swathe through his enemies if he was so inclined. The man's pale skin and dead eyes gave away his true nature, so there was no denying the fact that he was one of the undead. He glared at Aaron, running a hand over a large scar that bordered his buzzed haircut, his mouth upturned in a menacing snarl.

Flanked by Sam Mitchell and the soldier stood a slender, blonde haired woman who was a little too skinny in Aaron's opinion. Although, he couldn't deny that she was still somewhat pretty in her basic, utilitarian clothing, if you liked that sort of thing. He suspected that she was a vampire too, but it wasn't so easy to tell. It would be interesting to see if she would actually be of use in a combat situation as she didn't strike him as the violent type.

A young Cuban man waited at the far right side of the table and Aaron could only describe him as a thug with a goatee. He wore his jeans so low that he was likely trip up if he ever had to run, with a six shooter tucked into the waistband of his boxers where it was only partially hidden by his basketball jersey. It was likely that he couldn't hit a barn door at fifty paces, but he would make good cannon fodder when the time came.

A much older man, who looked as though he appreciated a clean shave, was standing to the thug's immediate left, leaning on a thin, wooden cane for support. It was highly likely that he was the younger man's elderly uncle or even his grandfather as there was a definite familial resemblance. He had made more of an effort than the others, donning a cheap suit and a matching fedora that looked a little worn, as if it had been purchased back in the thirties. From his heavy breathing, it was clear to see that this man was indeed human, but he was in poor health and probably wasn't much longer for the world.

Aaron didn't break his stride as Tommy entered the room behind him, his arrogantly loud voice echoing throughout the building. "Smells like somethin' died in here! Oh wait..."

Continuing to walk with purpose, Aaron quickly closed the gap between him and the rest of the group, stepping over various upturned chairs that were scattered around the disorganised room.

"I love what you've done with the place!" He spoke with sarcasm, the anger in his voice plainly obvious. His eyes scanned the rest of the room, checking for anyone who might be hiding in the wings, but there was no sight nor sound of anyone else being present there.

Sam seemed to shrug off the comments, nodding his head in greeting to the pair as they approached. "I'm glad that you made it."

The bearded thug placed a hand on his weapon, his eyes narrowing into slits as he watched Aaron and Tommy with suspicion. Aaron noted that it was a dangerous move, but having faced off against all manner of supernatural threats throughout his life, a common street thug didn't come close to intimidating him.

The large soldier on the other hand was something else entirely. He glared at the pair of them with obvious anger on his face, his hands balling tightly into fists. "Hunters? Really?!? Do you have any idea how many of my friends have been killed by their kind?" His rage was directed towards Sam Mitchell more than anyone else. It seemed that there was dissent in the ranks already, which wasn't promising if they were all meant to be working together to achieve a common goal.

To Aaron's surprise, Sam didn't back down and stood his ground against the man who overshadowed him. "I know it's not ideal, but they have a personal stake in this too."

Tommy couldn't help but poke fun, placing himself by Aaron's side once they reached the table's edge. "Hah! Stakes! Vampires! Get it?!?" He grinned widely as the soldier and his female companion both scowled. It definitely wasn't the right time for jokes, nor the right audience, but that never mattered to him. "Lighten up, will ya? It's a fuckin' joke!"

Aaron sighed loudly and shook his head with disapproval. "Seriously, man?"

The wide, goofy grin was wiped from Tommy's face when the tall soldier snapped at him and slammed his hands down on the table. "That's enough!" Once again, he addressed Sam and seemed to ignore them altogether. It was as if he didn't want to waste his words on mere mortals. "You put Alice in danger by inviting them here! Now they know our faces!"

Alice? Was this the Alice Delaney that Sergeant Ellis had told them about during their original investigation in Kansas that now seemed so long ago. If she was the girl that had been tormented by the townsfolk of Birchfield, then Aaron felt pity for her. However, whatever her origins, she had since fallen from grace and had become yet another monster in a world much darker than most would ever know.

Before things could escalate further, the girl stepped in and rested her hand on the soldier's forearm as she spoke softly. "Easy there, big guy. I can speak for myself." The man's whole body seemed to relax as he gave in to her soothing tone and took a step back. Whoever she was, she had hidden powers that she used to calm the enraged beast with ease.

Aaron stopped himself from staring at Alice and looked over at the two Cuban men at the other side with curiosity. "Who hired the extra muscle?"

The younger man looked as though he took offense to his tone and was undoubtedly about to come back with an unwitty retort before he was hushed by his elder who spoke for them both in rushed Spanish. Out of everything that he had learned at school, a second language was sadly not something that Aaron had picked up along the way, and so he struggled to understand what the man had said other than the odd word. It was something along the lines of respect, being crazy and possibly even death.

Aaron couldn't help but feel disappointed. When Sam had promised an army, he had expected a number much greater than those who were present and his mind had yet to be changed. "This is all you brought for backup? Frankly, I'm feeling underwhelmed and more than a little insulted."

The soldier tensed up once more, his anger refusing to remain under control for long. "You're just two mortal men with guns! What can you do that we can't?"

It was Sam that jumped into the middle of the conversation this time, clearly agitated by the petty squabbling and continuing disputes. "So it's clear there's no trust between us, but we need to work together to take TJ down or any hope of a plan falls apart! Now you either need to start playing nice with each other, or if you can't do that, you need to stop wasting my time and get the hell out of here!"

The outburst drove everyone to silence. Aaron couldn't believe that the kid had it in him and stayed quiet out of a surprisingly new found respect. If he could get this group to shut up for just a minute, then perhaps he could lead them after all, although Aaron would never admit that out loud.

Sam looked around at those who were gathered and nodded with quiet satisfaction. "Okay, so now everyone's here we can go over the plan. By the end of the night, the only thing left of TJ and his little empire will be ash!"

There were no further objections as he began to go through the motions. Everyone present was given a task to carry out in the upcoming battle, their own piece of the bigger picture. Aaron was actually impressed by the level of preparation and detail that had gone into the plan, making a mental note of the part that he had to play. It likely wouldn't go smoothly, as such plans rarely do, but he was determined not to let the side down. He wouldn't give the deplorable vampires the satisfaction of seeing him fail. Not now. Not ever.

"Is everyone in? Are we ready to do this?" Sam queried with eyes full of hope.

The question was answered by a single nod from the elderly man and a shrug from his younger companion. The soldier on the other hand was the first to verbally reply after making brief eye contact with his female companion who inclined her head towards Sam. "It looks like I'm in, for better or for worse." His rough voice didn't sound so convinced, but it caused the woman to flash a satisfied smile in his direction before responding herself.

"You know I'm in this until the end, Sam. We both are." Alice turned to look at Sam as she spoke, a look that he returned with thankful appreciation.

As soon as she had finished talking, all eyes were on Aaron and Tommy as the group awaited their confirmation. Aaron felt a little resistant and was ready to drag his feet, but his friend spoke up before he could even open his mouth. "I'm not doing this for you, Mitchell. I'm doing this for Christie. Let's kick some ass!"

The swift elbow in the ribs was Tommy's way of letting Aaron know that it was his turn to talk. The long pause that followed was enough to show Aaron's reluctance at working with those that he considered to be no less than evil monsters in their own right. The whole situation went against everything that he believed in, but his friendship with Tommy was far more important to him than his personal tenets. His friend needed closure from the Christie saga, and this was a way for it to finally come to pass. Maybe then they could forget that this ridiculous series of events had ever occurred and they could both move on with their lives.

Aaron sighed as he locked eyes with Sam Mitchell, with feelings of disgust still bubbling away in his mind. "I guess we're in too. Now, are you going to finish sharing your 'master plan' or do we have to beg?" The snarky tone seemed to have no effect on Sam, but Aaron could see that his attitude was irritating the soldier who crossed his long arms in front of his chest. He couldn't help how he sounded, as the past few months had grated on the last of his nerves. It was hard enough to be in the same room as such creatures without taking action, let alone conversing with and working alongside them.

It seemed that Sam had picked up on Aaron's feelings of

intolerance as his burnt face cracked a smile, the scar tissue around his lips twisting wickedly. "Begging really isn't necessary. All I require is your full and undivided attention."

As Sam finalised the outline of his plan and official introductions were made, Aaron couldn't help but make a plan of his own. He was skeptical that he could take down the larger vampire, but maybe him and this so called Huntsman would destroy each other. The girl shouldn't be as much of an issue, and then all that was left was to kill the kid and get the hell out of there. That would be three more vampires out of the picture, another notch on his belt and potentially countless innocents saved. Of course, Tommy wouldn't help him with Sam due to some misplaced loyalty to his dead girlfriend, but he had already said that he wouldn't stand in the way. The night was finally upon them. Samuel Mitchell would meet his end.

CHAPTER TWENTY SIX: A FLAW IN THE PLAN.

The guards at the west entrance of the warehouse hadn't put up much of a struggle and had easily been dispatched by the group without much trouble at all. From there it was a straight shot to the back stairwell and a steady climb up three flights of stairs to the main hall where TJ resided. From the look of it, it seemed that he preferred to rely on manpower instead of technology as there was no automated security or cameras to speak of. The lack of prying eyes didn't stop Sam from feeling anxious however, especially now that his time for vengeance was near.

The stairs themselves were fairly narrow and poorly lit, forcing the group to proceed single file as their footsteps echoed off the concrete surfaces. They slowed their ascent to a crawl in an attempt to reduce the noise, but even the sound of the hunter's breathing and the constant beating of their hearts could easily be picked up by sensitive ears. Fortunately, such sounds couldn't be heard by mortals, which most of TJ's men were.

Sam led from the front, assuming responsibility for the safety of the group by taking point and being the first to enter the building. He clutched a pistol tightly in his hands, unsure if he knew how to use it effectively. Everyone present was there because of him, so he wanted to make sure that he was the first to be in harm's way. He knew that his plan was laughable at best, but he had to keep it relatively simple so that no one would mess up its execution.

Just behind Sam was Matthew, who was surprisingly light on his feet for someone so tall, especially because he was still wearing his big, sturdy combat boots. He had opted not to carry a weapon, instead relying on his bare hands to knock out the guards that had been posted outside, with no assistance required from anyone else. Alice was close by, hidden somewhere just behind him and so quiet that Sam kept forgetting that she was there. She had changed into all black clothing, with leggings and a hooded sweatshirt helping her blend into the darkness. Like her companion, she had also decided to come empty handed, causing him to wonder what other abilities she brought to the table.

The hunters took the rear, despite Tommy's protest at being at 'the ass end' of the line. Whereas Aaron seemed to prefer being back there as he liked to keep an eye on the 'blood sucking fiends' who couldn't be trusted to 'keep their fangs to themselves', a fact that Sam had overheard from their not so subtle conversation outside. The pair of them were dressed as casually as usual and were armed to the teeth with shotguns, machetes and at least one handgun each. They were definitely ready for a fight, which was handy as they were likely in for one soon.

As they reached the top step, Sam came to a halt and the rest of the group fell in behind him. He raised a hand to make sure that the others stayed put as he crept over to the door to press his ear up against it. Listening intently, he could hear muffled voices on the other side. He couldn't be sure, but he guessed that they numbered at least a dozen men. Sam could swear that he could smell them too, but he couldn't pick the specific scents of individuals. They were definitely mortal and he had no desire to hurt them, but if all went to plan he wouldn't have to.

    A set of footsteps casually approached the door and Sam could see shadows moving through the gap at its base. In the corner of his eye he caught sight of Matthew moving into position, ready to strike, but he raised his hand to get the large man to stay put, which he did somewhat reluctantly. Whoever stepped through the doorway would likely alert anyone else within the room to their presence, but Sam couldn't risk the soldier breaking their spine or crushing their skull in the same manner that had almost happened to the other guards outside. From what he had seen, Matthew was so strong that he almost didn't know his own strength and could cause crippling injuries to others in the heat of the moment, whether he intended to or not.

    As the handle began to turn, Sam's body tensed as he stepped back away from the door and towards where the rest of the group still waited at the top of the stairs. Where were the Locos? They were supposed to have caused a distraction by now to draw TJ's goons through the front entrance and into the street, but so far there had been no sight nor sound of them. He felt a lump in his throat as his thoughts were overrun with worry. Perhaps the gang had decided to stand back and see how events played out without their involvement, or maybe they were too scared of the Huntsman to show their faces. Either way, without their help the plan was doomed to fail.

Watching in silence as the door cracked open an inch, Sam knew full well that Matthew would act if he didn't come up with something in the next few seconds. He could feel the eyes of his hunter companions boring holes into the back of his skull as they waited for him to take charge, with Alice still quietly hidden out of sight somewhere close by. He froze on the spot as the door opened further and the toe of a shoe could be seen stepping through. Sam was unsure of whether he should leap at them or try to hide behind the door itself, but he knew that at least one of them would be spotted in the stairwell no matter what. Fortunately for him, a late intervention kept his plan on track.

A massive explosion shook the foundations of the building, sending a shockwave through the concrete pillars and causing tremors to move the ground beneath their feet. The deafening sound echoed up the stairwell and reverberated down the empty halls, making it impossible to determine its point of origin. Chunks of plaster and dust fell from the ceiling as the rumbling continued, but the building somehow remained standing despite the sheer destructive force.

What Sam presumed to be the Loco's over the top distraction had achieved the desired effect, as the door slammed shut behind the man who was likely making his way back towards the explosion's epicenter, somewhere near the front of the building. That hopefully meant that all the rest of TJ's guards would be rushing to defend the main entrance too, leaving the way open for their small group who had been waiting for their cue to enter.

Sam had instinctively covered his ears to protect them from the loud bang, but that didn't stop them from ringing. It took a moment for him to recover before he turned to see the concerned expressions upon the faces of his allies. He could only just make out the words of Tommy who sounded as annoyed as he looked. "Great... Way to alert the cops, douchebags. Trust a bunch of street thugs to go overkill!"

Despite it being his plan of attack, Sam hadn't expected the Locos to start with such a large explosion either, but he now understood how they earned their namesake. There was no point complaining about it though, as it had drawn out TJ's men with a head on assault, and he knew that it was time for them to play their part. "That's our signal!" His own words sounded louder in his head than they likely did to the others, a result of his temporary loss of hearing.

As the ringing in his ears began to die down, Sam heard the usual complaints coming from Matthew who had wanted to run a professional operation, not realising that most of them had no clue at all about military tactics. "Are they trying to bring the building down on us?"

Sam ignored the usual cynicism that spouted from the man's mouth. He refused to dignify the question with a response as he returned to the door and slowly opened it just enough to see inside. The modest sized room beyond was a hangout of sorts, a disorganised home for those who had sworn fealty to TJ and his gang. It was a place for them to kick back and relax, with beaten couches angled to face a large entertainment center complete with oversized speakers, rows of CDs, and a white bed sheet that had been nailed to the wall to act as a screen. The projector still displayed some sort of racing game that had been muted and left on pause, the friendly competition having been rudely interrupted.

As Sam surveyed a table loaded with stacks of cash, drugs and scattered bullets that surrounded guns in various stages of disassembly, he noticed that the chairs around the tables had been overturned as if their occupants had left in a hurry. The open door to the far left of the space was wide open, showing another stairway from which a great deal of commotion could be heard. Voices cried out in panic, with another barking orders as gunshots rang out. The Loco's assault was in full swing and TJ's goons had been caught off guard. They would hopefully be distracted for a while, which would give Sam and his team the time they required to find TJ and deal with him accordingly. The big question that had yet to be answered was the current whereabouts of the Huntsman.

To the far right, past the boarded up windows and stained cots, lay the double doors that led into TJ's inner sanctum. It was a place that Sam had only briefly visited before, but it was a memory that had been permanently seared into his mind. Confident that the coast was clear, he pulled the door open all the way and stepped into the room itself, beckoning for his allies to enter behind him.

The rest of the group filed into the room, with Matthew taking the lead. His eyes darted around the corners as he searched for signs of an ambush, not seeming to trust Sam's conclusion that it was safe for them to enter. Alice followed him in, making her way around the edge of the room as she idly ran her delicate fingers across the smooth concrete surface. She didn't appear to be concerned by any potential dangers at all, a feeling of calm emanating from her like some sort of aura that made even Sam feel a little less apprehensive.

Aaron and Tommy burst in a moment later, their guns trained on each and every shadow that moved. They seemed even more on edge than Matthew, which was likely due to the fact that they were mortal and much more fragile than a vampire who could take a bullet to the chest and keep on moving without too much trouble at all. It was understandable that they would feel that way, as they were deep in enemy territory with a team that they had no love for and with whom they shared very little trust.

Sam edged across the room with caution, his pistol still gripped a little too tightly in his hands. He had set his sights on the double doors that led towards his target, but kept glancing around the room nervously as he made his way towards it. It was as if he expected the very walls to leap out and attack them. "Stay alert! Getting in to the building was the easy part..." He tried his best to sound assertive and full of a false confidence that had slipped away the moment they had entered the premises.

Aaron's lowered voice startled Sam as it came from a closer proximity than he had expected, the hunter having crept up behind him at a much faster pace. "Maybe we got lucky and your 'Huntsman' isn't here."

The booming voice of a hidden assailant caught everyone by surprise and instantly filled Sam with dread as it responded sinisterly. "Luck is not on your side!" It was the familiar, foreign accent of the very man they had only just mentioned. Akoni the Huntsman had found them before they had even laid eyes upon him and it was from that moment that the plan fell apart.

The towering figure of a well dressed man stepped out from the shadows, positioning himself between the group and the door to TJ's sanctum. He adjusted the cufflinks of his shirt as he flashed a grim smile, the whites of his teeth standing out in contrast to his ebony skin. The man's bloodshot eyes were open wide with an intense stare that made Sam feel weak and unprepared. He knew full well that the Huntsman's power was far beyond him, but that was the reason that he had brought along backup.

Matthew strode past Sam and the others, taking his place at the front line as he stood up against Akoni in defiance. Considerably tall himself, his muscular form was still overshadowed by the sheer size of the Huntsman who must have been almost a foot taller. The toughened soldier bravely faced his foe, looking somewhat scruffier in his practical clothing compared to the man who had appeared before them in his finely tailored suit. He was the guardian of TJ's chamber and wasn't about to let anyone past without a fight.

Tommy stifled a bought of nervous laughter. "I expected him to be taller..." Sam was quickly learning that if you could count on him for something, it was his smart-aleck wit and consistent wisecracks.

Matthew seemed unphased by Akoni, despite being dwarfed by his near gargantuan size. "You must be the Huntsman." He said as he cracked his knuckles before raising his fists up in front of him. "I've heard a lot about you."

Sam began to draw from the confidence of his allies to bolster himself as he too spoke up against their adversary. "Are you scared yet?" His bold gaze was returned with a terrifying look from Akoni that felt as though it was overpowering his will. He appeared to have more than just physical might at his disposal, as he crushed Sam's spirit with a single glance that looked through him as if he wasn't even there.

The Huntsman took a step forward, the wicked smile disappearing from his face as it was replaced with the serious look of a man who meant to tear them apart limb from limb. "I do not know fear, but fear knows me." And with those words he set upon them at lightning speed, his motion nothing but a blur.

A gut wrenching blow to the abdomen sent Matthew staggering. He had barely moved an inch before the Huntsman reached Sam, who he sent spiralling across the room and into the wall besides a large speaker that rocked precariously on its stand. Sam's body crashed into the plaster, leaving a crack in its surface before he fell to the floor. After the impact, he found that it was a struggle to pick himself up, instead having to watch in bewilderment as the rest of his team was dispatched all too quickly.

"Surround the son of a..." Tommy's words were cut short as he was tossed into a table at bone shattering speed, the Huntsman continuing to run rings around them with seemingly little effort.

Aaron tried to catch him with a quick blast of his shotgun, but the pellets hit nothing but air. In the blink of an eye, he found himself empty handed, his foe having disarmed him in an instant. Akoni bent the barrel of the weapon with ease before using it to club the shocked looking hunter over the head, causing him to drop like a sack of potatoes. His body sprawled out over the floor and it looked as though he wouldn't be recovering any time soon.

Not wasting a second, the Huntsman turned to face the final member of the group, the blonde haired girl who stood her ground despite the knowledge that she was outmatched by her opponent. He took a moment to adjust his tie, smoothing a crease in the red silk as he grinned at her wickedly. Alice didn't even attempt to move out of the way as the man lunged at her, raising an arm to strike her with his unnatural strength. Fortunately for her, his hand didn't even get close to making contact as his wrist was caught in the powerful grasp of someone who he thought he had already taken down.

"You don't get to touch her!" Matthew's voice was stern and carried the weight of his words with grim determination. He had quickly recovered and had moved to intercept the Huntsman with surprising speed. It seemed that Akoni wasn't the only one in the room with an impressive degree of strength and resilience. Even if the soldier wasn't his equal, perhaps he could keep him distracted long enough for the plan to get back on track.

The Huntsman looked serious for a split second as his hand was suspended in the air by someone of comparable power. His blank stare didn't even acknowledge Matthew standing there as he paused for a brief moment of silent contemplation. Another second later and he flashed a deadly grin, nodding at his new rival with satisfaction. "Finally, a challenge."

Akoni somehow managed to break his hand free of the vice like grip and turned to face Matthew. The pair of them instinctively raised their fists and began to trade vicious blows, duking it out in an impressive display of brawn and aggression that the others were hesitant to interrupt. It was a clash of titans, with only one able to emerge as the victor. The other would surely meet their demise.

****

Aaron awoke to a splitting headache, with the sounds of a nearby scuffle only adding to it. The first thing he laid his eyes on as they opened was the face of his best friend coming into focus as a wooden chair shattered against the concrete wall behind him, a little too close for comfort.

"You okay, man? This isn't a good time to nap." The smirk on

Tommy's face barely concealed his obvious look of concern.

"What... what happened?" Aaron noticed the cuts and red marks on his friend's face that would no doubt swell up and leave behind some impressive bruises.

"You got nailed. We both did..." Tommy cringed a little as he spoke, clearly hiding more than just a few bumps and scrapes. He flinched just a little as another loud crunch signified the destruction of yet more furniture, causing him to quickly glance back over his shoulder. "We're out of our fuckin' league on this one, dude."

Aaron nodded, his neck aching as he sat himself up straight to see the vicious duel that was still raging between the Huntsman and their own powerhouse of an ally. "Maybe, but I'm not giving up."

Tommy shook his head slowly as he forced another brave, but goofy smile. "Did I say I was giving up? Come on, man... You know that's not my style."

Aaron picked himself up and quickly dusted his clothes off as Tommy stood by him, facing out towards the ongoing chaos. The fight was still going strong, with both them and Sam's friend Alice giving the large men a wide berth.

The carnage caused by the battle of the powerhouses was almost immeasurable. An immovable object had met an unstoppable force and the building around them was paying the price, with structural damage that was beyond repair. The walls were dotted with fist sized holes and even the concrete pillars holding up the ceiling were in danger of collapsing, meaning that the threat of the structure coming down upon their heads was very real indeed. The pair seemed oblivious to the extent of the destruction that they had left in their wake, colliding with each other over and over as they moved at speeds so fast they were exhausting to watch.

It was then that Aaron realised that Samuel Mitchell wasn't present within the room and was nowhere to be seen, but it was Tommy who beat him to the punch, voicing his concerns. "Wait... Where the fuck is Mitchell?"

Aaron was tired of letting Sam give him the slip, but he knew exactly where he had gone this time. "I don't see him... He must have snuck inside while we were distracted."

Both of them peered back towards the battle that was still raging, where it finally looked as though the pace was beginning to slow down due to overexertion. It seemed that even these immortal beings could eventually tire, albeit much slower than a human would. Unfortunately, Matthew's strength appeared to be fading a little faster than his opponents and he was showing signs of obvious weakness as he struggled to keep up. He was definitely tenacious, but was becoming increasingly reckless in his wild attempts to strike at his foe. The Huntsman would soon have the upper hand if they didn't do something to even the playing field, which was easier said than done.

Aaron knew what had to be done, but he couldn't risk leaving Sam Mitchell to face TJ alone. They were supposed to be the ones that finished him off, not some stranger that neither of them had ever laid eyes upon. "Tommy, go find the kid. I'll do what I can in here." However resistant he had been to coming along in the first place, he was invested in the outcome of the mission now and had to see it through to the end.

Tommy nodded, patting his hand on his friend's shoulder. "Got it. Don't get yourself killed!"

Aaron couldn't help but smirk, knowing full well that death was always a high risk in their line of work. "Likewise."

Tommy handed over his shotgun and nodded a second time, drawing his pistol as he turned to head in the direction of the doors to TJ's inner sanctum. Aaron took a moment to watch his friend leave before turning his attention back towards the chaos. He could see Alice edging around the room and made brief eye contact with her, a look that was returned with a surprisingly warm smile. Aaron wasn't sure what that meant, but it looked as though she was biding her time for something. Was she waiting for the Huntsman to grow tired before she made her move, or was she avoiding the conflict altogether? He wasn't sure, but he wasn't about to wait and find out.

Checking to make sure that his gun was loaded and ready to fire, Aaron prepared to enter the fray. He would try to keep his distance for as long as possible, taking pot shots at the Huntsman in an attempt to stagger him, or slow him down long enough for Matthew to land some vital hits. He longed for the days of fighting skin stealing slime monsters, confirming the fact that he was out of his depth this time.

Wiping the beads of sweat from his forehead, Aaron raised the barrel of his weapon. He then began to track his target, his finger moving up towards the trigger as he steadied his shaking hands. As he took a large gulp, his mouth felt so dry that it was as though his throat would crack. It was unlikely that his buckshots would have much effect, but if he could distract their gargantuan foe for just a moment then perhaps they could have a sliver of a chance at achieving victory. Perhaps he could survive the night after all, or maybe he would simply anger the beast and bring the man's wrath down upon him.

CHAPTER TWENTY SEVEN: IT ALL CAME CRASHING DOWN.

The lone figure upon the throne remained seated as Sam entered the inner sanctum through the double doors. The room itself was exactly as he remembered, a stage engulfed in darkness, other than the dwindling light of the burning twin braziers that were slowly dying out.

"Big man come to take my throne!" The tone in TJ's voice was that of annoyance as he glared at Sam with wide eyes, his hands gripping the arms of his chair.

Sam strode further into the room before stopping a few feet from the skulls that lined the raised platform. He scowled at the self proclaimed lord who refused to stand in his presence, his own words shooting from between his lips like venom. "No! I've come to burn it to the ground!"

TJ leaned forwards, his massive fur coat shifting as if it was part of him. He raised his voice in anger, spittle flying from his mouth and landing on the floor between them. "Who are you to challenge my power?"

Sam maintained eye contact, provoking the man at every

opportunity. "Me? I'm no-one. You made sure of that the day you took everything away from me." He paused a moment to let his words settle in as TJ studied him with calculating silence. "That was a mistake on your part, as now I have nothing else to lose..."

Appearing to be increasingly aggravated by Sam's insolence, TJ stood from up from his throne and shed his coat, letting it fall in a pile on the floor around his feet. A tapestry of scars and unusual tattoos marked the man's skinny torso and arms, with runes and unidentifiable symbols covering the majority of his skin's surface. The meaning behind the markings were obscured in mystery and Sam didn't let himself linger on them long enough to make any new discoveries.

Sam hadn't noticed it before, but TJ had hidden a long revolver under his baggy sleeves, only now displaying it as he felt threatened by the intruder within his domain. He brandished it wildly, waving the weapon in the air as he aggressively pointed it in Sam's general direction. The custom barrel of the six shooter was far too long to be practical, only serving as a method of intimidation instead of having any real use. The gun would surely be unwieldy and difficult to aim, likely requiring two hands to steady it in a manner that didn't quite suit the man's style of casual violence.

"All bark, no bite. You have no guts, boy." TJ cackled, still waving the gun around as if it was a toy instead of an instrument of death.

Sam ignored the loaded weapon and began his slow walk toward the stage, biding his time as he savoured the moment. It didn't take TJ long to pull the trigger, the first bullet missing by mere inches as it ricocheted off the wall behind him. Sam wasn't so lucky when the revolver went off again, the hot lead leaving a thumb sized hole through his left shoulder. The man upon the stage didn't have the decency to lay off for a second and wouldn't give him a break as a third bullet imbedded itself in his chest, causing him to stagger backwards as he tried to regain his balance.

The agony caused by the bullet wounds was immeasurable, but it was still nothing compared to the pain that Sam had experienced in recent nights. It didn't take long for him to regain his composure, continuing the push towards the stage once more with teeth gritted and fists balled up with all the bravado that he could muster. His tenacity caused TJ's face to twist with horror as the gap between them continued to close.

A fourth bullet struck Sam in the chest again, burying itself inside one of his dead lungs. It hurt a little less this time, his mind overcoming any physical limitations with sheer willpower alone. Where a mortal would have fallen, the Forsaken continued to drive himself forwards through the pain barrier, pressing on towards a final confrontation with the man who had occupied his thoughts for far too long.

A fifth shot grazed Sam's cheek as TJ struggled to hold the weight of the revolver out in front of him, with the sixth and final bullet hitting the ground between his feet. The lack of ammunition didn't deter the man as he continued to pull the trigger over and over, the gun making a metallic clicking sound as his panic overrode rational thought and prevented him from coming to the realisation that it was in fact empty.

Sam used TJ's bout of temporary insanity to his advantage and leapt over the row of skulls that lined the platform's edge. After weeks of planning and biding his time, Christie's murderer was finally within his grasp and he couldn't wait any longer. He lunged towards his foe with arms outstretched, but instead of wrapping his fingers around the skinny man's throat, his hands collided with an invisible wall that sent white hot fire through his veins.

TJ's look of terror faded and a sly grin crossed his face. It seemed that his fear had all been a ruse, as Sam found that the barrier was impassable. His hands struck against solid air over and over as it continued to wrack his body with a pain that was impossible to ignore.

"Did you think it would be that easy? Not so observant are you, big man." TJ gestured down towards a strange circle upon the ground that surrounded Sam on all sides. The shape was formed by a complicated arrangement of runes and symbols that were written in red, the scent of which smelled like dried blood. It wasn't human blood however, as the aroma was a lot less potent and much less appetising. Was this the magic that TJ supposedly dabbled in? Sam knew that the man had a few tricks up his sleeve, as Christie had told him as much, but he had never expected to be trapped within a kind of warding such as this.

"I knew you would come." TJ continued, the smug look on his face only serving to infuriate Sam further. "Did you forget that I have eyes everywhere? You are mine!"

Sam was trapped like an animal in a cage, with no idea of how to escape from this new predicament. He had foolishly stormed into the sanctum without thinking about potential hazards and was now paying the price for his arrogance. "I'll never be yours to control!" He spat out his words, his arms still burning from his desperate attempts at breaking free of his bonds. "You may as well kill me!"

TJ began a slow walk around the runed trap, circling Sam like a hungry shark as he bared his teeth. "Do not tempt me... Ending your miserable existence had already crossed my mind, but I still have use for a vampire that can walk under the sun."

A feeling of hopelessness set in. One that Sam hadn't felt to this extreme degree since the day he had watched Christie die. He had no knowledge of the mystic arts or how to break such enchantments, and the more he struggled, the more the barrier resisted with intense pain that hurt him far more than a simple bullet to the chest.

Both of them were caught up in the finality of the moment, and neither Sam nor TJ had heard the door open at the far end of the room as someone else slipped inside. In fact, Tommy's presence had gone completely unnoticed until his handgun blew a hole in the wooden boards that made up the stage, leaving a large gap where some of the runes had once been. Sam wasn't sure if the act had been carried out due to actual knowledge of the arcane or if the hunter had simply taken an educated guess, but he instantly felt a great weight lift from him as his invisible prison was destroyed. The energy from it dissipated in a shockwave that almost snuffed out the brazier's flames.

"Don't just stand there, you fuckin' moron!" Tommy yelled offensively from the shadows just out of reach of the brazier's flickering light. "Let's finish this douchebag!"

Sam didn't hesitate for another second as he dashed towards the stunned gangster who had already lost the smug look from his face. If he had any other tricks up his sleeve, he better use them soon as there wasn't going to be anymore holding back. Sam was about to unleash the beast that he had kept locked up inside of himself for so long and he was sure that there was no going back after that.

****

Aaron checked his clip, having already discarded Tommy's shotgun after running out of shells. The amount of ammo he had expended made it hard to believe that anyone could still be standing, yet the Huntsman had barely lost momentum and Matthew was still clearly losing ground to the gargantuan man who had gotten the upper hand some time ago.

Nothing seemed to hurt Akoni at all. Not the sledgehammer blows of Matthew's fists, nor point blank shots from the business end of a firearm. Aaron had considered trying his machete, but their adversary moved far too quickly to make a decent strike, and his wounds seemed to heal almost instantaneously anyway. The well dressed man was nigh invulnerable and could apparently withstand any punishment that was thrown at him.

Despite his obvious shortcomings, Matthew still tried his best to go toe to toe with his opponent, continuing to trade blows as his body was gradually beaten to a pulp. It was impressive that he had lasted so long, but from the look of him he didn't have much fight left in him. He was battered, broken and bruised, and yet he still continued to swing at the Huntsman with all his remaining might. Unfortunately for him, it seemed that physical force was completely ineffective against the man whose suit was now in tatters.

As for Alice, she had tried to intervene, but as fast as she was, the Huntsman was faster. Aaron had begun to wonder why they had even brought her along as she hadn't contributed much to the fight. She mostly waited at the edge of the room in between her weak attempts at assisting her large companion. He couldn't work out if she was actually waiting for a specific moment or if she was completely useless in a combat situation.

Matthew took another blow to the face and then another, with the Huntsman moving his head to dodge Aaron's bullet with an ease that was sadly no longer surprising. He fired again, trying to distract the man long enough to buy a few seconds for Matthew to break free, but once again he hit nothing but air. Aaron began to realise that he felt as useless as he believed Alice to be, but that didn't mean that he would give up the fight. He never gave up.

The Huntsman continued to pummel Matthew's skull as if it were a punching bag and showed no sign of relenting as he held his opponent in place with his other large hand. Once again, Alice rushed in to help but was swatted away like a pesky fly, her small frame ceasing momentum as it struck one of the crumbling pillars. Aaron went to fire his pistol, but the resulting click let him know that his clip had been emptied. It was too late for him to assist anyway, as Matthew was lifted into the air and his broken body was tossed through the boards of a nearby window and into the street far below.

"Matty!" Alice gasped, rushing over to the shattered window to peer down at whatever was left of her friend.

The Huntsman took the opportunity to dust off his torn suit jacket and adjust his shirt collar, taking his time as if his victory was assured and the battle was already over. Aaron knew that he didn't stand a chance against the giant, but he wasn't about to surrender. Whatever he chose to do, it seemed that his death was assured and he would rather die on his feet than on his knees begging for his miserable life. He unsheathed his machete from when it hung at his waist, knowing full well that it was his only option left despite the fact that he probably wouldn't be able to land a single blow.

It wasn't clear if Akoni had noticed the blade in Aaron's hand, as he paid it no heed and stared straight ahead with a deadpan look that held no hatred or malice. "You cannot hope to defeat me, for I am death incarnate."

It was now or never as Aaron began to charge, lifting his weapon in a desperate attempt to swing at his enemy. Perhaps he would get a lucky hit, but then what? He wouldn't get a second chance to cause any damage as the Huntsman wouldn't let him. His doubts clouded his mind, but he did his best to push them aside as he focused on the moment at hand.

Aaron didn't see what happened next, but he must have been stunned by a severe blow, as when he came to his senses he found his sore body slumped against the cracked plaster of the far wall with his machete lying a few feet away from him. As he looked up into the room he saw Akoni still standing, but his focus wasn't on him, it was on the smaller, skinnier form of the blonde haired girl who stood up to him as if she was his equal in both size and strength. The pair faced each other across the open space in a standoff that left Aaron feeling baffled. He couldn't believe that she had the guts to face a man who could crush her in an instant as if she were nothing.

Aaron watched as the Huntsman began to stride towards Alice with certainty, yet she still didn't back down. She didn't move a muscle as his massive form approached her like the unstoppable juggernaut that he was. Akoni wouldn't even make eye contact with her as his steady pace stopped just shy of where she waited. The girl's will remained unbroken as she craned her neck to look up at a man who had declared himself to be death itself.

No words were exchanged between them as Akoni widened his bloodshot eyes and curled his mouth into a sneer. Alice on the other hand looked saddened, as if something truly upsetting had happened or was just about to happen. Her own eyes were full of regret, for a reason that Aaron had not yet been made aware of. She looked so small and fragile next to the Huntsman, who was a mountain of a man in comparison.

Raising a massive hand into the air, the giant of a man prepared to strike her with a powerful backhand that could shattered her bones like ice, but Alice didn't try to move out of the way. Instead she raised a hand to lightly touch the man's face, an act that had resulted in an outcome that neither Aaron, nor Akoni could have predicted as he suddenly dropped to his knees.

Oddly, Alice towered over the Huntsman now as he cowered by her feet, both hands now resting upon either side of his face. His mouth silently pleaded with her as his expression of abject horror displayed only part of his inner turmoil. He appeared weak and pathetic as his body quivered while he was emotionally drained by her slightest touch. From the look of it, she too was feeling the effects of whatever she was doing to him, as her mental strain was clear and easy to read. Who was this girl that she could take down a man so much bigger than her with ease? And why did Aaron get the feeling that she was holding back the full extent of her true power?

Aaron felt his stomach churn as Alice turned her head to look at him, her face a disturbing image of blood rolling over her porcelain cheeks. Red tears streamed from the corners of her hauntingly blue eyes in an unnatural sight that sent chills down his spine and made it hard for him to breathe. Her thin lips called out to him as he recoiled with a fear that overwhelmed his senses. "Finish it... Now..." She looked back at the debilitated form of the Huntsman who was no longer intimidating in his pitifully helpless state.

Aaron felt his own strength return as Alice turned away from him, his mind regaining control over his body as he scrambled for his machete. He plucked it from the floor, grasping the leather binding of the handle tightly as he picked himself up and made his way over to them with unsteady legs. Turning his wrist to adjust his hold on the blade, the light reflected along its polished finish. In that moment, the weapon became an extension of his will and all he wanted was for the chaos to end.

As Aaron approached the wretched form of Akoni the Huntsman, the man still didn't seem to acknowledge his presence. He was a broken creature who begged to be released from his torment, his twisted expression praying for it all to end. Whatever Alice had done to his mind, he was but a shadow of his former self. It seemed that the hulking man had picked a fight with the wrong vampire and had finally paid the price for his transgressions.

Aaron couldn't bear to see anyone this way, even a monster such as the Huntsman. He believed that even evil beings such as this should be shown some form of compassion and should be killed as humanely as possible. Akoni's misery had to be ended, and so he placed the edge of his sharpened blade against the base of the man's neck and took a mighty swing. If he was lucky it would be a quick and a clean death. If not, it would be an unpleasant experience for everyone involved, and one that wasn't wise to dwell on.

****

"The throne is yours. You can have it... All of it. Just spare my life..." TJ whimpered between strained breaths.

Almost snarling in anger, Sam looked down at the skinny, tattooed man who grovelled before him and his fury quickly faded. The blood that leaked from his open wounds had no trace of the supernatural in its scent, meaning that TJ was mortal through and through. He wasn't anywhere near as powerful as he pretended to be and was just a regular human being who had learned a ritual or two. Sam still hated the man for what he had taken from him, but killing him now would only turn him into a monster. In his rage he had beaten TJ within an inch of his life and the thought of that sickened him.

"End it, Mitchell. What the hell are you waiting for?" Tommy stood close by, his hatred emanating from him in waves. He had kept his distance as Sam let his bestial side take over, only coming close once he deemed it safe enough to do so. It seemed that the raw savagery on display was enough to keep even a hardened hunter at bay.

"I can't..." Sam said as the last of his anger left him. "I'm not a killer."

The tone in Tommy's response was that of surprise. "What? You're a goddamn bloodsucker! You're meant to kill... It should be easy for you!"

Sam glanced over at the hunter who was looking more than a little confused, as if the very nature of his existence had been challenged. He frowned at him, disappointed that anyone could presume to know who he was based off so little information. "Well it isn't easy and I won't do it."

The trembling lump on the floor that was TJ reached out to touch Sam's leg, a gesture that caused Sam to take a step backwards as Tommy studied his reaction with peaked curiosity. "You're a strange one, Mitchell. I can't figure you out."

Sam wanted to smile at that statement, but found that he couldn't as he looked down at the man by his feet and felt pity for him as if he were a homeless beggar in the street. "That's one way of putting it..."

There was a brief silence, with only the sound of crackling fire and pained whimpering echoing throughout the dark room. Tommy seemed to ponder for a minute or so before speaking up again, his words honest and true. "Take your friends and get outta here before Aaron comes lookin' for you."

Sam turned to look the hunter in the eye, feeling sceptical at first until he could see how genuinely sincere he was. Tommy continued. "I'll deal with this asshole. You really don't want to see what happens next, as it's gonna get ugly..." He gently patted the handle of the machete that hung from his belt, turning his attention back to TJ who was still a mess.

Tommy was right. Sam didn't want to see what happened next, nor did he linger there long enough to think about the hunter's exact meaning. He turned to leave, with TJ's pleading only growing louder as he hopped down from the platform and made his way to the exit.

Before he could reach the door, Tommy had some final words of warning. "Oh, and Mitchell?" Sam stopped for a second, but didn't dare turn to look back. He couldn't look at TJ's face without feeling guilty for leaving him to this dreadful fate. "If I ever see you again, I'll fuckin' kill you."

There was no response required as Sam knew that Tommy meant everything he said. He instead pushed open the door and squeezed his way through into the room beyond. Somewhere behind him in the darkness, a blood curdling scream was soon silenced by a wet hacking sound that echoed out as metal met flesh and bone in a gruesome display that wasn't meant for the faint hearted. The deed had been done and it was all finally over. Sam's vengeance had come, but at what cost?

CHAPTER TWENTY EIGHT: LIFE AFTER THE FALL.

The battle between the Locos and TJ's crew had taken the news by storm as the fighting spilled out from the building and into the streets. Without TJ to lead or the Huntsman to back them up, the Loco's sheer number dominated the fight, leaving little remaining of the rival gang that had given them so much trouble for so long. With their bloody victory achieved, Sam's promise to their leader had been upheld and his debt to them was paid. The gang quickly reclaimed TJ's territory as their own, allowing them to increase their control over the city streets. Even though the change over was noticed by those living within the local area, the exchange of power was barely noticed by the rest of Miami's population as a whole.

In the aftermath, the police had little choice but to crack down on gang violence, funneling their budget into task forces that were specifically equipped to deal with the rise of organised crime. Fortunately for Sam and his band of misfits, no trace was found of their involvement, or at least nothing concrete enough to incriminate anyone. The images of TJ's dismembered body were deemed too graphic to be released to the public and were kept under wraps as part of the ongoing investigation, with a couple of the Locos marked as chief suspects.

The story of the brutal fight was dwarfed by news from Canada that still dominated the airwaves after a couple of weeks. Massive explosions and a possible terrorist attack had shaken Calgary to its core, with chaos running rampant in the streets. It had taken a great deal of resources to stabilise the situation and bring some form of order back to the once peaceful city. Clean up crews had already spent days sifting through the rubble as they worked hard to pick up the pieces and yet no one seemed to take credit for the attack. Not one person would have guessed that it hadn't been a terrorist plot at all and that it was just another chapter in the vampire hierarchy's age old war for control.

****

It wasn't a common occurrence for Tommy to let Aaron drive the truck as it was his baby, but this was one of those rare exceptions. The pair were heading north along the highway, braving the usual traffic as they finally left Miami in the rear view mirror. Even with the visor down, the sun was still causing Aaron to squint as it reflected off the hood and directly into his eyes. The windows were open, but the hot air coming in from outside defeated the point of having them open in the first place and sweat stained shirts had already become commonplace.

Aaron couldn't wait to leave Florida and its humidity behind, and he knew that Tommy felt the same way. The past few months had brought nothing but misery, causing him to doubt his principles and his level of integrity. At times his friendship with Tommy had been placed on the line and thoroughly tested as their differing opinions had left them at odds. Despite the feeling of betrayal that had come from his friend letting Samuel Mitchell get away, Aaron had forgiven him due to the fact that he had been going through a tough period in his life.

Aaron glanced over at Tommy who was beginning to snore in the passenger seat, his chair fully reclined as he had tried to make himself as comfortable as possible in the limited space. He couldn't bring himself to lose faith in someone who had stood by him through thick and thin, but he also couldn't quite fathom what had gone through his friend's mind as Sam managed to escape unhindered. However annoyed he had been when it happened, trust and loyalty were a rare commodity in their line of work, and Tommy had earned his several times over. The loudmouthed goofball was his blood brother and his closest friend, and he couldn't see that changing at any time in the future even though they had almost come to blows on more than one occasion.

Although his quarry had managed to evade his grasp, Aaron was sure that it wasn't the last he had seen of Samuel Mitchell. He was bound to slip up sooner or later, leaving a trail that would lead them right to him. Tommy had promised that he no longer owed the kid anything and his debt to Christie had been paid in kind. He had sufficiently honoured her memory and claimed that he would kill Sam if he ever laid eyes upon him again. The way he had stated it meant that Aaron was inclined to believe him, as his tone had lacked his usual level of gusto and humour. He still didn't understand why his friend had made the decision to let such a dangerous monster go and probably never would, but he was glad that their relationship was no longer stuck in limbo.

"Where we headin' next?" Tommy's mumbled words let Aaron know that he was actually awake despite outward appearances and the fact that his eyes were still closed.

Aaron kept his own eyes on the road, managing to stay calm even when he was cut off by a midlife crisis driving his brand new sports car. "Pennsylvania. There's been a series of unusual murders that have left the locals stumped."

Pulling himself upright, Tommy raised the back of his chair before adjusting his posture to lean against the door. He used his elbow for support, sandwiching his hand between his head and the truck's interior. "Unusual how? Don't you dare say bite marks... I'll fuckin' freak!"

Flashing a smile, Aaron kept both hands on the wheel as he indicated to change lanes. "No. They drowned. Their lungs were full to bursting, but they weren't found anywhere near water and their clothes were bone dry."

"A witch?" He caught Tommy glancing over at him with curiosity.

Aaron shrugged his shoulders. "Maybe. That's what we're

going to find out."

Tommy closed his eyes again, shifting his positioning a little as he tried to relax again. "Sweet. Wake me when it's my turn to drive."

Before he could let his friend return to his well deserved rest, Aaron had to ask the question that had been eating away at him all morning. "Tommy... Are you doing okay?"

His words caused Tommy to open one eye and peer over inquisitively. "Yeah, I'm fuckin' peachy. Why?"

It was difficult to find a way to phrase the sentence without instigating another argument, but Aaron needed to know what was going on in his friend's head. "You killed a guy, Tommy. TJ was human, not a monster... and you butchered him."

Tommy sat up straight again and craned his neck to look directly at Aaron, frowning slightly. "Yeah, he was human, but I don't regret a damn thing. The things he did to people... to Christie... He was still a fuckin' monster. You don't need to be undead or have powers for that."

It was a jarring response that came as more than a bit of a surprise. They were hunters, not officers of the law. Hunters were supposed to protect humankind from the beasts that stalked them, not kill the people that they were supposed to protect. They didn't have the right to decide the fate of humans, never mind become their judge, jury and executioner. If Tommy could commit murder without remorse, then perhaps he was capable of becoming what he had so despised in TJ.

Aaron cleared his throat. He could feel Tommy's eyes upon him, but he didn't know what else to say. Perhaps his friend would come to think differently given time. Unfortunately, the way Christie died would likely act as some sort of morbid justification for his actions, which meant that he was unlikely to change his mind on the matter.

Whatever happened, Aaron would do his best to support his friend and keep him out of as much trouble as possible. He was still concerned about Tommy, but there wasn't much he could do other than keep an eye on him and be there for his friend if and when he needed it. No doubt his feelings would be buried deep down as he lost himself in his work in true Tommy Hughes fashion. There was always the possibility of his emotions building up inside him until he snapped, which was something that Aaron would have to deal with when the time came. Until then, there was no telling what the future held.

Instead of continuing the conversation, Aaron decided to change the subject altogether, not daring to hear what else his friend had to say on the matter. "...Are you hungry?"

The serious look on Tommy's face was replaced by his usual cheeky grin. "Does a bear shit in the woods?"

Aaron sighed loudly, rolling his eyes in a manner that was all too common. "Let's grab some food then."

"Hell yeah! Fried breakfast?" Tommy sat up straight and drummed his hands on the dashboard with renewed enthusiasm.

A single nod from Aaron sealed the deal as he looked back

out at the lanes of back to back cars stopped ahead and slowed the car to a halt. "Sure. I think I saw a sign for a diner at the next exit. If we ever make it there…"

As Tommy began to sing loudly about his favourite breakfast foods, Aaron did his best to hold back a chuckle. His friend's ability to pick himself up following a serious discussion, or after such a trying series of events, never ceased to amaze. Pennsylvania could wait another hour until the morning rush was over, and hunting on an empty stomach was never a good idea anyway. Once they had eaten their fill and traffic was moving again, they would continue the long drive north and do what they do best, hunt and kill the beasts that preyed upon the innocent. After all, it was their calling in life. It was what they were always meant to do.

****

"What started as a typical night of gang violence quickly turned into bloodshed and mayhem as an explosion rocked the Miami industrial district in the early hours. Several civilians were caught in the crossfire and at least a dozen people are reported to be dead, with yet more being rushed to the local hospital in critical condition. A number of arrests have since been made, but the police are yet to discover what triggered last night's events."

Sam felt sick. It had never even crossed his mind that anyone other than TJ and the Huntsman would be dead once the dust had settled, and he was disgusted that he could have been that negligent. Had he already lost so much of his humanity that he had become a monster? The road to his revenge hadn't ended his misery, it had only led to more pain and suffering, and for what reason? Nothing had changed and Christie was still dead.

The news report continued to blare, but Sam couldn't pay attention to it any longer, instead getting lost in the guilt that welled up inside him. It didn't help that the volume on the television seemed to be stuck on high, with the sound close to deafening as it filled the small area of the waiting room with maddening noise.

Having grown tired of standing around outside as he waited for the others to get back, Sam had made his way into the gloomy room with the aim of making himself as comfortable as physically possible on the plastic formed chairs that made up the rows of cheap seating. However, he soon regretted his decision after his senses were assaulted by the stench of urine and the poor quality, static ridden sound of the old television that sat in its cage in the far corner of the room.

Sam could no longer stomach the images of the atrocities, knowing full well that they had been committed in the aftermath of events that he had put into motion. He had to get out of there and get some air, despite the fact that he didn't actually need it. Rushing towards the exit, he pushed his way out into the night and doubled over a few steps later, resting his hands on his knees as the door slammed shut behind him. The safety glass rattled in the frame, coming dangerously close to shattering as the wire barely held it in place.

Sam wanted to breathe. He felt as though he needed to, but it was all in his head. It felt as though he was suffocating, as impossible as that was. For the first time since he clawed his way up from the earth, he missed being able to fill his lungs with air and had almost forgotten what it felt like. Even though he was out in the open, he felt a sense of claustrophobia kicking in. There wasn't enough space left in the world as the ground seemed to fold in around him in a deadly embrace. However, the difference this time was that Sam had dug the hole himself and there was no hope of getting out unscathed.

"Sam? Is everything okay?" It was Alice. He couldn't see her yet as his vision was spotty from his onset panic attack, but he could recognise that voice anywhere.

A hand lightly touched Sam on his shoulder and everything suddenly stopped closing in on him. He felt calmer somehow as his senses returned, the warm breeze and ever present sounds of traffic letting him know that he was out in the open and he had space to move around if he needed. As he opened his eyes, he looked over his shoulder at the concerned, yet welcoming expression of his oldest and dearest friend. When Sam's eyes met the pale blue of Alice's he felt calmer still, but he also felt the need to open up to her. It seemed like as good a time as any for confessing his guilt over everything that had happened the night before.

"How could I have been so stupid? Innocent people were hurt! I didn't consider the consequences of my actions and people died because of my lack of responsibility." Sam paused a moment, his mind beginning to race once more, his thoughts swirling like a tornado inside his head. "The hunters were right, I'm a monster and I should be treated like one..."

Alice helped Sam stand up straight and gently turned him to face her, resting a hand on each of his shoulders as she maintained eye contact. "You're not a monster, Sam, you didn't mean for it to happen. The important thing is that you realise that you made a mistake and..."

Sam exploded, raising his voice as he almost yelled in frustration. "And what?!? I can't change what I've already done!"

Despite him lashing out, Alice still spoke in a calm and collected manner. The concern on her face surrounded her ever pleasant smile as she attempted to sooth his anger. "Exactly, but you can still strive to make yourself a better person and try to prevent any disasters such as this from occurring ever again." She waited a few seconds to let her wisdom sink in before continuing. "Think about what Christie would want you to do. Do you think that she would want you to give up on yourself after everything you've been through?"

Sam couldn't help but think about Christie's face as she burned under the light of day. It was difficult for him to see her any other way, as he could still picture it as clearly in his mind as the moment it happened. "No... She wouldn't want that at all. I just don't know how to go on as I am. Not without her." Without Christie Reece by his side, Sam felt as though he was completely useless. He no longer felt like he had a purpose in life, or any goals to fulfill. Once again he found himself feeling lost and alone.

Alice could clearly see Sam's thoughts trailing off as she moved her head to the side to stay within his field of view. "Then let us help you." She emphasised her words, trying her best to let him know that he wasn't on his own and that there were still those who cared for his well being.

Sam appreciated the sentiment, but he couldn't change his perception of reality so easily. "I'll try..."

An awkward and lingering silence followed as Alice stared at Sam, as if she was waiting for him to say something more. It took a few long moments before he could think of anything to talk about, deciding to change the subject entirely as it hurt too much to keep thinking about his lost love. "I'm a big brother now, Alice." Sam managed a smile as he spoke with mixed feelings of pride and sorrow. "I went to see my parents and they have a baby girl. I only saw her through a window for just a second, but she was so perfect."

Alice's smile widened from one of sympathy to that of joy. "That's amazing news! I'm really happy for them and for you." The odd thing was she didn't sound surprised by the news at all. It was as if she had already known about his sibling, but that couldn't have been possible unless she had been keeping tabs on them somehow.

Sam thought nothing of his friend's peculiar reaction and proceeded to further describe his feelings on the situation. "I know it's great for them, but I can never meet her or see my mom and dad ever again. I can't control this hunger enough to be around them...

It's just too dangerous."

Seeming to understand Sam's pain all too well, Alice let go of his shoulders and carefully took him by the hand. "We can help you deal with that too. It just takes time, but you'll get better at controlling your instincts." A gentle squeeze from delicate fingers was her way of letting him know that she was there for him. Sam knew that she would help him in any way that she could, but the thought didn't make him feel any less alone. He could be surrounded by dozens of friends and loved ones and still be the outcast among them, as his social anxiety seemed to have only gotten worse.

Sam snapped himself out of his self pitying stupor and took a few moments to look around the immediate area. The surrounding bus depot was completely empty of commuters and would be for at least another hour or so. It was unevenly lit by bright fluorescent lighting that attracted almost as many flies as the bags of trash that had been left lying around in piles, waiting to be collected.

It seemed that Sam and Alice were the only people present, which made him wonder what had happened to the third member of their group. "Where did the big guy go?"

Releasing Sam's hand from her grasp, Alice glanced down the street towards the busy main road that was still bustling with traffic even at that ungodly hour. "Matty went to get his motorcycle and to secure some more transport for us."

"Is he going to be alright? He looked a little rough earlier." The last time Sam had seen him, the soldier had been battered and bruised beyond recognition, and left in a state that would have put any human in the hospital or left them for dead.

Alice moved her attention back to Sam and gave him a thankful nod to acknowledge his interest in her companion's health. "Don't worry, he'll be fine. He's been through worse." Worse than the beating he received at the hands of the Huntsman? That was almost impossible to believe, but he knew that she wasn't lying.

Sam tilted his head to one side, raising his eyebrows inquisitively. "Are you sure you want me to come with you guys?" He still wondered whether he should try to find his own path instead of following someone else's, but he also wasn't sure if he could walk it without a guide.

"Of course I am. I wouldn't have it any other way." Alice's invitation was welcome, but Sam was still torn as to whether he should go with them or not. The easiest route through life wasn't always the wisest one to take.

"I don't think he does though. He doesn't seem to like me much." Sam couldn't help but doubt each and every decision he made after seeing what damage a single poor choice could do.

Alice quirked an eyebrow, studying Sam's face as she tried to work out what was going through his head. "Matty? He has trouble trusting people, but he'll come around."

Sam was convinced that it was something more than that, as his own experiences seemed to show that the man resented other people getting close to Alice or having any sort of relationship with her. "But I'll just slow you down. I really don't want to be a burden to either of you." He stubbornly continued to try and talk his way out of travelling with companions, with no real reason as to why he thought he should be alone.

Placing her hands on her hips, Alice glared at him with determination burning in her eyes. "Really, Sam? You won't be. I'm not leaving you behind this time!" There was more force behind her words now as she drove her point home. She clearly didn't want Sam to be alone and somehow knew that he didn't want to be on his own either, not really.

Sam had quickly found that there was no bargaining with Alice when she was trying to do something for his own good and he didn't have much argument left in him anyway. It wasn't as if he had anywhere to go by himself. He had nothing driving him anymore, so he may as well play the part of the third wheel. She had managed to convince him that he needed friends around him right now and it was true that there was no one better to act as his guide through the endless nights than her. At least no one who wasn't already dead or lying in a pile of ash.

Despite Alice's constant reassurance, Sam couldn't help but worry about almost everything and from the way she acted around him, it was obvious that she sensed his unease. Stepping forwards to wrap her cold arms around him, Alice gave Sam a friendly squeeze that made him feel surprisingly safe and secure. "And I thought I was the one that worried too much... Times really have changed haven't they?"

Sam gave in to her embrace, returning Alice's affection with a hug of his own. "You can say that again…"

Alice was right, the times had indeed changed and that had led to Sam questioning his own existence. Something had clearly gone wrong when he had been turned, but the reasons for that failure were still a mystery to him. He knew what he had been labelled as Forsaken, but he had no real idea of what that meant other than being physically weaker than your average vampire, lacking the implements that he needed to feed and having the ability to walk in daylight at least for a while. It was true that Sam wasn't the same person that he had been before his rebirth, but as to what he had become since then, he still had no clue.

Alice pulled away, ending the hug prematurely as she took a couple of steps back. Sam would have thought nothing of it if it wasn't for the look of woe that hardened her features. "I had a dream the other day... A glimpse of the future, some might say. There's a great darkness on the horizon and it's coming our way."

"Is it worse than what we've already been through?" Sam frowned, lowering his hands back down by his sides as he watched her with curiosity.

Alice gave a single, solemn nod. "Much worse..."

Sam could feel himself tensing up again as his own insecurities pushed their way back to the surface. "Let me guess... It has something to do with Katherine Louviere."

Alice began to sway a little, her feet still firmly planted on the ground as her body moved from side to side. "I don't know for sure, but yes I believe so."

Crossing his arms in front of his chest, Sam could already feel that he wasn't going to like what he heard. "Tell me what you saw..." He braced himself for bad news as Alice started to recount what she had seen. She began to pace as she spoke, no longer making eye contact with him while she concentrated on recalling the most important details of the dream.

"I saw a spider in its web, engorging itself on a feast of flies as her offspring watched and starved to death. Beneath it, a wasp was caught in a trap amongst squirming larvae, its legs damaged from the struggle to break free as a neighbouring butterfly tried to find a way to live on broken wings. Not far from there, somewhere in the wild, a lion and her mate hid from a pack of vicious wolves, as a single dove sang out for a flock of diseased pigeons, deep within a concrete jungle."

It was difficult for Sam to imagine how these images were relevant to them or how they would relate to anything that was going to happen, but he waited patiently as he heard Alice out. She continued to describe what she had seen with vague, yet vivid detail, her voice full of emotion.

"Surrounding them all, in a field of pure white powder, a crystal river meandered around a city that burned bright in a raging inferno. The red hot flames pumped smoke into the night sky as it melted both ice and snow without mercy. The web caught a spark and went up in flame, the fire engulfing the spider and everything else in its path. The wasp couldn't escape, nor the butterfly whose slow crawl wasn't fast enough to carry it to freedom. The heat caused the larvae to hatch into moths that carried the flames out towards the concrete jungle, unaware of the danger that they possessed. As the birds continued to sing their beautiful song, they were too distracted to notice the smoke in the sky and were completely oblivious to the destruction heading their way. Somewhere in the fields below, the cowering lions and the wolves that hunted them were disintegrated into nothing but smouldering ash in a sea of fire."

Sam's eyes opened wide as Alice spoke of a possible future that sounded closer akin to an apocalypse than anything else. He didn't know who the different animals represented, but he knew that all of them would die if the vision came to pass. Could this be the reason to live that he had been searching for?

"You weren't joking..." Sam said in a wondrous, yet slightly nervous tone. "Whatever the dream was about, it sounds awful and we can't let it happen."

Alice nodded in agreement, her pacing having stopped a just few feet away. "But first we need to leave town. It's likely that Katherine already knows where we are and she'll be coming for us."

Sam wondered if Katherine was the spider in the dream. If she was, then her descendants were the starving offspring, and if that was the case, then they would be amongst the first to burn if they didn't act. "Where should we go?"

Alice seemed to ponder his question for a moment before replying. "Maybe out west. Somewhere peaceful and away from busy cities. Somewhere where we can work out what to do next."

It was a simple plan, but one that Sam was inclined to agree with. "A place in the country sounds nice about now."

Alice smiled softly at him, seemingly satisfied by his answer. "It sure does. Farms, dirt roads and crops as far as the eye can see." She looked almost tranquil as she pictured the countryside that they had both grown up in and had left behind so long ago.

Sam knew that he didn't have much to offer, but he would dedicate himself to helping Alice stop the encroaching darkness in any way possible, unless it meant hurting innocent people in the process. That was a line that he didn't want to cross, not again. Not ever. Despite having so little left to give, there was still one thing that Sam could offer her. His complete and undying fidelity.

An unmarked van pulled into the bus depot, slowing to a stop by the curb. Matthew waved his hand from the driver's seat, looking pleased with his choice of ride.

Alice beamed with joy. "Are you ready to go?" Whoever Matthew was and however Sam felt about him, he was someone who seemed to make Alice happy, and that meant that he would work as hard as he could to get along with him.

Looking around the bus depot one last time, Sam silently took in the sights and sounds of Miami at night. He had never truly felt comfortable there, but it has become a home of sorts. Perhaps he had grown too used to the hustle and bustle of the city and he wouldn't be able to settle down out in the country. Sam hoped that he would be able to adjust given time, but he would let it happen naturally and wouldn't force the issue. There would be no more noise or light pollution. Just him, Alice, Matthew and the endless fields that made up the majority of the landscape.

Leaving Miami was admittedly going to be tough, with so many memories both good and bad reminding Sam of all the experiences that he had somehow survived through. However, the amount of friends that he had lost there had transformed the place into little more than a graveyard. Jacko, Mikey P, Chavs and Skid. He would cherish their memory forever, but he didn't want to stay there to be haunted by the spirits of the dead. The city had introduced him to Christie Reece and had given him the precious time that he needed to get to know her, but it had also taken her away from him, and that was something that was impossible to forgive. It was time to say one last goodbye.

Sam mouthed his farewell, but no sound escaped from his lips. He finally felt as though he was ready to move on and was done wasting time. Turning his head, he looked back at Alice who had inclined her own to one side as she awaited his response. "Yeah, I'm ready." He said weakly with a half smile. "Let's get out of here."

<u>EPILOGUE:</u> **THE QUEEN OF HER CASTLE.**

Katherine couldn't concentrate on the proceedings at all. In fact, ever since she had discovered the existence of her bastard child, she had struggled to focus on her duties as queen. She was in danger of neglecting them altogether, as she had become distracted in a similar manner to that which had begun the downfall of her predecessor. She of all should know. After all, it was Katherine who had personally overthrown the old ruler, a woman who she had once counted amongst her elite and particularly exclusive circle of friends. Their differences in opinion had left them divided long ago, and she knew better than to cultivate real friendships now. Vampires didn't have friends, not really. Just rivals and those that they wished to control.

The pitiful creature who knelt before Katherine's feet was a newcomer to her city whose petition to become a citizen of Calgary was falling on deaf ears. Like her failure of a child, he too was Forsaken, and weak blooded wretches such as this were not welcome in her pure blooded, totalitarian state. In fact they had no place within the city limits at all. They were mistakes, plain and simple, and needed to be wiped out as their very existence was a blight on vampire society.

Katherine had worked hard to make Calgary a city free of the abominations that plagued other kingdoms. However, she felt shame for the part that she had played in bringing such a thing into existence, a fact that she had only recently been made aware of. Sam Mitchell was supposed to have been bait, she had no designs for him beyond that. He was a tool that she was meant to use to lure Alice to her, but it was a plan that she had believed to have failed when his body refused to rise. What she didn't understand was how someone with her potent blood could create something so weak and pathetic. Was it because she had stolen her strength from others over the years? Was this a punishment for all her past sins? No! She had earned her power through her skill in guile and cunning, and it was hers by right.

As Katherine looked down from her throne to lay her eyes upon the skinny man dressed in rags, she couldn't help but draw a comparison with that which she had somehow spawned. He was still cowering before her and pleading for mercy that would never come, his terrified face replaced by that of Samuel Mitchell. Like all Forsaken, Katherine's child was a problem that had to be dealt with. She had no real connection to him, they had only met the once for an admittedly intimate but brief moment, and she could crush him so easily without feeling remorse. She would have to kill Samuel and Matthew too, even though the latter would be a much tougher task, and anyone else who had ever disappointed or betrayed her. But not Alice. Alice was different. She was special.

It was easy for Katherine to admit that she had always craved power, for as long as she could remember. Ever since her rebirth, she had sought it out and had grasped it wherever possible. She had clawed her way out of the brothels and whore houses of the old colony and had carved a path across the continent as she searched for her place within the world. Her power had been claimed, it hadn't been handed to her, and she would never let anyone take it from her. Not ever.

With everything that Katherine had gained along the way, she knew she had also lost so much in the process. The transformation had taken its toll on her soul, removing the very parts of her that had once made her human. Her conscience was a tattered mess that she had to try and balance out with common sense, otherwise she might just go on a rampant killing spree that she wouldn't regret until her body had been destroyed. As much as she craved blood and destruction, her self preservation acted to kept her in check in a mind devoid of true emotion. Yes, she could still fake her way through social gatherings and the like, becoming quite adept through decades of experience at making others feel comfortable in her presence, but it was all just an act. Katherine Louviere was as dead inside as she was on the outside and nothing would ever change that.

The kings and queens of vampire society weren't voted in to office, and the vampire hierarchy was far from a democracy. It was a vicious pit of politics, sinister plots and backstabbing that had to be braved if you wanted to make your way up the deadly food chain.

Taking calculated risks could result in the highest of rewards, but reckless and poorly timed actions could mean death or worse... exile. Katherine knew that it was a dangerous game that she was playing, but it was one that she had always played to near perfection.

Despite her strength of office, Samuel Mitchell was still a serious threat to Katherine's survival and she knew it. The social stigma of such a discovery would be too great to bear and it would cause her to lose the respect of her peers. She couldn't risk any of her rivals ever discovering his existence as they wouldn't hesitate to use that knowledge against her. The Forsaken wretch was a grubby little secret that they would wield as a weapon as they all turned on her in an instant. As queen, Katherine was faced with danger on a nightly basis, with the other vampires in the city constantly circling her like buzzards around carrion. If the vultures ever sensed any weakness in her, they would descend to tear her apart.

Katherine would never let anyone take her crown, not ever. She would raze the city to the ground and rule over the smouldering ruins before she would let anyone usurp her throne. Anyone who was foolish enough to cross her would be subsequently wiped from existence, leaving no one to dispute her sovereignty and her right to rule. She had worked too hard to lose it all. She had fought tooth and nail against all odds, rising up from nothing to become one of the most powerful and influential vampires in the New World. Alliances had been forged and old ties severed, with strategic planning and timeless charm getting her further than most had ever thought possible, but it still wasn't enough. Katherine still craved more. She would always want more. It wasn't greed that kept her motivated, not as she saw it. It was simply her fulfilling her destiny.

The throne room itself was a work in progress, with far too many reminders of the former queen that had yet to be disposed of. Renita Marquette had been a dreamer who was grounded in the past, with a penchant for times gone by. Her period of choice had been the French Renaissance, the memory of her former life in the old country refusing to fade, and her decor had mirrored that obsession. Whereas Katherine on the other hand preferred to change with the times, keeping her designs more contemporary modern and sparse. The dusty tapestries and expensive drapes had been torn down as renovations began, but the golden gilding and old fashioned tiles still remained, at least for now. It was out with the old and in with the new, but change took time and she had to remain patient. Her seat of power would mirror her elegance soon enough and then all traces of the old regime would soon be erased.

It was true that Calgary and its surrounding lands now belonged to Katherine, but Renita still lived. She had somehow escaped the city along with her bodyguard, leaving her most loyal supporters behind to face their terrible demise. The stripped monarch had no power, throne or kingdom anymore, but she was still out there somewhere. There was no doubt that she was in hiding, plotting her revenge and preparing to take back what she believed to belong to her. However delusional that belief and however sure Katherine was that her rival's plan was doomed to fail, it turned Renita into yet another threat that still loomed on the horizon.

Katherine didn't know what the future held or exactly what steps to take to ensure her eternal dominance, which is precisely why she needed Alice Delaney and her innate talent for foresight. Her enemies couldn't sneak up on her if she knew where they were and when they were coming for her. Alice was the key to her continued existence.

A robed figure entered the chamber from the elevator doors beyond, drawing the remainder of Katherine's limited attention away from her petitioner. They made their way around the edge of the circular room, seeming to glide over the tiled floor as they brushed past the well dressed guards. The same guards who were strangely oblivious of the mysterious figures presence as they continued to watch the proceedings in silence. In fact, no one else in the room seemed to notice the intruder except for Katherine who tracked their movements with increasing interest.

A smile crossed Katherine's face as she laid eyes upon the scraggly, black hair that poked out from underneath the robe's dark red hood and the pale, boney fingers that protruded from baggy sleeves. "Morgana... I trust you have news?"

The robed figure stopped just a couple of steps shy of the throne before bowing their shrouded head with respect. It was then that everyone else seemed to notice them, the guards reaching under their suit jackets for their weapons until they were stopped in their tracks by a quick wave of Katherine's hand. The pathetic thing that knelt at her feet scurried backwards on all fours, until he was stopped by a nearby guard's cruel kick that put him down in an instant.

Morgana spoke with an eerie whisper that somehow projected into Katherine's mind. "I have found them, my queen."

Katherine's smile changed to a wicked grin as she leaned forwards, balancing herself on the edge of her uncomfortable golden throne. Yet another object that needed to be replaced. "Good." She gestured towards the door as she addressed her guards. "Leave us!"

A single nervous voice called out from somewhere in the sidelines. "Beg your pardon, your highness… but what should we do with the prisoner?"

Barely acknowledging the Forsaken's presence, Katherine dismissed them with yet another wave of her hand, as if his life meant nothing to her. "Put him with the rest and execute them all in the morning." She didn't really appreciate being addressed as 'your highness', as it was an outdated term, but she found it acceptable under the circumstances due to it being intended as a form of respect.

Katherine gave Morgana her full attention as the man was dragged kicking and screaming out of the throne room, the other guards filing out behind them. "Tell me, witch… What have you learned?"

Morgana's face remained hidden beneath her hood and layers of unkempt hair as she spoke, her words still spoken with a hushed whisper. "Your offspring were easy to find, my mistress. It seems that they did not inherit your ability of masking their intent."

Katherine knew that the blood witch was almost as cold and calculating as she was, but she wasn't one for sarcasm. It was quite an honour to be shown respect by someone who was a powerful force in her own right. "Inexperience is the downfall of most of our kind and it seems that my children are no exception to the rule. So where can I find them?"

The witch raised her head until her dark eyes made contact with Katherine's. Any lesser vampire would have felt dread when met with such a gaze, but not her. "They are on the move, my queen, but I can still lead you to them. It seems that they caused quite the disturbance within the city of Miami."

"Interesting." The grin left Katherine's face, her expression turning to one of deadpan sincerity. This was business, not pleasure, and it was time that her demeanor reflected as much. "All three of them are together? Alice, Matthew and Samuel too?"

Katherine's question was answered by a single nod of Morgana's head, allowing her to continue her train of thought unhindered. "Well that will make things simpler... Call Vincent back from his hunt. Tell him that once he has aided our cause, I shall dedicate more resources to helping him find his brother and that miserable excuse for royalty that he protects."

"By your will, my lady." Morgana bowed her head, moving her arms out to her side as she bent her knees in a polite curtsey. The motion gave Katherine a glimpse of the glowing red runes that had been tattooed across the pale skin of her skeletal forearms.

Ancient runes with meanings that had been lost in the sands of time.

The strange woman turned to leave, her robe trailing behind her as she moved with an unnatural grace that would seem quite alien to the uninitiated. As she drifted out of the room through the golden doors that opened for her without a single touch, Katherine silently wondered how loyal her subject actually was. 'Act as though you trust them, but do not believe their lies.' The wise words of her maker echoed through her mind, yet his own failure to abide by that rule had resulted in his demise at her hand and she had since vowed never to become the victim of someone else's deception.

So Morgana claimed to know where her children were, but Katherine couldn't risk going after them herself. If she were lured away from her responsibilities, then the witch would likely seize the opportunity to take the throne for herself. After all, she had once tried to overthrow Renita Marquette without success and it was only a matter of time before she craved the seat of power once more. For that reason, others would have to go in Katherine's stead, which is why she sent for Vincent, one of the most skilled hunters that she knew and one without any ambitions beyond his station.

It was likely that Alice would sense Vincent's approach before it happened, but Katherine had faith that her visions wouldn't save them. The wolf had a knack for tracking that was unsurpassed by anyone else and he rarely ever travelled alone. Wherever he went, whatever was left of his pack would follow. They had been almost completely wiped out in the war for the throne, but those that remained were still loyal to a fault. Each and every one of them had given in to the beast inside of them, an act that made them crave little more than blood, survival and their freedom to roam. It had also converted them into useful tools that Katherine wouldn't hesitate to wield.

With Vincent and his pack on the prowl, assisted by Morgana's blood magic, there was no place that Alice, Matty and Sam could run to or hide. Katherine knew that they would all soon be within her grasp and that Alice's abilities would once again be hers to command. Perhaps it would be wise to keep the other two alive as well, or at least one of them to act as leverage. After all, Alice was a kind and loving girl who couldn't bear to hear the tortured cries of those she loved, which meant that it was a weakness that could be easily exploited.

Sitting alone with her thoughts, Katherine couldn't help but smile to herself. It was a sly, despicable smile, full of delight as she could finally see all the pieces coming together. She had played the long game, and the end was almost in sight. After hundreds of years, everything that she had worked for was almost hers for the taking. What she didn't possess already would soon be hers and there was little that anyone could do to stop her. With her immense wealth of power and her massive reserve of resources, the world would be Katherine's to devour... And she was ravenous.

A THANK YOU FROM THE AUTHOR

I truly appreciate anyone who has taken the time to read through my book, so thank you for doing so. I put a great deal of time and effort in to this novel, so I hope that you enjoyed reading it as much as I enjoyed writing it.

This is the second novel in a series of books that tell the tale of Alice Delaney and other characters who cross her path. For details of upcoming novels, please keep an eye on The Beast Inside Facebook page at:
https://www.facebook.com/TheBeastInsideNovel/

If you have the time, please leave a review of the book on the Facebook page or on Amazon.

Thank you once again for reading **The Beast Inside: Blood of the Forsaken!**

Manufactured by Amazon.ca
Bolton, ON